Twisted in Time

She finally knew forever existed...

Deb Laubach
Ray Caragher

ISBN-13: 978-0998529004

Also available in A Twisted Series:

A Lost Romance Found – Book Two

Coming next in A Twisted Series:

A Twisted Reality – Book Three

The Curse of Love – Book Four

Acknowledgments

We cannot thank The Powers That Be, the Cosmic Tumblers, Open-Mindedness and Awareness enough.

We thank our spouses and our children for *understanding who we really are* and believing in our dream. Thank you for loving and supporting us, while accepting each time we said, "Just one more chapter," knowing that it would turn into countless more hours and one less plate to set at dinnertime. We love you.

Endless thank yous to our visionary team of experts at CommunityAuthors.com: Traci Hall and Christopher Hawke for their tireless assistance.

May we all be filled with Love: Consideration, Compassion, and Compromise. Love is timeless and always reveals Herself and She knows no boundaries - for She is Love.

Chapter 1

Grant Robinson! he thought to himself. *I was just a damn farm boy from Madison, Wisconsin. And now I'm a successful fashion designer in New York City?*

Grant was thirty-four years old and six foot four. His salt-and-pepper hair gave him a distinguished look. His captivating cobalt-blue eyes and his chiseled facial features made him almost look like an Adonis.

However, his greatest gift was the boyish grin that radiated all over his face whenever he smiled. He had a lean, muscular build from all the summers of physical labor during his youth that were spent working on relatives' farms and later at the circus. Grant spent long days doing a variety of chores, which beefed up his body.

The rest of the year, he had lived with his father in Madison, where he attended high school. Each day after school, he would go to the University of Wisconsin to work as part of the grounds crew. By his senior year, Grant towered over his classmates at more than six feet and was as tanned as a lifeguard. He laughed when he recalled that he never dated any girls from high school, only college girls, who thought he attended the university.

Grant had met her years before while preparing for a fashion show. He was doing an internship for a small women's wear company, TerRae Sportswear, while finishing his fashion degree from the Art Institute of Chicago.

The husband-and-wife owners of TerRae had models flown in from New York and Los Angeles. They were boisterously arguing over the cost. The wife wanted models brought in early to ensure the fit for the show.

"Do you know why I want them here early?" the wife screamed.

"Yeah, I do! You just want to impress some of your cronies with all the little models you can fly into town so they can flock around you, making you feel like a big-shot fashion queen," he yelled back at her.

"Fuck you," she shot back. "You are a thickheaded moron. No. I want them here because these girls will go back to the fashion markets in L.A. and New York and fucking talk about us to other buyers. Maybe we can land some additional private-label contracts from the exposure—something perhaps you've forgotten, you asshole!"

Grant recalled the dead silence in the factory after their argument, only to turn around and look into the face of a stunning eighteen-year-old girl. Her auburn hair with blonde highlights framed her face perfectly.

"Hi, I'm Ginger Madison," she said softly with a smile. "I'm looking for Mrs. Vidal."

Ginger's eyes were an unusual mix of flecked green with a ring of deep blue around the irises. He often tried to remember anything else about her from that day—what she was wearing, if she was with another model, anything. Yet it was her *eyes* that burned into his mind and soul.

Smiling, he recalled being in bed with her. Just as he was about to reach his climax, he pulled out of her, ejaculating onto her bare ass and back. She was the most erotic lover he had ever been with. He would find himself just watching her walk around naked. She was so in touch with her body and soul; Ginger moved as gracefully as a cat. When she gazed into his eyes, the universe stopped.

He unfolded a tattered note from his pocket, which he read often. It *was* real. He finally knew the meaning of true love. He'd do anything for her. Tears filled his eyes. In all his thirty-four years of life, he never felt anything like her.

He thought back to what his life once was—a bad marriage, a year and half in Vietnam, a rough childhood. And then he met *her*.

But where does this love story actually begin?

Chapter 2

It was a typical scorching day in August 1984 in New York City. Grant woke at five thirty a.m. and reminded himself to be quiet, not wanting to wake the kids. He sneered at the thought of tiptoeing—his wife and children moved away to Chicago weeks ago. He could make as much noise as he wanted, because no one was there to hear it.

A memory flashed through his mind: lying in his bed as a nine-year-old boy after his mother died. He remembered waking up in the morning, wishing it was a bad dream.

He pictured her in the kitchen after driving his dad to

work at the University of Wisconsin. She wore an old pair of pants, white socks, and deerskin moccasins. She loved listening to music—*The Arthur Godfrey Show* was her favorite. The Mariners would sing some song or maybe Patty Paige would do her rendition of "How Much Is That Doggie in the Window?" Every morning she was singing or dancing, sometimes taking his hands and swinging him around to dance with her.

He would go downstairs into the kitchen and find that she wasn't there. After reality set in, he would go to her master bedroom closet and sit inside it with the door closed, trying just to smell her scent and crying in the silent darkness all alone. Here he was, twenty-five years later, remembering the silence.

Grant finally snapped himself out of his childhood memories and prepared to head down to the exercise room on the twelfth floor. Upon opening his apartment door, there stood Brenda, his neighbor from 34B, getting on the elevator, her two-year-old son in a jogging stroller.

"Hey," he mumbled while pushing the button for the twelfth floor and asking Brenda what floor.

"Ground." She looked at him as if she was trying to think of something nice to say. After a few floors, she finally spoke. "Looks like another hot day."

"Yeah, August in the city," he replied. "Going jogging?"

"Yeah," she halfheartedly responded.

Back in his apartment, while taking his shower, he began to think of his week ahead. *I'm flying into LIA—Love International Airport.* He smiled thinking about an airport named "Love." *Flying into Love? Wonder who came up with that fucking name for an airport? Love is such an overrated concept.* Pondering the question, he thought, *Is love even real? Is it real other than between a parent and a child, or another special family member, if you're lucky?*

He was already packed for Dallas; it was only seven forty-five. The limo wouldn't be downstairs until eight thirty. He poured himself another cup of coffee. Grant looked at the two empty bottles on the counter, reminding him of how empty he felt after last Thursday night's escapade.

Abigail, the property manager, noticed Grant leaving last Thursday morning. She had flirted with him consistently over the years, even when Margo was standing at his side.

"Grant," she called, with her usual smiling, sparkling face. "When you have a chance, I would like to get your input on my sister's wedding for her gown and the bridesmaids' dresses."

"Sure. What do you need to know?"

"Well," she replied, "the wedding is next year, late summer. I thought you could give me some trends and ideas because she's going to have everything custom made."

"Yeah, sure. No problem. I'll reach out when I get back from—"

"How about I drop by one night?" Abigail interrupted. "And we could have a glass of wine and go over your thoughts."

"Sounds good." He chuckled. "Just make sure you bring a chair with you."

"Oh? Why is that?"

It was obvious she was pretending that she didn't know every detail about the tenants in her building.

"I gave most of the furniture to Margo, and she always took care of the home decor."

Abigail's face lit up. "Oh, I *love* decorating! How about we trade info? You give me the trends and I'll help you with picking out furniture?"

"Bartering is always good." He left knowing it was more of a game of cat and mouse.

Grant arrived home that night around nine p.m. He noticed the light was still on in Abigail's office as he headed toward the elevators. Within five minutes of entering his apartment, there was a knock on the door. He opened the door and there she stood.

She was wearing a white baby doll dress. It was a

loose-fitting, sleeveless garment with lace spaghetti straps. To complete her look, she wore unmistakable brown "fuck me" stilettos and a "come hither" look on her face.

"Hey, Grant. Hope I'm not disturbing you, but I had to work late tonight and just finished up when I saw you walk into the building." Then she blurted out, "Mind if I come in?" She coyly displayed the bottle of vino as promised.

After yet another long day, his brain finally caught up with what was going on. He laughed, then said, "Sure, sure. Come on in. Where are my manners?"

She brushed by him, lightly touching her arm against his, leaving the scent of her perfume in the air. She smiled when handing him the bottle of merlot, remarking that it was already at cellar temperature.

"Oh, why thank you, Abigail. I was just preparing a shot of tequila for myself. What can I get for you?"

"I love tequila! After *my* day, I could use a shot. And please, call me Abby."

She walked into the living room, talking over her shoulder. "I'll take mine with lime and salt, please. Hopefully it's chilled. Oh, and I have the floor plans if you want to look at them."

"Um, sure thing." Going into the kitchen to make their shots, Grant felt like he was being a bad boy. His divorce wasn't final yet. Margo and the kids had been gone only a few weeks. Yet the thoughts he entertained about Abby's body had already made his cock semihard.

He handed her the shot of tequila. Abby was sitting on a leftover patio chair with her legs crossed. Adjusting her legs, Abby remarked, "Again, I hope it isn't too late to drop by." He wondered if she was wearing panties.

He looked at her curvy body, dark-brown hair, and full lips, wondering if she was a 36D or 38D. *Fuck me!* he thought. The red flags were going off in his mind as he said, "No, not at all. It's nice to have some company."

She licked the salt seductively from her hand, slammed the shot, and sucked the lime like a bar pro. Not even quivering, Abby held her shot glass out to him: "One more, please."

"But of course." He went back into the kitchen to prepare two more shots. "How are the kids?" he shouted out from the kitchen, to which she didn't reply.

Entering the living room with their second shots, he stopped hard when he saw her standing there, completely naked.

"Fine, and yours?" she said smirking. She waited for his response.

"O-Okay." His cock became fully erect. *God, she's a good-looking piece of ass*, he thought. Grant handed Abby her shot and a fresh lime to suck.

"A toast?" They raised their glasses. "To good

times." Grant didn't even have time to respond before she slammed back the second tequila, and he followed suit. She placed the lime in her mouth and sucked it enticingly.

The next few hours were spent feverishly pleasuring each other with countless orgasms.

When Grant woke, she was gone. The only proof she had been there were the empty bottles and the panties she left behind for him.

Chapter 3

He stood there looking out his window at the incredible view of Central Park. The phone rang at precisely eight a.m.

"Good morning, boss."

It was Howard Golden, the owner of H&M Designs and a first-class narcissist. H&M Designs was one of the biggest private-label houses in New York City.

"Look, Grant, get that bitch Rebekah at Neiman Marcus to commit on these designs and write an order. Go and kiss the ass of your buddy, Steve, her boss—hell, kiss everyone's ass!"

"I understand. We talked about this yesterday."

"Get your fucking ego out of the way. If she wants an extra fucking inch of fabric on a goddamn dress or skirt, give it to her!"

"Okay, okay, Howard. Calm down."

"Farm boy, we *need* this account. Call me after your meeting tomorrow." Click.

"Asshole!" Grant said. "Never 'Good luck' or 'Good-bye.' You would think I've never closed a difficult deal for the company before today."

He walked away from the phone and stared out the window. He lived in a three-bedroom, 1,400-square-foot Midtown Manhattan apartment facing east toward Central Park—the perfect place to live.

What the hell happened to my life? Money wasn't an issue. Margo's dreams had all come true. Her dreams had actually become my dreams. But something got screwed up along the way.

Grant grabbed his bag and portfolio and rode down the elevator. Entering the lobby, he saw Abigail slip into her office and close the door, as if avoiding him.

Well, fuck me! She hasn't said hi or good-bye or even a "Kiss my ass" since the night we were together. What am I supposed think about that? He felt his face turn slightly red with frustration. *Just another woman to be a pain in my ass. Can't please them all—or any of them. They all want something that apparently I can't give.*

Chapter 4

Walking toward the exit, he saw Evan, his driver, outside standing by the shiny black Lincoln Continental stretch limo.

"Good morning, Mr. Robinson," Andreas, the doorman, said, holding the lobby door for him. "How are you today?"

"I'm fine, Andreas. You?"

"Great, sir."

Evan held the door open to the limo. "Where are you off to today, Mr. Robinson?"

"Today is Dallas, Evan," Grant said, climbing into the

cool air of the limo. "And, Evan, how many times do I have to remind you that you and all the people I work closely with need only call me 'Grant?'"

"Right you are, Mr. Grant." Evan closed the door and placed Grant's bags in the trunk. "I heard it was ninety-six degrees yesterday in Dallas. You packed some shorts, Mr. Grant?"

"I'm afraid not. What's important, though, is how was your daughter's wedding? Sorry I couldn't make it. I was finishing up with the divorce and spending some time with my kids. But you did receive my card?"

"Yes, I did. Your gift was very generous! So was that designer gown for my wife, Emma. Did you know that we've been together since she was fourteen? Twenty-eight years, Mr. Grant! Time flies."

"Holy shit. Twenty-eight years? How do you do that? Sorry, I didn't mean to curse. But really, is there a secret that someone forgot to tell me?"

"That's all right, Mr. Grant. Luck, I suppose. I wasn't always a good man, but she's always loved me for just being me. Yessir, I guess I'm just lucky. When I came back from 'Nam, I was pretty messed up. She put her arms around me on bad nights, telling me I was a good man—even when I thought differently."

"You're one lucky SOB, Evan," Grant said with a smile.

Driving toward the airport, Grant's mind slipped backed to the night he told Margo some things about Vietnam. He came back so emotionally fucked up; he was usually drunk during the first two months after returning home.

One evening after dinner, when the kids were in bed, Grant and Margo sat on the front porch. He poured himself another scotch and began unveiling some details about the eighteen months he spent in 'Nam and his feelings of overwhelming guilt.

He was nowhere near finished, with tears in his eyes, needing his wife to show him some understanding and sympathy.

"You need help, Grant," she barked.

"I know. I feel so out of touch with the world around me."

For a moment, he felt that she cared—until she tersely said, "Are you finished? Howard called me again yesterday. He's wondering when you're going to start. Do you know the strings I had to pull?" Margo paused, "Or maybe you don't want it?" She glared at him. "Jesus, Grant. Look, I know you've been through hell. But you're not the only one. You need to fucking pull yourself together."

He was stunned by her words and said nothing.

With no emotion, she flatly said, "I have things to do."

Margo left him alone with his emotions lying on the floor. Grant vowed never to speak of Vietnam again.

Hearing Evan's story, he wished he had been so lucky.

"American, correct?" Evan asked, pulling Grant from his unwanted remembrance.

"Yes, Evan."

"When do you come home, sir?"

"Sunday the eighteenth, three thirty p.m."

"I'll be here, Mr. Grant. Safe trip and God bless you."

"Thanks, Evan. I'll need it."

LaGuardia wasn't busy for a Tuesday morning. He quickly shot down to Concourse D and entered the Admirals Club.

"Good morning, Mr. Robinson."

"'Morning, Jack."

"Your usual, sir? Extra hairy Bloody Mary?"

"You know me, Jack."

Jack mixed his drink. "So where are you off to today, Mr. Robinson? Dallas or Chicago?"

"Dallas."

Jack smiled, then placed the drink down and walked away.

Grant downed the drink as he thought about seeing Rebekah Scott. She was the contemporary women's wear buyer who held the reigns tightly for the last twenty-six years at Neiman Marcus. Every design he showed her always needed to be tweaked by her. Last season's sales of his line were flat due to changes she demanded.

Jack returned. "Ready for your second?"

"No, thanks, Jack. I'm in a hurry today," he said, placing a ten-dollar bill on the bar.

"Thank you, Mr. Robinson. Have a safe flight and see you soon."

Chapter 5

Grant exited the lounge and headed to D4, where the gate attendant, a hot, young brunette with blue eyes, was already boarding first class. He handed her his ticket, eyeing her up and down. "Have a nice flight, Mr. Robinson," she said with a flirtatious smile.

"Thank you." He wondered if she smiled the same way for the coach passengers.

Walking down the ramp, he ritualistically patted the side of the 747. Entering the big bird, he saw the familiar face of Tina, a flight attendant who was always working first class.

"Well, good morning, Mr. Robinson. How are you?"

"Great, Tina. I haven't seen you since last month."

She held open the curtain to first class. She gently touched his arm as he walked by. "You know where your seat is, Mr. Robinson?"

"Yes. Thank you, Tina."

"It's nice to see you again, Mr. Robinson." She leaned in close enough for him to smell her hair and notice her cherry-flavored lip gloss.

Tina was a brunette and wore her hair in a bun, showcasing that her hair clearly reached the top of her ass when unfurled. She was five foot four with a small waist, twenty-four years old at best, clearly a 34D, size four, with a nice ass and legs to match. Tina's lips were perfectly shaped, with a bottom lip that was slightly bigger than the top—completely kissable. She had a cute dimple in her chin, a nose that turned up as if designed by a plastic surgeon, and hazel eyes that were clear and happy.

Grant sat down in his seat on the portside, wondering why he always wanted to sit on that side of the plane.

Just as he was snapping his seat belt, Tina walked up with her apron on and a sultry smile on her face. "Would you like anything from the galley? Coffee? Tea?" Giggling, she then said, "Me? Oops, sorry. Didn't mean to be sassy, Mr. Robinson. Milk?"

Smiling at her with a slightly naughty look in his blue

eyes, he replied, "I'll take a glass of champagne. Call me Grant."

The air from the vent above began to turn colder as Tina brought him his champagne and then walked away to serve the only other two passengers in first class. The 747 taxied down the runway. The whine of the engines had Grant wondering what it felt like to be a pilot in the cockpit. *Why do I love flying so much?* He watched the ground fade away as the plane soared into the blue-and-white-covered sky. *If I ever had a chance to do it all over again, I would be a pilot.*

In less than fifteen minutes, Tina was back to serve him. Grant ordered a cup of coffee with cream and sugar, needing to sober up. He asked Tina if she was from the Big Apple.

"No, I'm from Sioux City, Iowa. How about you?"

"Madison, Wisconsin. Where's your home base?"

"L.A. I'll be right back." She pardoned herself to assist the other two passengers.

After a few minutes, Tina returned with a Bloody Mary. "So, are you married, Grant?"

"I suppose you can hold the cream and sugar on that Bloody Mary?" He laughed at the puzzled look on her face.

She laughed and said sheepishly, "Oops, that's right. You wanted coffee. Got your order mixed up. Clearly there are just *too many* first-class passengers today. You know how it goes on a Monday—no, Tuesday morning?" Tina tried to hide her embarrassment.

"Guess I'm not the only one who's drinking Bloody Marys—or perhaps just the vodka?" He winked at her and smiled.

When she returned, he was serious. "Well, I'm technically still married until Thursday, which is when I sign the final divorce papers. So, yeah, I guess I'm married at the moment."

"Oh, I'm sorry to hear that." She walked away.

When the seat belt sign went off, Grant unbuckled and headed toward the lavatory. As he passed the galley, Tina looked up and smiled.

As he exited the lavatory, Tina said, "I just finished my divorce last month. It's so crazy to be alone. The silence is the hardest part." Her eyes watered and the smile left her face. Reaching out, he put his hand on her shoulder. "I know. We'll be okay. In time."

She looked into his eyes, and a small smile returned. For a moment, he felt like someone understood him.

A few minutes later, Tina walked up to him, handed him the menu, and asked sweetly, "What would you like for brunch, Grant?"

"It's not on the menu, Tina."

"What would *that* be?"

He gently laid his hand on hers. They shared the same

unspoken sexual desire. Nothing was said for a moment. Tina broke the silence: "Give me twenty minutes."

Grant watched her take the menu to the elderly couple sitting in the back of first class.

Nearly a half hour went by before she returned. Tina leaned over to Grant. "Can you follow me? I'd like to show you something."

Grant nearly jumped out of his seat to follow her.

"Caroline, I'd like to give Mr. Robinson a tour of the crew's quarters below." Tina winked at the other flight attendant.

"Take your time. I've got you covered," Caroline responded with a knowing smile.

Tina opened a door leading into a small elevator. The elevator began its decent into the belly of the plane. When the doors opened, there was a lounging area with a couple of beds front and center.

She removed her blazer and pulled him toward her. Before he could even react, she passionately kissed his lips, sucking his tongue into her mouth.

Tina slipped out of her skirt and removed her blouse. She kept eye contact with Grant, enjoying the expression on his face. She took off her bra and stepped out of her panties, revealing the beauty of her naked body.

Her breasts were God given and overly proportionate to her petite size. Her nipples were fully erect, waiting to be touched. Grant stood there visually devouring her body for a moment and began to remove his shirt and tie. She lunged toward him and attacked his belt. His pants hit the floor and he stepped out of them. She freed his cock from his boxers, inciting her excitement—she loved how virile he was.

She was on her knees within seconds and couldn't wait to suck his dick, but he wanted to taste her first. Leaning her back onto the bed, Grant whispered, "I'd like to pleasure you first, if you don't mind."

"Me first? Oh, my!"

She propped herself up on her elbows, spreading her legs as he crawled between the silkiness of her inner thighs.

With the first lick of his tongue, she knew this was going to be a fun-filled sexual experience. Adding a few fingers while eating her clit, she quickly climbed higher and higher and came on his face. Grant could taste her orgasm in his mouth and loved that he could please such a hot little number.

Tina had multiple orgasms and was breathless as they repositioned themselves in countless ways. Finally, while fucking her from behind, deeply inside her, his climax began.

"That's right, baby, give it to me. Oh, how you fill me up!" Those words put him over the edge and he came hard, reaching deeper and deeper with each thrust of his hips.

He rolled off her, and they caught their breaths. She

kissed him and said, "Well, Mr. Robinson, I'm glad I could give you the tour. Welcome to the mile high club."

He was in shock that he just fucked the hot little stewardess.

"However, I do have to get back to work now. You know your way around?"

"Sure do," Grant said. "Go do your thing." He wondered how many men she'd brought to the crew's quarters—he was probably just a number to her like she was to him.

She jumped off the bed and cleaned up while Grant watched her get dressed quickly. Once her uniform was back on, she reworked her hair into a perfect bun and freshened her makeup.

"Less than thirty minutes left on the flight, so hurry your sweet ass up," she said grinning.

"I'll be right up, Tina."

She was gone in a flash. Grant returned to the cabin. *What a way to start off a week from hell*, he thought as he buckled himself into his seat. *Maybe it's a sign of good things to come.*

Grant felt an adrenaline kick when thinking about the day ahead of him. Working at H&M Designs for ten years, he still had to earn his keep. Grant knew what this meeting represented to his firm and his personal future.

He unbuckled his seat belt and grabbed his briefcase.

Tina waited at the exit with a big grin. She removed the wings from her jacket. “Here, you earned these. If you ever need me, just look in the clouds above.” She shook his hand with a wink of approval.

Grant winked back. “See you again, Tina.”

He smiled while heading toward baggage claim. *Jesus Christ, no one would ever believe that just happened.*

Chapter 6

Grabbing his luggage, he headed outside and saw a man holding a sign that read, "Neiman Marcus—Robinson."

He walked up to the driver. "Hi, I'm Grant Robinson." He shook the man's hand.

"My name is Ralph, sir, and I will be your driver for the next few days." Ralph held open the door.

"Ralph, I'm staying at the Mansion."

"Okay, Mr. Robinson."

Grant sat back in the limo. His apprehension about his meeting with Rebekah Scott permeated his thoughts, though he had to admit that he was looking forward to staying at the

Mansion. Sue, his secretary, made him an appointment to have a massage after his meeting with the CEO of Rosewood Resorts, Wilbur Franks.

Rosewood Resorts owned and operated the Mansion. The company was always looking to be fashion forward, wanting to be just a step ahead of the competition, including the staff uniforms.

The Mansion was a ten-thousand-square-foot house rebuilt in 1923. Linda Hunt of the Hunt Oil Family bought the property in 1981 and converted it into a resort. She spent more than twenty-seven million dollars to renovate the property, making it one of the highlights of Dallas, just in time for the Republican National Convention.

The fact that Grant stayed there was incredible to him, and his room was always comped by Wilbur. The last time he stayed in one of the executive suites, Wilbur joked that he was afraid he was spoiling him. The suites were a thousand dollars per night.

Wilbur's daughter married a few months prior. Grant arranged for Wilbur to pay half price for his daughter's wedding gown from Neiman Marcus.

Wilbur trusted Grant and recognized his ability to forecast and create the latest trends. Because of Grant, he had won two awards from the Hotel Association of North Texas for best-dressed staff.

The limo pulled into the circular drive of the Mansion.

Grant was always amazed by its beauty. The fountains, the colorful gardens—it was like stepping into a different era.

The doorman, JP, opened the limo door for him and immediately recognized Grant.

"Good morning, Mr. Robinson! Welcome home."

"Thank you, JP."

JP retrieved Grant's luggage and briefcase from Ralph.

"Ralph, I'll be leaving in thirty minutes."

"I'll be right here."

The domed entry and lobby had twelve-foot ceilings and arched windows with marble floors. Not a single detail was overlooked: flowers on every table, crisp linens everywhere, soft lighting, soothing music softly playing, and fabulous antique furniture. It was a beautiful and romantic place to be, a world of decadence that made it feel healthy to indulge.

He was immediately greeted by Kent McCleary, the general manager. "We've been expecting you, Mr. Robinson. You will be staying in the Terrace Suite. JP is bringing your luggage up."

"Thank you, Kent. I'll be meeting Mr. Franks at three o'clock."

"Yes. The meeting will be in the FDR Suite."

"Thank you, Kent."

The Terrace Suite was larger than his apartment in

New York City. He straightened up his shirt and tie and began to think about how wild his flight had been. He was teetering between being half-disgusted and half-proud of the fact that he could lay just about any woman he wanted.

Grant relaxed for a few minutes before heading downstairs to the limo for lunch with Steve Williams.

Grant sat back for the fifteen-minute limo ride. His brain flashed back to the fall of 1967, when he read the letter notifying him about his roommate assignment at the University of Wisconsin. He remembered wondering why a guy from Texas would want to attend UW.

Grant had considered asking his dad for a favor, since he didn't want to share a room with Hank Williams Jr. He hated asking his dad for help. His father always made him feel inadequate without even saying a word.

On August 26, 1967, Grant walked down the hallway of the Harold C. Bradley Residence Hall. When he opened the door of room 1059, his new roommate, Steve Williams, was fucking some blonde chick that was clearly high on something and certainly out of it.

Steve stopped midstride: "Hey, you must be Grant!" Steve hopped off the girl with his cock rock hard and glistening with her wetness. He walked over, extending his hand in a gesture of introduction and new friendship—acting like this was a completely normal way to meet someone.

"Yeah, I guess you're Steve. I suppose this bed will be mine," he said, pointing to the unused bed.

"Say, Grant, you want a turn? I'm pretty used up, came twice already. She's pretty good, I'd say." Steve turned to the girl. "You don't mind if my new roomie joins us, do you?" She smiled as she laid there, spread eagle with cum dripping out of her.

Grant stood there looking at the pretty blonde. *And I was worried about sharing a room with a guy who would want to listen to country music all night instead of the Beatles?*

"Thanks, but, um, I'll just toss my stuff on the bed and head to the bookstore. Maybe another time."

"You sure don't want at least a blow job? It's good luck to start the semester off with some sort of sexual act, ya know?" Steve turned toward the girl. "Come over here. Uh, sorry, what the fuck was your name? Susan, right?"

"No, no." She smiled. "Heather." She dropped to her knees in front of Grant. She pulled on his belt and slid his jeans down to his ankles. His cock instantly became hard when she ripped his boxer briefs down and stuck his cock in her mouth.

He fell back on the bed and she began to suck him.

Grant had never cum with another guy watching. Steve lifted Heather's ass up so he could slide his dick inside her from behind. With Steve sliding in and out of her, each thrust caused Grant's dick to go deeper down her throat.

Heather climbed on top of Grant, guiding his thick cock inside her. Steve mounted Heather from behind again, and Grant felt Steve's cock slide inside her pussy with his. After a few minutes with the tips of their dicks grinding in perfect rhythm, Grant, Heather, and Steve all came at the same time.

Heather stood up and smiled at the two college boys she just simultaneously fucked and went to the in-dorm bathroom to wash up.

"Welcome to college, roomie! I think we got off to a good start!" Steve proclaimed with a shit-eating grin on his face.

"Not what I expected, but yeah, I think it's going to be a good year."

When she came back out, Heather began to dress.

Steve stood there, going through his wallet. "So what's the damage?"

"Well, are you calling me again?" she replied with a slurred voice.

"What do you think, roomie? Lady wants to know if we'll be playing with her again."

"Um, sure?"

"Okay. One hundred dollars will cover today, pretty boys."

Heather stood with one hand on her hip and one hand

out. Grant sat there watching Steve fork over the money.

After Heather left, Grant asked, "Man, so she was a hooker?"

"Yeah, and a good one too, huh? Wham, bam, thank you, ma'am. No strings attached."

Grant reached into his pocket, knowing he only had twelve dollars and change, attempting to offer up some cash. Steve laughed. "Keep your money, buddy. It's my treat."

So began his freshman year with Steve Williams—who only partied, fucked, and drove fast cars. Grant wasn't sure if he ever went to class. He grinned, thinking how many times he got laid during college.

What a memory. Steve Williams, now the big boss man at Neiman Marcus, my old roommate. Who would have taken a bet on that? He shocked the hell out of me when he called two years ago and told me about his new position.

Ralph pulled up in front of 1201 Elm Street. It took a moment for Grant to reset his mind to meet with the present-day Steve after reliving that memory. When the elevator doors opened, Shirley, Steve's newest receptionist, greeted him with a sultry smile, eyeing Grant up and down.

Shirley was in her mid-twenties, a size two, with huge tits that someone, possibly Steve, bought her.

"Mr. Robinson, Mr. Williams is expecting you. Did you have a nice flight?"

"Yes, thank you."

"Something to drink?"

"No, thanks."

"Please have a seat. I will inform him you have arrived."

Grant sat for less than a minute before Steve burst into the reception area. He stuck out his hand. "Grant fucking Robinson. Good to see you, roomie! Hey, I'm starving. How about you? Lunch at the French Room?"

"Yeah, sure."

Riding the elevator, Steve inquired about Margo.

"Hey, roomie, how are things working out with the divorce?"

"Just short of the cost of the Republican Convention coming up next week." Both men laughed.

Steve's personal driver was out front waiting for them. "Well, buddy," Steve started, "again it seems our stages in life aren't that different. My wife filed for divorce two weeks ago. Hey, maybe we could be roommates!" He laughed. Steve got serious. "Roomie, I do need a *huge* favor. There's this hot model I've been banging for a few years. I need to get her a job out of town for a while. Catch my drift?"

"You mean like disappear?"

"Yeah, just for a while, or possibly forever." Steve grinned. "You know how it goes when it's time to end things with a side dish."

Grant sat there for a minute, the wheels turning in his head, deciding how to turn this situation into something that could benefit him.

"Well, I need a favor from you too, roomie. Rebekah Scott. She's always changing my line, add an inch, remove an inch, fabrics are not soft enough. She's constantly screwing up the line and blaming it on me."

Steve got serious. "Whoa! It's almost impossible to touch her; she's friends with Stanley Marcus."

Grant sunk back into his seat, feeling defeated.

Almost as if a light bulb flickered on, Steve's demeanor changed. "However, *for you*, there may be a way to take her down. What time's your meeting tomorrow?"

"Ten a.m."

"Okay. I'll have Shirley send for you to come to my office around ten twenty. You leave, but just go to the men's room. Wait five minutes, and casually walk back into the conference room, saying some shit like, 'Oh, excuse me, I forgot my briefcase.' And leave again."

Steve's smirk was devious. He threw his hands up, finishing with, "Voilà."

Grant's expression was one of pure confusion, "Voilà?"

"Trust me, roomie."

Grant decided not to push the issue any further. They made plans to meet around six at the Mansion Bar, and Steve would be bringing his *favor* plus a *playdate* for Grant.

After lunch, Steve dropped Grant off at the Mansion, adding his last words regarding his much-needed favor: "She's not stupid. I need this to look like it's a great opportunity that you *happened* to mention to me at lunch. And I just *happened* to have the perfect model in mind for you."

"Of course. I got you covered, Steve."

Grant's meeting with Wilbur went well. He designed a few new looks while making alterations on some current garments, reinventing the staff's look.

Back in his room, Grant updated Howard on the meeting with Wilbur Franks, reviewing the orders he placed. He then enjoyed the two-hour massage followed by the steam room.

Chapter 7

Grant arrived at the bar just before six p.m.

The bartender, Bobby, greeted Grant as he approached.

"Hey, Bobby. I'm entertaining a few friends and will need a table."

"No problem, Mr. Robinson." Bobby guided Grant to a table close to the bar so he could serve him.

No sooner had he sat down before Steve walked in, hailing him from across the room in his pretentious way. "Is that you, roomie?" he shouted.

"Hey, pal."

Steve sat down at the table. "I know you won't be disappointed with the company tonight, and I don't mean with me. My favor has picked out someone just perfect for your viewing pleasure tonight. Who knows where the night will take us, roomie."

Steve pushed back his chair and stood up. "Ginger!" Grant got up and recognized her immediately. She was the model he had met many years before when he was interning in Chicago. He had never forgotten her. In fact, she was a locked-away fantasy he had hidden in his heart.

Their eyes met briefly while she neared them. Every sound in the room faded. He could hear his heart beating. *Air!* His lungs were on fire. She stood before him more beautiful than the day she showed up at TerRae Designs in Chicago.

Ginger was wearing an emerald-green dress. The long, flowing sleeves were sheer, revealing the natural beauty of her arms, shoulders, and neckline. Her hair was in a wispy braid, off her left shoulder, reaching down and kissing what he imagined to be the world's most beautiful breasts.

Steve introduced Ginger to Grant. "This is my roommate from college I told you about, Grant Robinson."

Reaching out her hand to Grant and locking eyes, they held hands for the first time in their lives. In that moment, Grant felt a startling shock shoot up his arm. With just a touch, he could feel her hands were tender yet strong. She just had a way about her that reminded him of Audrey Hepburn in *Breakfast at Tiffany's.*

After what felt like forever, she pulled her hand from Grant. The two of them turned to Steve. "Ginger, Grant, how does champagne sound?" Steve said. "A bottle of Veuve Clicquot?"

"Uh, yeah. Great idea, Steve." Grant was still reeling from the touch of her hand.

"Steve, a rosé, if you don't mind," Ginger said.

"Sure thing. Ginger, Grant mentioned this afternoon that he has an opportunity for you in the Big Apple."

Ginger was standing with her arm draped around Steve's shoulder. Ginger looked at Grant pensively. She waited for them to say more.

"Listen, babe," Steve said, "I know you've been waiting for something big to come along. Grant's company has a chance to land a new account in Paris. He needs someone to do some fashion shoots for their new line. I told him how great of a model you are and that you would be the perfect choice!"

She remained silent, allowing Steve to ramble on, excluding Grant from the conversation. "This will get you some European exposure. Paris, babe! Who knows? It may give you the opportunity you've always dreamed of. Where the hell's that bottle of champagne? Let's celebrate. My

Ginger in Paris!"

Ginger gave Steve a halfhearted kiss on the cheek, which was far from warm and fuzzy. She knew Steve well enough to know that this had to be beneficial for him but wasn't exactly sure how Grant fit into the equation.

Grant felt the tension slightly ease at the sound of the champagne cork popping. Bobby poured three flutes. "A toast!" Grant held up his glass. "To the stars, may they guide us all to the happiness each of us has dreamed of."

The three raised their glasses and clinked, smiling as they took a sip. Grant thought about what he was doing to Ginger. The real reason he had agreed to *help* was for his own gain—making him feel like a shithead. *If I knew it was her, would I have done this?*

Grant tipped his glass a second time toward Ginger. He instantly vowed to himself he would never do wrong by Ginger Madison, wondering why he so strongly felt the need to protect her.

"Ginger," Steve said, "where's Sarah?"

"She'll be here shortly. She had to meet someone about a fashion shoot at four." Ginger finally said her first full sentence since hearing about her "great opportunity."

"So, Grant, when do you need her in New York?"

Grant took a deep breath. "Um, a week from today? Of course, if you still have unfinished work, Ginger, I can wait a few weeks."

Ginger looked at them both, making sure she had their undivided attention. "Have you seen the movie *Mommie Dearest*? It's based on Joan Crawford's life. Of course, I think it's safe to say you've never read the memoirs of Christina Crawford, her adopted daughter. My favorite part of the movie is when Faye Dunaway, portraying Joan Crawford, stands up to the board of directors of Pepsi-Cola, fighting for what she believed in, and says, 'Don't fuck with me, fellas!'" Ginger smiled. "Keeping that in mind, I haven't accepted the job yet, *fellas*. Did I miss the part about pay, cost of living, and how this affects my employment—and what about us?"

"Whoa, whoa, love!" Steve responded. "You've been telling me forever how you've been waiting for that big break."

"I actually thought I already found that at Neiman Marcus," she sarcastically responded to Steve.

"This is all about you, babe! Grant's company has a relationship with Rosemont Resorts, which owns and manages the Carlyle Hotel on the Upper East Side. You can stay there if you wish—at my expense, of course. Obviously, Grant will pay you the going rate for a top model. You're *only* on loan right now—you are still a Neiman Marcus employee and still *belong* to me, baby." Steve squeezed her.

Ginger took a slow and thoughtful sip of her

champagne with obvious mistrust in her eyes. "Let's make this clear, Mr. Robinson: I belong to *no one.*" She slid a subtle glare toward Steve. She turned to Grant. "Your proposition sounds good. However, I will quit if you start any kind of BS with pay, sexual innuendos, and—most of all—lies. I really despise liars." She again turned to look at Steve.

"Understood, Ms. Madison. You won't have that problem with me."

For some inexplicable reason, looking into Grant's eyes, Ginger sensed his integrity and truly felt she should take a chance.

Perfectly timed, Grant likened Sarah's arrival to the sound of a bell going off at a boxing ring, saving the boxer who was getting his ass handed to him.

Sarah Gilman was twenty-five years old with a perfect model's body. She had a slightly elongated face, dirty-blonde hair, and a radiant smile. Looking into Sarah's blue eyes, Grant saw no light. *She's pretty enough for most men*, he thought, *but I wish Ginger was my date.*

Ginger and Sarah greeted each other with a warm hug. With her head resting on Ginger's shoulder, Sarah looked at Steve in a particular way, and Grant instantly read it: they were lovers.

"Sarah, come meet my good friend and roommate from college, Grant Robinson." Sarah slipped out of

Ginger's arms and planted a kiss on Grant's cheek. "So, *you're* Grant. Nice to finally be able to put a face with the name—and stories."

"Nice to meet you, Sarah."

Grant turned away from Sarah. "Bobby, I think we'll need another glass and more champagne, please."

Over the next few hours, they shared small talk and laughter while feasting on Texas-bred steak. Grant's intuition was confirmed throughout the evening that Sarah and Steve were having a tryst of sorts, even though she kept constant physical contact with Grant—touching his leg or arm, leaning into him, whispering how horny she was.

This is so fucked up, Grant thought. *I've got Steve's new girlfriend feeling me up and I'm supposed to get his current girlfriend out of town. I feel like I'm playing a game that I don't know the rules to. Honestly, all I'd like to do is spend an evening getting to know Ginger Madison. I don't understand why I'm so drawn to her, but all I know is that I want to protect her from Steve. Why the hell do I care about her? Who is Ginger Madison to me, really?*

"Well, roomie, it's about that time. Gotta run, being a family man and all," he said winking at Grant. "You and Sarah go have some fun. Kinda like the old days, huh, pal? If you can recall those blurred memories."

They all stood up to say their good-byes. Ginger leaned over to Grant and placed a soft, gentle kiss on his cheek, like a butterfly landing on a flower. Looking into his china-blue eyes, she said, "It was a pleasure to meet you, and I *do* look forward to working with you."

Grant was caught off guard and captivated by her innocent kiss. It was the first time her lips ever touched him, only to be rudely reminded of Sarah's presence when she grabbed his ass. Ignoring Sarah, he responded, "I'm looking forward to working with you too." He gave her a smile that completely melted Ginger's heart. She smiled back at Grant, wishing he could read her mind: *I'd rather be going home with you tonight, Grant*, she thought.

While walking away, Steve turned around with his arm draped over Ginger. "Sarah, don't forget about that photo shoot in the a.m. Try to be in my office by nine."

Sarah pretended to pout, looking at Steve like she was a teenager with a curfew, and then giggled. "No problem, boss! I won't let you down. I'll be there with bells on."

Sarah whispered in Grant's ear, "Let's go to your room and fuck our brains out, baby."

Grant and Sarah made their way to the elevator, and before the doors closed, she was pushing him against the mirrored walls and grinding her hips against his body. She felt his cock getting hard. She dropped to her knees and said in a baby voice, "What floor, *big boy*?"

Grant choked out, "Three."

She rose up. "Mmmm, too bad. I was hoping it was the thirtieth. I'd love to get a mouthful of you. Guess that's going to have to wait a few minutes."

He barely shut the door before she was completely naked and lying on the bed, leaving a trail of clothing along the way. Grant excused himself to use the bathroom. He found himself staring into the mirror, his thoughts consumed with Ginger. He couldn't get her eyes out of his head, the way she looked at him when they touched. *And what the hell was that perfectly sweet kiss? I'm hard because of Ginger, not Sarah. But there's no possible future with Ginger—doesn't she belong to Steve?*

Standing in the bathroom, he remembered the day he met Ginger and making love to Margo that night; he fantasized about Ginger's beauty and the secrets hiding in her eyes the whole time. Margo commented on how wild he was. He tried to disguise his desire for another woman with, "Well, it's been a long time since we made love. Guess you pushed all my buttons tonight."

"Grant!" Sarah yelped from the bedroom. "What are you *doing* in there?"

Entering the room, he glanced at Sarah lying on the bed with two fingers deep inside her cunt while massaging her clit with her thumb. He nonchalantly walked over to the minibar and poured himself vodka on the rocks.

After a few sips, Grant walked over to the edge of the bed and undid his belt. Sarah pulled her fingers out of her pussy and rolled over to yank down his pants, releasing his fully erect cock. She purred with joy at his size. Lying on her stomach, Sarah inched closer to him and took his cock into her mouth, almost gagging on it. She rolled over onto her back with her head slightly off the edge of the bed, making it easier to swallow his whole cock.

After a few minutes of fucking her mouth, he stepped back. Sarah rolled back over, pulling him with her. Grant was physically into the moment and buried his face into her dripping pussy. He slid three fingers inside her, then his whole fist as she begged for more, gripping his wrist, pulling him deeper into her, bringing her to a shattering orgasm.

"Oh my god!" she cried out, locking her legs around his head as the waves of pleasure crashed over, causing her body to tremble uncontrollably.

Grant rolled her over on to her knees and mounted her from behind. Sarah murmured, "Fuck me, Grant! Oh, baby, fuck me!"

Ginger's face filled his head as he felt his body building toward an orgasm. Grant called out "Oh, Ginger!" as he pulled out and blew a huge load onto Sarah's back.

They laid there for a few moments before he rolled off

her, trying to regain his breath. Sarah had a grin on her face. "By the way, my name is Sarah. Good thing I'm not your wife!" They both laughed: hers was devilish and his was a nervous chuckle.

"Well, I'm getting divorced on Thursday, anyway."

"You're some lover, Grant. You were Steve's roommate in college?"

"You know I was Steve's roommate."

"Well, he should have taken notes."

Sarah left the bed and jumped in the shower—like it was all done and she had to go.

She was fully dressed when she returned to the bedroom, attempting to sound sultry. "That was great, Grant. And I hope to see you soon." He was half expecting her to ask for payment. She kissed him on the cheek and left.

Grant thought about what she had just said, realizing that his instincts were right on: Sarah was already fucking Steve. And Steve wanting Ginger out of town had nothing to do with Steve's pending divorce.

Chapter 8

Ginger was lost in thought while leaving the Mansion with Steve. Everything she dreamed of during the last couple of years was quickly slipping away. Steve was rubbing her leg like nothing had changed, acting like he was excited to be with her. She was half listening to his babbling, knowing none of it mattered any longer. *Of course he'll want to get laid. Ugh.*

"Baby, aren't you excited about New York?" Steve sounded thrilled, bringing her back to the here and now.

"You really want to have this conversation right now, Steve? I thought you just wanted to screw me." She waited to see if he reacted to the double meaning.

"Jeez, why would you say that, Gin?"

"Really, Steve?"

"Okay, baby. I—"

Ginger cut him off with a wave of her hand. She turned on the radio to avoid additional conversation with him.

Back at her apartment, they fucked. Again, it was just for him. She felt used, just a piece of ass that he was obligated to fuck. Steve was even more distant than ever. He didn't even bother to put her in her favorite position. No, he left that out.

Ginger got out of bed without speaking and dressed in her robe, almost feeling like a whore. To protect herself from him emotionally, she wrapped the robe tightly around her body. She knew he was full of shit.

When she looked in the mirror, she felt disgusted. She gave him her all—especially her heart. She couldn't hide this truth from herself; she started sobbing.

When she returned to her bedroom, he was fully dressed and grabbing his keys. "God, baby, you're so beautiful. I just love being with you. I wish I could stay, but Lucy's keeping an eye on me. You're everything I ever wanted. Sorry you'll be gone for a while, but it's all for the best until the divorce is over, babe."

"Just looking out for me, huh?"

"Always. I gotta run."

"Yeah. See you tomorrow."

Without a real kiss, he left. Ginger thought, *Thank God I'm going to New York. That son of a bitch will never touch me again. I'm getting my key back from him—oh, hell, who cares? Screw him and all those liars. They don't give me credit for my mind. Beauty is a bonus, but that's all they ever see and want. God, please, I need somebody who can see me for who I really am. Lord, help me find that man—if he even really exists. Do I even need a man?*

Dressing for bed after a long shower, Grant popped into her head. Ginger found solace in wondering what it would be like to be intimate with Grant: *What are the odds? I met him so long ago. I wonder if he remembers me. I knew there was something special about him then, and obviously there still is. That look on his face while we were holding hands was incredible—the energy between us was indescribable.*

Ginger hoped he felt that electricity when they first touched too. Something definitely passed between them.

She knew he had left with Sarah. *God, Sarah will do anything. She's such a harlot. She'll screw his brains out, and I will be the last thing on his mind. She's so young and beautiful. I would love to be able to tell him that I'm not like her.*

I'm not with Steve just to get ahead. I wanted to build a future with him. He claimed he was separated and that I was the best woman he ever met. We planned to be a huge part of Neiman Marcus together. I believed him—I believed in *him. Well, now his wife is actually leaving him—but so am I. Ha!*

And now Grant's back in my life. Why? Who would guess that Grant Robinson was Steve's friend and roommate from college? And my, my, the years have been good to him! I pray to the powers that be that he's not like Steve.

Lying on her bed and thinking about Grant, she let her fingers find her slippery lips between her legs. She usually palmed herself for a very long time, but this night was different. She rolled her hard clit between two fingers, thinking of Grant touching her, kissing her, playing with her body. Before she knew it, she was bucking her hips and losing her breath with the most intense self-induced orgasm she could remember.

With her clit throbbing longer than normal, she moaned aloud, picturing Grant's face and body.

After her breath slowly calmed, Ginger drifted off into a blissful sleep, hoping that Grant was thinking of her, even though he was with Sarah.

Chapter 9

Grant grabbed two minibottles of vodka and poured them over a cup of ice. *God*, he thought, slamming back his drink, *what a fucking crazy night.* His thoughts drifted back to Ginger, knowing everything happening was a setup to get rid of her. *Why do I feel guilty for being a part of this?*

He was sure she didn't remember him from all those years before.

Steve, Ginger, Sarah, Margo, Howard, Rebekah. Jesus Christ! Of all the people surrounding me, I'm feeling guilty about letting Ginger down? What the fuck is wrong with me? I might as well be five again.

"Grant, honey, I made you your favorite cake. It's cherry cake with cream cheese frosting!"

His mother happily held the cake for him to see the red lettering: "Happy Fifth Birthday, Grant!"

"I don't want that cake, Mommy."

"But why, honey? It's your favorite!"

"It has the wrong name on it!"

"Well, my baby boy," she said with a smile, "what name should be on it?"

"Tommy!" he shouted.

His mother had a puzzled look on her face. "Why Tommy, Grant?"

"Because that's my real name!"

"Well, honey," she said, losing her patience, "your name's always been Grant." She lowered the cake for him to see again.

"I don't want that cake!"

"Grant Lee Robinson! I've had enough of this nonsense. I have worked all morning on this cake. You're being an ungrateful brat. Go to your room, now!"

She started to cry. Feeling horrible, he hugged her. He felt so guilty for disappointing someone he loved. "I'm sorry, Mommy. I'll be a good boy. I'll be your Grant."

She smiled and wiped away the tears. They hugged

tightly.

He was standing in the shower to wash away all his dirty feelings, including his tryst with Sarah. Steve and Sarah were identical, and he needed a deep cleansing from both of them.

Grant stood in the shower until the water ran cold. His brain churned about the meeting in the morning with Rebekah Scott, realizing he needed to be up in less than four hours.

He climbed into bed and was half-asleep before his head hit the pillow. And then . . .

"Tommy!" Her hands were on her hips. "Thomas Smith, where's your head? You're not a fly-boy today; you're on leave. Can you please stop getting lost in the sky? Today, you're all mine! I made you your favorite lunch."

He responded, "And what would that be, baby?"

"Spam sandwich, of course! Mustard or mayo?" She giggled. "Come on, my sweet Tommy. We don't have much time left before your leave is over." She wrapped her arms around him. "Let's pretend the bloody war is over and we're just a young couple in love, enjoying an afternoon in the countryside, okay?"

"I'm so in love with you."

He stared into her face: her vibrant, green eyes, filled with love and desire for him, her dark-auburn hair pulled off to one side. The birds were singing and green was everywhere, it was perfect. And yet, he looked back up into the blue, cloudless sky.

"Tommy, will you stop thinking about being a B-17 pilot?" His gaze returned to her face, which now had a slight frown on it. "Don't leave me, my love. I love you so much, words cannot describe. I just know you're my soul mate. So be *with* me and spend the rest of today enveloped in us before I go crazy and really make you eat a Spam sandwich!"

The alarm went off, tearing Grant from his dream. The woman in his dream quickly faded, but he didn't lose her eyes. *Those eyes! I can't get them out of my mind—like I know them.*

The knock on the door further removed him from his dream. It was food service delivering his morning coffee, juice, and assortment of pastries.

He poured his coffee and began to organize his thoughts for his meeting with Rebekah Scott. He'd already sent her some fabric samples, line drawings, and pictures, requesting any comments regarding her thoughts on the line. Per usual, the witch had not responded, wanting to make him sit on it until they were face to face. She was sure to rip him a new asshole on every item she could.

The phone rang, and Grant knew it would be Howard.

"We need this fucking contract, Grant! Don't screw it up!"

Grant pictured him screaming through gritted teeth. "Howard, how are you doing?"

"If she wants an inch, a fucking inch, give it to her!"

It was a repeat of the conversation from yesterday. He let Howard spew his anxiety but did not allow his negativity to infiltrate his being.

"Grant! Are you listening to me?"

"I've always delivered whatever you've asked for in the past—in fact, I always give you more. Why would today be any different? Trust me on this one, okay? And just a heads up, I've made a deal to perhaps get us more than a million-dollar contract."

Howard laughed. "What did you give away, farm boy?"

Grant ignored his tone. "Steve Williams needs us to create a job in New York for a female acquaintance of his for a while."

Howard barked, "Come on, Grant. Focus! Get the

contract signed and that bitch will get work for as long as she wants, and I'll give you a bonus!"

"I want more than a bonus, Howard. I've earned it."

Howard's ragged breathing was all Grant could hear. "Well, if you can bring in the Neiman Marcus account with a large order and the new lead in Paris, I'll give you whatever you want—within reason, of course. Grant, you know . . . you sound like a different man."

"I mean it, Howard! *When* I land these two accounts, I want twenty-five percent of the business at a minimum."

"Okay, okay. We will work something out," Howard mumbled.

"Seriously, Howard."

"Okay, I get it. What's happened to you down there? Did you have an awakening or something?" Howard laughed. "Well, anyway, good luck. I look forward to hearing good news from you." The line went dead.

Chapter 10

"Good morning, Mr. Robinson."

Ralph held the door open to the limo.

"Good morning, Ralph." Grant climbed into the cool air of the limo and leaned back in the seat.

"Corporate offices, Ralph."

"Yes, sir."

As the limo sped off, Grant looked out the window and noticed all the political banners, reminding him about the upcoming Republican National Convention. Ronald Reagan was running for reelection. *And I'm surprised by a World War II dream? My dad made me watch all those war movies. He just loved Ronald Reagan, Rita Hayworth, John Wayne, Clark Gable—most of them had a rank in the service, but they rarely saw action, just photo ops.*

The limo came to a halt in front of the building. Grant looked at his watch: 9:51 a.m.

"We're here, sir."

"Thank you, Ralph."

Grant walked into the building and rode the elevator to the second floor, knowing he would soon be face to face with his archnemesis. Rebekah Scott was a sixty-two-year-old spinstress who decided what women ages twenty-five to forty-five should be wearing to attract men or look glamorous in. *What a fucking joke—might as well have Captain Kangaroo's opinion on designing the clothes.*

Knowing Rebekah Scott was waiting to torture him, always fucking with his line and mind, left his stomach in knots. As he rounded the corner, he spotted her standing by her door with a scowl. Her countenance contrasted the image of Ronald Reagan's wide smile on the pin on her lapel.

Grant forced a smile. "I see you're ready for the convention, Ms. Scott."

"And who are you voting for, Grant?"

He hesitated for a moment, deciding how he should reply. "Well, if I said Ronald Reagan, would that get me a contract signed right now?"

Rebekah showed no response.

"Okay, well, what if I said John Anderson, the independent. Would that be better?"

Rebekah looked him dead in the eyes and grinned. "You're a kiss ass, Grant Robinson."

"I assume you're voting for President Reagan," he said.

"Obviously, Grant. How did you figure that one out?" Her tone was clearly condescending.

It was a welcomed distraction when her new assistant arrived. Rebekah's hands were staunchly placed on her hips. "Beth, this is Grant Robinson, the head designer from H&M Designs. He'd do anything to keep our account."

"It's a pleasure to meet you, Mr. Robinson. I've heard a lot about you."

"Nice to meet you, Beth. And who are *you* voting for?"

"Well, President Reagan, of course."

Rebekah turned to her assistant. "Beth, is the conference room ready for our meeting?"

"Oh, yes, ma'am." She looked like Bambi caught in the headlights.

"What time is our fit model coming, if needed?"

Beth answered, "At one, Ms. Scott."

"Great, that will give us enough time to review your line and go over the notes I made."

Grant jokingly said, "Let's get the war—I mean, the meeting started."

"Isn't that just a tad bit dramatic?" Rebekah retorted.

Looking at his watch, it was 10:05. Steve told him his assistant would be fetching him at 10:20. *Can't wait to see what* voilà *means.*

They walk into the conference room, and he noticed in Beth's hand pages of notes regarding his designs.

They sat around the conference table while Grant pulled out his paperwork. "Where should we start, Ms. Scott?"

"Well, how about the sportswear tops."

"Sounds good." He began to put the tops up for display.

"Stop right there, Grant. Let's talk about the neckline." Paging through her notes, she said, "Isn't that a little deeper than it should be? Exposing a little too much, don't you think?" Turning to Beth, she said, "Would you or any of your friends wear a top with a neckline that shows your cleavage that much?"

Beth walked over to examine the top, already knowing what she personally thought. Rebekah was rambling on about how Neiman Marcus maintained a certain look for their clientele. Beth held the top up to her body, pushing her breasts against the fabric, "Well, Grant—Mr. Robinson—it *is* slightly revealing."

Grant was just about to respond when he was interrupted by Steve's assistant. "Excuse me, Ms. Scott. Steve Williams needs to speak with Mr. Robinson."

Rebekah tossed her pen on the table. "Oh, of course. Not a problem." Turning to Grant with a clearly fake smile, she said, "We'll be waiting for your return. No rush." She flipped her hand into the air.

"Hold that thought," Grant said to Beth and Rebekah with a smile. He tried not to look nervous. "Feel free to look at anything else while I'm gone. You know how long-winded Steve can be at times."

"Sure do, Grant. After all, *he's* the boss." Rebekah's tone clearly displayed her distaste for Steve's interruption.

Grant followed Shirley down the hallway and told her he would be up shortly after visiting the men's room.

Grant's brain was all over the place. *Fuck, fuck, fuck! That son of a bitch. Watch the time! Five minutes. Three minutes and counting. Keep it together, you stupid shit!*

After counting the minutes, he left the restroom and returned to the conference room. He felt his heart was about to jump out of his chest as he stood outside the door.

Grant opened the door and saw a sight that made him almost shout, "Holy fuck!"

Rebekah Scott had her legs spread and her panties dangling from one ankle with her feet resting atop the table. Her head was leaning back on the chair and her hands were grasping Beth's hair, pulling her deeply between her legs. Beth was on her knees and finger fucking Rebekah, while her mouth was feverishly licking Rebekah's crotch.

Grant said, "Whoa! Excuse me, ladies. I forgot my briefcase." Beth jumped up, banging her head on the table, and Rebekah almost flipped backward in the chair. Looking directly into Rebekah's eyes, he saw the total surrender in her face. He turned and walked out of the room, thinking, *Voilà! Thank you, Steve fucking Williams.*

Less than three hours later, he held a signed contract for the next five seasons from Neiman Marcus, totaling seven million dollars. Standing outside the Neiman Marcus building, he finally allowed himself to soak in the feeling of victory. *Even the best stumble and fall sometimes, but not today!* He couldn't wait to call Howard. But even more than that, he wanted to see Ginger.

A Neiman Marcus limo stopped at the front door of the building, and Ginger got out. Grant nearly tripped over himself to assist her exit.

Chapter 11

Ginger exited the Neiman Marcus limo, and to her surprise, standing there, extending his hand, was Grant. Their touch once again was electric, yet her brain went straight to work mode.

"It's great to see you, Grant. But honestly, you're the last person I expected to greet me. Is the meeting over already?"

"Well, Ginger, it went better than I thought. Rebekah approved a lot of items, for once, placing a sizable order. I hope we didn't waste your time."

She had a sweet smile. "No, you haven't wasted any of

my time. That's how it goes in this industry. Are you always such a gentleman, Grant?"

He looked down at his feet for a second, trying to hide the fact that she was capable of making him blush. "Only when I'm with the right person." He smiled that boyish grin, and his blue eyes captured her again. He continued, "I've followed your work for years, and you're an exceptional model, Ginger. I don't know if you remember, but we met in Chicago, over ten years ago when I was completing my internship."

"Thank you for the compliment. I sort of thought I was under the radar. No, I haven't forgotten our first meeting. It was my first modeling job outside of New York. I was just eighteen years old." She blushed herself. "I'm really looking forward to working with you in New York." Ginger smiled and turned to walk away.

"Hey, Ginger? Please, don't take this the wrong way; it's meant to be a compliment. If I was Steve, I would never have let you out of my sight. You're way too talented to get lost in this industry. And just a heads up—I may end up trying to steal you from Neiman Marcus."

"Thank you, Grant. We may be just what the other needs." She disappeared into the building.

Ginger walked into Rebekah Scott's office.

"Hi, I'm Ginger Madison. I have a meeting with Ms. Scott," she said to Beth, Rebekah's assistant.

"Your name again?" Beth said snidely.

"Ginger Madison. She is expecting me."

"Give me a second. I'll let her know you're here."

While looking at Ginger, Beth picked up the phone. "Ms. Scott, a Ginger Madison is here for the fit model meeting."

Rebekah yelled out from her office, "We won't be needing her. The line meeting finished early. Send her my best wishes in the Big Apple. Mr. Williams informed me yesterday that she'll be moving to New York."

How the hell did she find out yesterday that I'm going to New York when I only heard about it last night? Who else has Steve told in the company?

Ginger composed herself. "Thank Ms. Scott for me. Have a nice day."

Ginger rode the elevator straight to the third floor and burst through the reception area looking for Steve. Shirley attempted to stop her but backed off as soon as she saw the anger on Ginger's face.

Ginger walked into Steve's office. "You fucking liar!" She slammed the door behind her. "Why the hell did you think it was okay to tell Rebekah that I'm leaving Neiman Marcus before you tell me or even ask me if I want to go to New York? Who the hell do you think you are? Last night was the last time you will ever have a piece of me, you . . . you—I can't even come up with a shitty enough word to describe you!"

"Baby, what are you talking about?" he said flatly.

"Don't you 'baby' me, you bastard! You know exactly what I'm talking about! So who's my replacement? Sarah? Just say it, you pompous ass. So she's younger than me—is that what you want? Why don't you speak the truth for once in your life? Just say it! Say her name! Say 'Sarah'!"

Steve was shocked into silence. She continued, "I can't deal with a liar. You know this. And yet I've shared a bed with a liar for over two years now." She slammed her hand on his desk and glared into his eyes. "Who do you think I am? A cheap whore? I'm done!"

"But, babe—" Steve tried to interject.

"Shut up! You lost the privilege to call me anything other than my name. How long have you been planning this? You know what? I don't care, because I'm going to make it without your help."

"Okay, if you think so," Steve said under his breath.

"I heard that, you asshole! And you will pay for everything you said you would, unless you'd like me to call your Lucille. I gave you my everything! My heart, my love, my knowledge of fashion, and all you did was use me!"

"Ginger, I'm sorry you feel this way," Steve stoically responded.

"The only thing you're sorry about is that you got caught in your own web of lies."

She stood tall, whipped around, and headed for the door. "This will probably be the last you see of me, unless you renege on your promises. Because I do expect that at the very least!"

Ginger opened the door, turned, and added, "Enjoy Sarah for what she's going to take from you," and then she quietly closed the door.

Walking past Shirley, who was eavesdropping, Ginger said, "Sit down, missy. You have bigger fish to fry than me. Good luck with the next one. Her name is Sarah, and then, who knows?"

Riding the elevator to the lobby, Ginger thought, *New York, watch out! Ginger Madison is coming home.*

Chapter 12

Grant slid into the limo. His thoughts were everywhere. He could barely decide what was more exciting: the thrill of landing the biggest order of his career or the unexpected conversation he just had with Ginger. And to boot, the limo was filled with the scent of her hair and skin.

"Mr. Robinson, where to?"

"Oh, sorry, Ralph. Back to the Mansion."

"That Ms. Madison is one of the nicest people around."

Grant didn't respond.

"I thought you two were friendly."

"We are—well, just old acquaintances."

He knew that the Neiman Marcus corporate limo drivers knew everything about everybody. Grant didn't want to put Ginger or himself in a compromising position. God forbid it got back to Steve that his thoughts were more focused on Ginger than the record-breaking deal he just closed.

He remained quiet, because all he could think of was Ginger. Her natural beauty, her grace, the unbelievable ease he felt when being around her—he couldn't understand it.

The limo pulled up in front of the Mansion. As Grant walked into the lobby, he saw Kent. "Could you fax this paperwork to my office, attention Howard Golden, please?"

"No problem," Kent said.

"And could you FedEx the paperwork to my office for me?"

"Sure thing, Mr. Robinson. Anything else?"

"No, I'll be checking out shortly. Thanks for all your help, Kent."

The phone was already ringing when he entered his suite. He knew who it was—Howard. He must have already gotten the fax. *That cocksucker will be screaming per usual, but at least he won't be condemning me to hell this time.*

Grant decided not to answer it. His thoughts were searching for a reason to call Ginger. He just wanted to hear her voice. *Why am I calling? I need a good excuse. Oh, maybe to see how her meeting went?*

He decided to call, but when the answering machine picked up, it occurred to him she was still at Neiman Marcus.

No sooner after hanging up did the phone ring again. "Hello?" he answered, hoping it might be Ginger's voice on the other end.

"Well, fuck, farm boy! How the fuck did you get that contract?"

Grant didn't respond.

"You son of a bitch! You did it!" Howard carried on with a million questions. "You're just like me, kid! I can still remember landing my first big contract. I guess Margo was right about you. I sure as hell didn't see what she saw in you, no matter how many times she tried to convince me."

Grant started tuning Howard out. His thoughts drifted back to Ginger.

Suddenly, Grant snapped back from Howard's loud celebratory hoots.

"Well, Grant, I'm impressed! Next stop, Paris, buddy boy. Let's see what the hell you can do there. See you Monday. Oh, almost forgot. Who's the piece of ass you'll be bringing back for me?"

"Come on, Howard, she's not a piece of ass. However, she is a kick-ass fashion model. Her name is Ginger Madison."

"Whatever, whoever. See you then, kid!" Click.

Grant sat in silence. *Was that a compliment? He's proud of my work and now I'm finally good enough? I've landed him so many accounts. And what the hell does Margo have to do with my work? Screw him!*

The phone rang again. *Jesus Christ! Did he forget to tell me how wonderful he is or what?*

"Hey, Howard," Grant said when he picked up the phone.

"Well, how did the meeting go? Didn't let you down, did I, roomie?"

"Steve, how in the—?"

Steve cut him off. "I've got sources, Grant. No worries. But here's the *real deal*, roomie: I have been at war with Rebekah Scott forever. She's been trying to bring me down since I started. With Stanley Marcus in her pocket, I've been like a soldier on the field without a weapon—until Ginger showed up and helped me out."

Grant responded, "Why are you letting her go?"

"It's time, Grant. You never had a killer instinct, did you? When you realize the danger of the person who knows your shortcomings and could use them against you, it's time to let them go."

"Steve, what the hell are you talking about?"

"The main reason I called is you need to deliver your end of the deal along with the product. Just get her out of here ASAP and I will keep you so friggin' busy your head will be spinning. But you have to keep her happy."

"Steve, I already talked to my boss about her, and the next stop is Paris. Why are you so freaked out? I wouldn't let you down, you know that."

"Honestly, Grant, this just happened. Ginger stormed in here and handed me my ass on a silver platter. I should have kept my mouth shut about her leaving for New York, but Rebekah loves to drive the dagger deeper than anyone I've ever met. That fucking cunt let her know that *she* knew she was going to New York yesterday. Bitch!"

"So what happened with Ginger?"

"She's not stupid, Grant. Remember I told you that already? Well, she figured out that I was getting rid of her. Call her and talk about the future, whatever. Just fucking calm her down. She's probably already ripping my pictures into bits or burning everything I've ever given her. Well, except maybe the jewelry." Steve nervously laughed.

"All right, all right. I'll call her right now. So let me take care of my end. I'll catch up with you later, Steve."

Grant dialed Ginger, waiting with anticipation as the phone rang, wondering if the answering machine would pick up again.

"Hello?" Her voice was shaky.

"Ginger?"

"Grant?"

"Yeah, hi, Ginger. I just wanted to catch up with you about getting you set up for next week. Would there be any chance that you could fly to Chicago first? We could spend a few hours on our flight prepping ourselves about work and the fut—"

"Sure, Grant. I don't mean to interrupt you, but I think that's a great idea."

Grant could hear the change in her tone.

"Believe it or not, I'm definitely ready to get out of here. A flight from Chicago to New York would be a fabu place to start getting to know you and going over what we will be doing."

"Great! I'll make the arrangements. Chicago will be flight 174, and it usually leaves Dallas around nine thirty a.m. and arrives in Chicago around eleven thirty. We can meet at the gate and catch the afternoon flight to New York. Does that work for you?"

"How do you know there's a flight at nine thirty from Dallas to Chicago just like that?"

"I have kids that I visit in Chicago—my daughter, Lyla, and my son, Jason. In fact, that's where I'm headed now."

"Oh, sorry. I'm suddenly a little gun-shy with people

making arrangements for me."

"I understand. I'll see you Sunday?"

"Yes, Grant. And thank you. I'm looking forward to it."

"Me too. Be safe this weekend."

"You too. Enjoy your children."

Grant reluctantly hung up the phone, whispering her name, "Ginger Madison. Wow."

Ginger couldn't pack fast enough. She even started wondering what she was going to wear on the flight. "Screw Dallas. New York will be my home; it's always been good to me. I can't wait!"

Chapter 13

Settling back into the limo's leather, on the way to the airport, Grant realized a change in himself: all the negative energy was leaving him and the rest would be gone soon. There was certainly something different about his entire being, something that he hadn't known or ever felt before in his life. The tension was melting away while thoughts of his children and Ginger began swimming around in his mind.

Upon arriving at the airport, Grant checked in and decided he had time to hit the Admiral's Club for a drink. Grant took a sip of his drink. *Why do I feel like I've known her since the beginning of time? I cannot wait until Sunday.*

Her eyes are embedded in my brain, her touch, her voice. I already feel addicted!

Grant slammed back his martini, paid his tab, and headed toward the gate.

After Grant buckled his seat belt, a young, pretty stewardess walked over to him. "Good afternoon. Can I get you something to drink?"

"Yes, a dirty martini will be fine. Thank you."

"I'll be right back."

The martini arrived, and taking his first sip, Grant tried to recall the last time he was in Baraboo, Wisconsin. *I remember it was fall, the leaves were just changing into their brilliant colors. It was just after I got home from 'Nam in 1973.*

He and Margo were in the process of moving from Chicago to New York City to start his new job. They visited with his cousin, Dan, and his wife, Karen, and they met his new niece, Aimee. Lyla was just two years old.

Grant reminisced about the summers spent there, skinny-dipping in Devil's Lake and camping under the darkest sky loaded with millions of stars. He was living with Old Lady Pete at her dairy farm, where his mother had grown up.

The thought of those hot biscuits and strawberry jam

made from scratch made him smile. He could almost smell the jam. Grant drained his martini.

Grant opened his briefcase, taking out the work orders to review the details for TerRae Sportswear, the subcontractor for H&M Designs. He wanted to be ready for an instant meeting, not knowing if Terri wanted to look at the orders right away or wait until the morning. She was picking him up at the airport. Terri was the business-savvy and "just do it" girl at TerRae.

As he exited the plane at O'Hare International, he saw Terri, looking as beautiful as she did during his last visit—like she hadn't aged a day since his internship: dark, naturally curly hair; olive completion; twinkling brown eyes; and red, blazing lips. She had a smile that had every man staring as they walked by her.

"Hey, Grant!"

She was so tantalizing, you would have to be blind not to notice her.

Grant whispered into her ear, "My God, Terri. You are as beautiful as ever."

Terri wrapped him into her breasts. The smell of her body cream slightly aroused him.

"Oh, come on, Grant! I know you say that to all the women in your life."

Terri and her husband, Richard, owned TerRae Sportswear. She had a great eye for fashion and forecasting future trends. Terri taught Grant to look at garments like they were puzzle pieces and how simple it was to create a new pattern by *changing just a few pieces.* She showed him how different fabrics worked and would fit better with certain designs. Although only a few years older than Grant, she was a great mentor; she made him feel like an artist, helping him find the confidence to finally believe in himself.

Near the end of his internship, Terri and Richard hosted a Christmas party at her home for all the employees and special buyers. That night, he drank a little too much, got a little too high from the free-flowing bongs. Terri insisted on him sleeping over and that she would handle it with Margo. She led him to a guest bedroom in her house, where he passed out instantly.

He remembered waking up later that night to Terri gagging on his cock. His dick was hitting the back of her throat, and she was unable to take his entire length. He reached down and pulled her hair while she then rhythmically slid his cock in and out of her mouth.

Finally pulling her up by her hips, he placed her body so her pussy was perfectly hovering over his face, and he devoured her. She was grinding her hips on his face when she came undone, enjoying the naughty pleasures of the flesh. Grant slid her body down onto his throbbing shaft. He drove it deeply into her wet pussy with the tip reaching the back of her cunt.

The next hour was spent eating, sucking, fucking, and playing with each other. Nothing in the world mattered except their physical feelings, not even the fact that Richard could have walked in on them at any moment.

The next day, Terri took Grant aside. She thanked him for the most sensual experience she had ever had. However, in the end, she said, "I'm sorry, but we shouldn't let it happen again."

"I can respect that; we're both married."

"Grant, thank you for reminding me what it feels like to be a woman. That was something I haven't felt in years."

"Last night will always be one of the hottest memories of my life, Terri." She smiled and hugged him, knowing that their secret was safe.

Driving toward the Ritz-Carlton in downtown Chicago, they caught up on recent activities in their lives. A half hour later, they arrived at the Ritz. Grant began the check-in process. "I have a reservation for three nights. Grant Robinson."

"Ah, I see your reservation, Mr. Robinson. You and your wife will love the view of the lake from your room. Do you need two keys?"

Grant turned to Terri, with his boyish grin. "Sweetheart, would you like your own key?"

Terri jabbed him in the arm. "But of course, baby. Just in case we get separated and I find myself in need of someone else to entertain me." Terri giggled.

Grant smiled. "One key will be fine. Thank you."

Riding the elevator to the eighth floor, Terri said, "You are such a tease, Grant. You think he knew you were fucking with him?"

"Nah. He only saw how beautiful you are and wondered if I'm fucking you."

"Sure." She winked.

They walked into a suite with a balcony that had a beautiful view of Lake Michigan.

"Terri, I need to clean up before we go out."

"Go freshen up," Terri said, "while I help myself to a drink."

"Thanks, Terri. Mind if I take a quick shower?"

"Of course not! Take your time."

After the relaxing, hot shower, Grant wrapped himself in a towel and walked into the bedroom. To his surprise, he found Terri lying on the bed naked. He admired her spectacular body.

The silence lingered far too long, only to be broken by Terri popping up into an Indian-style position. "Well, look at this. Grant Robinson is in love!"

Grant responded, "What?"

"Or am I repulsive?"

"Of course not, Terri. Repulsive? Never! You've always been a looker."

Terri said, "Come on, Grant. Let's get a drink and some dinner. I'm *dying* to hear about this one. When a desirable, divorced man like you is not in need of a freely offered lay, he's either become gay or fallen in love." She smirked. "So which is it, Grant?"

"It's a tale of all tales."

"Great!" She hopped out of bed and got dressed. "Come on, my little farm boy. I can't wait to hear all about her!"

Chapter 14

Terri and Grant enjoyed the luxury of a relaxed meal together, talking about something other than work.

Taking another sip of his wine, Grant recounted the first time he met Ginger.

Terri listened intently. Then Grant explained how she suddenly reappeared in his life through Steve.

"So you've been brought back together now. And?"

"Terri, when we touched, it was explosive between us, like an electrical charge went off."

"Grant, do you understand what's happening? Cosmic forces that exist beyond our control have drawn you back together and given you both a second chance! Maybe at *true* love. This has something to do with your past life—*and* hers. Most people aren't so lucky."

Grant had a dumbfounded look on his face. "Past lives?"

"There are a lot of mysteries in the universe, and past lives are one of them. Don't question it, Grant. Your soul is talking to you." Trying not to cry, Terri paused, "Look, I missed my opportunity to embrace true love once. Ginger was brought back into your life to complete something. But it's always your choice."

Grant sat back with a stunned look on his face. He sipped his wine and took a deep breath. "And I thought I had the tale to tell. I know there's something special about her. And it scares the hell out of me, but I won't let go of her."

"Cheers to that!"

Walking out of the restaurant, Terri and Grant hugged each other.

"Thank you, Terri. Your friendship has always been a gift to me."

"Grant, listen to your heart." With a friendly kiss on the cheek, they parted ways.

Grant stood on the balcony of his room and watched the moon rise over Lake Michigan. *God, what a crazy evening. Past lives and cosmic forces? What the hell? Maybe it is real—it could explain why I'm so drawn to Ginger. Sleep, that's what I need!*

He climbed into his bed and drifted off to sleep.

The young pilot had just flown eighteen hours eating army rations. "Spam," he mumbled. "I'd like to meet the asshole who invented it and shove it up his ass with the can and key intact."

It was nine p.m. when he entered little English pub looking for real food. The young woman behind the counter looked up at him while carrying three pints of ale.

"Have a seat, fly-boy," she said with a smile. Tommy sat down at the long, wooden bar.

The girl came back to the bar. "So what's it going to be?" she asked. She was petite, slender, and perfectly proportioned. She had chestnut-brown hair and green eyes with distinct blue on the rims of her irises.

Tommy almost got lost in those eyes. "Well, honey—"

"Not available, fly-boy!"

"Huh?"

"All you American fly-boys think we Brit girls are here for the taking. My name is not 'honey.' And in case you haven't noticed, this isn't a dance hall! So, are you hungry or are you thirsty?"

"Hungry and thirsty, miss." He was humbled by her words.

"Great," she replied, "I suggest the shepherd's pie and a pint of ale."

Tommy looked up at her and saw she had a grin on her face. He watched her as she walked away, almost swaying.

She returned with his pint, adding, "And it's not cold like you Americans like it, but cellar temperature." She stood there with her arms crossed, waiting for him to say something after taking a sip.

"Mmmm, that's perfect!" He wanted to appease her. She turned and walked away.

Wow, what a fireball! Tommy noticed every detail about her, embedding every element of her face and body into his brain. She was wearing a forest-green crepe dress that hung on her body perfectly. Her legs and her ass moved in perfect unison, precise yet smoothly like a cat.

She served him his shepherd's pie, standing there like a girlfriend tending to her sweetheart who was in need of a homemade meal. The food tasted so good, he started to gulp it down.

"Hey, blue eyes. You are supposed to chew."

He looked up at her. "Tommy."

She stood there a second and then walked away. Over her shoulder, she casually replied, "Rachel."

He ordered another pint and nearly licked his plate clean. "Well, Tommy, how would you like some of my fresh, homemade apple pie with ice cream?"

He looked into her beautiful smiling face and couldn't believe what came out of his mouth. "Only if it comes with a kiss from you."

"Well, you fly-boys are all the same, aren't you? I am a nice, proper English girl. So I'll ignore that last comment, assuming you are suffering from bloody high-altitude sickness."

Tommy watched her sway away in complete control, and he sat there feeling like a fool for ever saying something like that to a lady.

Rachel placed the warm apple pie with melting ice cream in front of him, grinning while pouring him a cup of coffee. "I know you Americans don't drink tea."

Rachel leaned on the counter and watched him eat his first bite.

"Wow! This is amazing."

"Glad you like it, Tommy. So where's home?"

"Madison, Wisconsin. Sorry if I insulted you before. I forgot my manners."

"It's okay. It must be strange to be so far from home. I need to finish up, Tommy. Don't be a stranger."

By the time he finished and was paying the tab, almost all the patrons were gone. “Rachel, thank you for making me feel at home and almost forgetting about the war. You are a very special lady for some lucky guy.”

Tommy turned to leave.

“Hey, you forgot something.”

He turned around, wondering if he forgot to tip her.

“I thought you ordered a kiss.” She walked right up to him and tenderly touched her lips to his. Then suddenly, her tongue was wriggling its way into his mouth. She stood back bashfully for a moment and giggled, looking at the ground and then back at Tommy.

“Really? And here I thought you were a proper English girl,” he stammered.

“I am. But what’s a girl to do when she finally meets the love of her life?”

Chapter 15

The scream of the alarm clock pulled Grant from dreamland. *Jesus! Why am I having these dreams?* He lay there trying to remember her name, but everything was quickly fading. *But those eyes! Those ravishing, green-and-blue eyes!*

Grant began prepping for the meeting with Terri at the factory, yet he was still distracted by the woman in his dream.

His breakfast of assorted fruits and yogurt arrived to his room. He sipped his coffee. *She was so vivid! I can almost smell her hair, feel her skin, her lips. What a captivating and beautiful creature. So is this a message from the universe? Ha! Terri can always influence me . . . all that past life shit. I need a lobotomy.*

An hour later, Grant exited the elevator into the hotel lobby. "Mr. Grant!" a voice called to him.

"Charlie! How's life treating you?"

"Fine, fine, sir!" They shook hands and walked toward Charlie's black 1980 Lincoln Continental stretch limo, nicknamed Betsy. He had been his personal driver for his business trips to Chicago for years. Looking like a retired linebacker from the Chicago Bears, his size and stature were deceiving, since he was just an oversized teddy bear.

"Charlie, Betsy looks beautiful."

"Doesn't she, though?" Charlie said with pride, his voice smiling. Grant settled into the limo.

"Where are we off to, Mr. Grant?"

"The factory on West Irving Park Road."

The car drove off. Suddenly, it clicked in his head. *Holy shit! Full circle. I'm returning to where I first met Ginger Madison. I'll be standing in the same fucking factory.* His mind for the next twenty minutes was spinning with the notion.

"All right, Mr. Grant, we're here." They pulled up to the TerRae warehouse. "If you need anything, and I mean *anything*, I'll be here. Just call me." Charlie hopped out of the limo and opened the door.

"Thank you, Charlie."

Grant rang the doorbell of the warehouse. The door swung open, "Grant Robinson," a woman screamed, with her arms wide open. She giggled uncontrollably at just the sight of him. Mary Ellen wrapped around him before he could take a step inside.

Mary Ellen was a spinster, a seamstress extraordinaire. She introduced Grant to the magic of creating with a sewing machine. "I have a surprise for you. I made you some of my world-famous pignoli cookies when Terri told me you were coming."

"Perfect!" He hugged her back.

Grant followed Mary Ellen down the hallway. The first door on his left was opened, and he saw the cutting table where he spent countless hours as a younger man—the very space he first saw Ginger Madison.

"Mary Ellen, I'll be in the cutting room for a minute."

Sitting in the chair, Grant placed both hands on the table. Memories began to emerge that were buried. Perhaps having Ginger in his future furthered his desire to rediscover some part of himself that he left behind. Closing his eyes, he recalled the morning Ginger would enter his life. He could almost smell her hair, the scent of her body lotion she wore that day, the music of her voice, and most of all, the beauty in her eyes. *My God, her eyes.*

Mary Ellen walked into the cutting room and saw Grant sitting there with his eyes closed. "Grant! Where the hell are you?"

His eyes opened and he laughed, slightly embarrassed.

"I just went to tell Terri you're here and you look like you went time traveling. You need a cookie and a double espresso! By the way, it's 1984," she said, giggling.

"Right. I need an espresso for sure."

Grant grabbed his briefcase and entered Terri's office. Terri was reaching for some paperwork near the top of a shelf when he entered. She wore painted-on jeans paired with a blue three-quarter-sleeved top, exposing a shoulder. Her ensemble left very little to the imagination.

Terri's office walls were lined with patterns that were neatly organized, making it known that she was the reason that TerRae was still alive and kicking. Her large antique wooden desk was slightly cluttered with orders and sketches.

After a warm welcome, she sat in her chair. "So, my sweet soul, let's see what you've brought me."

Grant and Terri went over the patterns for the Mansion's latest designs. Mary Ellen arrived with more coffee and cookies. "Mary Ellen, take a look at this and see what you think."

"Jesus, Terri. That's simple. We can update the patterns in no time."

Grant bit into one of Mary Ellen's cookies and jumped up. "Honey, I know this is sudden, and I'm not sure if I love you or your cookies, but will you marry me right after my divorce is final, about three thirty this afternoon?"

Mary Ellen screamed, "Oh my God, Terri! I have a fiancé! It took you long enough, Grant."

"Don't they say timing is everything?" They all laughed.

Grant and Terri went for a quick bite at Bella Lisa's Pizzeria, watching the passersby while sipping their wine.

"How does it feel to finally be almost rid of that albatross?"

Grant stared at Terri. "Huh?"

"God, you're such a naïve, sweet farm boy. Where the fuck is Baraboo, Wisconsin, anyway? Because I'm sending my kids there to finish growing up!"

"Well, about an hour—"

Raising a hand, Terri cut him off. "You know, Margo and I go way back. We even played when we were kids, but I never truly liked her. She only looked out for herself. She was always a user, looking to control every situation and climbing the ladder. For the last decade, she never cared who was in her way."

Grant was confused. "I really don't know what you're

referring to, Terri, other than the fact that she is a bitch."

"You know the old saying, 'While the cat's away, the mice will play'?"

"Terri, stop being coy."

"Grant, darling, how do you think a farm boy from Wisconsin, albeit super cute, would land a job in New York's premiere garment industry?"

"Margo had connections," Grant replied simply.

Terri was unable to look into Grant's eyes and took another sip of wine and broke off a piece of bread. "Try the bread, Grant."

He buttered a piece of bread. "What *are* we talking about, Terri?"

She sighed. "Okay, Grant. You know this industry. What do most models do to get ahead of their competition? Fuck any models lately? Anyone at Neiman Marcus offer you a piece of ass recently?"

Grant started to defend Margo, but Terri cut him off. "Shut up, Grant. You're going to make me spell it out for you? Damn it, you're such a sweetheart! I never wanted to be the one to say it, something that would really hurt you."

"Hurt me?" He was attempting to connect the evasive dots.

Terri looked out the window. "Remember, she was modeling in New York while you were away in 'Nam. You could have died at any moment. Just give thanks that you're about to be free of her. The most important thing is that you still and will always have your children. They're yours, honey, no matter what the story is."

Grant decided not to push the subject for fear of what could follow such a loaded statement. Whatever Terri was alluding to, he didn't care any longer. Terri smiled a sad smile and left it at that.

As Grant and Terri walked back to the factory just a few doors down, his mind drifted back to Ginger and how he couldn't wait to see her.

"Hello? Grant? Where are you?" Terri knew him well enough to recognize that faraway look in his eyes. "Already in Bara-fucking-boo?" She laughed.

Grant replied, "No, I was just lost in the most beautiful eyes I've ever seen. I've thought about what you meant by the universe and following the cosmic forces that crisscross in life. I think I finally get it, Terri. I know where I'm going. Thank you."

He hugged her. Terri released him after a few moments, saying, "She's one lucky lady. I hope she knows it. I have a feeling she does. But be patient until she discovers it herself."

After Charlie arrived with the limo, Mary Ellen handed Grant two bags of goodies for his kids. Terri rolled her eyes with laughter at Mary Ellen's farewell statement: "Don't forget, I want a big diamond! Size six."

"Charlie, my freedom awaits me at 1465 Cermack Road in Berwyn."

"Yes, sir, Mr. Grant. Sit back and enjoy the ride. How about a little music?"

"Sure, sure."

Grant's thoughts wandered off to what Terri said about Margo. He tried wrapping his head around it, but in the end, he decided he'd just sign the divorce papers and let it go.

Once again, Ginger infiltrated his mind. He hoped she was packing and not dwelling on Steve. *I am so happy that I will be working with her, that I'll just be around her.*

"We're here, Mr. Grant. I'll be waiting right here."

"Thanks, Charlie."

Grant opened the door to the massive entryway. *Thank God Margo agreed to use the same lawyer. For once in her life, she was reasonable about money—probably because she's getting more from me that way.*

He put on his game face, knowing that signing the papers was merely a formality at this point. A jolt of strength-sucking negative energy passed through him when he saw her in the lobby.

Grant gathered himself. “You look nice, Margo.” She rolled her eyes, looking away silently. “Always on top of the latest look.”

The receptionist announced, “Mr. Naughton is ready for you.” She led them down the hallway.

Before Grant knew it, the papers were signed. The ink was barely dry when Margo found him in the hallway for her last-minute dig. “Well, Grant, that’s it. Wish you could have kept it together.” Leaning in closer, she whispered, “Guess I don’t have to worry about a paternity test now. You’re such a dumbass.” She cackled viciously, walking away.

Grant was numb and motionless at her statement. He swallowed and said, “I’ll be getting the kids in about a half hour from your parents.”

“Just have them back on Sunday before noon, Grant.” She said his name like it was a bad word.

That’s what Terri was alluding to! Holy shit. She was fucking Howard, wasn’t she? And that’s how I got the job! Whoa. Is Lyla mine? Fuck them! Either way, she’s mine. She’ll always be my little girl.

Grant walked out the front door of the attorney's office and gave Charlie two thumbs up.

Charlie opened the door for Grant. "Looks like you've survived. Where are we off to?"

"Let's pick up my kids. They're going to stay with me for a few days of fun. But don't worry, I won't let them destroy Betsy."

"Now, now, you know Betsy and I love kids, Mr. Grant. I have six grandchildren of my own. Just sit back and relax, especially if you're going to be spending the weekend with your youngsters, you'll need it. If you don't mind me asking, what are your plans?"

"Tonight we're going to Grant Park for some music and a picnic. Tomorrow morning, the Museum of Science and Industry, and then off to Baraboo, Wisconsin. I've been instructed by my ex-wife to return them Sunday around noon. Ah, ex-wife sounds so good to me! Never thought I'd feel that way."

"Whatever makes you happy, Mr. Grant. So how are you getting to Baraboo?"

"Was planning to rent a car."

Charlie looked in the rearview mirror. "Well, Mr. Grant, I have two cousins who live near Baraboo. What if me and Betsy drive you there? It will probably cost the same as you renting a car. We could pack up Betsy, and the kids could even stretch out and nap if they wanted. You could relax all the way to Baraboo and have yourself a well-deserved drink. I like treating Betsy to a vacation every once in a while. If you need me to drive anywhere while visiting, I'll be glad to do that also."

"Then it's a done deal, Charlie."

Fifteen minutes later, Betsy pulled up to Margo's parents' townhouse. He wasn't particularly looking forward to seeing his now ex-in-laws, Fred and Patricia.

"Unit seven, Charlie, right there on the corner. Hopefully it'll be quick."

"No problem, Mr. Grant."

Walking toward the door, he saw Jason and Lyla looking out of the second-floor window of the brick townhouse and disappearing instantly. He could hear the kids screaming, "Grandpa! Grandma! Daddy's here!" Grant smiled hearing their excitement. He didn't even have to knock on the door before it swung open, with Lyla jumping into his arms and Jason hugging both his legs.

"Daddy!" they screamed.

"My babies! It's so good to see you!" Grant bent down so he could wrap his arms around both of them, overwhelmed with their love.

Fred and Patricia greeted him at the door. Patricia looked at him with distaste and immediately walked back inside.

"Come in, son. How about a drink?" Fred asked.

"Fred, I could use one, but I really don't have the time. I've got the limo waiting. Thank you." He smiled.

Patricia appeared in the foyer with the kids' suitcases and rudely commented over Fred's shoulder, "We've been waiting for you for more than an hour." She sported the same disapproving scowl that Margo usually wore.

"Got here as soon as I could, Patricia. See you on Sunday," he said, keeping his cool.

Turning to Fred and shaking his hand, he said, "Thanks for helping out with the kids."

"My pleasure, Grant. They're great."

"If you ever need anything, Fred, let me know." Grant turned toward the kids while grabbing their suitcases. "You kids ready to go?"

"Yes, Daddy!" they both sung out in unison.

"Daddy, is that your limo?" Lyla piped up.

"Did you bring it all the way from New York?" Jason added.

"No, son. But you'll like Betsy."

"Who's Betsy?"

"Lyla, Betsy is the name of the limo, and Charlie is our driver. Best behavior for the ride, okay?"

"Of course, Daddy." Lyla laughed. "Betsy. That's weird to name a car."

After the introductions and settling into Betsy, Grant asked, "How about a picnic at the park tonight?"

"What park, Daddy?" Jason asked.

"It's called Grant Park."

"They named a park after you?" Jason questioned.

"No, Jason. I think it's about a president or something." Lyla rolled her eyes at her little brother.

"That's right, Lyla. So there's a really big fountain with colored lights. Lucky for us, I happen to have a pocket full of coins to make wishes! But you can't tell me what they are, you know?"

"I know what I'm wishing for, Daddy," Lyla said, giggling.

"Can you wish for the same thing more than once, Daddy?" Jason asked.

Grant responded, "Yes, but careful. A double wish is a double wish."

"Oh, Daddy, I think it just makes the wish stronger."

Grant was silenced by Lyla's sweet and innocent wisdom. Jason squawked, "Then I'm really gonna wish for no school!"

They all laughed, and Grant said, "Yeah! I wish for no more work!"

Lyla scolded them both. "Now your wishes can't come true!"

Grant's kids were adorable at the park. They devoured their food and at times danced around to the music and sang along to the songs.

"Happy with your wishes at the fountain?" Grant asked later, when he was getting them ready for bed.

"Yeah, Daddy, I wished for—"

Lyla cut Jason off. "You can't tell us or it won't come true!"

Breaking up the bickering, Grant said, "Well, I only had one coin for myself, and I know my wish will come true. I hope all yours will also. Now let's get some sleep, kids. We have a big day tomorrow."

"What are we doing, Daddy?" Jason asked, clutching his favorite blanket.

"Well, tomorrow morning we're going to the Museum of Science and Industry, buddy."

"Oh, great. That sounds kinda boring," Lyla responded sarcastically.

"Relax, baby girl. You'll love the coal mine ride."

"Rides? Is it a real coal mine, Daddy?" Jason asked excitedly.

"I think it's as real as it gets here in the city. We'll see tomorrow. It's time for sleep. I love you both."

"Love you too, Daddy," they said in unison.

An hour later, Grant checked on them one last time before he visited the minibar, thinking he'd certainly earned a shot of vodka for the day. Taking a deep swallow of his reward in a glass, he thought about Ginger and what it would have been like to come home from Vietnam to her instead of Margo. *Why am I so drawn to her?*

Chapter 16

Ginger packed for her move to New York City, deciding what to take with her and what to leave behind. She wished she could obliterate any memory of Steve. The gifts he had given her didn't mean anything, just like his words. As the day went by, she kept finding herself thinking about Grant.

Ginger continued packing, only stopping to call her mom to share her news about moving back to the Big Apple.

"I've been put 'on loan' from Neiman Marcus for a gig at H&M Designs." Before her mother could respond, she began describing her new boss to her mother.

"You sound very excited about moving back," her mom said. "Although you seem more excited about this—what was his name? Grant?"

"Of course I'm excited to work with him! I met him years ago when he was just an intern, and now he's the head designer for a private-label company. Remember when I went to Chicago all those years ago for one of my first fashion shoots?"

"When?"

Ginger sighed. "One of my first modeling jobs, Mom. Anyway, that's where I met him."

Her mother laughed, "Well, maybe you'll grace some magazine covers again, honey. And I'm so happy you're coming home."

"Me too."

"Why don't you stay with us, honey? Your room is still available, and I know Dad would be excited to have you here."

"Thanks, Mom, but Neiman Marcus has a place for me already. Can't wait to see you and Dad, though. I'll call you as soon as I'm in the city."

"Oh, before I forget, Dad is closing the restaurant for the annual family picnic on Labor Day. You can bring your friend, Grant, if you'd like. You know I'd love to meet him, and so would Dad!"

"God, Mom. He's my boss, not my boyfriend!"

Taking a deep sigh, she said, "I'll let you know if he can make it. Don't start the wedding plans already, okay? And for God's sake, don't say anything about him to the rest of the family, please. Especially Aunt Sadie!"

Ginger's mother laughed, knowing she pushed it a little too far. "Oh, honey, I'm just teasing."

"Okay, gotta go, Mom."

"Be safe. And an October wedding would be great!"

Silence on the other line.

"Just kidding. You know I love you."

"Love you too, Mom. And give my love to Dad."

Ginger hung up the phone and thought, *Is it that obvious how excited I am to see Grant again?* Her thoughts wandered off to the last conversation with him: *I would never have let you out of my sight.*

Ginger sat on her couch and daydreamed about his eyes. She felt warm and fuzzy with just the thought of his touch. It rapidly spread throughout her body, only to end up in a tingly splice between her legs.

What am I thinking? This is just a modeling job. But he's so flippin' hot. And looking at him, those blue eyes! Mmmm—Jeez, get a grip, girl! I am bewitched by him. But . . . why do I feel like I've gotten lost in those beautiful blue eyes before?

Throwing away another picture of Steve, she thought, *Jesus, Mom! You've already got me thinking I'm going to live happily ever after with my new boss.*

After an exhausting day of packing and drinking a bit too much vodka, Ginger climbed into to bed and drifted off to sleep.

It had been a busy night at the little pub in England. Both Rachel and Isabella had been running ragged all night. The girls had been friends since they could remember.

Isabella had a voluptuous, curvy body and light-brown hair and brown eyes. She was full of life and had a promiscuous side that was out of control at times—particularly when it came to pilots.

The night was nearly over, and they began their nightly cleaning ritual. "God, Izzy, I wish you had seen my blue-eyed flyer from a few of days ago."

"Still enamored with that guy you kissed?" she asked. "Well, more like stuck your tongue into." She laughed hard. She noticed that Rachel's eyes were filled with tears. "Oh, I'm so sorry, hon. Sometimes my mouth gets away from me. Come here."

Rachel had been in love with Isabella's brother, Shelby. He was a pilot and had been killed in action during the summer of 1943. Isabella wrapped her arms around

Rachel and whispered, "I love you and the way you loved my brother. I hate this bloody war!"

Composing herself a bit and redirecting the subject, Rachel said, "It's been a few days since he came in. You don't think he's been in action already, do you?" Isabella could see the concern on her best friend's face.

"Rach, honey, you know those fly-boys. Why do you think he's so different?"

"Because I can't get him and that kiss out my bloody head! Buggers! He walked away without pressuring me like most of the fly-boys."

"Well, if he shows up again, see what happens. Chances are he won't, though—you didn't give him what he wanted that night. Just relax."

Isabella held Rachel's shoulders and shook her a smidge; she had her typical fiery look, trying to lighten the mood. "Maybe you and I just need to get shagged!" They looked at each other and burst into laughter.

"Izzy, stop it! You're such a harlot!"

"Always looking out for you. You're my best friend and my sister."

Just then, Isabella's mouth dropped open as she looked past Rachel. "Look at this one! Oh, my!"

Rachel turned and lost her breath for a second. "That's him, Izzy!"

"Well, hello, handsome! Now I see what you were

going on about! Go get him, lil sis."

Rachel contemplated her next move. "No, you wait on him. Let's see what he really wants."

Izzy snapped, "Fine. I'll gladly check and see what he wants."

"Don't touch him, Isabella. If he's here for me, he's all mine!"

"Of course, darling, slow down. I'm just testing the waters. But if he's just looking for fun, all bets are off, okay? That makes him just a fly-boy, right?"

Rachel rolled her eyes and said nothing.

Isabella walked up to Tommy as he sat in the same spot on the night he first met Rachel and greeted him. "What'll it be, fly-boy?"

"A pint would be great. And I was hoping I could speak to Rachel, if she's here."

"Well . . ." Isabella read his nametag. "Lieutenant Smith? I'll see if she's available. Dark or regular ale?"

"Dark, please."

"Coming up, Lieutenant."

Isabella walked back to Rachel and stuck her tongue out. "Well, he wants a dark, honey, *and you.* The bugger's all yours."

Rachel breathed a sigh of relief; she half expected Isabella was right about him and he was only after one thing: sex.

"Go and get his pint ready, lil sis," Isabella said.

Isabella quickly returned to the bar. She said very sternly, "Lieutenant Smith, Rachel will be bringing you your pint. However, look at me, cutie. I am Isabella. Rachel has been like a sister to me since we were kids. Be good to her."

He nodded his head with a surprised look on his face and remained silent.

Isabella continued, "She's already given her heart and soul to this war. If you just want a one-nighter, be a sport and move along. You're far away from home and lonely, but don't mess with my girl or I'll take you down. Understood?"

"Yes, ma'am." He felt as if he should salute as she walked away.

A few minutes later, Rachel placed his pint down in front of him. "Hey, Tommy," Rachel said excitedly.

"Hi, Rachel. Do you have time to sit with me for a moment?"

She walked around the bar and sat on the stool next to him, looking into his blue eyes.

He sheepishly asked, "Would it be okay if I asked you out?"

Rachel realized he was mustering up all his nerve. She decided to toy with him a bit. "Let me get this straight, are you asking me out or just inquiring whether or not you *can* ask me out?"

Tommy gulped down some of his ale. "I'm asking you out." He wasn't able to read her expression.

"I'm off in thirty minutes. Does that work?"

Tommy stumbled out, "Gr-great. Tonight would be . . . it would be great."

"Splendid," she snapped and turned away.

Rachel had a new pep in her step as she approached Isabella. "He's taking me out! Tonight!"

"Am I supposed to act surprised? I can tell all the way over here that you said yes. Now the question is, to behave or not? Hmm . . . *not*!"

Rachel blushed, and they both broke into laughter.

Ginger woke from her dream in a startle. *It felt so real*, she thought. *What was his name? Tommy? Rhymes with mommy. Leave it to her . . . Daddy always talked about being stationed in England.*

The images slipped away quickly. One thing remained though: *Those blue eyes. I don't think I will forget them. Jesus! Grant's eyes are that blue too.*

Her mind quickly became absorbed with thoughts of Grant. *I want to look really hot for Sunday's flight. Might have to go shopping. Make a casual yet grand entry—sexy but classy. After all, he's a manly man. Mmmm, a yummy one at that.*

Chapter 17

Tommy sat at the bar. He tried to contain his excitement after Rachel agreed to a date, but he could hardly wait. He watched as the two girls closed up.

Rachel grabbed her sweater and said to him, "One pound, please."

"Huh?"

"The pint, blue eyes. Maybe in the states it's free, but not here." She tried to masquerade her smile, holding her hand out. "And don't forget the tip. My friend Izzy will be bloody mad if she doesn't get a tip, and she's no one to mess with."

Tommy smacked his head and began to reach into his pocket. Rachel laughed. "No charge tonight, Lieutenant. I was joking. Ready to go?"

Tommy laughed at himself for not catching Rachel's sense of humor.

They walked outside into the cool, damp May night. Tommy gently grabbed Rachel's hand. Rachel gripped his hand tightly, letting him know she was just as excited to be with him.

"I'd like to go home and freshen up, if that's okay," Rachel said.

"Of course. Will I be meeting your parents tonight then?"

Rachel took a deep breath. "My parents died in a bombing raid nine months ago."

He looked toward the sky and sighed. "Rachel, I'm so sorry."

She held in her tears. "Honestly, it's okay. How would you know?"

"I can't imagine what it feels like to lose your parents to the war."

"I hope you never have to feel that loss." They continued their walk in silence, still holding hands.

Rachel suddenly stopped. "Tommy, are you married?"

"What? No. I wouldn't have asked you out if I was

married, Rachel."

She grabbed his other hand and kissed his lips, inviting his tongue into her mouth. When the kiss ended, they continued their walk.

She opened the gate to a small thatch-roof bungalow with whitewashed walls. The garden walkway was filled with flowers of every color and species imaginable.

Tommy stood at the gate for a moment. "My God, this is beautiful, Rachel."

She smiled. "Just like you. Come on, blue eyes." Tommy followed her up the stone path to the house.

Walking in, he felt like he was home. There were pictures on every wall displaying art and moments of Rachel's life. The living room was perfect, with a huge fireplace and high-beamed ceilings, and the furniture—

"What are you thinking, Tommy?"

"That I'm home."

She smiled. "Whiskey's on the armoire, and don't ask for any ice."

Tommy laughed, loving her sassiness.

"Think you could make a fire without burning the house down, Lieutenant?"

"Where's the hose?" He grinned.

"Sure it's safe for me to take a quick shower?" She begins to unbutton her blouse.

"You're in good hands, m'lady."

"Hmph. We'll see about that. Don't forget to open the damper."

Rachel disappeared into the bedroom, and Tommy poured himself a whiskey. *What an amazing woman she is. Jeez, it only took the Second World War for me to find the love of my life.*

The natural warmth of her home engulfed him, bringing him peace. He started the fire and then sat back on the loveseat facing the fireplace. He was eager for her to return from the shower. Suddenly, he felt guilty, thinking she deserved a man who will not leave because of a war. *I could be dead in a week and she's already been through so much. Why tangle her life up with mine? Should I just get up and walk out of here?*

Finally silencing his thoughts, all he could hear was the crackling of the wood burning. He decided to stay and sipped his whiskey.

Rachel opened the door. "Hey, fly-boy, could you pour me a whiskey?" She walked toward the couch wearing just a robe and a towel wrapped around her hair. "You mind if we stay in tonight?"

He made her a drink without hesitation. "Whatever you want, baby."

"Oh, we're at 'baby' already?"

When he handed her the glass, he could see her hands were trembling.

Tommy sat closely to her on the loveseat. "Rachel, I haven't been able to get you out of my mind since the day we met. I know there are a million reasons why we shouldn't be together—for one, there's a war going on."

"My sweet Tommy, I don't know what it is you should do—be a soldier and fly planes or fall in love? Leave, if that's what you think is better. But here's the problem: I am in love with you. I felt it since the moment our eyes met. Our kiss only confirmed what my heart already knew, what my soul was screaming."

Tommy responded by kissing her deeply, the way she first kissed him. "I'm not leaving home, Rachel. *You* are my home."

They sat on the loveseat kissing and falling deeper in love by the second. Drops of rain hit the roof. "Guess it was a good idea to stay in tonight."

Grant was once again pulled from his slumber. He looked at the clock; it was 5:21. He tried to capture every detail of the dream, but it was slowly fading. He closed his eyes again, wishing it was real.

Chapter 18

Lyla and Jason bounced onto Grant's bed. "Daddy!" they screamed repeatedly. It was seven a.m. He still had that dream on his mind—and Rachel's eyes. He shook off his thoughts.

"Okay, kids! Who wants pancakes with the smiley faces?"

They both cheered at that.

"Lyla, you're in charge of teeth brushing and hair combing."

"Okay, Daddy. Come on, Jason."

Lyla stopped in her tracks and said, "But first, Daddy,

let's hug. I miss seeing you in the morning."

"Come here, my baby girl. You, my little one, own your Daddy's heart!"

"Daddy! I can't own your heart." She giggled, hugging him back even harder.

"One day, when you're a mom, you'll understand. You stole my heart the moment I held you."

"Well, if *I stole* your *heart*, what part did Jason steal?"

"Um, my blue eyes? Hey, let's get this party started."

As they entered the museum, Lyla's fears of being bored were swept away by a loud whistle. "Daddy! What was that?"

"Oh, just the coal mine whistle," Grant casually replied with a smile.

"That is so cool!"

For the next four hours, they explored as much of the museum as possible, spending extra time in the areas designed for children.

When they climbed into the limo, Charlie could tell the kids were tired and had fun. Grant gave them Mary Ellen's cookies, which they gobbled up, and soon after, they zonked out.

Grant got comfortable for the ride to Baraboo as he watched them peacefully sleeping. He opened the bar that

Charlie stocked and poured himself a vodka on the rocks. His mind naturally wandered off to Ginger. *Is she as excited as I am? I need to hear her voice.*

Grant asked Charlie if he could use his car phone.

"Of course, Mr. Grant. Want me to put up the window so you can have some privacy?"

"If you don't mind, buddy."

He called her, hoping she would be home and available to talk, desperate to hear her voice.

"Hello?" Her sweet voice filled his ears, and he almost lost his breath.

"Hi, Ginger. It's Grant. How's it going?"

"Hi! Where are you calling me from? I thought you were traveling with the kids."

"I am looking at both of them right now. They are passed out in the limo on our way to Baraboo. We've had such a great time already."

"A limo to Baraboo?"

"Well, yeah, it's a long story. Sure is fun to be sitting here talking to you and drinking a vodka—and not driving. Didn't think my day could get any better."

"Wow! So I guess I don't have to ask how *you're* doing."

"Why?"

"Because you sound great."

"Yeah, but something is missing."

"What could that possibly be?"

"Some adult conversation, please!" he begged.

Ginger laughed at the tone of his voice. "Guess you're not going to be voted father of the year, then. It's only been since yesterday, you know?"

"Thank God for your laughter! You don't need a blankee or pancakes with smiley faces, right?"

"Well, I don't need the blankee, but I'll take the smiley pancakes. One of my favorites."

"That could be a deal breaker."

"Now you're gonna get smiley pancakes delivered to work every day, just you wait."

As they joked, he stopped feeling apprehensive about calling her.

For longer than he expected, they laughed and talked about everything—even about her pantyhose, which always seemed to run. Grant felt like he was talking with someone he'd known since the beginning of time.

"Hate to change the subject, but on a business note, do you have any questions regarding Sunday? You need anything else to get ready?"

"I'm good. Almost finished packing. I talked to my mother; she's thrilled. However, brace yourself—you've already been invited to the annual family Labor Day party." Laughing uncontrollably, he almost couldn't understand her when she was finally able to say, "And of course, my mother will probably be introducing you as my fiancé, not my boss."

"Should I bring my financial statement? I wanna be good enough for you." Grant laughed and continued. "So I will see you at the airport on Sunday. Do you need a ride? I can send someone to pick you up."

"Thanks, I have a ride."

"I hope I'm not overstepping any boundaries, but I enjoy talking to you."

"Not at all. I feel the same way. I'm really looking forward to a new chapter in my life, Grant."

"Me too, Ginger. It's a new beginning for both of us."

Wait, what? Ginger's head was spinning in delight and then stopped suddenly, singularly focusing on a part of the conversation. *I actually told him what my mother might say if he came to the picnic? Thank God he's got a great sense of humor!*

Ginger was on her belly, knees bent, twirling her hair—she felt like a teenager. She rolled onto her back while she absorbed their conversation.

It's so easy to talk to him! He actually wanted to hear what I had to say—about anything. And his laughter and openness lifts my spirits to new heights. I can't wait to see him again!

The woman in her head said, *Thanks, Mom, for always encouraging me to follow my dreams, even when I thought they were just fantasies.* The young girl squealed, *Time to shop! After all, I am finally following my dreams.*

Chapter 19

As they passed over the Baraboo River, Grant relayed to his kids a childhood memory when he would watch the elephants playing in the river. Jason nearly screamed, "Where are they, Daddy? I don't see any!" His face and hands were plastered against the window, bouncing up and down looking for the elephants.

"The elephants have gone home for the night. I'm sure we will see them over the next few days. One time, the elephants sprayed us with their trunks. We were soaked!"

"Eww! Isn't that from their noses?" Lyla said. "Did they have boogers?"

"I wish an elephant would spray all of us, right now!" Jason said.

They arrived at Dan's home. Dan, his wife, Karen, and their daughter, Aimee, all greeted the Robinson trio at the door of their old, two-story, white farmhouse. After the kids settled in, he asked Karen and Dan if going to Monk's Diner would be okay for dinner, offering to treat them for their hospitality.

"Sure, if that's what you'd like, Grant. Dan and I thought we could grill hamburgers, just to make it easy. Not really sure what the kids like."

"Let's not work too hard tonight. And honestly, if you don't mind, I wanted to let them see one of our old hangouts."

Both families piled into Betsy to enjoy an evening at Monk's. The next few hours flew by with the girls playing together and Jason spending more time than he should have on the *Pac-Man* machine. Just watching the kids laugh and play made Grant realize how much he had forgotten about being happy himself. He was shocked when he allowed himself to accept the truth that Margo always stood in the way of *his* happiness.

Grant silently solidified the reason he hadn't made it a point to get the families together sooner: Margo never wanted anything to do with his side of the family.

Karen almost seemed to be reading his thoughts. "We

should've gotten together sooner, Grant."

Grant nodded.

"We knew from the first time meeting . . . 'you know who' . . . that she thought we were just backwoods folk."

Grant raised his wine glass. "To real family. Thank you both."

"Cheers!"

After the kids were settled in for the night, Karen left Dan and Grant to catch up with each other. Dan grabbed his guitar, a few cigars, and a bottle of scotch as they headed to the back porch. He began strumming "Puff the Magic Dragon" by Peter, Paul, and Mary.

Grant said, "And to think everyone claimed that song really wasn't about getting high!" They laughed.

Nearly a bottle of scotch and two cigars later, Dan said, "Karen has plans to take the kids to the circus museum and berry picking tomorrow. And, buddy, I called my friend, Billy. He's pulling a few strings to make sure the elephants are there by the river, just like when we were kids. Karen knows exactly where to go so they can all get sprayed."

"That's perfect, bro. Now I can blame Uncle Dan when Lyla squawks at me!"

"Hey, on a completely different subject, there's a piece of property I'd like to look at tomorrow. Want to join me?"

"Sure, I'd be glad to."

"Great, cuz. Think you can still ride? A horse, that is." Dan chuckled at Grant's expression. "It would be fun to ride out to Shady Hollow Lane where the farmhouse is. You remember the Smith family?"

"How could I forget? The Smiths' farm was next to Old Lady Pete's dairy farm. Hell, I spent my summers playing with their son, TJ. Some of my favorite childhood memories are of us screwing around on the old dairy wagons."

After hours of chatting, the liquor got to Grant. They both stumbled back into the house. Grant just barely managed to get to his room, where he collapsed onto his bed. His mind, already fuzzy, easily drifted to a deep sleep.

Rachel stood up, removing the towel from her hair, and let her robe fall to the floor, revealing her naked body, baring her soul to him with an outstretched hand. "Tommy, I don't want to wait forever to make love to you."

Tommy pulled her into his arms, kissing her. "I want you too, but I'm so afraid I might cause you pain, Rachel. What if—"

"Shhhh, shhhh, Tommy, my sweet Tommy. Please

don't worry. I *want* you to make love to me."

She caressed his lips with hers, then guided him into her bedroom.

Tommy undressed. The rain ceased, and the moonlight illuminated the room, leaving the perfect amount of light for him to see her complete beauty.

Rachel was lying on the bed with her arms stretched over her head, legs slightly apart and bent at the knees. Tommy kissed her, both of them softly moaning. Slowly, his mouth caressed her neck, sliding down to her breasts. He sensually rolled his tongue around each of her pink, erect nipples. He was filled with the deepest desire he ever felt.

Moving his hand across her flat belly, Tommy finally reached down between her legs. She parted farther for him and again moaned aloud with pleasure when he slid two fingers inside her glistening lips.

Rachel could hardly believe the physical sensation flowing throughout her body, while her sweet Tommy reacted so perfectly to her needs, almost reading her mind. Touching the most intimate part of a woman, he gently massaged the soft, inner walls of her vagina, sending waves of pleasure throughout her body.

Finally lowering his face between her legs, he used his teeth and tongue to pull the most sensitive and sensual part of the female anatomy into his mouth. The sounds escaping from Rachel came deep from within her, from her soul. Her legs wrapped around his head, and her hands tightened her pull on his hair when she exploded into his mouth.

"You taste so sweet, baby."

Between her body movements and the pleasurable sounds escaping her, Tommy couldn't wait any longer. He climbed up and slid his throbbing cock inside her. Instinctively, she arched her back to accept more of his huge size, locking her legs around his waist. "You feel so good, baby!" Tommy could barely breathe.

"Yeah, Tommy, I need you!"

Thrusting his hips deep into her, they climbed together toward breathtaking orgasms. At some point during their shared climax, they found themselves looking into each other's eyes. An unspoken cosmic breeze passed between them. In that moment there was no one else in the world, only each other—they were one being, one soul.

"Daddy! Daddy!" Jason yelled.

Grant looked around, confused about where he was, his mind still reeling from the dream. Jason yelled for him again from his bed, which completely snapped him out of it.

Grant ran to Jason's room and climbed into bed with his son. He could feel his little body trembling. "What is it, buddy? I'm right here."

"I had a bad dream, Daddy," Jason meekly replied,

trying to stop his tears.

"Want to tell me about it?" Grant whispered while gently rubbing his head and hair, holding him.

"Not really. Daddy, you were a soldier, right? Did you kill people?"

Grant froze.

"It's wrong to kill, right, Daddy?"

"Must have been a bad dream, son. But let's ride the coal mine in our heads right now."

After a while, he felt his son's breathing change and knew he was sleeping.

Grant shuffled back to his bed. He shivered at the thought of what Jason said. The memory of his first kill started to creep into his head. It was in Vietnam, and he witnessed the life leaving the young soldier's eyes. *No!* He sat up. *I'm not going back there now!*

He settled back onto his bed, his head sinking into the pillows. *Now, who was that in my head before Jason woke me up? It was another one of those World War II dreams, right? What were their names? Tommy and Rachel? Who are these people?*

Chapter 20

The smell of freshly baked bread and coffee permeated the house, and for a moment, Grant was a child again, waking up at the Petersen farm. He remembered finding Old Lady Pete in the kitchen. She pulled the young Grant into her arms, wrapping him up in her apron, which was usually covered with flour, butter, and sugar. She always smelled so good.

He could hear her voice: "Land sakes, boy. I thought you were never waking up." Holding his little body at arm's length, she looked him over. "Why, Grant, you look just like your mother! She was my favorite girl, y'know. I loved her very much. Plus, she made the most wonderful little boy for me to love. Are you ready for a warm, sticky cinnamon bun?" Grant loved Old Lady Pete for her unconditional love and kindness.

Although it was only six forty-five a.m., Grant was the last one out of bed. He could hear the girls' laughter and the television playing cartoons—he knew where Jason was.

Karen greeted him in the kitchen with a hot mug of coffee and homemade blueberry muffins.

"Good morning."

He bit into the muffin. "These are delicious, Karen," he said with a mouthful.

Smiling, Karen responded, "Dan's already out by the barn readying the horses. Better get your coffee and muffins down. When did you ride last?"

"Let's put it this way: I hope you have some ointment for the inevitable saddle blisters I'm going to have."

She laughed. "It's going to be really hot out today—a perfect time for the kids to get sprayed by those elephants." She winked.

"Sounds great, Karen." He reached into his pocket to give her some money.

"No way, Grant. It's our treat. It's just so great to have you and the kids here. Besides, I haven't heard Dan laugh like last night in a long time. For that alone, thank you." She kissed his cheek.

"We always made each other laugh. Thanks for having us and reminding me what it feels like to be part of a family."

After spending a quick family breakfast together, Grant hugged his kids. "Remember, listen to Aunt Karen. She's in charge today."

"Of course, Daddy. I love you," Lyla said while hugging him good-bye.

"I love you more, my sweet baby girl."

"Love you even more, Daddy." Jason hugged his leg.

"And, please, nobody join the circus today." They all laughed, and he left, walking toward the corral.

"Where'd you get those damn fancy boots? Didn't think a city slicker could get a pair like that," Dan commented.

"Always been a farm boy at heart, I guess," Grant responded as they mounted the horses.

After an hour, they approached the Smith farmhouse. Grant was more than happy to get off the horse since his ass was killing him.

An elderly gentleman stood on the porch of the house.

"Mr. Smith, this is my cousin, Grant Robinson. Grant, this is Robert Smith."

"Pleasure to see you again, Mr. Smith. I don't know if you remember me, but I used to play with your son, TJ."

Mr. Smith analyzed Grant's face. He finally

responded, "Sorry, can't say that I do. I lost him in 'Nam, you know."

"Sorry to hear that." They shook hands.

Opening the door to the farmhouse, they all walked into the front room. Dan reached into his backpack and pulled out the contract for the sale of the property, and he and Mr. Smith discussed business.

Grant strolled over to the fireplace, and the photos on the mantel caught his attention. One old photograph in particular drew his interest: it was a black-and-white image of a crew of nine in front of a Boeing B-17. The name *Fifinella* was displayed on the plane's belly, which had a female cartoon character riding a bomb. Somehow, he felt like he knew these people.

Grant studied the picture. Mr. Smith interrupted his thoughts. "That's a picture of my brother, Thomas, who my son was named after, and his crew from World War II. He died just outside of Paris when his plane was shot down. This is him." He pointed to the picture. "August thirteenth of 1944 was his last mission. It's one of two dates I'll never forget."

"What's the other?" Grant's voice was almost a whisper.

"The day of my son's death."

Slowly riding back toward home, Grant and Dan reminisced about their childhood again. Grant nearly fell off the horse with laughter when Dan brought up his favorite story about Old Lady Pete chasing them with a broom for messing with the chickens. "I'll give you two little foxes a head start before I let Rusty out after you!" she had yelled. They flew out of the hen house, hoping the German shepherd wasn't after them.

They rode side by side down the wooded trail toward home.

"Dan, why are you buying all this farmland?"

"The future of Baraboo is changing rapidly. And what I'm buying today for three hundred dollars an acre could sell in ten years or less for three thousand dollars an acre. You have a stock that can give you that kind of return?"

"Hell, maybe I should invest with you!" Grant joked.

"We can always talk about that. But what's going on with you? Newly divorced—thank God—and working for that company for, what? Ten years now? What's your game plan, city slicker?"

Grant cleared his throat. "Don't you mean 'farm boy'? Dan, the more I listen to you, the more you're sounding like the damned city slicker. City slickers talk about land being an investment. Farm boys talk about the land being used." They laughed. "Anyway, I'm now the head designer for H&M, and I've got a couple deals I'm working on. Next is in Paris, and if I land that one, I've been promised a partnership—could be my chance to grab the golden ring."

"Damn. How about making some shit for men?"

"Maybe one day. But you wouldn't wear it, city slicker."

"Sally's is right up ahead. Wanna stop for some old-fashioned country cooking? Voted best fried chicken in the county. Could be an offspring from one those chickens we used to chase."

After they were seated and they ordered their food, Dan directed the conversation to women. "Any future female prospects, Grant? The ladies always flocked to you. What was that first chick's name? Your babysitter? Jeannie?"

Grant nearly choked on his coleslaw. "Hey, hey, you know gentlemen don't talk about that. At the moment, there are no prospects. However, I just hired a model that I had met years ago during my internship. She's beautiful, full of sass and class, and—"

"Whoa, buddy! Judging by the way your eyes lit up, she's not a prospect?" He threw his napkin on the table and got serious for a moment.

A silence fell between them. Grant sat back in his chair and sipped his beer. "Guess you really do know me, huh? I hate to admit it or even say it aloud, but I haven't been able to get her out of my head since the day I met her. I'd be lying to you if I said I didn't fantasize about her over the years, even when I was with Margo."

"I knew it! So what's she like?"

"Well, she *is* gorgeous, but she's so intelligent. Usually, those two assets don't come in the same package. We've had the most incredible conversations I've ever had with a woman. We only reconnected this past week, yet I feel like I've known her forever. I just can't explain it more than that."

Dan smirked. "So when did you fuck her?"

"Jesus Christ, Dan! I haven't even *kissed* her. It sounds really stupid, buddy, but the highlight of my sexual experience with her has been a kiss on the cheek."

"And you're this smitten already?"

"Well, a business acquaintance and friend of mine in Chicago has told me that when the cosmic lines—"

"Cosmic what?" Dan interrupted. "I hear Karen yammering on about that kind of stuff, why we ended up together and all that crap. I just think if it's meant to be, it's meant to be. However it happens. Fate? That's a Karen word. All I know is that I am happy."

"I know. When I saw you two together from day one, it made me question what the hell I was doing with Margo. Is true love real, brother?"

"Not to be sappy, Grant, but, yeah. I'm living the dream. I hope you find it too. You of all people deserve it."

After a few moments of silence, Grant said, "Thanks, man. I needed to hear that. Missed you, brother. Been too many years. I won't let it happen again."

"Good. I've missed you too. You're always welcome home. And we love the kids."

As they saddled up, Dan asked, "By the way, what's the model's name?"

"Ginger. Ginger Madison." Grant's face lit up at the mention of her name.

"I did that on purpose. Just wanted to see that smile again. Let's head back."

"Race you back to the stable, asshole."

Grant galloped away on his horse, feeling another level of freedom that was unexpected yet welcomed—the wind in his face and the power of his horse. He leaned into the horse as they raced off, leaving Dan in their dust.

Back at the stable, Grant dismounted and cooled the horse down with a slow walk. A few minutes later, Dan arrived. Both he and his horse were winded. Between breaths, Dan said, "Guess you really aren't the city slicker I thought you'd become."

"Well, let's make a deal. If you stop calling me a city

slicker, I won't let the family know you came in last by nearly twenty minutes."

"It most certainly was *not* twenty minutes!"

"History is written by the victors, bud. Should it be thirty minutes instead?"

"Touché. It's a deal."

As the horses cooled down, Grant felt an urge to call Ginger. He needed to hear her voice.

"Do you mind if I use your phone, bro?"

"Yeah, I'll take care of the horses. Take your time."

Grant entered the house and poured a little scotch on the rocks and dialed her number. He hoped the scotch would calm his nerves a bit.

"Hello?" Her voice was like a favorite song.

"Hey, Ginger. Hope I'm not bothering you."

"Grant? No, never. Just finished packing. Are you having fun with the kids?"

He could hear happiness in her voice.

"They're great. The kids are probably getting sprayed by elephants right about now. I just came back from horseback riding with my cousin."

"Great! Well, I'm itching to get out of here. Can't wait to be a New Yorker again!"

"I have an idea: why don't you have your stuff shipped to my apartment? I'm only a few blocks from the Carlyle. Gotta tell you, Ginger, you're a breath of fresh air.

Too bad we waited all these years to have a conversation."

"I couldn't agree more, Grant. And, yes, I will have my stuff shipped to your apartment."

They talked for a while until the kids burst into the house, squawking about the water and the elephants. Ginger could hear them excitedly recount their day.

"Grant, I'll let you go. Enjoy your kids. I'm looking forward to tomorrow."

He put his hand over the receiver and said to the kids, "Hold on one second! Slow down!" Then he pulled the phone back up. "Yep, I do have to go, Ginger. I'll see you tomorrow. Have a great day."

After she hung up, Ginger felt like she was floating. *I love his voice*, she thought. She danced around the room, holding her hands to the sky. She pinched her cheek—and then her ass cheek. *Yep, I'm awake.*

Chapter 21

Grant was nearly crying with laughter listening to his children recount their day: there was an elephant that shot water all over them with its trunk, dozens of clowns piling out of a tiny car, and fresh blueberries for the picking.

He wished Old Lady Pete was here to see his beautiful children. He was truly happy.

Later the water sprinkler was set up, and Jason ran through it and played with a water gun and laughed. Grant and Dan grilled up some burgers and chatted as they enjoyed some beers. The girls and Karen decided to make pie with the blueberries.

"Jason, you're just like us when we were kids," Grant said as he avoided his son shooting water at him.

Jason sat on his lap and asked, "Daddy, did you like being here as a kid?"

"Yes, buddy. It was good for me. Being here helped me begin to heal from my mother's passing."

"Passing, Daddy?"

"Yes, son. It was a difficult time for me when my mom died."

Overhearing their conversation, Dan said, "Jason, can you tell your Aunt Karen that the burgers and dogs are almost ready?"

"Sure thing, Uncle Dan." Jason ran into the house soaking wet.

"Grant, I hope I'm not overstepping here, but do you really want to talk to him about that now? I mean, he's a baby."

"You're right. I'm in a good place right now . . . don't know why I started with that."

"Well, it is a part of your life. But I know the real reason you're in such a good mood. What was her name again? Madison? Ginger? Mad-Gin?" He laughed.

Grant's face turned red. "Well, she's not the only reason I'm so happy. But yeah, I can't wait to see her tomorrow."

"Shit, I can't wait for you to see her tomorrow, either.

You need to take a cold shower, man. They might mistake your hard-on for a concealed weapon!"

"Shut the fuck up." They roared with laughter.

"Okay, kids, time for bed!"

"Aww, Daddy!" they protested. "We're having so much fun!"

"Come on. I've already given you a few extra *hours.* Besides, I know Charlie and Betsy will be happy to see you in the morning. Just be sure to bring a muffin for Charlie. Betsy doesn't need one . . . unless it's made of gasoline." He tickled them both.

"Good night, Daddy. I love you," Lyla whispered.

"I love you too, my sweetheart."

"I love you too, Daddy," Jason chimed in.

"Buddy, I love you."

After tucking the kids into bed, Grant headed to his room, exhausted. He climbed into his bed and was asleep in minutes.

After spending his leave with Rachel, Tommy reflected on how beautiful it was to be in true love. He had been engaged just before his deployment to England. He headed to Monk's

Diner to meet with Susan, his fiancé. Susan was a voluptuous brunette. She had aqua eyes with flecks of brown and was very feminine—beautiful and smart.

As he sat at the table, Tommy had a bad feeling—there was a different look in her eyes, a look of disconnect. She didn't even jump up to hug or kiss him when he arrived.

"Tommy, I'm going to say it before I change my mind, because I love you so much. But I can't be engaged to you anymore." She slid the ring off her finger. Tommy froze.

Susan continued as she placed the ring into his hands and folded them. "Do you know what it felt like when I found out that your plane crashed? I heard it from your *parents*, not even *you*. I was devastated." Tommy said nothing. Her voice quivered as she spoke. "My girlfriend, Helene, lost her husband a few weeks ago. I can't deal with that. I can't marry a soldier. I'm sorry, Tommy."

Tommy could barely speak. Tears rolled down his cheeks. Finally, he said, "Suz, I . . . I was afraid to tell you about the crash. It was just a training mishap. I'm so sorry you had to hear about it from my parents. I thought we had more than that. Is there anything I can say to change your mind? God, I love you!"

She shook her head. They cried and talked more, but the breakup was final. They both agreed that the engagement was off.

As they walked out of the diner, Tommy handed the ring back to her. "I want you to have it. I picked it out for *you.*"

"Do you hate me, Tommy?"

"Yes and no. But I do want one last kiss, Suz."

She was startled by his words. When they reached his car, she kissed him. "I love you, but I can't worry about whether or not you are coming back to me. If you survive the war, and I'm still here in Baraboo, maybe we can see where it goes."

Grant opened his eyes. This time he was able to retain more of the dream. *Tommy was from Baraboo? Wasn't that the name of Robert Smith's brother? Why the hell am I dreaming of this guy?*

After a breakfast of homemade blueberry pancakes, Grant packed the limo. "Okay, kids. Charlie and Betsy are ready to go. We have to be back at your grandparents by lunch time."

"Daddy, do we *really* have to go? I love being here."

"Come on, honey. We'll see Aimee, Aunt Karen, and Uncle Dan for Thanksgiving."

Dan and Grant share a brotherly hug, promising to keep in touch this time.

After a three-hour drive, they arrived at Margo's parents. The mood swiftly shifted from happy to somber as the kids exited Betsy.

"So you have to leave now, Daddy? When will I see you again?" she asked.

"Soon, baby girl. When I get back to New York, I'll call you. Don't be sad. Just because you can't see me, doesn't mean I'm not here," he said, pointing to her heart. "Remember, you own my heart. Be careful with it; it's breakable."

"I will, Daddy. I love you."

"I love you too, my baby girl."

Jason didn't say anything. He hugged Grant's leg tightly and darted into the house. Grant carried the suitcases to the front door with Charlie's help. Margo stood at the door with a distasteful expression. He tried to remember if she ever had a different look about her. She disappeared into the house without a word.

Fred walked out. "Hey, Grant. Have a good time with the kids?"

"It was phenomenal. Hey, Fred, mind if I use the bathroom to change for my flight home?"

"Use my office. I'll mix us up a couple Bloody Marys. I know you always liked them, and I think I make a damn good one!"

"I appreciate it, but I'm tight on time."

"Got it, no problem." Fred was clearly disappointed.

Grant changed his clothes and found Fred meandering near the front door. "Fred, if you ever need anything, I mean anything, do not hesitate to call me."

"You're a good man, Grant."

Grant reached out to shake his hand but was surprised when Fred wrapped his arms around him. "You'll always be a son to me."

Grant couldn't respond with words, so he just hugged him tighter.

Chapter 22

As Grant checked in at the American Airlines counter, he spotted Ginger approaching. She wore tight jeans with a loose-fitting, deep-salmon top and matching pumps. Her braided hair lay on her bare shoulder and pink sunglasses rested on her head. She held a small carry-on draped on her bent elbow.

Grant noticed how every male that walked past her did a double take; even men traveling with women companions sneaked a peek. Ginger was oblivious to the attention she naturally drew.

"Over here, Ginger." Grant waved.

When Ginger saw Grant, her entire face lit up. She almost overlooked Grant because she half expected to see him in his work attire, not in the athletic, fitted turquoise T-shirt, dark jeans, cowboy boots, and sunglasses. "My God, you look beautiful," Grant said.

"Why, thank you, Grant." She blushed. "So wait, is this look the *real* Mr. Robinson? And if so, I think it suits you just fine, cowboy."

"Cowboy?" he questioned.

"It's a compliment."

"Thank you. Can I ask you to join me for a drink at the Admiral's Club before we take off?"

"Why, yes."

They entered the club and sat in two overstuffed chairs side by side. Grant ordered his usual preflight drink, a hairy Bloody Mary, and Ginger asked for a glass of brut rosé champagne. The waitress served them their drinks shortly after.

When their drinks arrived, Grant raised his glass. "Ginger, I'd like to propose a toast." She raised her glass too. "To you."

"Me?"

"Yes, you! To your career and your future success . . . and to your happiness."

"Cheers." They sipped their drinks.

"You know, cowboy, I'm gonna have to keep an eye

on you. You sure know what a girl likes to hear."

"You got my number. Don't mind, do you?"

"A lady loves compliments. Feel free." She smiled. "So tell me more about your weekend with the kids."

After updating her, he added, "The weekend reminded me of when I was a kid. I would stay there for the summers, after my mom passed."

"How old were you when she passed?"

Grant turned his head away from her momentarily. "Ten."

Ginger quickly changed the subject. "I am *sure* you created great memories for your children, Grant."

"I really hope so. Lyla's got me wrapped around her finger. She owns my heart."

"I bet she does."

"So how was your ride to the airport?"

"Sarah insisted on taking me. She and I have been friends for a few years. She has a lot of good qualities. However, I know when I'm no longer wanted. I think the friendship has fizzled out some."

The waitress approached them. "You two are adorable. How long have you been together?"

Grant and Ginger laughed. Grant looked at his watch and replied, "Oh, about thirty minutes now, give or take."

"Wait," Ginger interrupted, "we met at the counter, so it's probably closer to forty minutes."

The waitress didn't know how to answer, so Grant saved her by saying, "We'll take the check, please."

Ginger loved how comfortable she felt in his presence and noticed how he made other people feel. Grant caught Ginger looking at him and pulled her from her revere. "Bottoms up, buttercup. We have a plane to catch."

Ginger snapped out of it and finished off the rest of her champagne, and though she tried to hold it back, she let out a soft burp. "Ooops! Pardon me." Her hand covered her mouth.

"Those damned bubbles," Grant said with a smile.

Following Ginger out of the Admiral's Club, Grant thought, *She is so fucking captivating. Am I really here with her? She makes me feel so alive.*

"You know, what's this about first class? I didn't expect that," Ginger said.

"Would you prefer to fly with the luggage underneath? Us cowboys like riding in style—it matches our boots."

She laughed. "Stop making me smile. You're giving me smile lines. Not good for a model!"

"Guess you've been hanging with the wrong crowd."

"I'm starting to figure that out."

In the first-class section of the plane, a female voice said, "Hi, Grant. So good to see you again." Ginger turned to see the flight attendant, Tina, palm Grant's shoulder.

Tina continued, "I see you've taken your wings off. Ready to earn another set?"

Grant was totally caught off guard. Ginger could tell, and she immediately jumped to his rescue. She took his hand. "Grant, baby, where are our seats?"

Tina responded, "Oh, let me see your ticket, ma'am." She eyed Grant. "Miss Madison, your seat is right here next to Grant." She turned to Ginger and forced a smile.

Immediately, Tina returned to Grant, refusing to let him go. "Your usual Bloody Mary, Grant?"

"Sure, Tina. And Ginger would like a glass of brut rosé. Isn't that right, sweetheart?"

"Oh, of course, baby. You know me all too well," she said, ignoring Tina's presence.

"Right away, Mr. Robinson." Tina disappeared.

"Guess I've flown a little too much lately. Sorry about that, Ginger. She was just a passing fancy. Thanks for saving me."

"It's obvious you and the waitress in the sky have been intimate. How recently?"

"Very recent."

"Grant Robinson, you are a hard man to get over."

"Thanks again."

"For what, Grant?"

"Not judging me."

Tina returned with their drinks, avoiding eye contact

with Grant. "Here's your drink, ma'am."

"Thanks, little one. You're doing a great job," Ginger responded while placing a possessive hand on Grant's leg. She raised her glass and said to Grant, "How about a toast to us?"

"Sure, Ginger."

"To *our* future."

"Cheers."

They began settling into a comfortable space between them, both physically and emotionally. After another round of drinks, Grant knew he was falling for her.

"I can't believe I'm ordering from a menu," Ginger said.

"Welcome to first class. You know, you can move back and get the peanuts and pretzels. If you're lucky, your bag might have more than two peanuts."

"I feel like royalty."

"The perks of working with me, I suppose. Enjoy yourself. Besides, I'm going to work you to the bone, and you won't be thanking me then!"

"Bring it on, cowboy."

"So, tell me more about you. I feel like we've only scratched the surface."

"Well, I got into modeling—"

"No, no. I know your modeling career. I want to know who *Ginger* is. Ginger Madison—given or staged?"

"Of course it's my real name! Jeez. Is your real name Grant Robinson?"

"I sometimes wonder, but yes, I was born Grant Lee Robinson from Baraboo, Wisconsin. And back to you, Ms. Madison," he said, pretending to hand over a microphone.

"Well, let's see. I loved to dance from the time I was three or four. I was always on a dance team, dreaming of performing on Broadway. My biggest dream was to be a Rockette. I pictured myself on the front line. I tried out for different competitions and Broadway productions all the time, and that's how my modeling career started.

"Long story short, while trying out for a Broadway production, I twisted my ankle. The producer of the show needed a pretty face for the cover of the handbill. He also used my photo to advertise the production in the papers. So modeling took over. I learned to walk the runway, and soon, I was going to fashion shoots and discovering fashion, fabrics, and design firsthand. The times between shoots and runways, I bused tables at my parents' restaurant in Queens, went to school, and spent endless hours practicing to be a professional model.

"I truly love the fashion industry and would love to think that one day I can do what you're doing. I have so many ideas. That's how Steve hooked me. Eventually, though, the truth always surfaces."

"Wow, you're obviously a multifaceted, talented individual. Do you realize that? I feel like I'm in the presence of a celebrity."

"Do you always say the right thing at the right time?"

"No, I just recognize the truth."

"Oh, please. I don't think of myself that way. But my greatest talent is reading bullshit artists, so watch it, cowboy! I have been fooled from time to time, though . . ."

"Who hasn't?" Grant said, thinking about what he just learned about Margo and how he got his first job in New York.

Ginger wondered who could have fooled Grant.

"Any sisters or brothers?" Grant asked.

"I have a younger brother, Andrew. I love him to pieces. He worked at my parents' restaurant for years while attending culinary school and is now the head pastry chef at the Ritz-Carlton in New York City."

"We need to check out his pastries while we're in town."

"That's enough about me. Your turn."

Before Grant could begin, Tina delivered their lunch: jumbo shrimp cocktails and another round of drinks.

"I've never seen shrimp this big." Ginger paused.

"Okay, so how in God's great name did a farm—oops, a *cowboy* from Wisconsin end up in New York City in the fashion industry? Was that your dream? You wanted to play dress-up with live dolls? And please don't tell me you're one of those closet cross-dressers!"

"Whoa, whoa," he said, laughing. "Nothing like that. As you know, I was born in Baraboo, Wisconsin, the winter headquarters of the Ringling Brothers and Barnum and Bailey Circus. Want to know whether or not I wanted to be a clown?"

"No comment."

"I think it was 1954 when we moved to Madison, Wisconsin. Ha, your last name! Anyway, my dad served in World War II in the Army Air Corps and was stationed in England. He was assigned to the ground crew for B-17s. He told me so many war stories. Come to think of it, that's probably why I'm having dreams about World War II. I hadn't really thought of them much until recently, with Ronald Reagan running for president. My pop used to make me watch all his war movies.

"My father changed after my mother passed away. He became angry with the world and disappointed with life itself. He was working for the University of Wisconsin then."

Grant's expression changed.

"It was during the summers after her death that he sent me to live with family in Baraboo. Well, I have to admit, I loved it and the circus, but the clowns scared the hell out of me. One day, my mom's cousin, Clara, showed me how the costumes were made. She was a seamstress who gave me lessons on sewing. When I was about thirteen or fourteen, I would go down to the circus and help her cut and sew all the garments for the performers. And so began my education about how fabrics and patterns work and how to mix and match those fabrics to make something beautiful."

"Okay, that's a better beginning than you led on. That's really cool."

"My father became angry and critical with age, and I think I reminded him of my mom. You know what sucked the most? We hardly spoke after I turned fourteen. He never even put a marker on my mother's grave. Years later, when he passed, I found a box of love notes and cards she had given him.

"I must admit, I always fantasized that I would find someone who loved me like that and would leave me notes, cards—anything to remind me of how much they loved me." They shared a long look. Grant broke the silence. "Anyway, I thought about running away from home and joining the circus many times. The bearded lady did have a crush on me, I think."

Over the next few hours, they became very comfortable with each other, sharing more stories about their lives while continually joking.

"Now, on a serious note . . ." Grant said, hating to change the subject to work.

"Oh, I knew this was coming. Wait, let me put on my work face." She slowly waved her hand in front of her face, changing from smiling to stern. "Okay, does this work?"

They both cracked up, the alcohol getting to them.

He shook off some of the haze in his head. "You haven't had the displeasure of meeting Howard Golden yet. Please promise me that you won't allow him to get under your skin. He's a first-class asshole who will most likely say some snide or lousy comment to you. It will make you want to shove him out the window of his office—but you can't because he's the boss. Unfortunately, Howard will try to provoke you. Probably accuse me of screwing you or some bullshit. My skin has gotten thicker through the years. He's such a narcissistic garmento that he may not even notice he said something offensive—or if he does, he doesn't care. That's just who he is."

"I appreciate the heads-up. I don't stand for bullshit. I know when it's time to open my mouth and slice someone in half or when it's time to smile and nod."

"To be totally honest, Ginger, I do want your input on the orders for Neiman Marcus."

"Absolutely! I look forward to doing anything I can to make you successful."

"Let me set you straight on that right now, Ginger. It's *our* success, *our* show, not just mine. I want to part the waters for you, for us, so you can make your mark in the fashion industry. And for that to happen, you must trust me. Do you trust me?"

She looked at him quizzically.

"It's a yes or no question. You know how anyone can get screwed over in this industry. Do you trust me, Ginger?"

She reflected on their conversation. Every fiber of her being told her not to say yes because of Steve. Yet looking deeply into those blue eyes, Ginger couldn't help herself: "Yes, I do, Grant."

"Good. I'm glad we got that settled. Gin, by the time we get to the city, it's going to be after six thirty and your stuff wouldn't have gotten there yet. Would you like to stay at my place tonight? I have an extra bedroom—and no funny business!"

"You want a sleepover? I guess we're too old to have our moms talk about it first?" Then she realized what she said and felt horrible. "Oh, wait, I'm sorry—"

"It's okay, really."

"So separate bedrooms, right? No purple?"

"Purple?"

"Come on, if you mix pink and blue, you get purple."

"Oh, yeah. No purple. I remember your rules."

As they departed the plane, Tina tried to make one last dig. "Enjoy your stay in New York, *ma'am.*"

"Why, thank you, *little one*," Ginger responded. "Sweetheart, it's nice to finally be back with you again." She grinned at Tina like a Cheshire cat.

"Thank you for flying American Airlines." Tina turned away from both Grant and Ginger.

Chapter 23

At five thirty a.m., Grant tiptoed around so he wouldn't wake Ginger for his early morning workout. As he entered the living room, however, he found her doing stretches. Ginger wore no makeup, her hair in a ponytail, tight midthigh shorts, a tank top, and sneakers, and she still looked gorgeous.

"Well, good morning, Grant. Just getting ready to go for a jog. Hope I didn't wake you. Coffee's ready. The Cheerios are stale, and I wouldn't touch the milk if I were you. I can grab a bagel or croissant after my run."

"Oh, um, well, I love croissants."

"Anything to go with it? Maybe egg and cheese?"

"Wow, sure. You're spoiling me."

"After what you've done for me?"

Grant smiled while tying his gym shoes.

"When you get back, I'll have it ready for you."

"Oh, wait, let me give you a key so you can get back in. After all, you might be here for a couple days—or maybe twenty or thirty years. Ha!"

He handed her a key. As they walked out to the hall, they ran into Brenda from 34B.

Crap! he thought. *She was always close with Margo. How much of our conversation did she overhear?* Grant shuffled to take control of the moment and said, "Well, good morning, Brenda."

Ginger quickly assessed the woman's demeanor. "Again, thanks, Grant, for letting me crash at your place last night while they're getting my place ready. What time do I need to be at the office? Don't want to be late for my first day at work."

Grant responded, "Around nine would be fine. We have a lot to go over."

He knew Brenda was listening intently and would report back to Margo.

All three walked to the elevator. Brenda said, "Hi, I'm Brenda. I live in 34B. If you ever need anything—"

Ginger cut her off. "Pleasure to meet you, Brenda.

But I won't be staying long. Thanks, though." Ginger smiled sweetly while she bent from the waist stretching her hands to the floor.

The elevator ride was excruciatingly silent and uncomfortable; Ginger decided to get off with Grant on the twelfth floor.

"Hey, mind if I check out the exercise room?" Ginger asked.

"Sure."

The elevator doors closed with Brenda's eyes locked on Ginger.

"Wow, that woman is a bitch, huh?"

"You have no idea," Grant responded with a deep sigh.

"I really didn't need the tour. I just wanted to get away from 34Bitch. But since I'm here, might as well check it out."

"Sure, why not?"

Grant showed Ginger around the exercise room, and she decided to run on the treadmill instead of going outside.

Grant and Ginger finished their individual workouts, returned to the apartment, and prepared for work.

"Do we have time to get that croissant? Gotta power up for our day."

"Yeah, glad you remembered."

Grant and Ginger took the subway downtown to Grant's office. As they rode the elevator to the tenth floor, Ginger felt butterflies in her stomach.

Sue, Grant's receptionist, greeted them. She had been his executive secretary for the last five years. Sue was a thirty-nine-year-old mother of two children. She always had a smile, a kind word, or just an ear to listen to others.

"Sue, this is Ginger Madison. She will be working with us and will be my personal assistant."

"Hi, Ms. Madison. It's a pleasure to meet you."

"Nice to meet you, Sue."

"Ms. Madison, if you need anything, let me know. Your first time in the city?"

"No, but it's been a while. I grew up here. May still need your help getting around. Thanks, Sue."

"Great to have you aboard." Sue handed Grant his mail and messages.

Grant's corner office overlooked Broadway and Thirty-Fifth Street with old-fashioned double-hung sash windows. A large, mahogany desk with a wraparound workstation was set up so he could see both streets at the turn of his leather chair. In the far right of the room sat a low, round working table with chairs. The bookshelves were stacked with all the latest and oldest trends of fashion.

On his desk was a picture of his children. This was the first time Ginger got a glimpse of Lyla and Jason; the two of them looked so happy in the photo.

"They're beautiful, Grant. Why don't you have any pictures of them around the apartment?"

"They're in the blue area. Off limits, remember?"

"Right, right."

"Make yourself comfortable while I go meet with Howard. If you need anything, Sue is at your disposal. These are all the line drawings that Rebekah Scott selected for Neiman Marcus, and I'd like your input on them. Later on, we'll go down to the seventh floor, and if you don't mind, I'd like you to try a few things on. If we're lucky, we'll get a pretzel for lunch," he said, laughing at his own comment.

"I guess this isn't first class? No jumbo shrimp? No Tina to serve us?"

"You're on your own, lady. Let me go meet with the devil and get my weekly ass kicking. Sue can show you where the kitchen and restrooms are."

Grant left, and Ginger took her time acclimating to her new surroundings. She looked at the wall with his degrees and photos of specialty garments he had made for various companies and celebrities. Ginger was impressed by his volume of work.

He called me his assistant. What a dream come true!

Grant entered Howard's office. Howard was an overweight Mediterranean man in his sixties with dark skin, brown eyes, and white hair. He was poring over some financial documents, his usual activity on Mondays, except that this Monday, he seemed jovial.

"How the hell are you, buddy boy? I don't know whether I should kiss you or fucking demand more from you, you son of a bitch! After all, I had to throw that fucking thirty-thousand-dollar Christmas party for you in 1972. Remember that night? That's when Margo was on her knees all afternoon begging me to hire you. Now look what you've accomplished. It's about time!"

He ignored Howard's abrasiveness. "Can we get started, Howard?"

After going over the orders, Grant reminded Howard, "If we don't do Neiman Marcus right, Howard, they will bury us. But on a good note, I have an asset of theirs with me."

"Oh, the little toy? What was her name? Bambi? She was the one who was fucking the big boss, right? Fuck her yet, farm boy?"

"Jesus Christ, can we stay on track? She's been the fit model for Neiman Marcus for the last three and a half years. She knows their fit; she knows what works. She's like having the playbook for the opposite football team before the Super Bowl."

"Yeah, yeah, I don't care what you do with her. Y'know, Grant, you're a lot like me. I can see why I should make you partner one day. Guess I was too busy looking at Margo's ass when I should have been paying attention to what you could accomplish."

Grant wanted to smash his face for bringing up Margo and dismissing Ginger as a toy, but he kept his cool. "Her name is Ginger Madison, Howard. She's not trash, so don't fuck this up with her. I'll be bringing her up to meet you shortly. Can you be a gentleman for maybe ten minutes, tops?"

"Oh, fuck you, farm boy. How do you think I got here?"

"I still wonder sometimes."

Grant scribbled "Ginger" on a sticky note and put it on Howard's desk. "You pronounce it *Jin-jer*. Anytime you can't remember her name, just look at this."

"You can't wait to fuck her, huh?"

"Fuck off, Howard."

Upon entering his office, Grant found Ginger sitting on the floor with her shoes off. The table was covered with photos and drawings, and she was surrounded by a mountain of the same.

Her hair was pulled back in a loose ponytail, and she still looked professional in her pinstriped jumpsuit. She was so wrapped up in her work and making notes that she didn't even notice Grant entering. He had time to admire the beauty sitting amidst the mess. It was uncanny how comfortable he felt watching her looking at his work.

"Whoa, I didn't see you there. I really got wrapped up here, Grant. I love most of it, but we can tweak a little here and there. Am I going to get fired my first day by saying that?"

"God, no! You ready to meet Howard?"

"I suppose. Let me get my shoes on."

"That would help."

"Do I look okay? First impressions last a lifetime."

He stepped toward her, gently swept back a few strands of her hair that were slightly out of place, then stood back. "You're perfect."

"Says my boss?"

"Yes he does."

"Thanks."

Ginger tried to control her anxiety about meeting the devil. Picturing a man with a pointed red tail and pitchfork made her smile.

Grant held the door open for Ginger to walk first into

Howard's office.

"Howard, this is Ginger Madison," Grant said.

Howard greeted Ginger with an outstretched hand. "It's a pleasure to meet you."

"She'll be putting the finishing touches on the Neiman Marcus line and working with me as my personal assistant—a second pair of eyes, if you will."

"Thank God we got someone to help him. Don't know how he's made it this far."

Ginger replied, "Really? I was quite impressed with his work. And it's nice to meet you too, Mr. Golden."

"Please, call me Howard. And if you need anything, my door is always open. Any problems or concerns, call me any time. Even after work. Whatever you need—" He quickly looked at the note to recall her name. "—Ginger."

"Okay, Howard. We have a lot of work to do. Just wanted to introduce you two."

As they walked out, Howard leered at Ginger and the hair on her neck stood straight up.

Chapter 24

Monday flew by. Ginger had tried on countless garments, and Grant snapped photos of his favorite pieces.

"Ginger, tomorrow we will go over the fabrics and-"

"Wait, when did we have lunch? I can't remember if we even ate. I need to shut down or I will be useless tomorrow."

Grant looked at his watch. It was almost eight p.m., and he noticed her eyes were heavy from exhaustion. "Sorry, I didn't realize the time. How does sushi sound?"

"Perfect. I could go for a large, hot sake. And promise me you won't breathe a word about work. I need a break."

"Okay. Would you like to walk or cab it?"

"Walking sounds great. I need fresh air. It'll wake me up."

Walking up Broadway, Grant watched Ginger become revitalized with each step, surrounded by all the bright lights of the city.

"Sorry I pushed you so hard today, Gin. Having you here, working with me, has reignited my inner fire. Thank you for that."

Ginger smiled. She stopped at a storefront. "Mind if we go in for a moment? It's been forever since I've been in the city."

"Of course not. Whatever you want."

Following behind her, Grant thought she looked like a kid in a candy store—even though she's clearly not a child. He watched her superb ass naturally sway back and forth, and his naughty thoughts took over, imagining her naked body.

She caught him gazing at her. "Ahem, Grant?"

"Oh, um, sorry. Better stick to the rules." He looked embarrassed.

Damn those rules, she thought. *Look at him! It's so hard not to get lost in those blue eyes. But I need to focus on my career.*

She held up a small, white top prominently displaying a heart, which would reveal her perfect midriff if she wore nothing underneath it. "Grant, isn't this pretty?"

"They are," he said, looking at her breasts and clearly not noticing the top at all.

"They?"

"I mean, it, *it*! It's a nice top."

"You've worked too hard today; you must be having double vision," she said. "Where's the sushi place? We definitely need some hot sake."

He sighed, happy she let him off the hook. "Not far. Would you like that? I'd like to buy it for you."

"What, dinner?"

"The top. Consider it a first day on the job gift from a friend."

"Are you trying to buy me, Grant Robinson?"

"I have a feeling you can't be bought, Ginger Madison."

"You're right, cowboy."

"If you'd allow me the pleasure?"

"If you insist, boss."

"Hey, no work talk! And please, don't consider me your boss. I'm just your friend right now."

Ginger blushed. "Thank you, Grant. That's very sweet of you."

They continued their walk to the restaurant, and Ginger took in all the sights. "Every block is wonderful. I forgot how good it feels just to wander down the streets at night and soak in the beauty of the city. It's good to be back home."

They reached their dinner destination and were seated immediately. "A large, hot sake for the lady, please, ASAP."

Their intimate space had a red lantern hanging over the low table and floor-level benches covered with gold-and-red cushions to sit on. The silk-screen partition with hummingbirds and lotus flowers printed all over completed the perfect Zen atmosphere. The waiter delivered the tokkuri and filled each cup full of the hot liquid.

"Kampai, Gin." They both slammed back the drinks.

Ginger analyzed her surroundings. "This could be very romantic—if we weren't working together."

"Hey, no talk about work," Grant reminded her.

"Right, no work talk. Well, in that case, it *is* very romantic. Oops. Too much sake, I suppose."

"Oh, bullshit. We only finished the first ochoko!"

"Yeah, but I didn't eat lunch. It must have gotten to my head already."

"Sure it did," Grant said as he filled her empty ochoko, then his. He raised the drink for a toast.

"What are we toasting to?"

"To your first day of work—and surviving Howard Golden. Kampai."

"Cheers." She never lost eye contact with him while she sipped her sake.

Their feet dangled beneath the table, sometimes briefly intermingling.

After dinner, Ginger and Grant sat on the steps in the restaurant and put their shoes back on. They leaned into each other, the sake in full effect. They decided, then, that it would be best to take a cab back to Grant's apartment.

Tuesday and Wednesday also whipped by in a flash, with their days starting with workout sessions and ending with dinner at Grant's apartment. They took turns looking through the peephole in the mornings to see if 34Bitch was stalking them, which became their inside joke. On Wednesday morning, they caught her roaming the halls, waiting for them to walk out together. She finally gave up and hit the elevator button.

Ginger could hardly keep the days straight or how long she'd been back in the city. She hadn't even had time to catch up with her mother, other than phone calls. Her mother constantly barraged her with questions about Grant and if she would be bringing him to the picnic. "Are you really going to leave him all alone on Labor Day?" her mom asked.

"Mom!"

Thursday morning, Grant and Ginger were barely keeping up with all the work they had when his phone rang.

"This is Grant," he answered while looking through some designs.

"Hey, roomie! How the hell are you?" Steve squawked so loudly that Ginger looked up, recognizing the voice on the other end. She noted the look on Grant's face and couldn't quite place his emotion—was it fear, shock, or what? He had nothing to hide, right?

"Roomie! I'm good," Grant replied while putting the call on speakerphone—a confirmation to Ginger that there were no secrets between them. She smiled at Grant and winked. He winked back at her and held his middle finger up to the phone.

"So what's been going on, roomie?" Not waiting for a response, Steve continued to babble about his life, even mentioning the Dallas Cowboys' roster for the start of the season. Grant pretended to shoot himself, using his hand in the shape of a gun. Ginger muffled her laughter. Grant shushed her with his finger, trying to hold back his own laughter.

Finally, Steve brought up Ginger. "On another note, buddy, Sarah told me that Ginger left behind some of her makeup. Didn't want her to be without it, so I called the Carlyle and found out she's not registered yet. Do you know where she's at? Staying at her parents, perhaps?"

Grant hesitated and looked at Ginger for direction, mouthing, "What do I say?" and pointing at himself, "With me?"

She had an evil smirk and nodded.

Grant gave her the thumbs up. "She's actually staying at my place."

Dead silence filled the room.

"Rebekah never had Ginger try anything on. She's been working with me. She's fitting all the garments for Neiman Marcus and making any corrections or tweaks that are necessary."

With still no response from Steve, Grant continued, "Honestly, man, I'm working her like a dog, and she hasn't even been able to visit her parents, let alone check into the Carlyle."

"Is she close by? Can I talk to her?"

Grant looked at Ginger, and she emphatically shook her head no.

"Sorry, pal, she's with the seamstresses, working on fits and patterns. You were right; she knows what she's doing. She's not just a pretty face."

"Uh, yeah, I told you so."

"Don't worry, man. You'll thank me for making you look like the most incredible head buyer Neiman Marcus has ever had! And if you really want, you can share some of your bonus with me."

There was still no response from Steve.

"Anyway, you can send her stuff to my office, roomie. I'll make sure she gets it."

"Great. Tell her I asked after her?"

"Of course, pal. I'm sure she'll reach out when she has time."

"Just make sure she doesn't call my house."

"Yeah, of course, man. I know the drill."

"I knew that you're my favorite farm boy for a reason. Dude, you should see the latest fit model I just fucking hired. Veronica. It's gonna be hard for me to keep my dick in my pants—or out of her mouth!"

"Jesus Christ, Steve! Wait until the ink is dry! You're not even officially divorced yet, you know." Grant mouthed the word "asshole."

All she could do is nod and think, *Oh, is Sarah in for a big surprise.*

"Don't worry about me. I've always got it under control. You got time to fly out next Tuesday to go over some of the line? Maybe a night out on the town?"

"Real work, Steve? Because I'm super busy here."

"Yes, damn it. I haven't asked for much. Besides, I opened the door for you at Neiman Marcus. Just one night."

"Sure. I'll be there."

"I'll take care of the arrangements. Just show up. I *need* a night out, roomie."

"If you insist, buddy."

They hung up. Ginger sat with her legs and arms crossed. "So, what do you think he has planned for this night out?" She pensively looked at him while waiting for his response.

"Ginger, I thought you trusted me. I didn't have to share any of his bullshit with you. And if you think I'm gonna fuck Sarah, you're wrong. That's all the past. For shit's sake, Steve is part of your past, right? Haven't things changed?"

She wanted to run, yet there was a stronger urge to stay by his side. Meekly, she responded, "Sorry, Grant. I'm just gun-shy."

"Gin, I don't hold secrets. That's the only way this relationship will work. You are my assistant. You need to know everything that's going on, and I have nothing to hide."

Chapter 25

After another long day, Ginger and Grant found themselves sitting on the floor of the apartment sharing a pizza and meatball Parmesan sandwich while sipping Chianti from paper cups.

"Grant, my mother continues to hassle me about this. Will you come to the Madison Labor Day picnic?" She wiped the marinara sauce from the corner of her lips, which Grant wished he could lick clean himself.

He looked her up and down. Her hair was a tangled mess, her camisole was covered in threads from working with the fabrics and patterns, and she had a light dirt mark on her forehead. Still, she looked beautiful.

"Yes, of course," was all he could say. "I think it'd be fun to meet your family."

They ate the rest of the meal in silence, both wondering where their relationship was heading.

Friday was another typical day at work. Their routine was down pat: workout sessions, showers, taking the subway to work, and busting ass through lunch. Their first workweek was winding down.

Grant asked Ginger, "Think you can come in tomorrow? No disruptions. We've just made so much headway on the line. But please feel free to say no. You have the right to sleep, you know."

"Hmm, let me think."

"Maybe you have a hot date tomorrow night?"

"If you haven't noticed, Grant, you've been my only date lately. Okay with that?" He glossed over the comment to her frustration.

"So I need to start working on what I'm going to bring to Paris. I need you to come with me. You have a passport, right?"

"What?"

"Well, you are my assistant and my fit model. If I can land this account, Howard is willing to give me a part of the company, which gives us both job security for a long time. And I can't do it alone."

She sat silent, letting Grant talk. "If I can break into that market, I'd love to have you standing beside me. Where would *you* like to be?"

"Right next to you, Grant."

"What a pair we make, huh, Gin?"

Ginger giggled. "Yeah, a farm boy from Wisconsin and a girl from the Bronx—wouldn't have put those two together under any circumstances."

"Damn, we're like a hundred to one odds. I think we have a chance though."

"So do I. I just wish we had champagne to celebrate."

"Must be your lucky day." He excused himself from the office and returned with a bottle.

"You never let me down, do you?"

"Never. Let's celebrate!"

As they sipped their drinks, Ginger thought, *I've always had men who were all talk, never a man of action. In less than a week, I've been practically handed the world—without as much as a pass or a kiss. I mean, I loved the flirtatious moments. He actually listens to me and sees me as an equal.*

Saturday seemed like every other day of the week, until about two fifteen, when Grant looked at his watch and said, "You like baseball? I have two tickets for the Mets game tonight. Wanna grab a beer and hot dog at the game?"

"Uh, sure."

"Although, in my other pocket, I happen to have tickets to a Broadway show, *A Chorus Line*." He smirked. "I mean, if you'd rather go to the ball game, I'll cancel the tickets."

Ginger scowled at him. "That's mean! Of course I'd rather do the show!"

"And since none of your clothes have arrived, you'll need the proper attire. That means we'll be shopping as well. I already called Bergdorf. They're expecting us. By the way, where *did* you send your stuff to anyway? Timbuktu?"

That took her aback. "But . . ."

"Wow, I finally figured out how to keep you quiet! We'd better close up shop for the day and get a move on. Bergdorf will be charging my card either way."

Ginger still hadn't said anything. "Gin, are you okay?"

"Um, yeah, just a little shocked."

"After the show, we'll get the best steak at Smith & Wollensky."

"Grant, is . . . is this a date?" Ginger stammered out.

"No, not really. Just two friends winding down a long

week. You okay with that?"

"Of course I'm okay with that. But I want to pay for—"

"Nothing. You pay for nothing tonight. It's my token of appreciation for how hard you've been working. I couldn't have gotten the line this far along so quickly without you. You have no idea what it means to me."

"I have a clue."

Ginger started cleaning up, but Grant stopped her. "Don't worry, Gin, we're the last ones out and the first ones in. I'm locking the door. Grab your bag and let's go."

"Yes, sir, boss! Friend! Pain in the ass!"

"God, I love your sense of humor, Ginger."

"Wouldn't be me without it." She smiled and elbowed him.

Riding down the elevator, Ginger was ecstatic but tried to keep her emotions in check. *I haven't felt like this since, well, jeez, senior prom?*

Grant stood behind Ginger in the elevator. She turned around to face him, leaving hardly any space between them. "Grant, just wondering something."

"What's that?"

"When did you have time to set this up? We've been working nonstop."

His boyish grin covered his face, turning his eyes to a deeper hue of blue than normal. "Oh, when I helped you out of the limo at Neiman Marcus in Dallas. I called Susan and had her set it up right away."

"What?"

"Just kidding. Yesterday, actually."

"You really didn't have to do this for me, Grant. But I'm glad you did. I can't remember the last time I saw a play! And it's been years since I shopped at Bergdorf."

"And today you will have a personal shopper to assist you."

"Every girl's dream! But can't I pay for some—?"

"Ginger, we've already talked about this. You pay for nothing tonight."

"You stubborn shit!"

"You ungrateful brat!" Grant retorted.

Laughing, Ginger leaned into him briefly. *I like teasing him, both mentally and physically. Hope he can handle me.*

As the elevator doors opened, Grant patted her on the ass and said, "Let's go!"

Surprised, Ginger thought, *Wait, who's teasing who here?*

Chapter 26

Entering Bergdorf, Grant clearly knew where he was headed. Passing through the fragrance section, he suddenly stopped. "Need any perfume?"

"I have enough at the apartment. But thank you."

"Whatever suits you."

Ginger felt like a princess being treated to a fairy-tale evening.

Stepping off the elevator on the third floor, Grant led Ginger to a door that read "Employees Only." He walked in like he owned the place. "Libby, darling, we're here!"

Ginger tried to hide her amazement. *What the hell? Is he some kind of department store rock star or something?*

"Grant, dahling!" an Italian woman in her late forties said. She looked at Ginger. "Oh, she's more beautiful than you described, mi amore!"

Grant blushed and avoided Ginger's eye contact. "Libby, I'd like to introduce you to Ginger, my new assistant." To Ginger, he said, "Libby's one of my longtime friends."

"Nice to meet you, Libby."

"Anytime she needs anything, please take care of her and send me the bill."

Ginger lost her breath and looked at Grant with a mix of chagrin and happiness.

"Oh, my gorgeous little dear, I've pulled some outfits for you. But of course, you're welcome to look around. Don't let me restrict you from anything special that catches your eye."

Following Libby to the private salon area, Ginger experienced for the first time what *this* lifestyle was like.

There were floor-to-ceiling mirrors all around, private dressing rooms, and a salon area. She saw a rack of clothing, shoes, undergarments, and accessories chosen just for her. Overstuffed chaise lounges with fresh-cut flowers on every tabletop. The classical background music created an atmosphere of pure decadent indulgence. Grant and

Ginger sank into a large, royal purple loveseat, but she couldn't relax.

Libby asked, "Would either of you like a drink? I have champagne and vino, of course. Whatever you desire."

Grant responded, "A rosé champagne would be great. Ginger?"

"The same, please. Thank you."

Ginger leaned over to Grant and whispered, "Personal shopper? Are you kidding me, Grant? This is insane! I feel like Cinderella!"

"Well, Cinderella, you've earned your keep thus far. Tonight, we go to the ball!"

"Thank you, Prince Charming." Ginger stood up and curtsied. "I'm already having a ball. Just missing my tiara, since Libby is clearly my fairy godmother."

"A tiara? That can be arranged."

The champagne cork popped in the background. "Girls," Libby said, clapping her hands twice, "we have work to do!"

One of Libby's assistants served the two their champagne, and then she grabbed Ginger by the hand and led her toward the clothing. Grant interrupted, "Pardon me, Libby?"

"Yes, dahling?" Libby's accent was sweetly thick, leaving Ginger to wonder if it was overly accentuated.

"I'd like to make a toast first, if you don't mind."

"How perfectly apropos, mi amore."

"To friendships—both new and old—may they last forever." All three clinked glasses.

"Now let's have some fun, my little beauty!" Turning back to her assistants, Libby said, "Chop chop, girls!"

Ginger modeled each look for Grant, but she refused to pick one, noticing not a single item had a price tag attached.

"They all look perfect to me."

"You're the one who has to look at me tonight. Isn't there one you favor?"

"Ginger, you look exquisite in every one. You pick, or they all come home with us."

Frustrated and knowing he would do just that, Ginger pleaded, "Give me a hint for a color at least then."

"Fair enough. Green."

"Thank you, dahling." She winked at him and disappeared behind the thick, purple velvet curtains of her dressing room.

The next two hours were overwhelming for Ginger. As a model, she catwalked on countless runways and appeared in dozens of magazines over her career, yet this entire event was just for her. Grant was treating her like a princess.

After her hair, mani, pedi, and makeup were finished,

Ginger stepped into her strapless, deep-emerald dress, which made her eyes an even more dazzling green. The hemline hit just about midthigh, revealing the length and strength of her legs. The silk and cotton blend made the dress flow with each step she took. Bold gold strappy heels and a matching clutch purse accentuated the jewelry that Libby picked out for her.

Ginger looked in the mirror and truly loved her reflection. Her auburn hair was in a half sweep, with a few ringlets draping around her face and down her back. She felt sexy and beautiful, and it wasn't for a fashion show; it was for her, compliments of Grant. She couldn't wait to see him.

Walking into the lounge of the dressing area, Ginger couldn't care less what she looked like as soon as she saw Grant in his tuxedo, looking completely delicious and dapper. The first thing she noticed after visually devouring him was that his cufflinks and buttons were a matching emerald green to her dress.

Neither of them spoke a word; they were both speechless and entranced by the other's beauty.

Finally, Grant cleared his throat and said, "I hope it's okay to compliment you."

"I'd like to compliment you first, please. You look perfect."

"My turn—to call you a pretty woman doesn't do you justice. You are *breathtaking*. Every person who looks at you tonight will be jealous of who you are and wonder who the hell I am to have you at my side."

Ginger blushed, not knowing what to say.

"Well, let's go to the ball, Cinderella. Your carriage awaits. Don't worry, though, it won't turn into a pumpkin at midnight."

"I'm ready, Prince Charming."

Libby appeared. "Ah, you both look magnifico! Fate una bella sera."

"We will. Libby, I can't thank you enough for today. I feel like a princess."

"Mi amore, you look like a *queen*!" She air-kissed both cheeks so as not to smudge the makeup.

"Grant, dahling, where shall I send the other dress? To your apartment or your office?"

"The apartment is fine. Thanks, Libby."

Grant put his arm out for Ginger to wrap her hand in, and she squeezed him tightly. "You little shit! Which dress?"

"Oh, relax. You'll see. Let's go enjoy ourselves, shall we?"

Chapter 27

By midnight, after hours of theater, dinner, and drinks, they arrived back at the apartment. Ginger's head was spinning from exhaustion. Riding the elevator, Grant held her against his chest.

Lost in a trance, she listened to the gentle but strong beating of his heart. She whispered, "Tonight has been one of the most wonderful nights of my life."

"I'm glad you had fun. I enjoyed your company. How about we sleep in tomorrow? Maybe a picnic brunch in Central Park and just relax?"

"Sounds perfect, Grant." She clasped her hands and

stretched her arms over her head, revealing her cleavage. He couldn't help but soak in the perfect lines of her body. His eyes were already removing her dress, wanting to explore every inch of this feminine feline in front of him.

Entering the apartment, Grant said, "I could use a day off myself. You can catch up with your parents or whatever, and I can get a hold of my kids again."

Standing in the hallway of his apartment, Ginger turned and kissed his cheek. "Well, goodnight, Prince Charming."

Grant watched her ass sway toward the pink room. "Goodnight, Princess."

Grant loosened his tie and poured a short vodka, then walked out to the balcony. Drink in hand, the late-night breeze was gentle but felt great against his face. The Broadway lights below danced and the streets bustled with people, yet he suddenly felt utterly alone, realizing Ginger could leave at any moment.

She's so full of life. Just knowing she's here is uplifting. My emotions for her are overwhelming. How can this be? And who is she, really?

Lost in thought, he sipped his drink. Then a voice startled him: "Grant? What are you doing? Are you okay?" Ginger softly asked, wearing only her bathrobe with her hair wrapped in a towel.

"Yeah, just decompressing from the week and looking

at the lights." He looked up at the sky. "It's hard to see a single star up there. Last week in Wisconsin, I could have captured a thousand stars in a paper cup, they were so plentiful. What a different life—a million crickets singing there. Here, there are a million people."

"Well, I suppose if you look hard enough, you can see one. Look right there." She pointed and slightly leaned into his body. Her touch sent waves of desire through him. "You miss them?"

"The stars?" Grant asked.

"No, your kids," Ginger said.

"Yes and no. Does that sound bad?"

Still leaning into each other, not waiting for her response, he continued, "Everything in life has trade-offs. I love being a dad. I love my children. But I sometimes think I would have been a better uncle. You know, that favorite uncle that showed up and gave you all the treats you could possibly want. Ever have an uncle like that?"

"No. No uncles like that." She pushed further into his body. "But I have the next best thing, my Aunt Sadie. Good news is you'll get to meet her at the picnic. She's going to eat you alive!"

"Think I'll get a present?"

"If you're a good boy!" She was thrilled to see his smile return, only to watch it fade away with his next statement.

"The problem with being too smart, Ginger, is that sometimes it makes you melancholy."

"I know the feeling."

Ginger's lips were just inches from his. "Yet what really counts is simple. It can be right in front of your eyes, and regardless of how smart you are, it's still unattainable."

Looking deeply into each other's eyes, Ginger didn't respond, she just soaked in his words.

He imagined reaching over and unwrapping her towel and pulling her in for their first kiss. Instead, he straightened up, finished his vodka, and said, "Well, thank you for a great time. Sleep well."

She whispered, "Good night, my sweet Grant."

Chapter 28

"Cap, are you sure this girl is fun?" Alex inquired yet again.

"Look, if I hadn't met Rachel first, Isabella would have turned my head. And they're best friends, so relax already!"

"Yes, sir!"

"Hey, we're not on duty. Just two friends on leave."

Stopping outside the entrance to the pub, Tommy turned to Alex. "Alex, this is *the one*. She is the love of my life. I won't be going back with you tonight."

"You're serious, aren't you?"

Tommy smiled. "Alex, I love her. I've never been more in love in my entire existence."

As they walked into the pub, the bartender yelled, "Hey there, Yankees! First round is on me tonight."

"Thank you, sir!" Alex said and ordered two pints of dark ale for them while they sat at the bar.

Rachel and Isabella were in the storeroom when they heard Ian, the bartender. Rachel held back the purple curtain so she could point out who Isabella would be meeting.

"That's him? Fantastic! Mmmm, I jolly well want a piece of that!"

"Slow down, Izzy. For Christ's sake, they just got here. Keep it together." Rachel laughed. "You're going to end up in bed or on a park bench somewhere, aren't you, you hussy?"

Rachel couldn't wait another second and burst through the curtains, running toward Tommy, who she hadn't seen in four long days.

"My sweet Tommy!" She cried and wrapped around him like a vine growing on lattice. Tommy spun her around and sat her on his lap, holding her so closely there was no space left between them. They kissed like they'd been apart for an eternity.

"Ahem," Alex cut in. "Hi, I'm Alex."

"Hi, Alex." She looked at him for a split second and then returned to kissing Tommy.

Isabella walked up to Alex. "Hi, Alex. I'm Izzy. Pardon those two—it must be true love." She rolled her eyes.

Alex responded, "So what will you be wearing to the wedding?"

"I don't know. I suppose we'll have to match, since I'll be the maid of honor and I'm sure you'll be the best man." They hit it off right away, moving a few seats down from the lovebirds to sip a pint and share some small talk.

After a while, Rachel and Tommy joined Isabella and Alex for a game of darts. Isabella already had Alex's hat on and was listening intently to whatever he had to say.

For a while, there was no war, just two couples having a good time; drinking, laughing, and enjoying each other's company. They made silly wagers on whatever they could bet on. Rachel kept teasing Tommy about his inability to hit the bull's-eye. "I'm just the pilot, not the navigator!"

Isabella said, "And I'm a great target!" She placed Alex's hand on her ass and winked at him seductively.

After a few hours of fun at the pub, Rachel whispered while grabbing between his legs, "My sweet Tommy, I need you."

Rachel barely finished her sentence before Tommy was pulling out his wallet and tossing bills at his friend for the tab. "Izzy, Alex, it's been swell. We're taking off."

Isabella pulled Rachel aside. "Have fun. I know I

will."

"I'm glad Alex is into you."

"Let's see *how far into me* he can get!"

"You bloody harlot. Enjoy!"

Rachel turned to Alex. "Alex, take care of my best friend, got it?"

"Oh, I plan to, Rachel." Alex looked at Isabella, who jumped into his arms and kissed him again.

"You two are bloody crazy!"

Once outside, Tommy said, "I have two days off. How long can you get off for?"

"As many times as you can make me, Lieutenant. Considering I'm much better than you at darts, I hope you're ready." She giggled.

They walked arm in arm down the street. "Ever think how difficult it is to fly with a group of sex-starved guys while having a huge distraction on your mind? I can't stop thinking about you. I nearly flew up the ass of the plane in front of me. Alex saved us by pulling me back into reality before I almost took out the tail gunner on the other plane."

"You're kidding, aren't you?"

"Yeah, baby, I'm just—"

"Tommy, you can't do that to me!"

"I'm so sorry." He wrapped her up in his arms. "Rachel, look at me. I love you. I will do everything in my power to always be with you." Rachel's tears spilled over her cheeks, and he gently kissed her eyes and nose, finally devouring her lips. "You are like a little white witch who's cast a spell on me."

"Then it did work after all." Rachel's tension eased.

The moment they arrived at her cottage and she opened the door, Tommy pulled her entire body against his. Her lips returned his kisses, and then her tongue slid into his mouth.

Rachel felt the stiffening between his legs with her hands and realized her mouth was watering with desire to taste and please her fly-boy.

Tommy's hand was unbuttoning her blouse by the time she closed the door. He could barely control his passion as he grabbed her ass. She pushed him back so she could seductively undress for him. He turned her around and pulled her into him from behind against his hard erection, sexually and mentally charged for her—only her.

"Tommy, baby, I'm *all* yours. Take your time; I'm your lover, not a mission."

There was no time to start a fire in the fireplace as the blaze was already lit between them, nor could they make it to the bedroom. Ripping his clothes off, everything disappeared in the world except the need to be one with each other. She pushed him onto the loveseat, the room dimly lit by the floor lamps. Then she climbed on top of him.

"Tommy, I need you. I love you."

"I love you, Rachel." She straddled his naked body and huge cock. He slid into her easily, for she was sopping wet with desire. She yelped with pleasure.

Rachel's grinding and Tommy's thrusting melded their bodies into one, when she cried out in pure pleasure. Losing her voice, he could feel her climax building with each grind of her hips. Tommy pulled tightly at her ass, burying his cock deeply inside of her, listening to Rachel's moans and indecipherable words. He knew by her body language she was begging for more. He was barely able to utter, "Fly for me, baby!"

Tommy felt his body give into the sensation—the promise of an orgasm while the walls of her pussy clamped around his cock, almost as if sucking on what was deep inside her. He *devoured* her like a feral animal, finally feeding and fulfilling his natural craving for her. The lion and the lamb had become one for a long moment, and time stood still.

Looking into each other's eyes, in perfectly wild sexual rhythm, they were one—totally lost in space. Again, time didn't exist—just the purest pleasure of their naked flesh and souls completely bared to the other. Both simultaneously exploded into ecstasy, sharing the most intimate and sensual orgasm either had ever experienced.

"Rachel!" he could barely say while his eyes were trying to focus on her beautiful face, surrendering to the utmost pleasure body and soul could offer, filling her with his passion. Rachel's orgasm was so intense, she could hardly handle the influx of the physical sensation completely overwhelming her body. As she grinded into Tommy, Rachel felt like she was falling off a cliff into an endless sexual abyss—even better than the first time they were intimate. She began to weep from the pleasure.

This was beyond making love. Rachel and Tommy coupled making love with a desperate need for fucking, intertwining both facets of the delicious, God-given gift of man and woman perfectly.

And so began the next two days of his leave—totally consumed with each other. Again, there was no war, no outside world, only their world, lost in each other yet hating the clock for stealing their time too quickly.

Chapter 29

Grant was sexually aroused by his dream. His mind was torn between two worlds. Needing to fulfill his body's primal need, he began stroking his already hard cock. Already so close to an orgasm after such a vivid dream, Grant thought of how desirous Ginger was.

Visualizing her naked body put him over the edge within seconds, feverishly trying not to call out her name while cumming. He lay in bed after climaxing all over his stomach, now fully conscious, wondering, *Who the fuck are Rachel and Tommy?*

Grant walked down the hallway toward the kitchen. It was obvious that Ginger was still sleeping since the aroma of freshly brewed coffee was missing. He decided to surprise her with a gourmet breakfast from his favorite corner deli.

Walking in the morning air toward the deli, he fervidly wished he could actually picture what Rachel looked like. Only her eyes lingered in his mind. *Ginger has the same color eyes—I guess I am falling in love with her. It's the only explanation for this Rachel character.*

Walking around the deli, he grabbed bagels, cream cheese, Nova lox, and a bottle of champagne and orange juice for mimosas. Feeling more drawn to Ginger than ever after last night's conversation on the balcony, he was lost in thought about her.

"Sir?"

"Yes?"

"That'll be eighty-one dollars and seventy-nine cents."

"I apologize. My mind is elsewhere." He handed her his credit card.

"Obviously a good place, judging by your smile."

"Have you ever tried to figure out the meaning of a dream?"

"All the time. I think they come from our subconscious mind, which may be trying to reveal something important."

"Great insight, Miss."

"Or just crazy. Here's your card, sir. Have a nice day."

The cute blonde winked at Grant, and for some reason, he blushed.

As he walked back to his apartment, he hoped Ginger was waiting for—and *wanted*—him.

When Grant entered the apartment, he found a note on the table: "Grant, I wasn't sure when you would be back, so I'm off to visit my parents for a bit. Be back around three—picnic then? Thank you endlessly for last night. It was wonderful! XO, Princess Gin." Next to her name was a smiley face wearing a tiara.

Grant kept reading "XO, Princess Gin" over and over. He folded the note and slipped it in his pocket.

Grant made a small breakfast and read the *New York Times*. Around midmorning, he called his kids, hoping his ex wouldn't answer. No luck.

"Hey, Margo. How are you?"

"Fine."

"Good. Are the kids available?"

"So why isn't your new assistant-slash-roommate or whatever the hell she is dialing for you?"

"Margo, give it rest. Just for the record, Gin—hell, you know what? It doesn't matter. Are the kids available?"

After a swift and cold silence, she replied, "Yes, and

just for the record, don't introduce *my children* to women that you're just screwing."

"Yes, sir!"

After fifteen or so minutes talking with Lyla, she handed the phone to Jason, who barely spoke—typical little boy. He liked being on the phone as much as anyone likes having their teeth pulled without Novocain.

Lyla got back on the phone: "Daddy, I just wanted to tell you I love you again. I miss you so much." Then she whispered, "And your heart is still safe with me."

"I knew it would be, my baby girl. I love you so much!"

"I love you too."

"Call me whenever you want. At work or home, okay?"

"Okay. Bye."

Grant could hear the tears in her voice and tried to hold back his own. The only good thing that came from his marriage to Margo was his kids.

Grant busied himself with weekend chores—laundry, straightening the apartment, and last-minute grocery shopping for his picnic date with Ginger.

Whoa. Date? That would make two dates if you count last night. And I haven't even touched her! I'm losing my shit.

Just then the door opened. "Grant, I'm home!"

"Hey, Gin! Back here in the bedroom."

"Oh, there you are," she said, leaning against the doorjamb to the blue room and watching him fold clothes. Ginger noticed a pile of her clothing already neatly arranged on his bed.

"You didn't have to do my laundry."

"Just being practical. I hope you don't mind that I tried on your bras. They don't fit too well. The panties, on the other hand . . ."

Ginger grabbed a pair of his boxers and held them up. "I'd like to try these on. It's only fair."

"Only if you put them on right here," he retorted.

"Fine." She pulled them over her cutoffs. "They fit okay." She turned to look in the mirror and saw pictures of his kids, and it emotionally transformed her in an instant, "God, they really are so cute!"

"I talked to them earlier."

"Everything good?"

"They're great. We all miss each other. How were your folks?"

"They're happy I'm back in the city, of course. And looking forward to meeting you. Sorry, but you may be tortured on Labor Day."

"You won't be wearing my boxers at the picnic, right?"

"Nah, despite the fact that they're really comfortable!"

Taking them off was more like a striptease for him. She felt sexy as she slipped her long legs out of his boxers. She held them against her breasts and slowly folded the purple-and-green plaid material. Her movements nearly commanded an uninterrupted gaze from him, which pleased her.

"Damn," Grant said, clearing his throat, "I think they look better on you than me."

"I wouldn't know," she said.

Grant wasn't sure if *she* knew what she wanted from him. His fear about losing her crept into his head. "I have a great bottle of champagne for this afternoon. And a few little treats. Still interested in a picnic or—?"

"Absolutely!" The temptress tempting the tempter, she grabbed a pair of her tiny sleep shorts and held them against her hips while folding them. "Then let me help you, um, finish the clothes."

Grant and Ginger packed the picnic basket, filling the air with conversation consisting of mostly small talk.

Walking into the park, Grant changed the subject. "So, when I called to talk to the kids this morning, Margo answered. Could have done without hearing her voice ever again, but she did hint at something."

"Hint? Let me guess, she talked to 34Bitch?"

"How quickly your brain works."

"You have no idea. So what's the issue?"

"Just a comment about not allowing the kids to meet a casual acquaintance."

Ginger stopped midstride for a moment, capturing Grant's full attention. "Well, then there's nothing to worry about, right?"

Grant nodded in agreement—to what, he wasn't sure.

"So I packed two bottles of champagne."

"Two?"

"One each for the two and a half blocks we have to walk—or stumble—back to the apartment. Because—don't tell anyone—I love an elevator ride with you leaning against me."

"Grant Robinson, are you planning to get me tipsy?"

"But of course not, Princess Gin! You don't want me to think you would accidentally end up in the blue room, right?" A brief silence followed, gauging her demeanor as best he could. "After all, it would be in the pink."

"You're a scoundrel! And if you keep it up, you *will* see me in your boxers at the picnic, just so you have to deal with my mother!"

They both felt comfort coupled with desire, the latter of which they both tried to ignore. Each silently wondered what the other was waiting for.

They decided on a spot just past Strawberry Fields,

close to the pond.

"I thought you said it was only two and half blocks."

"New York City blocks! You really have been gone a long time, huh? If we need it, there're a million places to stop for a drink and, if necessary, a million more cabbies available."

"Sounds good to me." She helped him lay the blanket out.

Grant and Ginger spent the next few hours relaxing, talking, and laughing on a beautiful late August afternoon. They enjoyed champagne and snacking on grapes and blackberries, marbled port wine and cheddar cheese, brie with strawberry preserves on water crackers, and sourdough bread with slices of prosciutto and honey glazed turkey.

Their conversation was light like a gentle breeze at times but also very telling about the other, a convergence of two becoming one with each puzzle piece falling into place. The sky was ablaze with hues of pink and orange as it began to set.

Ginger folded the blanket and looked at Grant, who was bent on one knee and repacking the basket. She blurted out, "Wow, I'm having a déjà vu!"

Grant looked up at her. "From when?"

"I don't know, but it seems so familiar."

Grant hopped up and said, "No more champagne for you, missy!"

"Oh, please!" She stepped closer, wrapped her arms around his neck, and whispered, "Thank you for this afternoon, Grant." She gently kissed him on the cheek.

Ginger stepped away before he could hug or kiss her back, leaving him ardently standing there.

"Uh, you're welcome." Though what he really wanted to say was, *I guess the rules are still the rules.*

Chapter 30

Monday was spent discussing and reviewing the Paris project. They needed to be sure they had a clear plan of action to accomplish their goals. After putting in another long day, both Ginger and Grant were sitting on the floor of the apartment, eating from Chinese takeout containers.

Ginger snapped at Grant, "How long ago was I sitting in first class with you and eating jumbo shrimp?" Ginger frowned when she held up a tiny shrimp in the air with her chopsticks. "I'd like to put this one back in the water and let it finish growing!"

"Not sure if it works like that, Gin. It was a

productive week, don't you think?"

"Week? I thought 'a workweek' consisted of forty hours, not forty plus ninety!"

"Guess we pushed it. How about breaking open the fortune cookies and see if we get the lucky lotto numbers? But one of us is going to have to drag our ass down to the corner to buy the ticket—and I can't, so it'll be up to you."

"Don't you dare think I'm going anywhere except down the hall into the shower and then bed, cowboy!"

Opening her cookie, she read her fortune aloud: "Confucius say, 'Hard work bring great success!'" Ginger started laughing uncontrollably. "Did you ask them to print this one for me?"

Grant handed his to Ginger to read it out loud: "Confucius say, 'Allow the cosmic breeze to guide you to true happiness and success.'"

Ginger snatched up her paper cup of wine and said, "I'll toast to that!"

Grant raised his cup. "Cheers. To the breeze and our dreams. Hey, how about we shop for some real dinnerware? I'm done eating and drinking from plastic and paper goods."

"Great! I mean, if you want my help. It's your apartment."

Grant didn't know how to respond at first, his smile slowly fading only to return. "Gin, if you can carve some time out while I'm gone, you can pick out whatever you like. Anyway, I will be back on Wednesday about midday. I'll head straight to the office to be with you—to work with you, I mean. You think you can handle everything while I'm gone?"

"I got this. Just don't change your plans and stay any longer."

It was just over nine days that they shared an apartment and almost every waking moment together. Nothing overtly physical had happened between them, which was starting to drive her crazy. Ginger wished that Grant would *finally* make a pass at her, because she knew she would acquiesce instantly. *I should be more careful about defining what I really want in the future . . . I want him!*

They were standing side by side in the kitchen while cleaning up after dinner. Grant thought, *Does she have any idea that I've fallen in love with her? She would probably hate me if I made a move.*

"Ginger, need to sleep in tomorrow morning? Evan can come back and get you at nineish."

"I'd rather ride with you to the airport, if that's okay. Then Evan doesn't have to double back to get me." *That way I won't miss a single day without your face and those eyes.*

Grant smiled. "I'd love your company."

"Yes, boss."

Her reply further confirmed what he thought: *I can't make a move on her . . . fucking rules!*

Tuesday morning came quickly, and they bumped into each other in the hallway. Grant tried not to act surprised when Ginger said, "Good morning! Coffee's ready, babe."

Heading toward the kitchen, he said, "Hey, babe?"

Ginger peered out of her bedroom door. "Um, Grant, did you just call me 'babe'?"

"Only because you said it first!"

"I most certainly did not!"

"Oh, you most certainly did so!"

"No, no, no!"

"Whatever, *babe*!"

She stomped her foot and yelled, "Grant!"

"Just teasing. Wanted to say thanks for the coffee. But you did say 'babe.'"

"You're welcome. And maybe I said it, but I'm pleading the Fifth. Almost ready for the gym?"

"Yeah, babe."

"Grant!"

"I'm not pleading the Fifth." He winked and sipped his coffee.

Grant and Ginger kept exchanging glances in the gym

mirror during their workout, both sweating profusely. She'd smile and look away when he'd catch her looking at him and he did the same, as if they were two teenagers.

Returning to the apartment, Ginger showered, thinking all the while, *What am I, fifteen again? We're twenty feet away from each other, both naked. I wonder if he's thinking of me in here. Oh my God! I* am *a fucking teenager again!* She pulled at her nipples with her slippery, bubble-coated fingers. *Watching him exercise is so hot! Shit, if I had the nerve, I would walk out of here and slither into his shower!*

Jesus Christ! Grant thought to himself in his own shower. *She's less than twenty-five feet away from me, totally naked, and here I stand with my hard dick in my hand wondering what to do. What's wrong with me?*

During the drive to the airport, he teasingly questioned Ginger regarding the upcoming Labor Day picnic. "So will there be any hot female cousins or other distant relatives at the party? I'm currently not dating anyone, you know."

Her reply came out nearly hissing like a cat: "Don't even think about it, Prince Shithead!"

"Then what does your mother look like?"

"Are you trying to get yourself uninvited?"

"Of course not . . . *babe.*"

Ginger harrumphed and they both laughed.

The drive passed too quickly for both of them, and before they knew it, they were at the departure zone. Grant reached for his carry-on and said, "See you tomorrow, Gin." Evan opened the limo door for him.

Ginger jumped out and raced around the back of the car. She jumped on Grant and wrapped her arms around him. He was reeling inside from the unexpected show of emotion and hugged her back, dropping his briefcase in the act.

They looked into each other's eyes. Grant asked, "Can we continue this when I come back?"

"I wish you were back already." She kissed him on the cheek, aware that he'd cracked her protective shell, the only thing that kept her emotionally safe from the rest of the world.

"Can I kiss you good-bye, Ginger?" Not waiting for her to respond, he gently leaned in and closed the space between their lips.

Grant and Ginger kissed softly at first. She pulled back, looking up into his blue eyes that seemed even deeper than the sky above, and then returned the kiss, bringing it into a full-blown make-out session. His hands were wrapped around her lower back; she was on her tippy-toes, running her fingers through his hair. Their tongues and lips moved in perfect sync.

After a few passionate minutes, Evan cleared his throat, reminding them that they weren't alone. Ginger blushed and giggled, not daring to make eye contact with Evan.

Her heart was racing. "Did that answer your question? Yes, please, let's continue this when you return."

Grant leaned in for one more kiss and then said, "Don't tell Lyla that somebody else has stolen my heart."

Ginger softly laughed. "So, cowboy, you want to wear my lipstick or should I wipe it off? Or maybe I should leave it on, in case that Tina girl is on your flight."

"Tina's the past, Ginger. This is the beginning of *our* future."

Ginger smiled. "Hurry back."

They parted with hands reached out to each other. At that moment, the "rules" she had made were silently renegotiated and sealed with a kiss.

Chapter 31

Ginger felt like she was floating when she walked into the office. She stumbled over the mess of papers and artwork covering the floor—work left over from the evening before.

Cleaning up his desk a bit, she found the two baseball tickets Grant had offered under a heart-shaped paperweight that Lyla made him. *Oh, come on! He really had those damned tickets just in case I said yes to the game?*

Trying to focus on work was difficult. All she could think about was their kiss—and what his lips said: *This is the beginning of our future.* As she tidied up, she kept glancing at the clock, knowing that Grant would call as soon as he landed.

When the phone rang around eleven, Ginger raced across the room and snapped up the phone. "Hi, babe! Thought you'd never call!"

"Babe?" the male voice responded.

Oh, crap! "Oh, sorry, Howard. I thought it was my mom calling me back."

"You can call me 'babe' anytime you want," Howard replied. Ginger felt disgusted.

"I need you to come to my office as soon as you can, Ginger. We have some things to talk about."

"I'll be up shortly."

Grant stopped by the Admiral's Club for his usual preflight drink, greeting Jack, his favorite bartender, with a huge smile. "Hey, Jack!"

"Good morning, Mr. Robinson. You seem more chipper than usual."

"I had a great weekend. You looking forward to Labor Day, Jack?"

Jack was already preparing Grant's Bloody Mary. "No plans for me. What about you?"

"Let's just say, Jack, I have plans and life is good right now."

"You deserve it. Enjoy." Jack walked away to serve his next club member, leaving Grant to his thoughts . . . thoughts of the kiss and what that meant for his future.

Suddenly his mind turned to the dark side—fear. *Will she have too much free time now to rethink her decision about breaking the rules?* He gulped down his whole drink.

He thought of calling Steve to reschedule their meeting. *Though if I cancel, that might make me seem too needy, and that may scare her away. Jesus.*

"Jack, another one, please."

"You lost your smile, Mr. Robinson. What happened?" Jack questioned.

"Business just crept into my head. *Work*—it's a four-letter word."

"*Work* . . . *life* . . . *love* . . . those are all four-letter words. But the best one starts with *f*," Jack said, placing the Bloody Mary on the bar.

Taking a sip, Grant said, "Four-letter words can be good and bad, I suppose. The one that will drive you to drink, though, is *love*." He downed his second drink, trying to remove the four-letter word that paralyzed his thoughts now: *fear*—the fear of losing Ginger *again*.

When the plane touched down and docked, Grant was the first one out, ready to get his meeting over. He found a row of payphones along the concourse wall and was middial when he heard a familiar voice. "Oh, Graaant!" He turned to see Sarah waving at him.

"Steve sent me to fetch you. He's tied up for a while. How about we go straight to the Mansion and have lunch? Maybe you can get tied up too?" Sarah's expression clearly showed what she was thinking.

"Hi, Sarah. What a surprise. I need to make an important call to my office. And then it's probably best to go straight to Neiman Marcus."

"Whatever you want, Grant." She tilted her head and pursed her lips, trying to remind Grant of their night not long ago.

"Um, thanks, Sarah."

His fingers trembled as he dialed his office number, praying that Ginger would answer.

"Mr. Robinson's office. This is Ginger. How may I assist you?"

"Babe!" He sighed with relief at the sound of her voice.

"Hey, cowboy. You've landed, I take it? How was your flight?"

"It was uneventful. And you'll never guess who I ran into."

"Who?"

"Sarah. Steve sent her to pick me up instead of the limo. I just wanted you to know." Grant continued in spite of the silence. "But more importantly, I wanted you to know that I haven't stopped thinking of you—and not just because we kissed today. You've been in my head since the first time we met all those years ago."

"You expect me to buy that?"

"I'm selling, Gin."

"Well, then, you have a sale." They both laughed nervously.

"Well, I got a surprise today too. And I accidentally called him *babe*."

"Who was it?"

"Howard. I'm supposed to go up to his office to discuss something with him."

"Be careful. He's an asshole."

"Oh, believe me, I haven't forgotten. Sarah isn't taking you to the Mansion first, is she?"

"Don't worry, I've already declined that offer."

"That bitch," she said through gritted teeth.

"That asshole," he replied in exactly the same tone, bringing them both to a giggle.

"Call me when you can. Bye for now, my sweet Grant."

"Be safe, love."

As he hung up, he felt dizzy from the conversation and smiled broadly. Then he jumped when he realized Sarah stood right behind him.

"Love?" she pouted.

Empowered by Grant's voice, Ginger was ready to face Howard. Although his door was opened, she knocked.

"Come in, sweetheart."

Kiss my sweetheart ass! She feigned a smile and walked in. "You wanted to see me, Mr. Golden?"

"I already told you, it's 'Howard.' Or 'babe,' if that's your preference." He winked. "I always like my employees to feel comfortable around me."

"Sure thing, *Howard*." She emphasized his name, making it sound like a bad word. "So what is it you needed to discuss? Grant will be back tomorrow."

"I didn't have an opportunity to catch up with him, and I was looking for an update regarding the Neiman Marcus account."

"Oh, I thought he met with you yesterday morning. Is there something he said that needs some clarification, sir?"

"What did I just—?"

"*Howard*. Sorry."

"You seem a little bit uptight. How about we have a

nice lunch, just you and I? Maybe a cocktail? We could get better acquainted. There are plenty of doors that I can open in this industry. Opening them for a *close friend* is one of my favorite things to do."

The look in his eyes was unmistakable, making her feel like the prey of a dangerous beast.

"Thank you for the invite, Howard, but I made lunch plans with my mother. Remember when I called you 'babe' on the phone? That's how I tease her because she still calls me 'baby.'" She hoped the lie would work.

"Then by all means, enjoy. Do you resemble your mother? Maybe we could all catch up for a drink tonight . . ."

"Howard, of all the days! I'm getting together with my mother for lunch so she can show me what she picked out for my father's birthday." She feigned a sigh to make it seem like the whole ordeal was a bother to her. "And tonight we celebrate." In her mind, she marked the day in case the subject of her father's birthday ever came up again.

"That's a shame. Well, if your plans fall through, that drink offer still stands, with or without your mother. Oh, and do wish your father a happy birthday for me."

The way he said that . . . he didn't buy it. "Will do, sir. Uh, Howard."

Ginger attempted a steady pace as she exited the office, trying not to look like she was escaping a predator.

She finally found solace, even in a miniscule form, when the elevator doors closed.

The drive with Sarah from the airport to Neiman Marcus felt longer than the flight. Her perfume permeated the car, leaving Grant wishing he *was* on his way to the Mansion—to shower off the scent.

As he entered, the scene in Steve's office reminded Grant of the day they met in college. A young, attractive woman, wearing only her panties, was bent over Steve. She jumped up when the door opened and immediately started dressing. Sarah gasped and stormed off.

Steve completely dismissed Sarah's reaction and said, "Hey, roomie! This beauty is Veronica, my latest fit model. What do you think?" He slapped Veronica's ass and said, "Honey, turn around and show him what you got."

She obliged without a word. Grant noticed the red handprints on her ass cheeks and shook his head.

"Just breaking her in. You know how that goes when you have a new model. It's good luck."

"That's Texas style, I think. New York has moved beyond that."

"We'll pick this back up later, honey. Gotta catch up with my buddy."

Veronica smiled at both men and shuffled off.

Once Veronica shut the door, Steve immediately said, "That was a short stay at the Mansion. I thought you'd be a while longer, leaving me with more time. What, Sarah didn't do it for you?"

"I'm trying to keep up my end of the bargain. I'm in the trenches right now with the Neiman Marcus order, and my Paris trip is right around the corner. So forgive me if I–"

"Okay, okay. Dinner tonight at the Mansion, though. You have to reserve another room, under your name, of course. Lucy's lawyer is checking every fucking detail of my life, down to the type of toilet paper I wipe my ass with."

"So what are the plans then? Four of us for dinner?"

"That's the idea."

"And what am I supposed to do with Sarah?"

"She's all yours, pal. Expect to spend some time with her tonight. I don't care if you fuck the shit out of her or tie her up in the closet. I am going to fuck the—"

"Steve—"

"Listen, I hooked you up with Rebekah, right? My divorce will be final in the next few months, which is why Sarah needs to be with you. They're watching *her* because they think she's who I've been banging. Gotta weave and bob, pal." He opened his top desk drawer and pulled out a piece of paper. He handed it to Grant with a smirk.

Grant sighed and looked over the info on the order.

"Are you bothered by another half-million-dollar

order for your company *and* a piece of ass? I should be your favorite person in the world right now."

"Yeah, right."

"When did you lose your edge, man?"

"Fuck off."

"That's my roomie!"

After an extremely long day at work—probably longer than usual because Grant wasn't with her—Ginger decided to call it quits. Throughout the day, it felt like she was on a covert mission: twice she crawled under Grant's desk because she thought she heard Howard's voice in the reception area.

Finally! she thought as she headed out. Her bed was calling her.

Back at the apartment building, Ginger rounded the corner and ran into 34Bitch, who stood by the elevator. "Hi, Brenda. How are you?"

"Fine, um, what was your name again?"

Ginger didn't reply.

"I thought you were here only temporarily?"

Again she said nothing. The elevator doors opened and they rode to the thirty-fourth floor in silence, with palpable disdain for each other in the air. The two exchanged glances as they exited the elevator.

Once inside the safety of the apartment, Ginger ran to the cupboard. "Where is that vodka?" She stepped out of her heels and dropped her clothing piece by piece, leaving them on the floor wherever they landed.

She sighed, finally ripping off her bra letting her puppies breathe. *Alone. Yet I don't really feel alone. Is it because I'm truly in love? I've never felt like this before.*

She put on a bathrobe and walked out to the balcony, enjoying the view while she sipped her second vodka and listened to the original Blue Eyes, Frank Sinatra; his voice was empowering. Ginger swayed and sang along to "That's Life": *And I know one thing / each time I find myself flat on my face, / I pick myself up and get back in the race! / That's life*—The phone rang, pulling her back into the present.

"Hello?" She was careful after her debacle with Howard.

"Is Grant available?" a female voice squawked through the phone.

"No, he's not home at the moment. Can I take a message?"

"You must be the flavor of the month. What's your name again?"

"May I ask who's calling?"

"The mother of his children."

"Hello, Margo. My name is Ginger."

"How perfect."

"He's in Dallas right now on business. Are Lyla and Jason okay?"

"Oh, sweetheart," Margo replied thickly, "if there *was* an emergency, I wouldn't be calling Grant for help."

"Then is there a message you would like to leave?"

"I heard you were only going to be there temporarily. Sort of the way he is with his eye candy."

"Margo, obviously you don't know me and—"

"*Know* you? No, I don't. But I *know* your type. Probably taller than the average woman, pretty, dark hair, possibly a model? Not that far off, am I?"

"Why are we having this conversation, Margo?"

"I just don't want any tramps around my children."

Ginger didn't respond for fear of her voice cracking. She was blistering mad but didn't want her voice to come off sounding fragile.

"And just for the record, he's not finished fucking me, honey. He never will be. Every time he sees our children—*our* babies—we always take a time out for each other, even since the divorce."

"Thanks for the info, Margo. I'll let him know you called."

"Don't bother. I'm sure he'll call me during his layover in Chicago. Which bedroom is yours? Oh, wait." She coarsely laughed. "You sleep in *my* old bedroom, don't you? Well, sweet dreams, Jennifer."

Click.

"Jennifer?! Oh fuck you, Mrs. Ex-Robinson!" Ginger yelled into the disconnected phone. She realized she'd be dealing with Margo for a long time to come, and so she made another drink.

Chapter 32

Ginger sipped her double vodka with three olives and celery—a saladtini—and enjoyed the city's lightshow that Grant shared just last night.

No, no, no! She tried to shrug off that feeling she had that Grant was just like Steve, always fucking around and only out for himself.

She finally broke through the negative thoughts and was certain that Grant wasn't doing anything that Margo claimed. *He doesn't even have a layover in Chicago! That bitch should focus on being a mother and not an ex-wife.* The sirens of a fire truck and an ambulance wailed in the distance, and the flashing lights and activity briefly soothed her thoughts.

Ginger walked back inside the kitchen, aimlessly meandering between the living room and bedroom. An hour or so went by before the phone rang.

Slightly frigid from the last time she answered, she cleared her throat in anticipation. "Hello?"

"Hey, Gin."

"Oh, Grant!" she said with a sigh of relief.

"Babe, you okay?"

"I'm much better now hearing your voice." There was background commotion on the other line. "Are you at a party?"

"Nope, just in my room at the Mansion. The clamor you hear in the background is compliments of Steve and Sarah. Long story."

Ginger said nothing, trying not to visualize Sarah in bed with her boyfriend—what a mess. She tried desperately to push away the thought of Grant fucking Sarah the last time he was in Dallas.

"Grant, let me say hi to my girlfriend. I miss her so much," Sarah squealed in the background.

"Hang on, babe. Sarah wants to talk to you." Then he whispered, "Sorry."

"Gin! When are you coming back to Dallas? I can't wait to hear about New York!"

"Missing you too, Sarah. Life is—"

Then Steve's voice popped in. "Hey, babe. How are you? Grant told us the city is treating you well."

"I'm perfectly happy here, Steve. Thanks for asking."

"Whatever you need, just let me know."

"I'll do that. May I talk to Grant, please?"

Steve paused. "Sure, sure."

Click.

Steve hung up and turned to Grant. "Sorry, roomie. She had to go. Sounded like she had a date or someone to get ready for. That one's always been saucy, you know what I mean? But never mind—let's go have fun!"

Grant suddenly felt extremely uneasy about the whole situation.

Ginger's heart was racing. *What the hell? I know Steve's MO. My ass!*

She chugged the bottle of vodka like water. Her hands shook while she dialed up the Mansion.

"Thank you for calling the Mansion. This is Cassie speaking. How may I assist you?"

"Grant Robinson's room, please."

"One second, please. Which room did you want? There are two registered under his name."

Ginger slammed the phone down, screaming, "Which room?" She took another swig of the vodka bottle and wished that she was already completely drunk.

Grant grabbed the phone and started dialing Ginger back until Steve snatched it and threw it aside.

"Asshole!" Grant said.

"Roomie, you're not fucking her, right?"

Grant's face turned red and he didn't reply.

"We need to get this party started. Right, Sarah?"

Sarah looked Grant over. "Nice room, baby. Can't wait to feel that soft bed. Just the two of us."

Again, Grant didn't respond, but he relented and decided to get the night started so it could be over already. The three descended to the lobby and headed to the Mansion Bar. Grant made sure he walked far enough away from Sarah so she couldn't touch him.

Bobby was at the bar again that night. "Welcome back, Mr. Robinson and friends. I have the perfect table right over here."

Steve called out to Bobby, "Three double shots of Macallan, eighteen. And a dirty martini for Sarah."

They slammed them back, and Steve ordered another round, making it obvious to Grant that his mission was to get Sarah drunk quickly.

"So, Grant," Sarah slurred, "is Ginger staying with her parents? I haven't been able to get a hold of her—well, besides tonight, of course."

Grant tried to be cavalier with his response. "Her belongings haven't gotten there yet."

"That . . . wasn't the question. Where's she staying?"

Both she and Steve stared at Grant, waiting for the answer.

Grant knew that Steve was fucking with him. He already knew that Ginger was staying with him. *So why the game?* "Come on, roomie. You're not hiding her from us, are you? After all, she belongs to all of us."

"She's staying at my place until she gets around to moving to the Carlyle. We decided she should wait for her stuff to arrive before she moves."

Steve guffawed. "Another round, Bobby!" Then he said to Grant, "Nice of you to be so hospitable to a girl who grew up in the city and has family just around the corner." He winked.

Sarah wasn't thrilled with the conversation and its focus on Ginger. "Excuse me, gentlemen. I need to use the restroom." She felt unwanted in the worst possible way.

Bobby delivered another round while Sarah was still

in the ladies' room. Steve reached into his pocket and pulled out a small vile. He poured a fine powder into Sarah's martini, stirring it while eyeing Grant.

"Relax, it'll just put her out. She's probably doing a couple lines in the bathroom. Like I told you earlier, she's sleeping in your room one way or another. I don't care whether you fuck her or not. Understand?"

He felt uneasy about Steve drugging Sarah and stared Steve down.

"I handed you an extra half-million-dollar order today, man. All I want is to fuck the shit out of Veronica without any worry in the world. It's the least you can do for me. And besides, now you don't even have to put up with Sarah's antics."

Grant remained silent, but his stomach flipped.

Chapter 33

Ginger slipped into a summer jasmine–scented bubble bath. She surrounded herself with a few candles, soft music, and another drink. She knew the only thing that would truly relax her would be an orgasm. Fighting the urge for a while, the music and the liquor finally took over, and she gave in.

Ginger began to squeeze her nipples while sliding two fingers inside herself; her thumb played with her clit while conjuring up images of Grant's face between her legs licking her.

She desperately tried to block out the last few hours. But her mind kept wandering too much, and she realized she wasn't going to reach a climax. Frustrated sexually and emotionally, she emptied the tub, wrapped her hair in a towel, and covered herself with a pink plush bathrobe.

Three women fucking with my head in the last three hours. Am I starring in A Christmas Carol?

Around nine thirty, she searched the fridge for a bedtime snack when she heard a knock on the door.

Jesus. Who could this possibly be?

She opened the door and was surprised at who she greeted: an attractive, voluptuous woman.

"Can I help you?" Ginger asked, hoping this woman was at the wrong apartment.

"Oh, hi. Is Grant available?" She eyed Ginger up and down.

"Grant?" Ginger choked out. "Grant is out of town on business. He returns tomorrow."

The woman's aura was sexy yet trashy. The caked-on makeup, the ankle-length pleather trench coat—she resembled a cheap whore. Ginger grasped protectively at the collar of her bathrobe, trying to keep control. "I'm sorry, who did you say you were?"

"Abigail. Grant and I were supposed to go over some ideas for furniture for his apartment."

Ginger ignored the bottle of tequila in Abigail's hand and lack of paperwork. "Is there a pamphlet or catalog that you would like to leave for him?"

"No. We were just getting started on ideas. I thought we would—"

"Did he hire you to redecorate the apartment?"

Abigail retorted, "Oh, no, no. I'm the property manager. Grant and I go way back, even when Margo was around."

Those last few words cut like a knife. Ginger counted to ten mentally before responding. "So you live in the building?"

"No. I was working late. Grant never minds late company. He likes having a real woman around, not just one of those fake models he's always surrounded by. He's beyond bored with them."

"I will certainly tell him you came by, Abigail."

"Oh, my friends call me Abby," she said. "And what was your name?"

"Ginger," she said flatly. She was already picturing herself in a cab with her suitcases on her way to the Carlyle. She couldn't handle any more of this.

"So nice to meet you, Ginger. And just for management's sake, of course, do you plan on staying for a while or—?"

"I'm leaving soon. Grant's a great friend. He offered his place for me to stay while I wait for my belongings. Hate to cut this short, Abigail, but I have to work early tomorrow. I'll be sure to tell Grant you stopped by."

"Thanks. Again, so nice to meet you."

Ginger nodded. "Good night."

Ginger fell back against the door after closing it and slid down to the fetal position. Her heart broke into pieces. *I know the past is the past, but why, Grant? Why do I feel like just another one of your toys?*

The tears streamed down her cheeks. *Why did I let him into my heart?*

She started packing her stuff feverishly, letting the tears flow. Knowing if she didn't move immediately into the Carlyle, Grant could weaken her resolve with just his voice or blue eyes.

Chapter 34

Grant's worst nightmare was unfolding in front of him.

Riding the elevator to the third floor, Sarah grabbed his crotch. "I need a good fucking like last time. And I want you in my ass this time. Come on, baby."

"Ginger," he started to say.

"*Ginger?* What's wrong with me? Why can't it be *me*? I always say yes. I do whatever they want me to do. Yet everyone wants Ginger. Fuck all of you!"

He could tell whatever drug Steve put in her drink was working. He felt horrible for her.

She stumbled into the room and dropped her dress to

the floor. "Don't you want to fuck me, baby? I want to *feel* it tonight. I want it to *hurt.*"

With the way she was weaving and bobbing, Grant was certain she would topple over into a piece of furniture. *Goddamnit. I don't wanna call the front desk with that type of an emergency!*

He led her to the bed while she begged him for his body; she deeply needed to be desired.

I knew I should have cancelled this fucking trip and stayed home with Ginger. What the fuck am I doing here?

Sarah passed out within seconds of him placing her on the bed. Stepping back and looking at her, he felt a mixture of shame and anger—and pity.

He covered her naked body. He considered calling Ginger and telling her about what a messed up night it was. Looking at the clock, he instead poured himself a vodka.

I love you, Ginger. I should have stayed with you and none of this would have happened! He slammed back his drink and listened to Sarah snore. He couldn't shake the feeling that he was betraying Ginger.

Fuck you, Steve Williams. This will never happen again, regardless of the consequences!

He walked into the living room area and climbed onto the couch. He covered himself with an extra blanket and finally fell asleep.

Tommy held Rachel in his arms, the two of them sitting on a blanket in a park. He ran his fingers through Rachel's thick, chestnut hair, but his eyes were distant and his mind elsewhere.

"Where are you?" she gently questioned him. Rachel crawled on her hands and knees to be in front of him. She straddled his lap and wrapped her arms around him, finally snapping him out of his trance.

"Where did you go?"

"To a faraway place, a long time ago." He stared at Rachel. "Do you believe in past lives? Sometimes I feel like I have known you since the beginning of time. I have dreams. They're so real, they *must* have happened. And somehow, I *know* it's your eyes I'm always staring into."

"Tommy, my love, you know how I feel about past lives. I knew the first time I saw you we were long-lost lovers." She kissed him. "Our souls recognized what our minds couldn't grasp."

Tommy wrapped his arms around her and pulled her against his body under the warm sun.

"I love that you're my soul mate, Tommy."

Grant's eyes popped open. Yet another dream about Rachel and Tommy. He felt so close to those two, as if he knew them. He finally concluded that the dreams were some kind of message: *Ginger is my soul mate.* Rubbing the sleep out of his eyes, he wanted to call her.

It was after six a.m. He decided to shower and pack up—get the hell out of there before poor Sarah woke. All he wanted to do was be with Ginger.

He left a note: *Sarah, you fell asleep as soon as we got back to the hotel room. Nothing happened between us or ever will. Best wishes, Grant.*

Chapter 35

Ginger tossed and turned in bed for hours after Abigail left. She couldn't erase the feeling that she was being used. It had been a mistake to trust Grant. She sobbed, realizing her dreams were slipping away.

It was 6:21 a.m. when the phone rang.

"Hello?"

"Hey, babe. I wanted to catch you before you went to work."

The sound of his voice softened her just a bit. The adrenaline pumped through her body and made her shake.

"Gin, you okay?"

"Oh, I'm fine. Just didn't sleep well. A lot on my mind."

"I didn't get any sleep either! I can't wait to tell you about it. What a crazy night!"

Ginger pictured Sarah in the hotel bed with Grant, screwing him for hours.

"Gin?" Grant said, feeling her distance, wondering what had changed since yesterday's kiss at the airport.

Ginger hesitated. "When do you get in?"

"Probably by twelve thirty."

"See you at the office?"

"How about a lunch date?"

"Where?"

"Feel like some sushi, where we had our first dinner date?"

"See you around one then?"

"I can't wait to see you, Gin."

"Okay, see you then." She hung up the phone without saying good-bye.

Grant's chest felt like it had a hole in it when he heard the line go dead. *She didn't even say good-bye or wish me a safe trip. I knew I should have cancelled this fucking trip!*

When he arrived at the airport, he went straight to the Admiral's Club and ordered a double shot of vodka, straight up. "Oh, three olives, please."

"Coming right up. You okay?" the bartender asked while preparing Grant's drink.

"That obvious?"

"A bartender knows."

"Yesterday, I was so thrilled to have that last ticket for the Titanic, and then today, I find out that it's going to hit that iceberg." Grant felt defeated.

"Hey, it may miss the iceberg this time," the bartender said while handing him his drink and bill.

"Here's to hope." Grant finished his drink, tossed a few bills on the bar, and left to board the plane.

And the hits just keep on coming, he thought while Tina held back the curtain to first class.

"Nice to see you again. Traveling alone today?"

"Yes." *I wish I had some of that shit Steve gave Sarah right about now. I'd slam the whole vile back.*

"Good," Tina said. Grant could barely make eye contact with her. He wondered how long a train would take to get back to New York.

Howard, toting two coffee cups, walked into Grant's office and found Ginger on the floor. She was surrounded by pattern paper and swatches and held scissors. She looked up.

"Didn't know what you took in your coffee, so I

thought I'd cover all the bases," Howard said almost sheepishly, looking at the unwelcomed expression on her face. Ginger nodded toward Grant's desk while wielding the scissors like a knife for protection.

"Hey, relax with the scissors," he chuckled. "I brought you a peace offering." He extended his hand out to help her off the floor. "Or maybe you want something else instead after last night?"

"Last night?"

"It was your father's birthday, right?"

"I'm just a bit on edge today. Probably been working too much." She stood up unassisted.

"Maybe just working too much *with Grant*," Howard retorted.

Ginger faked a smile. "I'm happy with the work. I love the lines and patterns and colors and—"

"So no dinner tonight then?"

"Um, no, Howard. I don't think it's a good idea. We need to stay professional. Just like I'm professional with Grant. Working relationship only."

"Of course. I wouldn't want it any other way. It was merely an opportunity to learn more about you. It's not every day that Grant Robinson jumps through fiery hoops for a girl."

Ginger could see right through his façade. "Thank you, but no. I have too much to do before Grant gets back today."

"Okay. You know, you really are a top-notch employee—*my* employee. Remember that." Howard exited and closed the door behind him.

Isn't life in the city just wonderful? She growled and threw the scissors across the room. *I guess I'll be back working the family business soon. Like Grant would keep me around after I break it off with him. Steve and Grant . . . I wish they weren't so similar.*

Tina plopped down in the seat next to Grant after takeoff. "So you're traveling without *her*. Is that over?"

"Probably," Grant said, looking out the window into the blue, morning sky.

"Then I think you should follow me. Maybe you need to rest your head on a real pillow for a few minutes." She unbuttoned the top of her blouse and pulled out of her pocket a gift for him: her panties. "Maybe you'd like to help me put these back on?" She crossed her legs and revealed the top of her laced thigh highs. "No strings, Grant, only wings."

Grant didn't respond.

"Seems like you're deciding on the menu. I'll be back to check on you." She leaned over him as she stood up to leave, pressing her cleavage together with her upper arms. Grant turned his face toward the window again, looking out at the clouds below. *Ginger sounded so distant and uncaring. I guess it doesn't matter if I fuck Tina, does it?*

Tina returned to get Grant's order. He noticed her scarf was removed. "I'd like to order the stringless wings, please."

"My pleasure, sir." Tina fluttered her hazel eyes at him and winked at her coworker for coverage.

Stepping off the elevator, he slipped off his jacket, and she dropped her blouse around her elbows, revealing her overly proportioned perfect twins. Grant loosened his tie and heard the zip of her skirt zipper. She stood completely naked in front of him.

He took a step toward Tina but suddenly pulled back. "I'm so sorry, Tina. I just can't."

Chapter 36

Ginger looked in the mirror, assessing her puffy eyes. *Guess I can say I had an allergy attack.*

She returned to a ringing phone in the office. "Mr. Robinson's office," Ginger said without emotion.

"Hey, babe. You want Evan and me to swing by and grab you?"

"No, I'm fine walking. I need the fresh air."

"Oh, okay. Blue Moon Sushi is still okay, right?"

"Yes."

"All right. Enjoy the air. See you soon."

Ginger was certain that Grant was deceiving her just like Steve had. She held her head high during her walk to meet Grant. *When I tell him I'm moving out, he's going to fire me. And the worst part about the whole mess is that I'd rather be with him than working for him—in spite of what I just went through with all these women.*

Ginger arrived at the Blue Moon first and ordered a hot sake.

"You okay, Mr. Grant?" Evan asked as he drove to the restaurant. Grant looked distant and unhappy.

"My head is all over the place."

"We all have those days. You gonna be okay?"

"I hope so."

Grant walked into Blue Moon, and spotted Ginger at a table. He leaned over to give her a kiss but landed on her cheek when she turned her head.

"Hi. I didn't know what I should order, so I didn't. Sake?"

"Whatever you want, Ginger. How about the seaweed salad you enjoyed last week?" He tried to make eye contact with her.

"That's fine."

"So can we continue with how we left things at the

airport yesterday?"

"I . . . I'm not sure where I stand. Things have gotten blurry since then."

Grant waited for her to continue.

"I've gone through so much lately. Grant, you're an exceptional man, and you will make a lucky lady happy. I wish it was me, but it's probably not. Yet I love working with you." She wiped away her tears.

"If we can't be intimate, then I suppose we won't be able to work together. I think it's best if I move into the—"

"Wait, we won't be able *work* together? Because we're not having sex?" Grant finally responded. "Since when did you think your job was based on being intimate with me?"

"I didn't mean to offend you, but I just assumed—"

"Assumed what? And by the way, I didn't act on Tina's or Sarah's advances because I'm in love with you. And *I* shouldn't be offended?" Grant tried to control his emotions while his heart beat heavily against his chest. The thought of losing Ginger, on any level, was unbearable.

"Grant, I'm sorry, I just—"

"Just what? You think I'm just like Steve fucking Williams, don't you?" Grant tossed money on the table and stood. "Hope I'll see you back at my office when your lunch break is over, *Ms. Madison.*"

Ginger couldn't breathe, let alone respond.

Grant somehow was able to calmly walk out of the restaurant, wondering what would happen next. In desperation, he began to count how many days he had left before heading to Paris—now without Ginger.

He arrived at the office at the same time as Howard was returning from his lunch break.

"Grant, how's my protégé doing?"

"Great," Grant responded. "Picked up an extra order from Neiman Marcus, making my overnight worthwhile."

"Fantastic," Howard replied as Grant held the massive glass door open to the building. They walked across the lobby to the elevators.

"Hey, I thought you were having lunch with your assistant."

"She had to run some errands."

"I tried to invite her out for lunch yesterday, but she had to meet her mom. She's a little jumpy about her personal space. You sure she can work with clients?"

Noticing one of the seamstresses standing at the back of the elevator, Grant felt he had to protect Ginger, regardless of whether she was coming back to work with him or not. He quickly changed the subject.

"Howard, has Gabriel Portier from Le Printemps talked to you this week? I called him on Monday and told him I would be back in the afternoon today."

"No. I'm going to let you deal with him. In fact, I will

be out of town starting Friday. I'm heading up to Maine for two weeks. Come up to the office later. I'm going to need you to run the show." The elevator stopped on Grant's floor, and he stepped out. "How about four? We can go for a drink. Bring your assistant."

Grant nodded his head while the elevator doors closed.

Walking toward his office, he stopped at the reception area. "Hi, Sue. Any messages?"

"Welcome back, sir. Mr. Gabriel Portier from Le Printemps just called. Here's the number for you to reach him."

"Thank you, Sue."

"Excuse me, Mr. Robinson? Is Ginger coming back today?"

"After she finishes with her errands, I hope she'll be back. I've been running her ragged, so I pray she doesn't quit on me."

"Are *you* okay?" Sue asked with true sincerity.

"Yeah, I'm fine. Just tired from my trip. Didn't sleep well last night." He held up the message. "This was weighing heavy on me also. Thanks, Sue. How are you doing?"

"There's my favorite Robinson smile! I'm great. Any plans for Labor Day?"

"Tentative plans so far." He wondered if he'd ever

meet Aunt Sadie.

"Well, if your plans fall through, let me know. We're having a barbecue with my husband's family."

"Thanks for the invite. I'll let you know either way."

Grant was always happy to speak with Sue. She knew how to gauge his moods and lift his spirits when necessary.

"Sounds great, Mr. Robinson."

"How many times have I told you to call me Grant?"

"Well, maybe if you come to the Labor Day gathering, I won't call you Mr. Robinson in front of my kids."

"Deal. But if I don't show, you can still call me Grant."

"Yes, sir, Mr. Robinson." She laughed.

He wished he could be at both parties at once—with Ginger. "By the way, I'll need the country code for France."

"Yes, sir. Coming right up."

Shit, Ginger thought as she watched Grant walk out of the restaurant. *What was I thinking? Did I misjudge him? I'm so fucking confused. Mom!*

She grabbed the payphone in the women's restroom. "Mom? I think I just did something really stupid."

Less than twenty minutes later, her mom entered the

restaurant. Ginger started crying the second she saw her.

"Come here, baby girl." She hugged her. "Did he fire you?"

"No, Mom. But how did you know it was about Grant?"

"Call it mother's intuition."

"We haven't been intimate, other than a fantastic kiss yesterday. But then I got hit with so many red flags, I don't know who I'm really dealing with. Why do I feel so . . . so—I don't even know what."

"Oh, honey."

"I'm afraid, Mom. He's so sweet, so upfront. But his past is driving me crazy! So I'm not sure if I should stay. What do I do? How did you know with Daddy?"

"What does your heart tell you to do *right now*?"

"To continue working with him and see what happens in the future—even if we're never anything more than friends. I need him in my life. It's like I've always known him, Mom. Since the beginning of time."

"I knew the first moment I saw Daddy. But I waited. And then when we shared our first kiss, I was all his, and we—"

"You can stop there, Mom. No details, please," she said through her tears. She managed a laugh, and it tempered her sorrow some.

"Love never comes without risk. It's up to you

whether or not you want to take that risk. He left the door open for you. Don't be faint of heart now, my love bug."

Chapter 37

Grant looked around his office. He saw the mess of work on the floor Ginger left behind. The scissors were stuck in the corkboard on the back of his desk. His office looked like a debris field after a tornado. He didn't mind the mess; what bothered him is that the mess lacked Ginger sitting amidst it.

Maybe I was too harsh on her. But I thought I made it clear enough that she didn't have to be my lover to work with me.

Sue chimed in over the intercom. "Excuse me, Mr. Robinson? The country code for France is thirty-three."

"Thanks, Sue."

He called Gabriel Portier. Portier wanted to know how soon Grant could be in Paris to personally review his line.

The door swung open.

"Monsieur Portier," Grant said, looking at Ginger, "my assistant is on her lunch break. Would it be okay if I called you back with an update of when a trip can be scheduled?"

Ginger held up a finger, asking him to wait.

"However, if you wouldn't mind holding for a moment, she just walked in."

He pushed the mute button, and Ginger spoke before he could say a word.

"I need about five days to finish the line."

"Can we be on the plane Wednesday evening, the fifth of September, and hold a Thursday presentation? Or am I pushing you too hard?"

"Whatever it takes, boss." She finally smiled.

"Even if we're late for your family picnic?" he teased her.

"Stop being a shit and tell him when we'll be there. That phone call isn't cheap." She winked.

Grant put the call on speaker and filled Portier in on the time frame. Near the end of the conversation, Portier said, "And how long should I expect your stay, Monsieur

Grant?"

"We'll be leaving your beautiful country by Friday night, Monsieur."

"No, no, no. My business is not just about myself but my family and their future. If you would be so kind to accept, it would please me if you and your assistant joined us at our country home outside of Paris until Sunday. Monday morning, we will discuss the line. I feel that we need to step back from our work so the passion of the moment doesn't cloud our thinking. It will also allow you to see and absorb the country and the flavor of the many people who live here. Do you accept, Monsieur Grant?"

Both Grant and Ginger looked surprised. She mouthed an emphatic yes.

"It would be an honor to spend time with you and your family. We appreciate your desire to get to know us better."

"Merci. My relationship with a vendor is like a marriage—that is, each of us desires to be fulfilled. It, however, requires us to spend time together to accomplish that goal. And what is your assistant's name?"

"Ginger Madison," Grant replied.

"Tell me a little about her. How do you know about her and her work?"

"I've had the pleasure of knowing her for more than a decade. She was previously a fit model and has transitioned into fashion design. She's detailed and creative. We work very well together. Sometimes it feels like I've known her all my life."

"Ah, you sound like me, a romantic. We are the best designers, I think. I look forward to meeting you both. Please fax my secretary your itinerary and my driver will be there at every stop."

"Merci, Monsieur Portier. We also look forward to meeting you."

Grant ended the phone call and noticed how swollen Ginger's eyes were. He decided not to mention it.

"We won't have a problem with being ready for Paris, will we?"

"No, boss. I can have us prepped to leave by Wednesday."

"Great," he said. "You had me worried for a moment." Grant picked up the phone and called Sue. "Sue, please make travel arrangements for Ginger and myself for Paris. The latest flight on Tuesday, the fourth of September, returning the following Wednesday, the twelfth."

"Yes, Mr. Robinson. Where would you like to stay?"

"At the Paris Hilton. We'll need a large suite so we can display the line easily. Thank you, Sue."

"You're welcome, Mr. Robinson."

"Voilà!" Grant clapped his hands together.

"Wait, that means we need to be ready by Tuesday

morning!"

"That's right. Are you up to it?"

Ginger looked deep into his eyes. "Not a problem, blue eyes—I mean, boss man."

"Grant will do . . . babe."

"Okay, then, blue eyes, or maybe Prince Charming. Let's get to work."

They spent the rest of the afternoon and into the late evening working side by side, without a word spoken regarding the catastrophe at lunch.

Chapter 38

Grabbing a cab, Grant and Ginger discussed what they should order for dinner.

"How about a pizza with eggplant and a beer?"

"No, pepperoni, blue eyes."

"Half and half, then, babe?"

The comfort level had returned between Grant and Ginger—they both felt it.

"Yes, half and half, boss."

"Boss? Just for that, you can treat *the boss* to dinner tonight."

They laughed as they exited the cab.

Halfway through the lobby, Deerpak, the doorman, called out, "Oh, Ms. Madison? There was a large delivery of boxes for you today. Would you like me to bring them upstairs for you?"

Ginger looked at Grant, not knowing what to say. Grant responded for her. "How about in the morning when we're fresh, Deerpak? We've had a long day."

"Sure, Mr. Robinson."

Rounding the corner and heading toward the elevators, Grant and Ginger nearly smacked right into Abigail, but all three halted just in time. The mood quickly changed from cheerful to ebullient.

Abigail said, "Hi, Grant. I stopped by last night to go over the furniture ideas." She ignored Ginger completely.

"Thanks, Abigail. I appreciate you following up, but I think I can handle it now. Please, if you would, just put anything in my mailbox." He instinctively put his arm around Ginger.

"Will do, Grant. Have a good night. And what was your name again?"

"Jennifer," she responded over her shoulder. "Good night, Abigail."

The elevator doors closed. "So, *Jennifer*, I see you've met Abigail. What was that about?"

"Yeah. I was a little shocked by the late-night intruder wearing a trench coat and toting a bottle of tequila," Ginger responded. She avoided eye contact.

"I apologize for not telling you sooner, but I'm sure you understand that my head has been elsewhere for the last couple of weeks."

Ginger still hadn't looked at him, and her smile had slipped from her face.

"Gin, remember how we said the past is the past? But I should have warned you of the land mines. Do you need any clarification about Abigail?"

"I'm not sure if I want any details, but just answer a question if you will. When was the last time you two had sex?"

"It was only once. Four or five days before we met in Dallas." Grant gently turned her head and looked into her eyes. "It wasn't romantic. It was just sex. I had no one at the time. But that's changed."

Ginger held his gaze. "Thank you for your honesty, Grant. And you're right, the past is the past. It just keeps popping up."

"I know."

Grant held her hand as they exited the elevator and walked into the apartment. Ginger was relieved that 34Bitch didn't make an appearance; Abigail was enough for one night.

While looking into the fridge, Grant said, "What beer should I order? Any favorites?"

Ginger had already shuffled down the hallway to unpack her suitcases. "Whatever you want. I'm not that picky."

"Yeah you are." He walked to her bedroom and stopped dead when he saw her suitcases on the bed.

"Are you packing or unpacking?"

"*Unpacking*. Like I said, it was a rough night."

"I guess we both had shitty nights. So Coors sound good?"

"Perfect. Order more than two, willya?"

"I think we'd need a case after the last twenty-four hours."

Grant knew she hadn't told him everything yet. *And now I have to add Sarah and Steve's antics to whatever she left out. Great. Just fucking great.*

"I've never seen the cancan girls in Paris. It's like coming here and not seeing the Rockettes." He took another bite of pizza.

"The Rockettes are amazing," Ginger said. "I still regret not pursuing my dream to be a Rockette back in my dancing days."

"Are you sorry that you didn't pursue that?"

"I don't know, sometimes. It didn't help that no one believed in me . . . *including* me. I know I could have done it. But everyone told me it was just a silly dream. So I let it go." Her voice was shaky.

"You should never let go of your dreams."

"I'm learning that."

"Look . . . I've learned in life that to know up, you must know down; to know happy, you must know sad." He leaned over and wiped away a single tear as it streamed down her face. "I know we have both known 'down and sad' all too well. How about we aim for 'up and happy' now?"

Ginger looked tired. "Agreed. But for now, I think I need to feel down in the pink room," she said and followed it with a yawn.

"You go. I'll clean up."

Chapter 39

Tommy slid away from her soft skin, trying not to wake her. "Damn it," he whispered when the bed squeaked and the wooden floor creaked under his weight—the sounds were augmented by the dead silence. He looked back at Rachel to make sure it hadn't disturbed her.

Hours had passed since they made love. The sex was so intense, his legs were still trembling.

Tommy's mind drifted to earlier in the evening. They had retired to her bedroom and were kissing. Rachel stepped back as she seductively untied her bathrobe, letting it pool around her ankles.

"Look at me, my sweet Tommy," she said, "Look into my eyes and hold onto what you see until you come home to me. I am yours until the end of time, my darling."

His eyes locked onto her gaze; her greenish-blue eyes were vibrant with love, almost like he could see the glow of her soul. Her body and the scent of her hair and skin were intoxicating.

"I missed you so much," he whispered. She closed the space between them and kissed him; their tongues danced and the taste of her mouth filled his.

"You're so beautiful, Rachel. Every time I see you, I fall even more in love with you."

"I missed you too, my love. Now that you're here, I need you inside of me. Let's not make love now. We have time for that later."

She dropped to her knees, unzipped his pants, and pulled out his hard cock. She swallowed his size as far as she could. He fell back against the wall, surrendering to her tantalizing tongue and lips.

Watching her mouth devour him for nearly four or five minutes was all he could take before he exploded into her, letting out a guttural cry of overwhelming satisfaction.

He pulled her up to his face. She still had some of his semen dripping from her mouth, and he licked her lips to taste himself. He shed his remaining clothes, not sure who tore off what, and climbed onto the bed.

Rachel lay back on the bed with her legs spread. She was so aroused that even her inner thighs were wet. Tommy crawled between her legs and began devouring her sweetness, causing her to explode into his mouth almost instantly.

His cock was once again fully erect, and he drove it deeply into her. "Rachel, I love you," he breathed. He focused on her eyes, peering deeper into her soul, he felt every bit of their physical ecstasy. He could feel the heat of his semen bursting deeply into her body.

He then buried his face in her pussy to taste their combined orgasms. Rachel took her turn licking the excess from his lips and nose. They continued kissing until they fell asleep in each other's arms.

A short time later, Tommy was awoken by a kiss on the back of his neck and slowly rolled over. Rachel climbed on top of him and bit his left nipple, not releasing for what seemed like forever.

"Baby! What's that for? Was I a bad boy or something?" Tommy rubbed his chest, smiling while looking at a teeth-shaped indentation on his skin.

"Just wanted to brand you. Anyone who sees your bare chest will know you belong to me."

"Will you marry me, Rachel?" Tommy asked.

"Oh, my sweet Tommy."

"Do you love me?" Tommy asked.

"Yes and yes! You already own my heart." She gently sobbed.

"I'm so in love with you, my sassy Brit." He softly caressed her face with his fingertips.

"Tommy, make love to me, please."

Still wet, he easily buried his cock deeply inside her. Feeling her beginning to quiver and knowing her body as they moved in perfect sensual rhythm, he couldn't hold back any longer. Tommy exploded into Rachel. She gave into the sensations that only he could create on so many levels, emotionally and physically.

Their eyes locked, knowing they were one, for no two souls could possibly be more intertwined and twisted in time. They shared the truest eternal love.

Thoroughly drenched in sweat, he rolled onto his back, and Rachel curled up into his arms.

"Tommy, there's something we need to talk about."

"What is it, baby?"

"You know how people can sometimes see things before they happen?"

"Yes?" he pensively replied, knowing where this conversation was heading.

"Then please don't fly tomorrow. I have a bad feeling about it."

He tried to reassure her that he would be just fine. After all, he had completed twenty missions and had only five left. She was not convinced.

Reliving almost every detail of their night, Tommy stood in the kitchen, drinking a glass of tap water. He looked out the window at some flowers he helped her plant. She had laughed at him covered in mud, calling him a farm boy.

Suddenly, Rachel's arms slip around him from behind, pulling herself tightly against him. "Come lie with me until you leave."

She took his hand and led him back to the bedroom.

Grant woke from his slumber. This dream was so vivid that he half expected Rachel to be lying next to him. *What an imagination. Ginger leaving me must have caused this one. But why is it always the same two people? And strangest of all, they always appear when I need them most . . .*

Ginger awoke completely refreshed but slightly disappointed that she didn't make it to the gym. That would be two days in a row before their Paris trip. *And I'm supposed to be the fit model? Grrr.*

She decided to do some yoga stretches, and as she did a one-legged pose, she mulled over the vivid dream she had last night.

Alex, Isabella, Tommy, and Rachel enjoyed a few drinks together at the pub.

"We're almost done, Izzy," Alex said. "We only have five more missions after tomorrow. Will you wait for me?"

"Of course I will. What kind of question is that, Alex?"

"Well, you know, if we got shot down and ended up as prisoners of war or hiding in France, or something . . ."

Izzy's face turned white.

"I didn't mean to worry you, Iz. Cap can get us home safely. He's one with our girl, *Fifi.*"

"And who the hell is *Fifi*?"

Rachel responded, "*Fifinella.* That's the name of their plane. Bless *Fifi*, don't curse her!"

Alex pulled Isabella into his arms and spun her in a circle. He called out her name to the whole pub, announcing his love for her.

Isabella giggled.

"It's her fifty-fourth mission. *Fifi* is a good girl to us." He kissed her.

"Get a bloody room, you two," Rachel squawked. Tommy pinched Rachel's ass.

Who the hell are these people? Ginger thought as she finished her stretches.

Ginger had a new pep in her step that morning—completely different from the morning before. She poured herself a cup of coffee and joined Grant out on the balcony.

"Good morning. Sleep well?"

"Yeah. But I had a crazy dream," she admitted.

"Must have been the pizza, because I had a dream that was over the edge."

"Really? What about?"

"It's a recurring, almost continuous dream. Probably nothing that I could ever figure out."

"Sounds mysterious. Have you ever written any of them down?"

Grant wondered if he should tell her about it. "No, I haven't, actually. Dreams are just your mind escaping reality. Like when you visit the zoo as a kid and then have a nightmare about the lions. Sometimes I think dreams could be us reliving actual events or experiences from the past or the future. Maybe even from somebody else's life. Does that sound crazy?"

They looked at each other tenderly, arms touching like the night they went to theater. Grant contemplated kissing her again—he longed to—but then the doorbell rang.

He rolled his eyes, set down his coffee on the kitchen counter, and walked over to the door. Grant looked through the peephole and then instantly pulled the door open.

"Good morning, Mr. Robinson," Andreas said. "Where should I place the boxes for Ms. Madison?"

"Ginger," he called out. "Andreas is here with your boxes. He would like to know where you want them."

Grant held the door open while Andreas started bringing in his delivery cart. Grant helped and noticed 34Bitch was eyeing him. *Perfect*, he thought. *I wouldn't be surprised if 34Bitch calls Margo immediately . . . this is juicy gossip for her.*

After getting her boxes neatly placed in the extra bedroom, they realized the time. Both Ginger and Grant ran around like lunatics getting ready.

Making it to the office by nine thirty a.m., Sue smiled as they exited the elevator together. "Good morning, Mr. Robinson, Ms. Madison," she said enthusiastically.

"Good morning, Sue." Ginger stopped to see if there were any messages for Grant while he continued to his office.

As he entered the office, his phone rang. "Good morning. This is Grant."

"A *good* morning would have been two hours ago," Howard growled.

"What's up, Howard?"

"You never made it up here yesterday. I'm going on vacation tomorrow and we need to go over everything, including your Paris trip."

"Sorry, I got tied up yesterday. I can come up now," Grant replied.

"Now," Howard said and hung up.

Ginger walked into his office and saw Grant shaking his head.

"Going up to Howard's office, babe." Grant winked. "This won't take long. All he cares about is how much of an order we can secure."

"Okay, babe. I'll be working. If I'm not here, you can find me with the seamstresses."

The day flew by while they worked on all the line specs. Around seven p.m., Grant said to Ginger, "I'm going to call the kids. It's six o'clock their time, and if I wait much longer, they'll be in bed."

"Do you want me to leave so you can have some privacy?"

"Please stay."

"Okay. I was just working with this pattern for the Lycra miniskirt."

She busied herself and wondered how Grant interacted with Margo.

Grant dialed.

"Hey, Margo. Are the kids available? I'm leaving for Paris on business and I'd like to talk to them before I go."

"Paris? Are you bringing your latest conquest with you?" she replied.

He pushed the speakerphone button, placing a finger on his lips.

"Conquest? And who might that be?"

"Don't play stupid with me."

"Doesn't matter. I'm meeting a new account."

Ginger attempted to leave.

"Please hold, Margo." He pushed the mute button. "Ginger, don't leave. I have nothing to hide from you." Ginger stayed but felt uncomfortable.

"Margo?"

"Good for you, Grant, but you don't need to be coy with me. I know she's living in our apartment. You never took *me* to Paris."

Margo's disgust and jealousy filled the air. Ginger cringed.

"It's *my* apartment, Margo, and that's none of your business. Those papers we signed last week confirm that. Let's not make this ugly, please. Let me talk to the kids."

"I spoke with her a few nights ago, you know. She's just another flavor of the month for you."

"Let's be adults here. Can I talk to the kids now?"

Ginger stood and wrapped an arm around his waist for

comfort. She knew this was difficult for Grant.

"Here they are, *Super Dad*," she sneered.

Just hearing their voices lightened his mood. Ginger enjoyed watching him as he listened to every little detail of whatever they had to share with him. It reminded her of the one man that she always trusted: her father.

Grant hung up the phone and turned to see Ginger admiring him through puppy eyes and a broad smile. He knew there was more to Tuesday night.

"Ginger, what else happened Tuesday night? You spoke to my ex-wife. What did she say?"

Ginger avoided his eyes, and Grant sat on the floor in front of her and took her hands in his.

"Please look at me, Gin. What happened?"

"Honestly, so many things bothered me about that night. What hit me the hardest was when I asked Steve to give you the phone and I was hung up on. And you never called back. I didn't get to say good-night after our first kiss." She wiped tears from her face. "Then I called the hotel to try to get a hold of you and found out that you had reserved two rooms. So which one was yours? Which one did Sarah sleep in?"

"Mine," he said flatly, not letting go of her hands.

Grant gave her the details about Tuesday night, including the fact that Steve drugged Sarah and that the other room was for Steve, per his request, so he could fuck

Veronica, his latest conquest.

"I just can't go through another relationship being lied to, Grant." She reached her arms around his neck. "If you need more time, I understand. Just don't play with my heart. Please."

"I would never play with your heart."

The rest of the evening was spent putting together the Paris portfolio.

When Grant left to use the bathroom, she called her mom. "Mom, thank you for yesterday. You've always been there to hold me steady. I love you."

"Oh, honey. Moms are supposed to be there when we're needed. So, did you patch things up with Grant?"

Ginger blushed. "Well . . ."

By ten p.m., they had worked so long, their vision was blurred and their muscles ached. They rode back to the apartment in a comfortable silence. It had been an enlightening day, and they once again enjoyed the palpable attraction they had for each other.

Grant crashed into bed without showering. He thought about all the World War II stories his father talked about as he fell asleep.

Chuck, Grant's father, looked distant.

"Where are we, Dad?" Grant asked. Somehow, he knew he was dreaming. They rode in his father's old Ford pickup down an unfamiliar dirt road on some farmland in Wisconsin.

Finally, his dad pulled the truck over and turned off the motor. "Let's watch the sunrise, Tommy."

"Dad, my name is Grant. You know that!"

His father looked at him with an odd expression. "Does it really matter, son? Let's look at the beautiful sky. You hear the birds?"

Chuck lifted his arms up as if to embrace the blue early morning. "Son, they told me I wasn't the best guide for you in life. After your mom died, I was filled with such anger. I'm so sorry."

"*They*?" Grant inquired.

Chuck turned to his son. "The Master Spirits allowed me to come back to guide you. You are much more than you think. When you're ready, you'll know what I mean. I love you, Tommy."

His father slowly faded, his arms still stretched toward the sky. Grant called out in his dream, "Dad, come back! I don't understand!" he yelled as everything turned black.

Chapter 40

Ginger banged on Grant's bedroom door. "Grant, are you okay?" She could hear him saying something, but it was muffled through the door. She opened it and found him in bed, still asleep, suffering through some nightmare. He kept repeating, "Dad, I don't understand." She draped her body on top of him like a blanket, trying to comfort him.

Hours later, Ginger woke. Grant slept calmly; clearly his nightmare had passed. The scent of his body permeated all her senses. Reliving the sensual kiss they shared at the airport just a few days prior, she felt her body tremble with a longing for him.

Ginger's mouth watered as she felt his smooth skin. She caressed his back and moved her hips against his body. She envisioned flipping him over, crawling between his legs, and sucking him awake. Mustering all her will, Ginger slowly slipped out of his bed.

Why am I so afraid? He's shown me who he is, you stupid little girl. I need to dowse my brain with caffeine and a workout.

Leaving the blue room, she thought, *Blue room, blue eyes, blue skies—why am I running? I really love every hue of blue. When will it morph into purple?* Ginger continued down the hallway to the kitchen and brewed a pot of coffee.

On the balcony, Ginger began her pre-exercise stretching in the morning air, admiring how the moon and the sun kissed the sky. It was just for her, she thought.

"Morning, Gin. Did I oversleep or are you up extra early?" Grant rubbed his eyes and then stretched his arms over his head, wearing only his boxers and an old, raggedy University of Wisconsin T-shirt. The bottom of his shirt lifted when his arms touched the doorcase above him, revealing his beautiful abs. She wanted to rip his shirt and boxers off right there on the balcony.

"Coffee's ready, sleepyhead. I hope to God you don't plan to pack that shirt for Paris. It's just"—she used air quotes—"too 'holey.'"

"I'll consider it. God, I had the craziest dream. It was about my father." He looked apologetic. "I'm sorry, babe, you must be getting sick of this. They're just dreams. The wildest part was, at one point, I felt like there was an angel trying to soothe me. I could feel her arms around me. Pretty crazy, huh?"

He hadn't realized she was that "angel," comforting him in the night. "Do you believe in angels, Grant?"

"I believe in a higher power, God, whatever you want to call it. Although I never used to when I lost my mother. No matter how much I prayed, I couldn't save her."

She saw his pain and started to reach for him, but he turned to pour himself a cup of coffee. *Why won't he touch me again? Who am I fucking kidding? I am the one who keeps running away.*

Grant stopped suddenly and turned. "Can I get a hug, Gin? I could really use one right about—"

Ginger's arms wrapped him in a hug before he finished his sentence. She relaxed into his body, feeling his heart beat, and time stood still.

"Babe? The phone is ringing," Grant said, pulling her back to reality.

"Oh, sorry. I didn't hear it," she replied, letting go of him and blushing.

"This is Grant," Ginger heard him say into the phone.

She was afraid it might be Margo again or another woman from his past.

"I'm so sorry to hear that! I hope she feels better. No, no, tomorrow is fine. Okay, don't worry." Grant hung up and walked back out on the balcony.

"Dulce, you know, our head seamstress, her daughter is sick and she won't be in today. We're going to have to work tomorrow to make up for this—maybe even Sunday."

"Whatever it takes," Ginger replied.

"We better get to the office and see what's left to do. Thank God Howard's gone. We'll have the office to ourselves."

"If it were the time of day for a drink, I would toast to that. Guess we'll be skipping our workout today."

"After work, maybe?"

"What, midnight?" They both laughed and walked back in to get ready.

"Grant, I'm getting hungry," Ginger said. Friday was half over and they hadn't eaten.

"Pretzels with mustard?" Grant teased her.

"Jumbo shrimp, if you don't mind," she said.

Pressing the intercom, Grant said, "Sue, we need to order some food, please."

"Yes, sir. I'll be right there."

"Thank you." Grant winked at Ginger. "Probably won't be jumbo shrimp though."

"Whatever you have to offer, I'm in," she said, hinting at more than food. Grant's mind drifted to their hug that morning on the balcony.

"Grant? Hello?"

"Sorry, what?"

"I asked you how many inches do you want on this skirt. Where were you just now?"

"On a balcony."

"Oh, really?"

"I've visited that spot a few times today." Grant didn't want to push it too far for fear of scaring her again. "So what was your question again?"

"You're too much," she giggled. "How many inches for the—"

"Oh, how about twenty-five? Sound good?" *I've got more than seven inches that I would love to bury inside of you right now.*

"Good."

"It's always the extra inch that counts." Grant grinned and noticed the smirk on her face.

As time kept ticking, the sunset turned the sky into an array of oranges and pinks, and the city lights soon illuminated as the night took over.

Ginger knew they had food delivered at some point,

recalling it was delicious sushi, but had trouble remembering what kind it was. She talked to her mother during the day—they were only supposed to bring wine to the picnic Monday. She couldn't recall a time when her mind and body ever felt so alive yet exhausted.

After a grueling twelve-hour day, Grant said, "Babe, I want you to know something. What you have done is the most incredible thing. I'm proud of you."

She watched while Grant touched each garment like he could feel the energy it gave off.

Then he walked over to her and held her hand as they admired the garments lining the walls. The presentation was perfect, less the few changes that Dulce had to complete.

It was around midnight when they climbed into the cab. Ginger slid over and leaned her head against Grant's shoulder.

Looking down at her wavy, auburn hair, he gently placed his lips on her forehead.

"Gin, I'm sorry I've worked you so hard, but can you wake up long enough to get upstairs, or should I carry you?"

Chapter 41

Saturday morning, Ginger woke up in her bed, not recalling how she got there. *I'm losing it. How did I even get out of my clothes?* She had only her panties on but was completely under the covers. She looked at the clock and sprung from the comfort of her bed.

Throwing her robe on, she wandered down the hallway and found Grant on the recliner. He was studying *Frommer's Guide to Paris* and sipping a cup of coffee.

"Good morning, Sleeping Beauty."

"Exactly how did I get into bed last night?"

"I carried you to your room."

She looked embarrassed.

"Oh, relax. I kept the lights off while undressing you." He grinned. "Although, is that a freckle or a mole on your left breast?" He laughed.

"And to think I was about to call you Prince Charming."

"Ah, but you see, m'lady, the prince in *Sleeping Beauty* was named Phillip, not Charming."

She laughed, attempting to hide how aroused she felt at the thought of him undressing her. "Did you leave any coffee for me?"

"Of course. But you've got to look at this travel guide and see all the things to do in Paris."

"Caffeine first."

Sitting by his feet, Ginger confirmed, "So we'll get to see the view from the top of the Eiffel Tower? Magnifique!"

"And the Louvre," he said, attempting a French accent.

"Monsieur, do not talk like that when we're in France!"

"Why, whatever do you mean? Do you not like the way I talk? Perhaps, you, how do you say, sleep on the wrong side of the bed?" he said, again in his miserable French accent.

She laughed at how childlike he could be. "You have *way* too much energy for all the hours we put in yesterday.

When are we going to the office?"

"Whenever you're ready. I already spoke with Dulce. She's been sewing since eight o'clock. We just have to double-check what she's working on and then we can start packing."

"Great."

"Maybe we can go shopping today if we have time."

"What for?"

"I need some things for the trip, and I'd like your opinion. Do you mind?" His hands were together in a pleading gesture. "After all, if I'm going to be in Paris with the most beautiful woman in the world, I need to look my best. I wouldn't want people wondering why she's with me."

"Oh, please." Ginger blushed.

"Why, just look in the mirror, and then you will understand my dilemma, m'lady."

It was after six by the time Grant and Ginger felt like their line was ready to be packed. They accomplished more than they hoped for, even changing a few more minor details along the way.

Both agreeing that there was no time left to shop, they decided Sunday would be a better day to spend at Bergdorf.

They were walking back to the apartment when Grant remarked, "How about we pick up a few groceries and I'll cook you a nice dinner? You can soak in the tub and finally relax. You've earned it."

"I'd feel guilty if I didn't help with dinner, Grant."

"Okay, fine. You can help me by, um, not telling me if it sucks. Don't forget, I'm the boss."

"You're going to play that card? Fine, I'll be in the tub for two hours, and you'll need to wake my wrinkled body. How's that for a visual, *boss?*"

"If that makes you happy, I guess. At least I'll know how you'll look at ninety. Feel like a glass of vino on our way home? It's not too far from here."

"Sure, boss. I mean, Prince Phillip."

Entering a small hole-in-the-wall Italian restaurant and settling into a booth, Grant called out, "Hey, Nick. How are you?" Nick was the owner of the restaurant, a bald Italian in his early fifties with a booming voice.

"Grant, where the hell've you been? And, oh my, who's this lovely lady?"

"This, my friend, is Ms. Ginger Madison, a very good friend of mine. We work together."

Nick wiped his hands on his flour-covered apron and reached out his hand to Ginger. Being a romantic through and through, he kissed the top of her hand. "What a pleasure to meet you, Ms. Madison. I'm sorry you have to work with such a jerk." Nick turned and yelled, "Hey, Tony, I'll need a bottle of wine and some bread for two of my pals."

"I was going to cook for her, Nicky."

"Are you trying to kill her or somethin'? I'll take it from here. No questions." He slapped Grant on the back affectionately and disappeared into the kitchen.

And the food never stopped coming. Grant warned Ginger not to finish any course, as there would be seven—and plenty of leftovers too.

Walking into the lobby just after eleven, Grant said, "Gin, I can't see straight. Between the work and the food, I'm ready to pass out. How you doing?"

"Are my eyes crossed? I feel like they are."

Their conversation was interrupted when 34Bitch exited her apartment. She held a small bag of trash and headed for the garbage chute down the hall. She seemed flustered, like she was caught spying.

Grant held up the bag of leftovers. "Oh, hey, Brenda. Ginger and I are leaving for Paris. We have all these leftovers and I'd hate to throw them away. Why don't you take some? You could eat something while you fill Margo in on my life."

She said nothing.

"I guess that's a no, then? Oh, well. Good night."

Ginger unlocked the door and said loudly, "Come

now, Prince Charming."

Grant smirked at 34Bitch. "Coming, m'lady."

Chapter 42

Ginger was the first one to open her eyes Sunday morning. She drew back the curtains to see the start of what she hoped would be a wonderful day. Grant's bedroom door was slightly ajar, and she listened to him breathing peacefully. She made the coffee and walked onto the balcony.

Ginger was leaning against the railing wrapped up in her cozy bathrobe. The energy she felt was like a newborn bird who just gained her freedom by learning to fly. She was overwhelmed with every aspect of Grant. He crept into her every thought.

Ginger could no longer deny her true feelings. She whispered, “I’m in love with you, Grant Robinson.”

“Good morning, Gin.”

She jumped at his voice. Had he heard her?

“Good morning, babe. What’s with the robe? Are you cold or just hiding something?”

Grant’s faced turned red, wondering if his cock was still hard enough for her to see. *I’ll wait a bit before I ask for a hug. God forbid she discovers what I’m thinking, for shit’s sake.*

“Um, just a little cool this morning. Think I should pack it?”

“Aren’t the robes complimentary?” Ginger playfully commented. “I pictured us lounging around in matching his and hers. Only if there’s time, of course.” Her eyes never stopped devouring the sight in front of her: a sleepy-faced Grant, hair tousled and so beautiful.

“On another note, what do they allow us to put on the balcony?”

Of what she said, his brain registered on only one word: *us.*

“What did you have in mind, Gin?” he said, triumphantly smiling at her.

“Well, wouldn’t it be lovely if we had a few comfy chairs, about right here, to enjoy the mornings and evenings? Or late nights, if you keep working me like this.”

"Whatever you'd like. If we have time before Paris, we could look around. And I'd really like to add a little more furniture inside."

Ginger held up her coffee mug. "A toast to new furniture without the help of the property manager."

"Cheers."

They toasted with coffee cups and laughed at how silly they were, silently acknowledging the groundbreaking moment in their relationship.

"So how about some brunch at Tavern on the Green before we go to Bergdorf?" She didn't hear a word of what he was saying—she was too focused on his beautiful face, his kissable lips, and those blue eyes.

"Gin? Hello?"

She swallowed and said, "What, babe?" Their eyes were locked on each other and neither could or would move, just feeling the energy pass between them—it was electrifying.

"Brunch? Shopping? Any thoughts?" Staring into her eyes, almost laughing, he was dying to tell her how beautiful she was and that he knew he was more in love than he'd ever been in his entire life.

"And what are you grinning about? If you want something to smile about, Grant, I'll take my robe off."

"I'll take off mine if you take off yours."

She was silent, seeming to ponder his offer. "Brunch

and shopping sounds great—for now."

"Okay. Then I suppose sharing a warm shower is out of the question?" He was unable to hide his desire.

"Hmph, are you trying to get lucky before we pick out the furniture?"

"Well, maybe we should have some comfy chairs out here . . . ASAP!"

Ginger replied, "I'm hopping in the shower alone—*for now.*"

An hour later, Ginger and Grant were getting into the elevator. Now completely comfortable with sharing their personal space, she grabbed his hand without looking at him.

Entering the lobby, Andreas held the door open. "Good morning, Mr. Robinson, Ms. Madison. Today is a beautiful day. And it's also my seventeenth wedding anniversary."

"Congratulations," Grant said. He reached into his wallet, pulled out a hundred-dollar bill, and palmed it to him. "Treat your wife to a nice dinner tonight, Andreas."

"No, not necessary, Mr. Robinson."

"Love is something worth celebrating. I insist."

"Thank you, Mr. Robinson. And may I add, you and

Ms. Madison make a beautiful couple."

Neither of them replied. Holding hands again, they walked out of the building, both silently wondering when they would consummate the fact that they really were a couple, both afraid to push it too quickly.

Only two days into the month of September, fall was already in the air. They walked down Sixty-Eighth Street toward the park.

"Grant, do you really think we have a shot at landing the Paris account?"

"Together? We could take on the world. Why?"

"What happens if we don't? Will you still, um, need me?"

Grant was about to respond when the walk sign illuminated. They crossed the street. After passing the corner, Grant stopped and grabbed both her hands and looked into her eyes. "Are you asking if, after I'm done with Neiman Marcus and Le Printemps in Paris, you will still have a job?"

Ginger looked to her feet. "That's an unfair question, isn't it? It's just that we have been on such a crazy pace since I arrived, both personally and professionally. We never really discussed my job or its future."

"It's not unfair. Your job isn't just those two accounts. It's about a larger scope of work that I haven't shared with you, primarily because of the priority these two accounts hold."

She looked confused. "You're not a temporary employee, Gin. I want you to work with me whether I'm at H&M or on my own. I've needed someone like you to reignite the fire in me that I lost over the past few years."

Ginger took a deep breath. "Thank you, Grant. Guess I just have some leftover insecurities from Steve."

Grant looked toward the park and changed the subject. "The eggs Benedict are to die for."

He realized how deeply she had been hurt, despite her tough exterior.

Ginger slid her arm around his waist.

Arriving at the restaurant, Grant watched Ginger taking in the décor. The brick building was adorned with cobblestones and green vines. "God, look at the nest of blue jays on the vine. I've only been away for three years and I feel like a kid seeing everything for the first time."

Grant loved looking at things through her eyes. The world seemed like a better place just with her by his side.

The maître d' held open the door. "Mr. Robinson, we have missed you."

"Good to see you, Felix. A table outside by the flowerbeds would be great."

"Yes, sir."

"Felix, we're not in a hurry, but we would like to order a couple of drinks for starters."

"A Bloody Mary, Mr. Robinson? And for you, my beautiful lady?"

"A mimosa would be lovely."

Felix turned just in time to catch a waiter who was delivering a tray of drinks to a table and intercepted a mimosa and Bloody Mary.

"Madame," Felix said when handing Ginger her drink.

"Merci beaucoup," Ginger said.

He handed Grant his drink. "And for you, Monsieur."

"Thank you, Felix."

Looking around the courtyard, Ginger asked, "Did you come here often with your family?"

"Well, not at first. We lived in the Village. But after we moved to Midtown with the children, Sundays were spent here in the park."

Felix appeared again to lead the way to a table under a huge oak tree that was surrounded by a raised flowerbed of yellow mums. They ordered their brunch and sipped on another round of drinks. Grant and Ginger soaked in the ambiance of the beautiful setting: the park, the sunlight that poked through the trees in beams, the gentle breeze.

After some easy conversation, Grant took a deep sigh.

"I know we agreed that our pasts are just that, the past, but unfortunately, the past sometimes creeps into the present, and oftentimes into our future."

He continued, "This may be a difficult topic, yet it's very necessary for us to attempt to be successful, on any level."

She noticed his irises had taken on a greenish hue, which was the first time she'd seen his eyes change color.

"My feelings for Margo ended long before we actually signed the papers. The reason our marriage fell apart is because she was jealous of what I was able to accomplish without her involvement. It angered her each time I won an award or received a bonus. It eventually grew worse and worse, until there was nothing left and we ended it." He took a sip of his Bloody Mary.

"Earlier when we spoke about your future, Steve's name came up. He's like a constant shadowy figure in both our lives. The way he treated you makes him my nemesis. But it's not like we can totally cut him out of our lives in this industry.

"Which leads me to something I'm afraid to ask. What if he were to call to tell you his divorce was final and he wanted you back? What would you do? Do you still love him?" His voice cracked with overwhelming emotion.

Ginger placed her champagne glass on the table and folded her hands under her chin. "Grant Robinson, you are no Steve Williams. Can we start with that?"

"That's a good start, I think."

"I did fall for Steve. He claimed to be separated when we began dating. I thought I found someone who understood and loved me. I was excited to be with him and be a part of his vision for Neiman Marcus.

"After some time had passed, I realized he wasn't just going home to 'work out financial matters' or 'take care of sick kids' or any of the bullshit stories he fed me. He was still married and using me the wrong way in this crazy industry. How did he even get the job of head buyer?

"Anyway, I began falling out of love with him about a year ago. When Sarah came along, I saw how he looked at her. I'm not stupid; I knew what was happening.

"At first I was pissed that I could be tossed away so easily. You know how girls are. I don't want you, but I want you to want me? That kind of nonsense? That was my initial reaction.

"Then you came along, Grant Robinson. *You* have reminded me so quickly of who I really am, who I wanted to be, how I can make my dreams come true. Is it scary? Hell yeah. But I'm staying right here."

Grant sighed in relief.

"Ginger, I'm deeply in love with you."

"Oh, Grant. I never forgot meeting you in Chicago all those years ago. Call it fate, but I was *supposed* to be there. I was *supposed* to meet you. But nothing came from it—until now. I want you to know, and of this I am certain: I am just as in love with you as you are with me."

"Thank God."

"Besides, I haven't moved out yet, right?"

"Only because I haven't told you what your portion of the rent is."

"Eh, you can call your 'roomie' and get his dumbass to pay for it."

"I'd like to make a toast," Grant said, raising his glass.

"Why am I not surprised?" She raised hers.

"To our future."

"To us."

Chapter 43

Grant and Ginger decided to shop at Raymour and Flanigan Furniture on Broadway before hitting Bergdorf. After an hour browsing, they realized how overwhelming it was with the limited time they had. Deciding to leave the inside furniture selection for another time, they picked out some overstuffed patio furniture, which surprisingly could be delivered the same day.

Grant called his building, knowing that the rules emphatically enforce no Sunday deliveries. He realized that Abigail would need to be the one to approve it. Luckily, Deerpak answered the phone.

After the conversation, Grant smiled triumphantly and declared, "Well, m'lady, we will have the lounges to relax upon this evening."

"Perfect." Ginger grabbed his hand, and the two headed off to Bergdorf.

Walking inside the department store, Grant asked for Libby. She was off for the extended weekend. Her staff knew there would be trouble if she found out that Grant Robinson had been there and she wasn't notified. He ended up on the phone with her.

"Libby, really, it's fine. Enjoy your family. Ginger and I can do this."

Grant handed the phone back to Renee, Libby's head assistant. Renee was a beautiful woman in her mid-thirties. Her tall and slender build led Ginger to think she could model if it weren't for her age.

"Yes, Ms. Libby. Will do." She hung up. "Okay, we have work to do, girls." Renee popped the cork on a bottle of champagne. "Ms. Libby wants Mr. Robinson and Ms. Madison to have the best experience as they prepare for their trip to Paris."

Ginger sipped her champagne, wishing she could follow him into the dressing room and devour him. She thought about fucking him senseless the moment they got back to the apartment. Her mouth started watering as she began to imagine how his cock would taste, what it would feel like in her hands and mouth.

He appeared in a pair of deep-brown slacks with a blue shirt. "You like, m'lady?" Grant modeled for Ginger.

"That color blue looks good on you. It compliments your eyes." Ginger noticed that the three associates were all looking at him. *He's mine, bitches.*

After a few hours shopping for his clothes, Grant said, "Your turn." He plopped himself down next to her on the couch, accepting a glass of champagne.

"My turn for—?"

"You heard me. I'd like to see you naked—er, I mean, in that black-and-white Versace dress."

"You *are* a clown!"

With each dress and ensemble she tried on, the sexual tension grew between Grant and Ginger. Their eyes no longer concealed what they were feeling, not even trying to keep it in check while in public.

After their shopping spree was complete, Renee inquired whether they wanted the packages delivered. "I think we'll take them with us. We just may need assistance carrying the bags to a cab, if you don't mind."

"No problem. I'll take care of that for you."

"It's been a pleasure as always. I'll be sure to tell

Libby you and your team did a fabulous job, as usual."

She loved how people so easily ate out of the palm of his hand—he just had that way about him. And she was thrilled that regardless of how many beauties surrounded him, all his attention was focused on her.

Followed by the entourage of sales associates carrying their bags filled with hats, outfits, suits, and shoes, Grant stepped momentarily behind Ginger as they left Bergdorf. He admired the beauty of her body in motion. *She still moves like a cat*, he thought.

He fantasized how he would rip off her clothing, unwrapping her like she was the sweetest strawberry-filled Godiva chocolate, slowly tasting her just to see how her naked body would respond to his touch. He planned to savor every moment.

Deerpak was gone when they arrived at the building. Andreas, whose shift had just started, helped them unload their bags. Abigail stood by the entryway. She stared at the couple with her foot tapping and her arms crossed.

"Mr. Robinson," she said in a condescending tone, "you *do* know there are no deliveries on the weekends, correct?"

Grant stepped toward Abigail.

"Rules?" he said. "Which rule says it's okay for the property manager to drop by a tenant's apartment late at night to seduce him? Y'know, I still have your panties you left behind . . ."

Abigail took a step back. Grant closed the gap between them, almost like a wild animal stalking his prey.

"And furthermore, you wouldn't want me to—"

"I think Abigail gets your point," Ginger interjected, grabbing at his arm. "Don't you, Abby?"

Abigail nodded in agreement.

"Well, then, good night, Abigail." She pulled Grant toward the elevator.

The elevator arrived and Grant and Ginger boarded in silence until the doors closed. "Well, Grant Robinson, where did that come from? I guess I don't know everything about you! On some psychotic level, that was really hot and exciting. Sexy!" She put her arm around him and pulled him into her, nuzzling her face into his shoulder.

Grant's anger was immediately replaced with lust. *If I'm a lion, I know what my next prey is—this sexy lamb right in front of me. Roar!*

As they stepped off the elevator, they found Andreas at the door with all the packages on a cart. Grant unlocked the door, and Andreas pushed the cart inside. He nearly tripped when Ginger squealed at the sight of the furniture.

"Oh my God, our first furniture! Let's keep them

forever, okay?" She jumped back into his arms.

"God only knows what they will look like after forever, but I'll remind you about that comment when you're looking to replace them." He hugged her back, kissing her forehead.

"Ahem. Mr. Robinson, I think I've covered everything here. Unless you'd like some help with the furniture?"

"Oh, no. We can do that. Here, this is for you." Grant handed him a twenty-dollar bill.

"Thank you, Mr. Robinson. Good night, Ms. Madison."

They were left alone, surrounded by dozens of bags and plastic-wrapped furniture.

Ginger grabbed a pair of scissors. "We need to use this furniture at once, especially after your brave battle with Abby to have them delivered today."

"Agreed." Ginger tore the plastic off the furniture. "Be careful, Gin. You're a maniac with those."

"Oh, please. The sun is setting. Don't you want to watch it tonight?"

"Okay, I can't watch this. While you're cutting off your fingers, how about I make us a cocktail? Any preference?"

"A ladyfinger martini?"

"Yeah, that ain't happening. How about a

cosmopolitan?" He prepared the cocktails when he heard no reply.

By the time he finished the drinks, Ginger had already torn off all the plastic and was attempting to drag the first chaise lounge onto the balcony.

"Jesus, Gin, I got it."

"Well, hurry up then!"

Out on the balcony, Ginger wedged the oval cocktail table between the lounges. Adding yellow blackjack orchids on the table, everything was perfectly in place by her standards.

She asked which lounge he wanted to watch the sunset from.

He gave her a naughty look. "Think we could fit on one?" He sat down on the closest lounge. "Sit here," he said, patting the spot in front of him. She climbed in with him and sensually crawled between his legs. Briskly kissing him on the forehead, she flipped over, surprised by his steely erection forging into her back.

"Mmm, this *is* nice," she purred.

He wrapped his arms around her waist, and she covered his hands with hers. Leading one hand to the hem of her dress, he slowly explored the bare skin of her thigh. She was still wearing the black-and-white dress Grant picked out for her. She kicked off her shoes while getting lost in her lust for him when he slid his hand up to her inner thigh.

Relaxing and spreading her legs, enjoying the pleasure of his erotic touch, she guided his hand farther and purred again with desire. He responded by kissing behind her earlobe and pulling her hair back, exposing the nape of her neck. His right hand, still guided by hers, began gently massaging her panties, discovering her warm wetness beneath.

Ginger turned to kiss him. Grant's eyes closed naturally, but she wouldn't have any of that. Her thumb gently rubbed his eyelid, prompting him to look into her eyes, making their kiss even more intimate. Grant's free hand slid into the scooped neckline under her bra to caress her erect nipples.

Both breathing deeply, not even noticing the sun had already set and the city lights were aglow, the kiss they shared was beyond what they experienced at the airport. They both knew the barriers had been removed from their relationship, and it was finally time to take it to the next level.

Until the phone rang.

"Goddamnit! Really?" Grant spat out. His cock was rock hard, and Ginger had just started to grind her ass into him.

"Do you have to?" she begged, pulling his lips back to hers.

"Oh, baby, I'm sorry. No one would call me this late

on a Sunday unless it's an emergency. And my kids . . ."

"Oh, right, I didn't mean to be so selfish, baby. I'm just so—"

"I know." He kissed her. "Me too. I'll make it quick." She reluctantly leaned forward to give him room to move. She smiled when she noticed the wet spot on his jeans.

Ginger sipped her cosmopolitan and prayed it wasn't anything to do with his kids. Hopefully it was just Abigail apologizing.

"No, no, Dulce. Don't worry. We'll be right there. Ginger and I were just, well—we'll be there. It's okay. You're welcome. Oh, don't cry. She'll be okay . . . All right. Bye."

Ginger was at his side before he hung up. "Babe, I can't tell you how sorry I am about this, but we—or I—have to go to the hospital. Dulce's daughter's fever is nearly one hundred and five. She has no insurance, thanks to Howard. She can't get a hold of her husband, and—"

"Let me get my shoes on. I'll go with you. She needs you, and I just adore her."

"You are one of a kind, aren't you?"

"They broke the mold! Don't worry, the furniture isn't going anywhere."

"How did I get so lucky?"

"Almost!"

Chapter 44

It was nearly five thirty a.m. when Ginger and Grant returned to the apartment. Barely able to walk yet still holding hands and leaning into each other, Grant unlocked the door. The living room area was still cluttered with their shopping bags and boxes.

"Grant, it really was beyond sweet of you to take care of Dulce's medical expenses. I'm so relieved she'll be okay. It was emotionally taxing, though." She leaned against the counter.

"It's the least I could do for her. She's worked with me for so many years. Hell, I've watched her daughter grow since birth."

He laced his fingers around the small of her back and kissed her gently on the forehead. "I suppose we need to actually *sleep*, don't we?"

She sighed. "I guess you're right. The picnic will be starting before we know it, and I'd prefer to not wear a ton of makeup to cover dark circles from sleep deprivation. And you, Prince Phillip, will need to be ready to meet my family."

"I'm especially looking forward to meeting your Aunt Sadie. Ahem. Think she's with someone having fun?"

"Ew! Turn it off already or I'll introduce you as Prince Shithead." She kissed him on the cheek and walked to her room.

Grant stood outside her door, watching her pull her dress up over her head, revealing the beauty of her back, ass, and legs; he immediately felt aroused. *Is that a subtle invite? No! Calm down, boy! Tomorrow is a new day. God, I love her.*

Grant slipped into his bedroom with a raging hard-on. *Wait . . . I should've just given Dulce a credit card number to pay for her daughter's treatment. Fuck! But I had to be there for moral support. At least Ginger was with me. She said I was a good man. Am I really, when all I want to do is run into her room and fuck her?*

Grant tossed and turned for over an hour before he

fell asleep.

Tommy had been lost in thought, staring out the kitchen window. Rachel led him back to her bed and removed his skivvies. She only had one thought encompassing her mind: *him*. She took his cock into her mouth. "Mmmm, you taste so good. Where have you been?" Rachel slid his entire length into her watering mouth.

"Inside the most beautiful girl in the world. Maybe you know her?" he sighed, trying to catch his breath. "I hear she's into fly-boys."

Nibbling just a bit harder than usual, she looked up into his eyes. "Nope. Only one."

"Me." His voice cracked from the physical pleasure and emotional pain.

"Then I know who you're talking about. Forever and ever, right?" Rachel whispered, sliding her tongue up and down his thick shaft.

Tommy lifted her up and pulled her on top of him so he could slide into her. "Always and all ways." Rachel's body responded immediately to his deep penetration, her wet pussy took every inch of him. She gasped.

Within seconds, she was climbing toward a climax, trying to focus on his eyes. Rachel's knees dug into the bed and her toes curled on top of his muscular thighs while she rode him.

Tommy couldn't hold back any longer when she cried out, "My sweet Tommy, yes! So . . . good . . ." Moans of satisfaction replaced her voice.

"I love you, Rachel Smythe, I love you . . ."

She collapsed onto his chest, with him still fitting perfectly inside her. Intertwined as lovers, they fell asleep.

Grant was still dreaming and hard when Ginger gently knocked on his door. She quietly peeked into his room. The sheets were down around his waist, and he had a slight mist of sweat covering his body. His hand was tightly wrapped around his cock, stroking up and down through his boxers. He picked up the pace, almost as if he knew she was watching, which excited her immediately.

It became clear that he was dreaming, and she didn't want to disturb him. She hoped, though that it was her he was dreaming about. Leaning against the doorframe, she slid her fingers down to her clit. Ginger was nearing her own orgasm and thought about climbing into bed to clean his cock with her mouth. *That's not how we will do it for the first time.* She tiptoed out of his room and started brewing coffee in the kitchen.

Grant hadn't awoken to himself covered in his own semen since he was a kid. Still foggy from the dream, he thought, *Wow, what great sex Rachel and I have. Wait, I mean Tommy. Me? We? Oh God, I'm losing it!*

He could smell the freshly brewed coffee and looked at the clock. "Shit!" He jumped out of bed and quickly changed his boxers, tossing the soiled ones to the corner of his room.

In the hallway, Grant nearly smacked into Ginger. With a bashful face, he said, "Good morning. Sleep well?"

"Like a rock. How about you, babe?"

Grant blushed again. "Yes, but it took me a while to fall asleep. It was hard to get this ethereal vision out of my head."

"Ethereal? Like angelic?"

"Yes, exactly."

"Part of your dream?"

"Yes . . . no. Wait . . ." He gathered his thoughts. "Before going to bed, I watched this incredibly sexy woman slowly undressing in the hallway. I sure liked what I saw . . ."

It was Ginger's turn to blush. Grant lifted her chin up to make eye contact, kissed her softly on the tip of her nose, and said, "I better get ready, huh?"

"Time's flying, fly-boy."

Fly-boy? Grant thought while showering. *I just heard those words in my dream. Why would she call me a fly-boy? I always wanted to be a pilot, but I don't recall telling her that . . .*

He ended his shower and started picking out an outfit. He felt he had to look perfect to meet Ginger's family.

"How's this for the party, Gin?" He modeled his khaki shorts, a yellow-and-blue-striped polo shirt, and sandals.

"Are you kidding me? You're not wearing your University of Wisconsin T-shirt? Come on, babe. You look perfect."

"Good, because you look gorgeous." Grant eyed her up and down, showing his appreciation at the sight in front of him. "You're just missing your angel wings, Gin."

Ginger was wearing a white tank with a deep, ruffled neckline; flower-printed midthigh shorts, and orange kitten pumps.

"Who, me? Why, thank you, Prince Phillip."

"Come on, m'lady. Time's flying." He kissed her glossed lips.

"Wait a second, mister. Let me take care of that." She reached up to his face, cupping it with both hands, and continued the kiss, letting their tongues dance.

Grant slid his hand down the back of her shorts and under her panties and grabbed her ass, pulling her into him. Ginger could feel his erection and lost her breath. They kissed and touched and panted until Ginger finally found the strength to pull away.

"Grant, baby, we need to stop. I don't want our first time to be rushed because of family plans." She tried to catch her breath.

They gathered themselves and headed out.

They walked out into the sunlight and headed toward Broadway locked arm in arm. Grant's hand slid down her back, hooking his finger at the waist of her shorts. He was intoxicated by the fragrance of her hair and scent of her body mixed in the light breeze.

Ginger and Grant turned the corner, heading toward Lincoln Center to catch the subway. "So, baby, I never asked you, but how many people do you expect to be at the picnic?"

"Let's see. Louisa and her two kids, Elmer and Elaine—no, wait, not them."

"Under thirty, right?" Grant pressed her.

"Wait! I'm still counting," Ginger said, slightly annoyed that he interrupted her thought process.

"So, have you made all the men you've dated meet the *entire* family before they get lucky?"

Ginger snapped at him. "If you want, you can return

to your ivory tower and see if you can get lucky."

"Oh, Gin, I'm just messing around. I can't wait to meet them. Actually, I am really looking forward to meeting your parents." He pulled her into his body.

She reached her hand around his neck and kissed him. After a long, passionate moment, she said, "Forty-three. Plus us, which makes it forty-five."

Grant pinched her ass while boarding the train. She let out a small yelp. "Listen, you can't do that to me today. I have a hot date tonight and wouldn't want to explain any marks on my body."

"Really? Is he cute?"

"Well, not in a conventional way. But when the lights are off, it doesn't matter what he looks like, right? As long as he has the right equipment, anyway." She pinched the inside of his leg.

"Ow! You brat!"

Chapter 45

Twenty minutes later, they stepped off at 111th Street.

She looked off in the distance. "Wait, stop. There's my brother and his wife." Ginger shouted, "Hey, Andrew!"

Her niece, Paulina, and nephew, Adam, screamed and ran at her. "Auntie Gin! Daddy, Mommy, it's Auntie Gin!"

She knelt down on the sidewalk to brace herself for the impact, and they both jumped into Ginger's outstretched arms.

"Oh, my favorite babies. I've missed you!" Realizing this was the first time she would be introducing him to her family, she stumbled a bit to say, "This is my, uh, a very special friend of mine, Grant."

Adam was only six, but he stuck out his hand like a gentleman. "It's nice to meet you, sir."

Grant knelt down to meet him eye to eye and shook back. Then Adam yelled, "Mom, Dad! Come meet Auntie Gin's boyfriend!"

Paulina, who wrapped herself around Ginger, looked at Grant and whispered, "Auntie Gin, he's cute. I want to hug him. Is that okay?"

"Of course. There's enough of him for both of us."

Still whispering, she said, "Are you in love with him?"

"Yeah, I think so."

Ginger smiled, passing Paulina into Grant's arms. She hugged Grant and smooched his cheek. "I like you."

"I like you too, Paulina."

"Grant, this is my brother, Andrew, and his wife, Clara; two of the most special people in my life."

"It's truly a pleasure to meet you both." Grant reached out his hand toward Andrew and then Clara.

"Your children are sweet," Grant said as they walked toward the park.

"Thanks, Grant. It's all the beatings," Clara teased.

Walking up to the park, Lois, Ginger's mother, was adjusting her dress and her wide-brimmed sun hat. She was already hugging Adam while Paulina wrapped around Ginger's dad, Bill. He was wearing a weathered Giants T-shirt with a Yankee's baseball cap that looked like he'd worn it since he was ten.

Ginger kissed her dad and then hugged and kissed her mom. "Mom and Dad, I'd like you meet Grant Robinson. Grant, these are my parents, Lois and Bill."

"We're glad you could come to the picnic, Grant," Lois said. She kissed Grant on the cheek.

Bill extended his hand. "Grant, it's nice to have you join us." Ginger watched how her dad measured Grant up, looking into his eyes.

Grant shook his hand. "Thank you for inviting me, sir."

"Want a coldie, son?"

"That would be great," Grant responded. Bill handed him a beer out of a nearby cooler.

"I'm in charge of the grill, so I need to get it going."

"I'll be glad to give you a hand, Bill," Grant said, taking a swig of his cold beer.

"Thank you, but I've got help. I have my old army buddies on kitchen patrol. Spent two years overseas with these guys in the Ninety-First Army Air Corp."

"Really? Where, if you don't mind me asking?"

"England. Hey, let me introduce you. Guys, head on over here for a moment."

Three men walked over, each holding a beer.

"Grant, this is Elmer, Kenneth, and Gene. Grant is

here with Ginger, boys. And if I know my daughter and wife, they're itching to show you off. So make them happy, son. Never keep a lady waiting."

"Yes, sir. Pleasure to meet you, gentlemen."

Ginger appeared. "Hey, fellas," she said, and then she pulled Grant away.

After meeting so many people at once, Grant's head spun. He wasn't sure who was who and couldn't possibly remember anyone's name. The only exception was Lauren, the nineteen-year-old girlfriend of Ginger's older cousin Henry. She kept seeking Grant out to talk about the latest fashion looks. After three or four attempts and feeling a bit protective, Ginger took Lauren aside and told her she would personally talk to her after their business trip, emphasizing that this was their day off.

"Ginger, darling! How are you?" Aunt Sadie said. The elderly lady was dressed like an aging actress. Despite her seventy years, she wore heavy makeup, over-the-top jewelry, a vintage purple knee-length dress, red shoes, and a bright-red sunhat.

"Finally, Aunt Sadie. How are you?" She squeezed her spitfire aunt and kissed her cheek.

"Good, my love. And who's the hot piece of ass you brought?"

"He's a special friend I—"

"Honey, all my lovers have been 'friends.' What does he do for a living?" Aunt Sadie said while she looked at Grant like a piece of meat, trying to decide whether she wanted him raw or well done.

"He's in the fashion industry. A designer for a private-label company. He hired me as his assistant."

Ginger turned in Grant's direction. He was speaking with her father and his friends again. She caught his attention. "Grant, come meet my Aunt Sadie."

He excused himself and joined Ginger.

"Aunt Sadie, I'd like you to meet Grant Robinson. Grant, this is my Aunt Sadie."

He held Aunt Sadie's hand and placed a gentle kiss on it. "It's an honor to meet such a lovely lady. I've heard so much about you."

"Oh, I like this one, honey. He has class. He knows exactly what a lady expects from a man," Sadie said with a naughty little smirk.

Sadie eyed Grant for a moment. "You leave me wanting to read your palm, honey. Palms always have a story to tell. Do you mind?"

"If it makes you happy." Grant winked at Ginger. "But you don't need to read my palm to keep holding hands. All you have to do is ask."

Sadie ignored his comment and studied his palm like

she was reading an important manuscript. Suddenly Sadie dropped Grant's hand. "So, you were in a hurry to come back, weren't you?"

Grant was confused. "Excuse me? Back from where?"

Sadie turned somber.

Ginger chimed in. "Grant lives here in New York."

"Grant, would you be so kind as to get me a vodka on the rocks, please?"

"Sure, Aunt Sadie. Would you like anything, babe?"

"The same, please."

After he walked off, Ginger asked, "What's going on, Aunt Sadie? You look upset. Do you need to sit?"

"I've been waiting for that SOB to come back to me for forty years, Ginger. I waited and hoped that every young man I met who was twenty years my junior would be him."

"What do you mean? You were waiting for whom?"

"The uncle you never met, Allen. He died on D-day. He promised me that he would come back for me."

Just then Grant returned with their drinks, inadvertently silencing her. Sadie took the plastic cup and slammed it back in a single shot. Grant watched her in amazement; Sadie handed him the cup and asked for another one.

Ginger turned her full attention toward her aunt. "I'm not sure I follow, Aunt Sadie."

"It's in his palm." She nodded toward Grant. "Just look at him. He's having a reunion with his comrades."

Grant conversed with Ginger's father and his friends while preparing the second vodka.

"Do you know who those guys are?" Aunt Sadie asked.

"I know they're Dad's childhood friends. They grew up—"

"They all enlisted in the army together. Originally, though, there were five friends, but only four returned from the war. Your Uncle Allen died on Normandy Beach saving the life of two wounded soldiers. He promised he would come back to me."

Grant returned with Aunt Sadie's drink.

"Thank you, Grant." She slammed it down in one gulp again.

"Hey, Grant! You've got to come over and hear this one," Ginger's dad hollered.

"Pardon me, ladies, I'm being paged. Aunt Sadie, can I get you anything else?"

"Oh, honey, are you trying to get me loopy? No, thank you."

"I can see where Ginger's sense of humor comes from." Before he left, he kissed her hand and then kissed Ginger on the cheek.

"So is he any good in bed, honey?"

"Aunt Sadie, you're too much! We haven't gotten that far."

"Yet. And when you do, I think you will discover something very special about him." Ginger hugged her aunt who was slightly trembling. "Also, my little one, pay attention to the numbers. Numerology is very telling."

"And what should I be looking for?" Ginger inquired.

It was six thirty in the evening when the crowd had thinned out. Grant and Ginger were helping her parents pack up their van when Grant discovered a bottle of champagne left in the cooler.

Ginger was in the middle of a conversation with her mother. Grant turned to her father. "Want to finish this last bottle of champagne?"

"Hell, yes."

Grant popped the cork. "I'll take that as an order, Sergeant."

"Damn right, Private. And you know what? Next year, you're on Kitchen Patrol. I've had enough of Elmer's lip. He's been dismissed from duty."

Hearing the cork pop interrupted their conversation, but Ginger and her mother were happy to see Grant and Bill bonding.

"I think Daddy really likes Grant, baby girl."

"And I think Grant really likes Daddy. It's as if they've known each other their whole lives. At least that's what Aunt Sadie said. Is she losing it, Mom?"

"She's always been like that. Your aunt has a special talent, and I'm not really sure how to describe it. She can see the past, as in past lives. Sometimes the future too."

"So she's a psychic?"

"I suppose you could say that. She's never wrong. Why do you think I married your father?"

"You never told me that."

"Timing is everything, my dear."

"I firmly believe in that."

"Ladies, I'd like to make a toast," Grant said, raising his plastic cup as the girls approached.

"To relationships, old and new, may they continue to blossom and grow in friendship and love, forever."

"Cheers!" all four responded in unison.

"Might want to drink quickly. Look at those clouds brewing," Bill remarked after his sip.

"Oh I hadn't noticed," Ginger said.

"How about I give you both a ride back into the city?"

Grant responded, "Bill, thanks for the offer, but you'll be stuck in Labor Day traffic."

"Besides, Daddy, we'll take the subway and be home in twenty minutes." She took another deep sip of her favorite champagne. "Mom, do you like it?"

"I sure do. It's already hitting me," she whispered, although the men could still hear. "And I really can't wait to get your Daddy home!"

Ginger spread the next word into two syllables: "Mo-om!"

Both Grant and Bill laughed. Bill elbowed Grant, winking at him. "See? Already working, Private."

"Ahem . . ." Grant kicked a rock, feeling slightly embarrassed for what he was already thinking about doing to Ginger; it was like Bill read his mind.

"So, Mommy, Daddy, we really should be going."

"Thank you for today, Bill, Lois. One of my favorite Labor Days that I can remember." Grant leaned in to hug Lois.

"Remember, Mommy, we are leaving for Paris tomorrow night. It will be a week-long trip, so we won't get home until the following Wednesday. I'll call you next Thursday, okay?"

"Of course, my baby girl. Good luck and *be safe*." Ginger's mother hugged her tightly.

"Take care of my daughter, Grant," Bill said, shaking

Grant's hand and putting an arm around his shoulder.

"Yes, sir. Always."

A branch of lightning flashed in the distance and was followed by an elongated thunderclap.

"On that note, I think we should go, Gin." They waved and started running toward the subway.

Chapter 46

When they reached the 111th Street subway entrance, Ginger came to an abrupt stop. "Make a wish, Grant! We are standing on an angelic street."

"What?"

"Aunt Sadie said that in numerology, one hundred and eleven is one of the highest, most powerful angel numbers. It's like the universe takes a picture of your thoughts and hands you exactly what you're thinking. If you believe, of course."

They both silently made their wishes. It was easy to know what they both wanted: each other.

When Grant opened his eyes, he noticed that Ginger's irises were the deepest green he'd ever seen on her. She kissed him so passionately that his eyes watered.

When one teardrop trickled down his cheek, Ginger licked it up seductively. "I want every drop of you, Grant."

"I can't wait to get you home. I need you, Gin."

"Mmm, I need you too," she purred. "I can hardly wait to strip off your clothes."

"Then we better board the train, and *fast.*"

Running down the steps to the platform hand in hand, the Number 2 was just pulling in. Crowded with people heading home from the holiday weekend, they had to stand. Grant grabbed a pole and positioned Ginger between his body and the two inches of stainless steel that reached from floor to ceiling.

The best way to steady oneself on the subway is with your feet at least shoulders width apart, to which Grant took full advantage of.

Ginger's clit was perfectly placed between the unmovable pole while his huge erection split her ass cheeks. All her sexual senses were stimulated while the subway bounced around, causing Grant's cock to thrust against her. Ginger pushed back into him—a not-so-subtle hint of what she really wanted.

He nuzzled his lips against her neck, right below her ear, sending needy chills down her spine. Ginger wished the train was empty, because she would slide Grant inside her wet and throbbing kitty instantly.

Surrounded by strangers, she was nearing an orgasm as the subway came to their stop at Lincoln Center. Ginger knew if there was one more stop, she would have exploded in public, which filled her with more desire than ever. *I've never been an exhibitionist, and now I can't wait to do that again!*

Walking up the steps, Grant and Ginger found that the sky had opened up. They were immediately soaked to the bone.

"Of all days for me to wear white," Ginger growled. Grant, on the other hand, smiled, admiring how her top clung to her skin, outlining her perfect physique.

"Too bad there's not a wet T-shirt contest going on somewhere—you would certainly win, hands down."

"Oh, really Prince Bullshit Artist?"

"I love how you constantly change the name of your prince."

"It solely depends on my mood." Ginger grabbed his ass, pulling his hard cock deeply against her as they kissed in the pouring rain. "Prince Naughty. That was the best subway ride ever."

They walked three blocks in the rain, splashing in puddles like children yet stopping every few yards to kiss and tug and grind into each other.

Finally arriving at their building, Andreas opened the door for them. "Oh, Ms. Madison! You're soaking wet. Hurry in. Were there no cabs, Mr. Robinson?"

"Why take a cab? I'd miss out on this!" Grant eyed her wet body, to which Andreas looked at the floor and gave no verbal response.

Just before rounding the corner to the elevators, Grant stopped and held Ginger's arm up. "Winner!"

"I reluctantly accept this award, thanking my greatest fan, who probably fixed the contest." She took a bow.

Upon entering the elevator and just before the doors closed, Grant grabbed her two hands and pinned them over her head against the elevator wall. He feverishly kissed her. Her response mirrored his passion, as they grabbed and tugged and pulled at each other.

Knowing that the first twenty-five floors were usually nonstop, Ginger let herself indulge in his animalistic need.

Exiting the elevator on the thirty-fourth floor, they both bolted for the door. Grant fumbled for his keys. Ginger couldn't wait any longer to please him in any way possible. She pushed Grant against the door, causing his keys to tumble across the hall while unzipping his wet shorts, yanking down his boxers. His huge erection sprung to freedom and right into her mouth.

"Oh, Gin, baby . . ." Grant sucked in air, feeling dizzy from the pleasure. He pulled her hair as he thrust his throbbing cock deeper into her mouth. Ginger took as much of his size as she could, enjoying the taste of his precum escaping his dick.

"You're so . . . tasty . . . baby," she was able to murmur.

Grant heard 34Bitch's apartment door open. Ginger was on her knees, and the both of them were dripping wet from the rain.

34Bitch screamed, "Oh my God! Take it inside, you two whores!"

Grant could barely hold up his hand, attempting to flip her off, slurring, "Go to hell." He exploded down her throat, and Ginger continued to eagerly suck and swallow his cum, not giving a damn that 34Bitch was watching. She had her legs wrapped and grinding on his ankle, nearing her own climax.

34Bitch retreated back into her apartment, slamming the door.

Crawling around the hallway floor, Ginger found the keys and unlocked the door while Grant was on his hands and knees, overcome with the orgasm she had just given him. Pulling her face to his, he kissed her mouth, tasting his own cum, and licked the leftovers off her chin, swallowing his own semen.

Grant and Ginger managed to get into the apartment, falling onto the parquet floor. He ripped Ginger's wet clothing off her needy body. She helped by removing her bra and panties.

Grant spread her legs and placed his mouth on her clit. He gently sucked it in between his teeth while tonguing it. He began to give her small cock a blow job. In all her sexually active years, Ginger never felt such physical pleasure. "Oh, Grant," she moaned.

Her fingers spread the lips of her pussy apart for him. Her legs fell open and her hips grinded upwards toward his mouth. She began to climb toward the most intense sexual experience she'd ever had. She felt like she was soaring up the side of a mountain and then falling deeply into an abyss of euphoric physical ecstasy. When he stuck two fingers inside of her, it caused her to climax like never before.

"Uhhh . . . yeah . . . baby! Yesssss! That's . . . perrrrfect! My . . . sweet . . . Grant . . ."

She no longer was able to control her body and bucked wildly into his mouth with each pulse of sensation. Grant wouldn't let go of her hips, pulling her against his mouth, drinking every drop. Even when she tried to crawl away from his mouth, he couldn't stop.

"Please, Grant! I can't take anymore," she begged him. "I . . . I . . . oh, babe! I need to breathe!"

Ginger was lying on the floor in the foyer waiting for the oxygen to return to her brain when she discovered Grant's cock was hard again. "Oh, baby, I need your perfect dick inside me! Please!"

He shed his remaining clothes, scooped her up, and carried her down the hallway to his bedroom.

Grant placed her on his bed.

"Make love to me, Grant," Ginger sweetly begged.

"Yes, baby," was all he could utter, realizing that he was moments away from fulfilling an eleven-year fantasy.

Ginger lay back on the bed with her legs spread; she was so wet, her pussy was glistening. Grant crawled between her legs, placing his erection against her wet lips. Looking at her, he hesitated for a second before slowly sliding his cock inside, wanting to savor the moment.

He penetrated her, feeling for the first time in his life a connection he had never had with another human being. The emotional and physical intensity was so beautiful that they both paused once he was completely inside her and locked eyes.

He began to slide his cock slowly in and out. "Ginger, I love you," he breathed. He watched her eyes roll back into her head. She already began to feel the tingle of another orgasm.

With each tender yet powerful thrust of his hips, Grant felt the burning heat of the walls of her pussy tightly holding onto his cock.

Ginger felt her clit begin to pulsate, but it was like her orgasm started from some otherworldly place within, encompassing every inch of her body.

Grant buried his huge cock as deeply as he could into her. He too released a raspy, euphoric sound himself; a sound that triggered a familiar emotion hidden in the depths of their souls.

Ginger's legs were tightly wrapped around his lower back. She held one arm around his neck and the other hand on his ass, drawing him deeper and harder into her. They came together, and Grant fell on top of her sweat-covered body, kissing her lips.

Something indescribable passed between them . . . the truest lovemaking and fucking combined, at last.

Eventually, Grant slid off her dampened skin. "Ginger, you are amazing, my love."

"I was just thinking the same about you, baby, and we're just getting started . . ."

When their breathing somewhat returned to normal, he reached over and grabbed her arm to pull her on top of him. He spread her legs, positioning her body over his face, and began to drink their sex from her dripping pussy. She instinctively began to grind her hips, moving up and down in a circular motion while he sucked on her swollen clit and lips. After a few minutes of riding his face, Ginger turned her body to suck Grant's cock. He loved the sight of her perfect ass being so close to his face.

He slid two fingers inside her totally exposed kitty,

causing her to lose focus. Ginger's pussy tightened around his fingers, making her moan.

"Oh baby," she cried out, and Grant slid another finger inside her. "I'm going to cum again!"

She exploded onto his face. She relished the fact that her orgasm lasted longer than the previous few while Grant licked the savory liquid dripping from her cunt.

Almost all her energy was drained as she felt the last few waves of her extended orgasm flow throughout her body. Exhausted and breathless, she rolled off him. Ginger licked their juices from his lips and nose.

"Grant, you've brought me more pleasure than I ever imagined I could feel."

"Gin, I am truly in love with you . . . and in *lust* with you too."

She twisted her legs into his while they lay next to each other. With her head nuzzled into his neck, they fell into a blissful sleep.

Chapter 47

When the sun rose early Tuesday morning, Grant awoke to Ginger's mouth wrapped around his cock. "Am I dreaming?" he asked her.

"If you're dreaming that I'm sucking your dick, then yes, you're dreaming." She smiled a wicked smiled before cupping and playing with his taut balls, sliding his cock back into her mouth.

"I love this dream," he moaned. It didn't take long before his body was surrendering to the wet warmth of her mouth, the sight of her perfect ass high in the air, and the touch of her long auburn hair as it brushed against his inner thighs each time she slid her mouth up and down. He no longer could hold back when she gently rimmed his ass with her finger.

"My God, Gin!" It excited her to feel his leg muscles stiffen and the tightness of his balls. He let out a guttural cry as he exploded into her mouth.

He came so hard and fast that she couldn't keep up . . . it filled her mouth to the point that it spilled over her lips.

Grant pulled her face up to his, kissing her wildly, swallowing his own cum while sliding his still erect dick into her slippery pussy. With his hands grasping around her hips, he rocked her back and forth on his hard dick. Ginger's eyes rolled back into her head from the depth of his shaft.

She moaned, "Ah, Grant . . . mmmm . . . that's perfect . . . Oh . . . my . . . God. I love you!" She fell forward onto his chest.

It seemed she was spent, but Grant felt her orgasmic tremors continue in wave after wave as the walls of her kitty contracted and her clit pulsated over and over again. Her breath was jagged with her mouth up against the side of his face. He could feel her heart rapidly beating against his chest.

"I love you, baby. You're the greatest, hottest thing that's ever happened to me. I didn't know this kind of love was real."

Mustering up all her energy, Ginger pinched his

nipple as hard as she could.

"Oh, yeah. Harder, Ginger! Don't forget to do that the next time we're fucking."

"Anything for you, blue eyes."

They lay in a lovers' embrace, waiting to catch their breaths.

"I hate to disturb our perfect afterglow, but we need to get our line packed up for Paris . . . so we can come back early enough today to explore a few ideas I have, all surrounding your body."

"Okay, Prince Insatiable. I like the sound of that."

Holding hands as they exited the office elevator, Sue greeted them with the biggest smile. "Good morning. Did you both have an enjoyable Labor Day?" Sue was happy for Grant. She knew how unhappy he was before and could see how Ginger changed him.

"Yes, we did. Thanks, Sue. How was your day off?"

"It was nice. Thanks, Ms. Madison."

"If you need anything, let me know. I know you're leaving tonight for a week."

"You're irreplaceable, Sue."

Grant was oblivious to the whole conversation as he looked through his messages and mail. He seemed focused on one particular piece of paper.

"Ready to pack up, buttercup?"

"Uh, sure, Gin. Let's go." He folded the paper and stuck it in his pocket.

Walking toward the office, Ginger inquired, "You okay, babe?"

"Yeah, yeah, I'm fine. Just more shit to deal with. But it can wait. Let's pack."

In his pocket was a message from Steve to call him back and that he wanted to come to New York and celebrate—his divorce was final.

While packing, Ginger noticed Grant was distracted.

"Grant?" He didn't respond, lost in thought. "Hello? Prince Brain Trust? Are you there?" She was slightly annoyed.

"Yeah, baby. Sorry. What did you say?"

"We discussed bringing the extra photos we had taken. Did you want them or not?"

"Yeah, of course. Thanks for reminding me."

"Where's your head, baby?"

"You love me, right, Ginger?" She heard the insecurity in his voice.

"I *really* love you. I'm *in* love with you. 'I love you' doesn't even cover it. Why? What's wrong, my love?"

"I shouldn't let it bother me, but, well, here. Just read it." He handed her Steve's message.

Not knowing what to expect, she took the paper and read it—then reread it.

I love her so much that I'd let her go if she wants to be with Steve, he thought, *but I just got her!*

"Babe," she said, wrapping around his body like a backpack, "do you want to throw this away or should I?"

"How does it make you feel, Ginger?" Grant asked.

"It saddens me to think that you've been worried about something as trivial as Steve, sweetheart. He is my past. Remember what we said about the past?"

"Yes, but you have a history with him, and we have only had a few weeks. And it's just, well, allowing my heart to be this in love with you is unchartered territory for me."

"I'm yours. Always and all ways." She was stretched on her tippy toes to reach his lips and wiping away a tear from his eyes.

"I don't know how to live without you, Gin. I feel like I've always known you."

She kissed him sweetly, letting their tongues twist and turn in tender, slow motion. Pulling back for a moment, she replied, "I love you, my Prince Crazy. Can we refocus on our work now that we've gotten rid of Steve fucking Williams again? Sure, we can entertain him when he comes into town. Let him see the love we have for each other. Hell, maybe Abby will fuck him. Two birds, one stone."

"You're the best." He planted kisses all over her face.

"Refocusing here, and that doesn't help."

"Good, because I did say I wanted to get out of here early."

She tossed Steve's message in the trash.

The entire line was finally packed. Grant and Ginger said their good-byes to their seamstresses and Sue and left for the apartment.

Back at the apartment, they rushed around like lunatics, packing for the trip. Well, at least Ginger was until Grant interrupted her fury by standing in the doorway of her bedroom. "Hey, baby, I called Evan, and he'll be picking us up around seven o'clock."

She didn't look up. "Sounds great, babe."

"Ahem. Think this looks okay?" He was wearing a green-striped shirt and plaid golf pants with a cowboy hat and mismatched sneakers.

"Jesus, Grant. Hurry up and finish so you can show me what you were hinting to earlier! Unless you're no longer interested?" She held up a pair of turquoise thongs.

"On it!" He bolted out of view.

Twenty minutes later, he was standing completely naked in the doorway with his cock fully erect. "Want to take a quick shower, lover?"

"I'd love to."

He visually devoured her while she undressed and then led her by the hand to the master bath.

Entering the bathroom, the shower was already running, and light steam enveloped the room. The counter was covered with lit candles, two champagne glasses, and a bottle of Veuve Clicquot champagne cooling in an ice bucket.

"I *love* your idea of a quick shower. Wait, did you really pack?"

Grant popped the cork on the champagne.

"Well, if I forgot something, I'm sure we can buy it." He handed Ginger a glass of her favorite bubbly.

"A toast to the love of my life." Staring into each other's eyes, they sipped the champagne. With the champagne still in his mouth, he leaned over and suckled her nipple.

"Baby, you are so good to my body," she whispered, running one hand through his damp hair.

Steam from the dual showerheads fogged the frameless glass door, and Grant opened it to invite her in. "Madame, Monsieur would like you to join in this steamy land of water play. Oui?"

"Oui."

Grant slowly ran his tongue up her back, starting at her ass and ending at the nape of her neck, sending shivers through her. He reached around from behind and tugged at her nipples. The sexual tingles went straight to her clit. "Such pleasure. You're spoiling me."

"*My* pleasure."

With the hot water enveloping their bodies, they shared a kiss. "Baby, I've always wanted to wash a woman's hair. May I?" He squeezed her erect nipples again.

"That would be a first for me. Yes, please." She turned around and leaned against him, feeling his erect cock slide between her legs.

Grant filled his hands with shampoo and began massaging her scalp. He gently leaned her head back into the running water. She relaxed her entire weight against his body as the water flooded over her.

With her eyes still closed and a slight buzz from the champagne, she enjoyed how he was pampering her body. Grant slowly rinsed the shampoo out of Ginger's hair. "Don't open your eyes yet, baby."

Adding conditioner, he gently ran his fingers through her hair, which nearly reached her ass, not missing a single strand. He kissed her neck, and she wrapped her arms around him. Ginger crossed her feet, creating a tight spot between her legs. He felt how wet she was as he slid his dick back and forth. She was dripping with desire.

Ginger knelt down in the shower, letting the water cascade over her face, and handled his thick shaft. "Is this what Monsieur had in mind for our shower?"

"A bonus, Mademoiselle."

She purred while sucking him, the water sometimes streaming into her mouth. She handed him the bottle of conditioner. "Monsieur, a little help?"

He squeezed some onto her outstretched hand, wondering where this was leading. She gently slid the tip of her index finger into his ass.

Grant was shocked at the intrusion at first but then felt fully aroused and relaxed into her.

She continued to slowly finger fuck him and suck him at the same time. Grant finally held onto her head for balance when he began to blow his balls into her mouth. She sucked him empty.

Lifting her up once he could see again, Grant whispered in her ear, "Hold onto the wall." He knelt down and slowly spread her legs. He began to lick her pussy, finding her little erect hot spot immediately.

Her breath hitched while he slipped three fingers inside of her. She hummed in delight as he fucked her rhythmically with his fingers and sucked her clit. She began to quiver, and her knees buckled.

They slid down the shower walls to the floor while he continued to finger fuck her.

Ginger found herself on her knees, her hands in his hair, pulling his face into her pussy. She let the first wave of ecstasy rush out of her. "My God!" She drew out her last word for what seemed like forever. Grinding out her delicious orgasm on his face, Ginger was breathless.

He lifted her up to the far end of the shower and bent her over the teak bench. "Your turn, baby," she said seductively. "Take me."

Grant growled and succumbed to his passion. He guided his cock into her from behind until it was completely submerged. He pulled her hair and deeply pumped his erection into her again and again. She held onto the bench, blocking her forehead from being pounded into the shower wall. She enjoyed every grind, thrust, and push, which were physically lifting her off the floor.

She could tell by his breathing that he was getting close to an orgasm. Just as he started howling, he pulled out of her and shot his load all over her back. Ginger waited for his final wave to pass. He bent down and licked her back, sucking up as much of his cum as he could before the water washed it away.

Evan was putting the suitcases in the trunk as Ginger and Grant entered the limousine.

Ginger settled in the middle seat so she could feel Grant against her body. "I love you, my sweet Grant."

Evan looked in the rearview mirror. "JFK, Mr. Grant?"

"Yes, Evan. American Airlines, international terminal."

"That's right. You're off to Paris."

"Yes, we are," Grant replied, and kissed Ginger again.

"Sit back and relax, you two. Leave the driving to me." Evan put up the privacy window.

Ginger and Grant slipped into a comfortable embrace, listening to soft music. Ginger kissed his nose. "I am so excited. Ever since I was a little girl, I've wanted to see Paris. My father once told me that French women have hair under their arms. Is that still true?"

Grant laughed. "Maybe some of them. I've seen some hairy legs that would put mine to shame."

"Really?"

Grant burst into laughter, and Ginger slid over to the other side of the seat. "Don't make fun of my naïveté!"

"Oh, baby, come back. I was only kidding. Your dad was there right after the war. It was a tough time then. I remember when I was in Eng—" He stopped midsentence, analyzing what he was about to say.

Ginger slid back to his side. "What? When you were where?"

"For a moment, it felt like I . . ." He shook his head. "Never mind, babe. Obviously you fucked my brains out."

Ginger remembered what her mother said regarding Aunt Sadie's supernatural abilities. She dismissed the thought and snuggled in his arms for the rest of the drive to the airport.

Evan unloaded the luggage and hailed a skycap.

"Thanks, Evan."

"Always a pleasure, Mr. Robinson, Ms. Madison. Best wishes."

"Gin, it's seven thirty-eight. We'd better be going."

Chapter 48

"Ladies and gentlemen, we will begin to board first-class passengers. Please have your boarding passes out for the gate attendant."

Walking down the ramp, Grant stopped to do his ritualistic pat of the side of the plane. When they entered, a friendly flight attendant directed them to their seats.

Ginger turned to Grant. "Do you prefer the window or the aisle?"

"The window, please."

Ginger stepped back so that Grant could enter the row first. He pinched her ass and then sat down. "I saved this one for you, m'lady."

Ginger and Grant spent the next few hours eating, drinking, and planning their downtime in Paris. The lights were finally dimmed for the nighttime flight.

Grant slid his hand under the blanket and between Ginger's legs. Pushing his luck, he slipped a few fingers under her dress, rubbing her panties. He slid her thong over and penetrated her wet lips with two fingers and rubbed at her soft but hardened clit.

Ginger kept her moans low and grabbed his face to look directly in his eyes. She breathed in his warm breath. The sheer pleasure he brought her was overwhelming. Being in public was an added bonus. She was on the brink of crying aloud but gulped it down and pulled his hair. She whispered, "Baby, I'm cumming so hard . . . How do you . . ." She breathed heavily on him.

It took Ginger a bit to recover. "Baby, that was so good. Is there any way I can repay you? How about I sit on your lap?" She found his nipple and bit him through his fitted gray T-shirt so hard that he nearly yelped.

"Unzip your jeans just enough. I *have* to fuck you right now."

"Really, Gin?"

"Wrap the blanket around us. It's dark enough. I want to feel your hot cock in me."

Grant draped the blanket across them while she slowly

straddled him facing outward.

They both let out hushed moans in unison as Grant penetrated her, slowly raising her ass up and down and guiding their minimal thrusting. She could tell by his quiet but ragged breathing that within moments, he would blow. Leaning her head back into his, finding his ear, she whispered, "Come for me, baby. I'm all yours."

With those few words, Grant silently exploded into her. Feeling his cock pumping into her, she pushed her ass against him to take his entire size into her cunt.

They caught their breaths, kissed, settled back into their seats, and fell asleep.

Tommy looked out of the cockpit window of his B-17. A simple farm boy would never have dreamt of flying a plane that would take up half a football field. His plane, the *Fifinella*, sat in a English countryside as its crew prepped it for their next mission.

How perfect life would be if there wasn't a war, he thought. *I could fly* Fifi, *delivering packages, and then go home to Rachel Smythe.*

He wondered if he would ever see her smile again, hear her voice, or listen to her laugh. He longed for the gentle touch of her hand, the kisses she gave him for no reason at all, the scent of her skin.

"Hey, Cap?" Calvin Sellers, his ball turret gunner, said. "You think we can get some fried chicken when we get back?" Calvin was always hungry; he always hid snacks in his pockets.

Leonard Rogers, the tail gunner, started laughing. "Calvin, you know that ball turret only holds two hundred pounds before it falls off, right?"

"Cap, is that true?" Calvin asked.

"Relax, okay?" Jess Briton, the waste gunner, admonished. "Hey, what's the name of that artist that designed *Fifi*'s logo?"

Del Spears, the radio operator, said, "Disney. Walt Disney is his name."

"That's the guy who makes the mouse cartoons," Briton said.

"I can't believe he stayed out of serving by designing cartoons on the side of planes," said Luis Stark, the copilot. "I mean, hell, if all I needed to do was doodle to help the war effort, I woulda gone to art school! Please, fellas, don't take my comment the wrong way, but I'd rather be drawing on a hot Sunday in August instead of sitting on three thousand pounds of high octane fuel and enough TNT to blow my ass to the moon!"

"Stop your bellyaching," Tommy interrupted. "You couldn't draw a polar bear blinking in a snowstorm."

The crew all laughed, but their merriment was

tempered with the knowledge that they'd soon be on their mission.

Tommy asked Charles Sturgeon, his top gunner and flight engineer, how *Fifi* looked.

"Shipshape and ready to roll, Cap."

Tommy asked Alex Calder, his navigator, "We all set?"

"Yes, sir, Cap."

"Ray, everything good?" Tommy asked Ray Rietschel, the bombardier.

"Yes, sir."

"We're going to be the lead plane today."

All Tommy could think of was Rachel waking up alone in her bed, the fluffy comforter surrounding her as she lay naked. He pictured her pink nipples on her perky, soft breasts and how he would gently squeeze them, causing her to moan with delight. He could feel himself becoming aroused at the mere thought of her.

"Let her roll, sir," Dell said, cutting through Tommy's fantasy. "We're clear to go."

Tommy cleared his throat. "Ladies, please buckle your seatbelts and keep your hands and feet inside at all times. Snacks and coffee will be served when we reach fifteen thousand feet. Enjoy the flight."

Tommy taxied *Fifi* down the runway. He locked the brakes as he revved the engines one more time, double-checked the generator, locked the tail wheel in place, and set the gyros.

Tommy ramped up the engines and released the brakes, causing the plane to surge down the runway. *Fifi*'s engines whined as he lifted her fifty-five thousand pounds into the sky.

Tommy eased up on the engines as he climbed into the blue sky.

"Landing gear up?" He looked out the left side. "How about it, Luis?"

"Landing gear up," Luis confirmed.

Ten minutes later, they could all see the English Channel down below. The sweltering ground heat that previously filled the cabin was replaced with cool, clean air.

"Listen up, guys, let's not fall asleep," Tommy said. "I know we all had fun last night and we all want to go home. It's not a training mission, so be on your toes. We don't want any surprises today, okay? I have a pretty little lady I plan on returning to. Del, put on some music."

"Yes, sir."

Harry James played through the speakers.

I'll get by / as long as I have you. / Though there may be rain / and darkness too, / I won't complain, / I'll see it through. / Poverty / may come to me, that's true, / But what care I? / I'll get by / as long as I have you.

The altimeter read fifteen thousand feet with the coast

of France just ahead. *Twenty missions down and five to go*, thought Tommy. *Come on*, Fifi, *old gal. Don't let me down now.*

Soaring through the blue, Tommy's thoughts continued: *Rachel didn't want me to go. She said she had an uneasy feeling. But who doesn't? Look at this: no clouds, no antiaircraft fire, no German planes. What could possibly go wrong?*

I'm so close. I just need to get through five more missions and I get to spend the rest of my life with that beautiful, hot English girl who stole my heart. Tommy slipped his hand into his flight jacket, rubbing his fingers over the mark she gave him when she bit his nipple the night before.

"Hey, Cap? You know what I could really go for right now? Some fried chicken," Calvin said.

"Calvin, shut the fuck up about food! We're almost ready to drop our load and then home we go, understand?"

"All right, sir."

"Cap," Alex said, "we're ten minutes from target."

"How's she looking, Ray?"

"Good, sir."

"Hey, Chuck, those guys falling into single formation?"

"Yes, sir."

"Ray, whenever you want, *Fifi*'s yours. Be gentle with

her."

"I'll take her now, Cap."

"Okay, Ray. I'm going to take a quick nap. Wake me when we're—"

A loud explosion shook *Fifi.* Suddenly, the cockpit erupted into smoke and fire, with every alarm blaring. Tommy couldn't breathe from the burning smoke filling the cockpit.

"Bombs away!" he heard Chuck scream out.

"Chuck!" Ray yelled out. Chuck grabbed a fire extinguisher as Tommy banked to the left to get out of the way of the other planes making their bombing run.

Tommy could see blisters forming on his right hand from the heat of the flames. His jacket was smoldering as he brought *Fifi* down to ten thousand feet so the crew could breathe.

"Engine two shutting down, sir!" Luis screamed.

All the hydraulic oil had caught fire and the oxygen exploded.

"Crew, report in!" One by one, he heard their names. Tommy looked at Luis and rang the bell three times—the signal to prepare to bail out. Then, as Tommy leveled out the plane, he gave one final, long ring.

"Go, boys! I'm going to hold her steady!"

"Come on, girl," he whispered to *Fifi.* "I'm not leaving you. Not 'til the boys get off. Just a bit more, baby."

Engine three began to smoke while he fought for control. Tommy banked around to distance *Fifi* away from the town below.

All the crewmembers jumped out when he heard the next explosion, followed by Alex screaming, "Cap, we need to go!" Tommy felt Alex's hand on his shoulder as *Fifi* was beginning to tremble.

"You go, Alex!"

"Tommy, we'll find a way to land her!"

"Not without losing our lives. And that village below! Tell Rachel that I love her, Alex. Will you do that for me? Promise me!"

"I'm not leaving you!"

"Alex, this is not your ride. Go! Tell my sweet Rachel that I'm so sorry and that I love her like I've never loved anyone in my life. Tell her that I'll be back for her, the next time around."

Alex screamed something before he jumped, but Tommy couldn't hear anything anymore. Smoke filled his lungs, and his skin burned.

Then, suddenly, it stopped.

Tommy lifted his head and found himself surrounded by a blinding light. He felt enveloped by it, almost like he was floating, and a sense of calm took over.

The only pain he felt was the physical loss of Rachel—he would never feel her body again, look into her eyes.

Tommy sensed a presence with him.

"May I go back now?" Tommy asked the presence. "I don't want to be here. I want to be with her."

The presence responded, "Your time there is complete. If you return now, it will not be as you remembered."

"But I left the love of my life behind! I would do anything to get back to her," Tommy said. "Please?"

"Your sacrifice saved many lives. You've earned your rest. Here, you do not have to suffer wars, or pain, or death."

Tommy pondered this for a while and then responded, "You said there's no pain here, right? So why am I in the worst pain I've ever felt? I miss her with all of my being."

"Because she's your soul mate—your souls are forever intertwined. But should you choose to go back, there's no guarantee that you'll find each other again. Your soul is still attached to your human emotions. That will pass. I promise it will."

"No, please! I *must* go back to her. I promised! Please!"

Chapter 49

Grant's eyes opened. Ginger was asleep, curled up in her seat with her arm wrapped around his, her head resting against his shoulder. He could smell her hair and skin and didn't want to disturb her.

That was the most intense dream yet. Rachel and Tommy—did they really exist? Is someone opening a window to the past for me to look through? Why me?

The whole thing was just so crazy to Grant. He laughed, which woke Ginger.

"Grant, what's so funny?" She rubbed her eyes.

"Oh, let's just put it this way: I don't think Aunt Sadie

should ever read my palm again."

"Okay . . ." Ginger said, confused. She looked around. "How long until we land?"

"About an hour and a half. They'll be serving breakfast soon." He started sliding his hand up Ginger's dress. "So, baby, what would you like for breakfast?"

"You can't have *that* for breakfast." She giggled and pushed his hand away.

"Just teasing." He looked away awkwardly. "Mostly."

Within minutes, a flight attendant approached them. "What can I bring you two lovebirds for breakfast?" She handed them a menu and flashed a knowing grin.

"A mimosa and an extra hairy Bloody Mary to start, please."

"Coming right up."

They touched down at Charles de Gaulle Airport, and Ginger was bouncing with excitement. Grant could only smile at her enthusiasm, which heightened his expectation for the week.

After exiting the plane, getting their luggage, and going through customs, they walked out of the airport. By the exit, there was a man who held a sign that read, "Robinson/Madison."

They approached the handsome Frenchman. He wore a tailored gray suit and kept a neatly trimmed goatee. He hid his green eyes behind black-rimmed glasses, complimenting his short, black hair and light-olive skin.

Grant attempted to converse with him. "Bonjour, Monsieur. Je m'appelle Grant Robinson." He turned to Ginger. "Madame Ginger Madison."

"Good morning, Mr. Robinson, Ms. Madison. My name is Fabio." The chauffeur responded in perfect English but with a naturally romantic French accent.

"Whew. Obviously my French isn't very good."

"You spoke very well, sir. Monsieur Portier informed me that I am to be at your disposal all week while you are visiting our country. Please consider me your guide, translator, and whatever else you wish." He handed Grant a business card with his pager and car phone number.

Ginger and Grant held hands and followed Fabio to a Mercedes limo.

"Your first stop would be the Eiffel Tower Hilton, oui?" Fabio inquired.

"*Oui*, Fabio. Merci beaucoup," Ginger responded flawlessly. Grant rolled his eyes.

On the way to the Hilton, Fabio treated the couple to the scenic route, pointing out some of the well-known attractions: Le Louvre, Arc de Triomphe, Champs-Élysées, Notre Dame, Place de la Bastille. Ginger's eyes were glued to the window, soaking in every ounce of the historic sites.

"Gin, there it is, the Eiffel! Want to go to the top and make out—I mean, make a memory with me?"

"Either way, mon amour, I can't wait to see the view with you."

Overhearing their conversation, Fabio interjected, "When you're ready to visit the Eiffel Tower, my cousin has connections. Regardless of the line or time, he can get you to the top in a private elevator that is only reserved for special guests."

"Merci. We will take you up on that, Fabio."

Fabio pulled the limo in front of the Hilton, opened the door for Ginger, and retrieved their luggage. Grant slid out and handed Fabio some francs. "Monsieur, no. I would be insulting Monsieur Portier if I accepted anything from you. He is a man of great kindness. He has cared for my family over many years. Merci."

In French, Fabio called for the bellhops to attend to his occupants and treat them like royalty.

Walking into the grand lobby of the Hilton, Ginger and Grant were greeted by the hotel manager, a tall, handsome Frenchman who walked with confidence and style. He handed them each a glass of champagne. "Monsieur Robinson, Mademoiselle Madison, my name is Hayden. Please enjoy the champagne. It's Veuve Clicquot, a rosé. Monsieur, as per your request, the other six bottles are chilling in your suite. I do hope this pleases you."

"Oui, merci," Grant responded.

"I also wanted to inform you that your additional parcels have been delivered to your suite, along with the garment carts as requested. You will find a basket of fruits, cheeses, and caviar awaiting you as well."

"Merci," Ginger replied this time. "And the champagne is magnifique."

"Enjoy your suite and your stay with us. Anything you need, please do not hesitate to ask. If I am unavailable, I have informed Liam, the concierge, to assist you."

Upon entering their suite, Ginger stood in the foyer and soaked in the décor. It reminded her of the Louis XIV era. She ran to the bed and flopped on it with Grant a step behind her, jumping atop her. The ceiling over their bed had carved and painted figures in sensual positions. Candles dotted the room and the bucket of chilling champagne was within arm's reach on the ornate cherry wood nightstand.

"Ah, in bed again . . . but in Paris, bébé!" She couldn't hide her physical excitement any longer. Their kiss was long and tender. Grant buried his face into the nape of her neck, gently brushing his lips against her soft skin. He whispered, "Do you love me, Ginger?"

"You own my heart, blue eyes."

"I often wondered if I'd ever see you again after that time in Chicago, but so many years went by—"

"My sweet Grant," Ginger said, beginning to tenderly sob.

He traced her jaw line with his fingertips. "What's wrong, Gin?"

"I'm perfectly happy, Grant. Take me again, please. And I mean *take me*!"

They removed their clothing and lay on the bed. Grant's voice was hoarse with desire. "I want to play with your body for little bit."

He started by butterfly kissing her face and then leading his tongue down her neck to her breasts. Then he began biting and sucking each nipple. Her body quivered.

Gliding down to her belly, he sporadically sucked, kissed, and nibbled on her skin with his mouth. She could feel the heat of his breath on her clit while he moved from one leg to the other, suckling the inside of her knees, which amped her desire and need to cum. He could tell the anticipation of what he would do next was driving her insane.

Ginger's body reacted to his every touch. He pushed her legs into a bent position toward her head and licked the rim of her ass, crippling her with need. She grabbed handfuls of his hair and tugged tightly.

"Mmm." His sound reverberated throughout her ass and into her pussy.

Grant penetrated her hole with his tongue, keeping her on edge. He slid his hands around her ass cheeks and softly kissed the glistening lips between her legs. Grant delicately isolated her clit, caressing and sucking it with his tongue. He gently clinched it between his teeth. Taking his thumb and forefinger, he began to massage the small, erect clit while his tongue caressed the very tip of it, giving her a mini–blow job that ended in a wild climax.

Grant continued to take her pleasure to another level when he inserted three fingers into her now pulsating pussy, slowly sliding them in and out of her. After the third or fourth thrust, Grant added another finger, making her gasp with pleasure.

"More please."

He added his thumb and pinkie finger; her hot, wet cunt accepted his entire hand while she again moaned with pleasure, feverishly squirming on the bed.

Ginger's hands were wrapped up in Grant's hair, pulling his face deeper into her clit. She moved her hips in perfect rhythm with his fist and fingers, crying out, "Oh my God! Grant! What are you—oh, baby, I'm cumming . . . so . . . hard . . ." She crashed through some physical barrier that she'd never experienced, something completely beyond her imagination. "Baaaaaby . . ." Her voice trailed off and tears spilled from her eyes, blurring her vision and heightening her physical sensation.

Grant pressed against her flat tummy with the open palm of one hand and continued thrusting his other inside her. Ginger's body finally collapsed, and her senses were all over the place.

"Grant, I . . . I need to breathe. Breathe!" She gently pushed his head away from between her legs.

"Baby, I'm not finished with you." He flipped her over. "Ginger Madison, you're mine!"

"Grant, baby. Slowly, please?" She felt her insides contracting, pleasure mixed with pain.

"Of course, my naughty princess."

Slipping a pillow under her hips to tilt her ass upward, Grant mounted her from behind. Ginger was still trying to catch her breath when he plunged his cock deeply inside her.

She cried out his name, and with limited but deep thrusts of his hips, he let out a guttural cry as he began to explode inside her. Ginger eagerly took every ounce of his cum. He finally collapsed onto her back with his cock still ejaculating into her. They curled into each other and passed out.

A few hours later, they awoke in the same position. "Do you really believe in soul mates, Gin?"

"Yes."

"I believe that you're my soul mate. And I'm never

letting you go."

"Good. Don't," Ginger replied while reaching up to his swollen lips and kissing him.

Grant pulled her up on top of him. "Why are we here, Ginger?"

"In Paris?" she asked.

"No. This life."

"I don't know. Let's figure it out together."

Chapter 50

Grant and Ginger decided to do some recon at Le Printemps, the French department store that may define their future. Fabio joined Ginger and Grant inside to assist in translating. They were astounded by the large selection of women's accessories on the first floor.

"Every color you could imagine," Ginger said. "And to think, these are just the accessories!"

"What floor is women's wear located, Fabio?"

"You mean where my wife spends most of our money, Monsieur? Let me show you."

Exiting the escalator on the fourth floor, Ginger

squealed at the multitude of colors and designs. Meandering through the maze of displays and racks of clothing, she said, "Do you see what's missing?"

"Our line?"

"Oui, mon amour. I think we've got what he's looking for . . . and if not, we can design it for him." Grant could see her design wheels spinning.

"The first garment you fall in love with, it's yours, Gin. It will always remind you of today every time you look at it."

Fabio approached Grant while Ginger flipped through the dresses. "Monsieur Robinson, I thought you might be interested in knowing that Monsieur Portier is nearby speaking with one of his sales associates. Would you like to meet him?"

"Let me ask my partner first."

Grant walked over to Ginger.

"We can meet Monsieur Portier now or wait until our allotted time tomorrow. What do you think?" he said.

"Absolutely! He needs to see how invested we are in his store." She smoothed her hair and dress. "Do I look okay?"

"Absolutely stunning, babe."

"I'll take your word for it, Prince Charming." She giggled nervously.

Grant turned to Fabio and nodded his head. Fabio

immediately headed off toward Monsieur Portier.

Grant and Ginger watched the exchange between the two gentlemen. Monsieur Portier stood about six feet tall, was in his late fifties with long, gray hair pulled back in a ponytail and a full beard. He wore a double-breasted navy pinstriped suit with a pink boutonniere attached to the lapel. He clapped his hands together and grinned widely as he walked briskly toward Grant and Ginger.

Fabio introduced Ginger first and then Grant. "Monsieur Grant, I see you brought your secret weapon with you." Monsieur Portier's amber-colored eyes sparkled with life as he shook hands with Grant. He then cupped Ginger's hand while leaning in to give her a kiss on each cheek.

"It's a pleasure to meet you, Monsieur. Your collection is beautiful," Ginger said. She returned the double-cheek kisses.

"Secret weapon? I can feel my credit card burning a hole in my pocket, Monsieur." Grant laughed.

Monsieur Portier returned the laughter. "Madame Ginger, have you found something that fancies you?"

"But of course. You truly are an artist."

"Merci, Madame Ginger. Although, I can only take some of the credit, as I have assistance from the love of my life, my wife."

A sales associate popped the cork of a champagne

bottle, pouring three glasses.

Gabriel raised his glass toward Ginger and Grant. "A toast to our future. May it be long, friendly, and prosperous!"

All three glasses clinked. After their sip of celebration, Gabriel asked, "Madame Ginger, which dress pleases you?"

"This one right here, Monsieur." She held up the emerald-green dress. It was strapless, fitted, and fell right above the knee.

He immediately removed the tag with tiny scissors from his pocket. "Call me Gabriel, oui? This is my gift to you. I want you to remember today as the beginning of our friendship."

"But I couldn't, Gabriel."

"Oh, I insist. It would be an insult for a friend not to accept a gift. Madame, I cannot wait to introduce you to my beloved."

"Then, merci beaucoup, Gabriel."

As they rode back to the hotel in the limo, Grant asked Fabio, "We are still a bit jet-lagged and will need to nap. Do you have a place to recommend for dinner this evening?"

"Oui. Guy Savoy."

"Merci, Fabio. Please make a reservation for us around seven thirty. You've already done more for us than you may realize."

"Monsieur Grant, I assume you would do the same for me if I were in your country and was in need of assistance."

"I would."

A comfortable silence fell between them as the Hilton came into view.

"Just an observation, but I believe Monsieur Portier thinks highly of you both. I have worked with him for many years and am able to assess his thoughts via body language. Enjoy your rest."

Ginger was only slightly aware of the conversation between Grant and Fabio, as she was lost in a realm between sleep and consciousness.

Ginger thought about the impromptu meeting with Monsieur Portier. She wished that she could have told him that she too designed clothing with *her beloved*. However, that might be too personal for their first encounter. And then she again closed her eyes and drifted to sleep.

Grant slowly coaxed her back to reality with a kiss on her forehead.

A few hours later, Ginger woke up in a startle—they still had to prepare their line for the meeting in the morning. She woke Grant, and they started unpacking and steaming the garments.

They worked into the early evening when the sun set and all the lights from the Eiffel Tower started streaming through their French-door balcony. "Bébé, you've got to see this," Ginger said. "Take a break and bring your drink."

Both were wrapped in the hotel's fluffiest robes. He walked onto the balcony and filled her glass. "Madame."

"Let's make a toast to our love and future," Ginger whispered.

They clinked, sipped, and passionately kissed.

While she gazed at the lights of the tower, Grant wrapped around her body and whispered, "Ginger, you are more beautiful than anything that my eyes have ever seen, including the Eiffel."

Ginger leaned back into Grant as he continued.

"These moments with you are more beautiful than anything I thought life would bring me." He swept a strand of her hair behind her ear, kissing her neck. "And the words 'I love you' could not possibly begin to describe the feelings you've evoked in me. How did you do that?"

"Magic?"

Grant and Ginger's kiss was illuminated not just from within but by the Eiffel . . .

"Hungry, baby? Fabio suggested a place to dine tonight, unless you'd like to order in."

Ginger kissed the tip of his nose. "Probably safer if we go out, especially due to the growth between your legs. You know that robe doesn't hide much."

"I'll call Fabio. And for security purposes, maybe I should have him come up here while we get ready?"

"Grant Robinson! You make me laugh so much. I'm going to have smile lines before my time. Don't forget, I need to be a fit model in the morning."

"Fine, fine. I'll be dull. How long do you need to get ready?"

"Half an hour, Prince Naughty."

Chapter 51

After a delicious French meal at Guy Savoy, Ginger and Grant returned to the Hilton. They slid into bed, and Grant spooned against her naked body, feeling his semihard cock on her bare ass.

The six-hour time difference hit them hard. It redirected any of their sexual intentions into sleep.

Ginger drifted off into a dream.

Rachel and Isabella were trying their hardest to keep their spirits up, despite the fact that they hadn't heard from

Tommy or Alex in days. Each time the pub doors opened, they both immediately looked. With every ring of the phone, they would trip over themselves to answer it.

"Izzy, listen, maybe we should go shopping or something. A change of scenery will do us good, don't you think?" Rachel wrapped her arms around her best friend, who began to sob into her shoulder.

"I . . . I can't go through this again, Rach. This bloody war took my brother, and now it could possibly have taken Alex and Tommy."

Isabella couldn't stop crying, but Rachel stayed strong. "Izzy, if our fly-boys had to jump, it's going to take them days to get back to Britain—maybe even weeks. I know that wherever they are, they're thinking of us. I just feel it." She wiped the tears from Isabella's cheeks. "I can't stand another minute waiting for the door or the phone. Let's go! If they do come by when we're gone, I'll leave Ernie with strict instructions to call my aunt. She'll cheer us up. Grab your bag. Now!"

Rachel didn't give her a chance to argue. They left the pub and ran to the train station to catch the express to London.

After an uplifting visit with Aunt Marilyn, the girls went shopping. They were in a boutique when the air-raid sirens bellowed. Hordes of people immediately scurried in every direction—it was mass chaos.

Isabella and Rachel ran with the crowd to the closest bomb shelter and held hands until they were torn apart by the sea of scared people.

Rachel finally reached the shelter and looked for Isabella. She could hear the explosions going off outside. The sound of destruction deafened the sobbing and wailing in the shelter.

Rachel called Isabella's name out as loudly as she could over the mayhem and clawed her way to the shelter's exit.

When she exited, she was stunned at what she saw: Isabella stood on the bridge. Rachel desperately screamed at her, knowing she couldn't possibly hear her. Yet Isabella turned to her and held her arms up just as a V-2 rocket hit the bridge.

The shockwave of the explosion was so intense, it threw Rachel to the ground, along with others near the entrance of the shelter. After the dust finally settled, she looked out again only to see the bridge was gone—and so was Isabella.

Rachel called out her best friend's name. Crying, she fell into a crumpled mess on the floor of the shelter. The constant barrage of explosions kept on outside, and Rachel curled up and covered her ears, hoping the noise would soon stop.

Rapping at the door woke Ginger up. "Izzy?" she asked, confused.

Grant jumped out of bed at the sound of her voice. "What? Did we oversleep?"

The knocking continued. Grant rubbed his eyes. "That must be room service." He threw on his robe and answered the door.

Grant walked back into the bedroom carrying a cup of coffee for her. He noticed that she looked perturbed. "It's not that big a deal, babe. We're just a half hour behind."

"No, it's not that, Grant. I had an awful dream."

"Want to talk about it?" Grant smoothed her bed head hair from her face.

"Not particularly. I've just had odd dreams lately. But it's not important. I've got to get my head into what *is*—the biggest meeting of our careers!"

"There's my girl. Always able to shake it off."

Before they knew it, it was ten a.m., and Monsieur Portier was promptly knocking on the door for their meeting. Grant welcomed him and two other women into their suite. Ginger stood next to him, excited and nervous.

"This is the love of my life, my wife, Monette," Monsieur Portier said.

Monette was obviously younger than her husband by

a number of years. Her auburn hair was long and flowing and a few shades darker than Ginger's. Her facial features were soft, with gentle cheek lines. Her blue-green eyes hinted at strength and happiness within. She was the same height as Ginger, and her body and posture indicated that she had once been a model but now was a lady of business who held herself high.

"Wonderful to see you both again. Ette, do you see how well she wears the gift we gave her?"

"Oui, mon amour." Monette took Ginger's hand and spun her around.

"It's an honor to meet you, Madame Monette. Monsieur Gabriel beamed when he spoke of you."

"Merci, Ginger. S'il vous plait, refer to me as Ette, as my friends do."

"I would like to introduce you to Francesca. She will be our fit model for today," Gabriel said. "Francesca does not speak English, so we will be interpreting for her today."

Ginger led Monette and Francesca toward the racks of clothing, and Grant and Gabriel followed. Gabriel noticed the champagne in the ice bucket. "Monsieur Grant, you must have a little French in you, or you've adapted to our culture very quickly. May I do the honors?"

"If it pleases you," Grant responded.

"Ah, a rosé. I could never get Ette to drink a brut champagne that was not rosé. This is her favorite. She is unlike anyone I have ever met, my wife." He popped the cork and continued. "I believe you have someone like that in your life, Grant?"

"I do, Monsieur Gabriel." Grant looked in Ginger's direction.

"I saw it instantly yesterday. Your chemistry is palpable."

"We have something indescribable together. She is one of a kind." *Why do I already feel connected to this man? Am I fucking crazy? Yes! Crazy in this industry is good, right?*

"I know in America, it is not looked upon kindly to consume alcohol at work—thankfully, we are not in America! I believe Francesca should have a glass as well."

Grant poured another glass. "I love France," he proclaimed, and Gabriel nodded in approval.

"Ladies, before we begin, a toast is in order." Gabriel raised his glass with Monette sliding into his arm. Ginger and Grant each took a glass.

Raising his champagne flute, he said, "To life and how timeless it is when you are in love." All five clinked their glasses, and then Gabriel double tapped Monette's glass, kissing her before sipping.

The next few hours flew by, and with each moment, Monette and Ginger grew closer. While they were dressing Francesca in one of the last ensembles, Monette said,

"Everything that you design is *magnifique* and very fashion forward."

Francesca modeled for Gabriel, who was taking notes regarding styles, from time to time commenting to Grant yet always asking Monette for her opinion.

"I would like to share something with you, ma chérie." Looking into Ginger's eyes, she said, "He is your soul mate. I can clearly see it. You and Grant remind me of the younger Gabriel and myself and how we fell in love. Once upon a time, I was his fit model, and he saw me for more than a pretty face. Grant looks at you the same way, as my Gabriel still looks at me nearly forty years later. It feels as if we've known each other since the beginning of time."

Ginger hugged Monette. "Thank you—merci—a thousand merci for sharing such an intimate part of yourself with me, Ette."

"No, no, jolie. It is I who thank you for sharing your heart and soul. For *that* is the true meaning of life."

Ginger wiped the tears from her eyes, apologizing for being so emotional.

After Francesca modeled the final outfit, Ginger and Monette joined the two men on the leather sofas.

"I will inform you of our decision on Monday after Ette and I have time to review everything," Gabriel said.

Ginger turned to Monette and suggested that Francesca pick out her favorite piece as a gift.

Monette translated, and Francesca kissed Ginger on the cheeks. "Merci, merci."

Gabriel continued speaking with Grant. "As per our first conversation, Fabio will pick you up tomorrow around four thirty to spend the weekend with the rest of my family. Pack for a casual weekend. We will see you tomorrow evening."

"We are looking forward to meeting your family, Monsieur."

Chapter 52

After farewell hugs and kisses were exchanged with the Portiers and Francesca, Grant shut the door and turned his attention to an excited Ginger.

"That was an amazing meeting. I think we made a great impression, bébé."

Grant was speechless. He gently leaned into her forehead, resting and relishing the moment.

"What do you think, mon amour?"

Grant kissed her forehead and walked over to pop the cork on another bottle of champagne.

"You won't tire of me, will you, Gin?"

"Absolutely not. Why would you ask such a question?"

"Because I have a toast to make."

"You and your toasts . . ."

"To the love of my life." Then he dropped to one knee. "I should have asked your father for his blessing, but, Ginger Madison, will you spend the rest of your life with me? Will you marry me?"

"Are you trying to get laid again?" She laughed at him.

"Always. Ginger, will you be my wife, my lover, my best friend forever?" Grant asked.

"You're serious, aren't you?"

"I have never been more in love. With you, I feel like a whole person."

She dropped to the floor to be face to face with him. Ginger gently cupped his cheeks in her hands. "And you make me a better me. Grant Robinson, I would be honored to spend the rest of my life as your wife."

They kissed passionately and fell to the floor, wrapped up in each other's bodies.

Grant pulled a ring box from his pocket that contained his mother's ring. "Gin, it's not big, but it was my mother's. I will get you a new ring, whatever you want."

"It's perfect. Thank you, Prince Charming."

Grant slid his mother's ring on her finger—only, it

didn't fit and got caught at her knuckle.

"Your mother's hands were petite, huh?" Ginger laughed.

"Well, she wasn't five foot eight like you, baby."

"I love it, Grant. When we get back to the states, we'll have it sized."

"Okay. Let's just put it back in the box for now."

"So are we not engaged then?" she teased.

"Too late. You already said yes." He tickled her, which eventually turned into kissing. In no time, clothes were flying off in every direction.

Grant scooped Ginger's naked body off the floor and carried her toward the bed. Their lips never parted. She grabbed his hair, pulling him tighter and closer into her, their breathing needy and desperate.

Ginger was dripping with want as Grant laid her on the bed. She wrapped her legs around him while he slid his throbbing cock into her slippery lips. There was no time for foreplay; they were too hot for each other.

"Oh, yeah. Harder!" Ginger cried out.

Grant's body responded with unleashed passion. "Oh, Gin! I'm gonna—"

"Get off!"

"What?"

Ginger pushed and flipped him over onto his back. "I want to swallow your cum, every drop."

"Jesus, Gin!"

"Oops, guess I have to wind you up again."

She slid his cock into her mouth and sucked him just the way he liked it—softly at first, licking and sticking her tongue into the apex of his tip. She began nibbling the head of his cock harder, stroking his length with one hand and finger fucking his ass with her ring finger that she lubricated from her pussy.

"You taste so good. Where have you been, Prince Naughty? Have you been playing with pussy?"

"Yes, yes, yes—I was just fucking my fiancé."

His breathing became ragged, and Ginger could tell that Grant was close to an orgasm.

Grant was thrusting and moaning, and he tightened his grip on her head, pulling her hair to where it almost hurt—that good, sexual pain. She kept up with his hips as he let out an animalistic cry, erupting into her mouth.

Ginger kept swallowing until she sucked him dry.

Grant suddenly jerked his body away from her lips and finger. "Sorry . . . I can't take . . . anymore." He was barely able to get the words out.

"Did that feel good, bébé?" Ginger whispered as Grant pulled her body up to his face, taking a moment to catch his breath. Kissing her, he tasted his sexual pleasure in her mouth.

After lying for a while in their afterglow, Ginger

kissed Grant and asked, "I'd like to take a shower. Want to join me?"

"Sure, in a minute. But you need to know something. *I more than love you.* The word seems trite, trivial, and meaningless. Love. Does it cover the emotion of adoration? Desire? Treasure? Cherish?"

"Grant, *love* covers it all. How else could we say it?"

"I don't know. But creative minds like ours will discover the word that means more than *love*."

"Well, aren't you ambitious, ready to add to Webster's Dictionary!"

"*We* will."

"I just know that you're a mirror of my emotions, Grant."

"That's just the beginning of finding the phrase that means more than 'I love you.'"

"And for now, I am you, I mirror you, Grant Robinson."

"I mirror you too. So get that shower started and I'll call Fabio. What time should I tell him to be here?"

"About an hour, if you can keep your hands to yourself, my fiancé."

"Then back away, you temptress!"

"An hour and a half just to be safe, I can't promise you anything when you're naked." She flashed a wicked grin and disappeared into the bathroom.

Grant grabbed the phone. "Good evening, Fabio. We were thinking about an hour and a half from now. Does that work for you?"

"Of course. I will be there, Monsieur Grant."

"And there's that other stop that we spoke about. Is your cousin working tonight?"

"Oh, you mean my brother-in-law? Oui."

"Merci, Fabio."

"Will we be walking a lot tonight?" Ginger inquired after their shower, deciding how to dress.

"No, not unless you want to."

"And there's a New York–style bar in Paris? I guess that's a novelty here."

"Yeah, it's Harry's New York Bar. You'll see. Trust me."

As she braided her hair to one side, Ginger looked into the mirror and thought how quickly her world had changed. *Why am I so comfortable with this? If any friend of mine told me they were engaged to a man after less than a month, I would've called her a fool. Yet I feel like it's fate . . .*

Ginger chose a pair of Lycra leggings in a deep magenta and a lighter hue long-sleeved top. The sparkly silver belt was the main accessory to her outfit, complimenting her silver stilettos, which were accented with straps that crisscrossed around her ankles. Happy with her reflection in the mirror, she sauntered out to find her fiancé.

Grant was wearing a pair of silky jeans, an off-white, long-sleeved shirt, and a navy-blue blazer.

"Come with me, Grant." She led him by the hand to the full-length, gold gilded mirror. "Look at us, bébé." She loved the fact that even when she wore four-inch heels, he still towered over her.

"What a pair we are," Grant whispered, kissing her naked earlobes.

"A perfect pair." She reached up to kiss his soft lips.

"I think Fabio is already downstairs. Let's go enjoy the night, ma chérie."

As they crossed the river, Ginger asked, "So where is this place? Have you been here before?"

"Yes. It's a jazzy place to eat. Not far away."

Fabio turned onto Avenue de Friedland, drove two blocks, and stopped. "Monsieur Grant, your first stop. Don't forget to ask for Sydney."

"Merci, Fabio."

They parked in front of Tiffany & Co. Fabio opened the limo door for Ginger.

"Grant, where is this Harry's place? Are we walking from here?"

"Tiffany's *is* our first stop, my love. I would like my fiancé to have something to wear on her finger so that everyone will know you are spoken for."

"What? Here? No way."

"Indulge me, Gin. Please?"

"Grant, Tiffany's? Have you lost your mind? I'd marry you with a piece of tinfoil wrapped around my finger. Don't you get it?"

"I do. That's why I love you. At least look?"

Grant grabbed her hand, led her into Tiffany & Co., and asked for Sydney.

A tall man greeted them. "Monsieur Grant, it is my pleasure to meet you. Fabio speaks highly of you. Is this your bride-to-be?" Sydney kissed Ginger's hand.

"Oui, Sydney. This is Ginger, the love of my lives—um, *life*." Though Ginger barely noticed the error, Grant wondered why he had just said *lives*.

"A pleasure to meet you, Mademoiselle. Follow me to the back, if you will. I have prepared a collection for you to select from as per your request."

Ginger was agonized by the mere thought of the cost and tried once again to reason with him. "This is crazy. I have a perfect ring at the hotel just waiting to be sized."

"Well, there's nothing wrong with having more than

one ring to wear." The look in his eyes won her over.

They spent two hours looking through the most spectacular diamonds, picking out the ring, and waiting for it to be sized.

"Now she wears a ring that mirrors her beauty, if that is possible. The lights of the city are dim compared to her glow. Wear it well and forever."

"Merci, Sydney," Grant responded.

"My friends, you are always welcome. Madame Ginger, don't forget your little blue box."

Back in the limo, Ginger wore her new two-carat sparkling round solitaire diamond on her finger. She couldn't stop looking at it; she held it up as they passed streetlights, igniting a rainbow of colors everywhere.

"Once we're married, I suggest I manage the funds, for you, mon amour, have gone mad."

After spending the next few hours drinking, dancing, eating, and laughing at Harry's, Ginger and Grant returned to the Eiffel Hilton. After making love, the two lay in bed.

Grant listened to Ginger breathe softly; it was soothing to his soul. She was curled up against him. He could feel the warmth of her skin against his. Yet he was struggling with the fear of losing her, like waiting for some tragic event to occur.

She nuzzled into him.

Why is this bothering me? Why do I fear losing her so much? Is it because of these dreams I'm having of this Tommy guy? Is that the root of my fears? But it's just a dream, right?

He held her closer, feeling their connection. Then he quietly slid out of bed. He grabbed a vodka from the minibar, opened the French doors to the balcony, and walked outside. Just like his apartment, the view told its own story. The city lights were on display, indicating that the area teemed with activity, even at that hour of the night.

Grant leaned against the railing and admired the illuminated Eiffel. Sipping his drink, he tried to clear his head of his demons and dreaded dreams. He slammed back the clear, cool liquid, waiting for it to intoxicate his brain enough to bring about much-needed sleep. Still feeling way too sober, he went back to the minibar and grabbed two more little bottles. *That ought to do it.*

Standing on the balcony, he raised his glass in the air. "To you, Aunt Sadie, the palm reader." He looked around, but there was no one to hear him. In the moment of solitude, he looked at his palm and wondered what it was that she saw. He slammed back the second vodka. At last, Grant felt the numbness and decided it was time to crawl back into bed with the love of his life.

Grant rolled over and reached for Ginger, finding that she was not there. The breakfast cart Ginger ordered was loaded with an assortment of croissants, fresh fruit, cheeses, and coffee. Returning to bed with his cup of coffee, he propped himself up on a couple of pillows while he listened to the water running in the shower and Ginger singing in her best shower voice: *If you're lost, you can look and you will find me / Time after time; if you fall, I will catch you, I will be waiting / Time after time . . .*

Grant smiled at the sound of her voice. Not able to contain himself, he sneaked into the bathroom. He pulled back the shower curtain and burst into song: *Time after time!*

Ginger jumped and then blushed. Grant admired every inch of her wet, beautiful body and noticed the sparkle on her ring finger. He passionately kissed her while the shampoo dripped down her back.

"I hope you don't mind. I couldn't take it off, even for a shower."

"I'm glad it makes you happy, my love." Stepping into the shower, he tilted her head back and gently rinsed the shampoo from her long hair.

"*You* make me happy, my love."

Fabio dropped them off at Musée Rodin, the gallery of the famous French artist, Auguste Rodin. Ginger and Grant were enveloped in the beauty of the sculptures and paintings. They particularly enjoyed *La Danaïd*, a sculpture of a nude female created from marble.

"She reminds me of you, mon amour." Grant pulled her into him and kissed her bare shoulder.

The piece was finished in 1889. This sculpture's inspiration was an eighteen-year-old art student, Camille Claudel, who Auguste Rodin had fallen in love with.

"Great ass, you know?"

"Is that what makes you think of me?"

"And then some. This museum is so sensually intoxicating that I'm not sure if we will make it back to the hotel before I tear your clothes off—or even fuck you with your clothes on."

Ginger winked at Grant, encouraging his behavior.

Further along in their tour, they stood in front of Rodin's *The Kiss*, circa 1898. They followed suit and mimicked the sculpture's kiss, although they left their bodies covered, unlike the lovers in stone before them.

"I feel so connected to this sculpture. Rodin captures the essence of their passion," Ginger said.

"You could have been the inspiration for this one

also."

"How—?"

"Pure beauty, ma chérie. A woman's body is a work of art. And you—lucky me—have the finest artwork."

Ginger giggled. "Prince Charming *and* Horny. You always know the right thing to say." She kissed his neck right below his ear.

Next was a sketch enhanced with watercolor from the 1900s: *Avant la création.* They were both aroused by the beauty of the naked woman, her legs spread while lying on her back.

"It's erotic and romantic at the same time."

"I couldn't agree more, my fiancé."

"*Fiancé!* I love that word! And after we're married, my new favorite word will be *husband.*" Ginger kissed his beautiful face.

They enjoyed a late lunch in the garden and decided to finish touring the last few rooms. Grant and Ginger were floored by the huge bronzed double doors called *The Gates of Hell.*

The demons on the door made the hair on the back of Grant's neck stand on end. Right in the middle of the transom sat a man lost deeply in thought: the Thinker. That reminded Grant of himself. The nude couple kissing troubled him; they were not depicted as being happy—it was more of a broken love. Grant gripped Ginger's hand tightly.

"Being that this is the last thing we've seen, I hope it isn't an omen of what's to come."

"No, no, my love. This piece represents Dante's *Inferno*, a fourteenth-century poem. Look at the date: 1879. It was *his* hell, *not ours*. We only have years of pure love and bliss ahead of us." Ginger hoped she comforted him—in reality, she was trying to reassure herself also.

Redirecting his thoughts to just the figures in lust, Grant whispered, "Ready to head back to the hotel, babe? I need to take a nap with you."

"Monsieur, it doesn't *feel* like you want a nap." She grinded into him.

"Perhaps we'll need a nap after we . . . *nap*?"

Ginger became quiet as they walked toward the exit.

"Gin, are you okay?"

"Will you always love me like this? Is it possible to be *in love* forever?"

Grant faced her, holding both of her hands to his heart. "Ginger, I've never been so in love, *ever*. And please don't take this the wrong way, but the way we make love is beyond anything I ever knew was possible."

"No man has ever loved me the way you love me, Grant."

Chapter 53

Grant and Ginger took a much-needed nap after indulging themselves in licking, sucking, fingering, and intense fucking. When they woke, they quickly packed for the weekend.

It was a beautiful seventy-degree September day. Inside the limo, Grant placed his arm around Ginger. He weaved his fingers through her hair, gathering a handful to tug on, just like when he took her body from behind. He leaned over to kiss her and moved his other hand onto the crotch of her pants. Ginger guided his hand to her exact pleasure spot.

The limo left the city and they were coasting through the countryside.

"Fabio, may we have a little privacy, please?"

"Oui, Monsieur." He closed the dividing window, leaving Ginger and Grant alone.

Due to time limits, they tried to keep it "civil." She pinched his nipples and grabbed his leg. "Bébé, you make my mouth water." She squeezed the base of his throbbing cock, never loosening her grip until she reached his crown through his jeans. Precum soaked through the thick material from his excitement.

"Your touch is magic, Gin."

Ginger couldn't undo his belt and unzip his pants fast enough. She knelt before him, sucked and licked the tip of Grant's velvety erection. She lifted her top, releasing her breasts and allowing Grant's dick to slide between them, masturbating him with her perky twins.

She already knew his sexual sounds by heart and was compelled to pleasure him. She sucked and stroked him with that sensual twist of her wrist. His hips thrust upwards while she gently rubbed her thumb on his most sensitive spot and tongued the tip of his pulsing, steely dick. She held his balls tightly, knowing his climax was beginning to take over.

Ginger wet her finger by sliding it into her sopping wet pussy and rimmed his ass, but not completely entering.

Then he came. Hard and long. She tried to swallow it

all, but she could scarcely keep up with the amount of semen that exploded into her mouth.

Ginger leaned up and kissed him; she saved just a little bit of his perfect taste for him. "I love the way you taste, don't you?"

He kissed her deeply.

The limo began to slow just as Grant was about to rip off her pants and mount her from behind. "Baby, I need to be inside you."

"Grant, we can't. We're almost here. Get dressed, my sexy lover."

"You're not off the hook, you know?"

"I don't ever want to be off *your* hook," Ginger shot back at him.

"I'm burying my cock inside you tonight—the first chance we get."

"Good. I *need* you."

Fabio spoke over the intercom and announced that they were arriving at the Portier property.

"Merci, Fabio," Grant replied, trying to hide the fact that he was out of breath.

Ginger and Grant looked out the windows and saw the beautiful farmland. There was a silo and two barns, with horses, cows, and sheep out in the field. The rounded home front had a water tower with a weather vane atop. The buildings were all connected and easily the length of a football field or more.

The two exited the limo. Ginger noticed the tall grass blowing in the wind. "Where are we, cowboy?"

Grant smiled. "It seems familiar, doesn't it?"

She couldn't contain her excitement. "I positively love it!"

Gabriel Portier was assisting his grandchildren to ride the ponies. He waved to his new guests. He was clearly in casual mode, wearing a straw hat, jean shorts, a white linen button-up shirt, and a pair of boots. He headed toward the limo to greet Grant and Ginger.

"Bonjour, bonjour! So happy you've arrived." Gabriel kissed Ginger on the cheek and shook hands with Grant, which turned into a gentleman's hug.

"Merci! We're so happy to be here, Monsieur Portier—Gabriel," Ginger responded.

"Come now, let me introduce you to my grandchildren." Turning toward his grandchildren, he said, "Je voudrais vous presentez mes nouveaux amis d'Amerique, Madame Ginger et Monsieur Grant."

A few jumped and squealed while two had hopped off the ponies, all lining up. Each child waited their turn to walk up and greet Grant and Ginger individually.

The boys kissed Ginger's hand while the girls kissed Grant's cheek.

They met Maurice, Olivia, Gaby, Mikel, Aiden, and

Edward. The eldest grandchild, Aksel, spoke English with that spellbinding French accent. "How do you do? My name is Aksel. It is a pleasure to make your acquaintance."

"It's our pleasure, Aksel," Ginger responded. Just then, Olivia grabbed Ginger's hand and said, "So pretty, you are. Would the pony like to ride with me and you?" Her English was broken, but it was clear enough for Ginger to understand.

"Oui, mon amour, oui!"

"You like?" Monsieur Gabriel inquired. "This, mes amis, is our favorite place to gather the family."

"Like? Amour!" Ginger spoke with such enthusiasm that Gabriel couldn't hold back his laughter.

At that moment, Madame Monette and Cherise, her daughter, joined them with outstretched arms. "Ginger, Grant, bonjour!" She hugged them both. "I see you've met our lovely grandchildren. This is my daughter, Cherise. She's blessing us with yet another grandchild in a few months. The rest of our children are relaxing on the porch. S'il vous plait, come and meet them."

Ginger turned to Olivia. "May we ride the pony later? I would like to meet your parents and aunts and uncles."

"Oui, Madame Ginger." Her innocent smile melted Ginger's heart.

Grant and Ginger entered the covered porch, finding a mass of people waiting to meet them. The next hour was spent exploring the new relationships while drinking a plethora of alcoholic beverages. Though each Portier family member worked for Le Printemps in some way, Grant was impressed that there was no shoptalk. He knew it was the family's opportunity to get to know them.

Relaxing and enjoying the evening, the early fall breeze swept across the porch, and the nearly full moon began its rise.

After some time, the chamberlain announced, "Le dîner est servi." The grandchildren went to the table set for them, and the adults gathered around the elongated weathered antique table in the dining room, large enough to seat fourteen.

Ginger was relishing in the beauty of the ornately decorated room. Photographs, paintings, and sculptures surrounded the table.

Gabriel raised his glass, to which everyone followed suit. "To the beauty of life, all it has to offer, and new friends."

They clinked glasses filled with the finest Pinot Noir.

Dinner was a French gourmet serving of fresh seared salmon and scallions in wine sauce. Ginger was grateful for the etiquette classes her mother insisted she attend as a child as she swiftly recalled which fork to use at the proper time. Dessert was a chocolate soufflé with a dripped lemon cream sauce, creating decadence on a dish.

After dinner ended, Gabriel and Monette joined Grant and Ginger on the porch for a late-night espresso. "The darker the bean, the less the caffeine," Monette said, reassuring Ginger that she would be able to sleep.

Gabriel asked if Grant would join him for a horseback ride in the morning.

"Oui, Gabriel."

"And I promised Olivia I would ride the ponies with her in the morning."

Monette giggled. "Ginger, we're so much the same. Small horses, oui; big horses, eh."

Ginger raised her cup of espresso to Monette. "I want to be like you when I grow up."

"Merci, mon amour. Tomorrow, I have arranged for the ladies, even our little ones, to be pampered by our coiffure. She will arrive with many assistants. They will work on your hair or nails or give you a body massage. Whatever you wish."

"Ette, you are spoiling me."

"We deserve it, mon amour. What do our men love about us? That we keep ourselves belle, attractive, and sexy, no?"

Though Gabriel and Grant pretended not to hear the ladies' conversation, Gabriel responded, "Mon amour, you are so beautiful. Do whatever you wish, for I adore looking at you."

Monette walked over to Gabriel, sat in his lap, and whispered loud enough that Grant and Ginger heard, "I believe it's time for bed."

Gabriel jumped up and said, "And goodnight, my friends. You know where your room is. Enjoy the home, the fields, everything like it was your own."

Gabriel and Monette left, and Ginger watched as Gabriel kissed Monette's neck as they walked upstairs, knowing exactly what they had in mind—the same thing she did.

"So, Grant, would you like to explore the property or—?"

"I'd like to explore more of your body. Let's tour our bedroom."

Entering their room on the third floor, Ginger and Grant found their suitcases were unpacked and their intimate belongings placed in drawers, their shoes and outfits displayed in the closet, and their toiletries neatly placed in the bathroom.

Ginger removed her top and was heading toward the bed when Grant grabbed the back of her pants and gently tugged at her while locking the door.

"And your pleasure, my prince?"

"You. All of you." He spun her around and pushed her up against the door. He unbuttoned her pants and fondled her ass cheeks.

Ginger removed her panties, and Grant dropped to his knees to assist her. While she slowly stepped out of the soft fabric, he stood up and held her wrists over her head against the door with one hand. With his other hand, he unhooked her bra in one fell swoop. "Show off," she said.

Sucking and biting her nipples, he finally lowered and honed directly onto her wet, throbbing clit while sliding three fingers into her. Grant knew after a few thrusts of his hand and the way she breathed that she was nearing an orgasm.

To her dismay, he stopped, her hips midstride. He carried her sex-craved body to the bed. She spread her legs. Obligingly, he slid his cock into her wet pussy. Grant could feel her inner feminine muscles gripping his cock. Her eyes rolled back into her head. He knew he owned her—the way she owned him.

Their rhythm was uniquely in sync for such a short romance, and Ginger began to quickly fly toward blinding ecstasy each time Grant drove his thickness in and out of her. Pumping. Thrusting. Fucking. Knowing she was getting closer to the edge, he let her grind upward into him, burying his dick farther into her.

He covered her mouth so no one else could hear her moans. He felt the knot in her cunt with each thrust until she quietly cried out, biting his hand. Tears rolled down her cheeks.

He watched her face, studying everything, even the batting of her wet eyelashes as she tried to regain her focus. Seeing her bask in the afterglow of such an incredible orgasm, his cock still inside her, incited his need.

Ginger locked her legs around him, not allowing him to pull out. She sucked the rosy-colored disc of his nipple.

He lost all control. Grant began thrusting deeply inside her. Ginger was still biting him when he soared into orgasmic bliss. She quickly placed her hand on his mouth, and he bit down on her palm while he came, still feeling her pussy sucking his dick, which drove him even more over the edge.

She breathed into his ear, "Feel that? It's what you do to me. Feel it. You're *mine*! Fill me with everything you've got. Feels . . . soooo . . . good!"

His extended orgasm shook his body to the core. He hovered above Ginger and wondered aloud, "Still want to marry me, Gin? I can't live without you."

Their faces were inches apart, breathing in each other's breath.

"Oui," Ginger whispered her response.

Grant's breathing slowed. They rolled onto their sides and fell asleep, still connected with him inside her.

Chapter 54

Tommy found himself sitting on the bench in Rachel's garden, watching her work with the dirt—one of his favorite things to do. She looked in his direction—almost as if she was looking *through* him. A soft smile crossed her lips. He smiled back and blew her a kiss, yet she didn't respond like she always did. He thought maybe she didn't see it and decided not bother her. Tommy leaned back and relaxed, enjoying the view: the birds singing, the butterflies flittering around, her body in the early morning sun.

He felt the warmth of the sun as it rose higher in the sky; however, there was a chill in the air. Tommy heard the gate open and footsteps walking down the path of the garden. It was Alex.

"Hey, buddy. It's about time you got here," Tommy said, but Alex didn't respond or even look at him. Rachel's face immediately turned red and blotchy when she saw him. She collapsed to the ground without Alex speaking a single word.

"Please tell me he's just hurt, Alex. *Please*!" Rachel pleaded. "He'll be okay, right?"

Alex bent down and wrapped his arms around her shaking body, trying to stay strong enough to do what he promised Tommy he would do. "I'm so sorry, Rach. He's gone."

Rachel cried out.

He held her tightly. "Rach, honey, he saved the entire crew and a small village in France. I would have gone down with him, but he wouldn't let me. He . . . he told me to find you and give you a message."

Rachel was curled up in a bawling mess of tears and dirt while Alex held her.

"What did he say?" she asked through her tears.

"He said . . ." Alex's voice broke. "He said that he's sorry, that he loves you like he's never loved anyone in his life. He said . . . he said that he'll be back for you the next time around."

With those words, she allowed the harsh reality to

shred her heart and soul to pieces. The truth that she lost her soul mate, the love of her life, was just too much to bear . . . there was no room for hope anymore.

Alex kept a hold of her while she wept, whispering, "My sweet Tommy," over and over.

"No, no, no, no," Tommy said. "I'm right here, my love. Rachel? Alex? Buddy?" At that moment, Tommy finally realized that he wasn't really there.

"I . . . I never did make it back, did I? What have I done to her?"

He cried out to her as his surroundings faded away into nothingness . . .

Rachel had finally gathered her composure. Alex sat with her inside her cottage. She was cooling her neck and face with a dampened cloth, leaning against the kitchen counter. Sipping a neat whiskey, her body still trembled.

"I'm so sorry, Rach. I went by the pub to get Izzy to come with me to tell you, but no one would tell me where she was. They told me that I should just find you, that you would be home. Where is she, Rach?"

Rachel again burst into tears, and she jumped back into Alex's arms, not able to look him in the face. Instantly, Alex knew Isabella was dead. "No . . . how? What happened?" Tears streamed down Alex's face. "I love her so much. What happened?"

Rachel could barely get the words out. She explained the bombing raid. "She lost all hope, Alex. She thought you were gone." She hugged him tighter. "She loved you so much, she couldn't live without you."

Alex dropped to the wood floor, and Rachel draped herself over his sobbing body.

"We've both had the most important souls taken from us because of this bloody war," Rachel said. "Who cares who wins at this point? You and I have already *lost.*"

A gentle knock on the bedroom door awoke Ginger and Grant from their deep sleep.

"Monsieur Grant? Madame Ginger?" Sybille, une femme de ménage, spoke through the door. "The time is eight thirty. You requested to be stirred after eight. Breakfast has been prepared and la famille Portier awaits your arrival."

"Merci, Sybille," Grant responded, nearly jumping out of bed. Ginger rolled over and stretched. Parts of the dream filled her head. She wiped a few tears away so Grant wouldn't see her sadness. It was only a dream, after all, and it quickly slipped away.

Grant pulled on his jeans, splashed water on his face,

and brushed his teeth. Still shirtless, Ginger watched him put his boots on. "Oh, my cowboy. You must have gotten in a cat fight last night."

"Of what do you speak, mon amour?"

"That, that, there, and there," pointing out a few bruises, hickeys, bite marks, and scratches.

"Jesus, Gin. What the hell did you do to me?" He laughed at his reflection in the mirror, examining his upper body.

"Don't put your shirt on yet, bébé. You look so hot. Hair tousled and cowboy boots. Lucky me!"

"Maybe we can take a 'nap' after I return from horseback riding with the guys."

"Sounds like a plan, Prince Hop Along. And I do mean *hop* and *long*." She guffawed. "Although, I'd be lying if I said I didn't want to *hop* you right this minute."

Grant crawled on top of Ginger's naked body, kissing her nipples, neck, and finally her lips. To her surprise, he suddenly flipped her over and bit her ass hard enough to leave a mark; she squealed uncontrollably.

"You brat! It's a good thing I'm desperately in love with you."

Grant pulled on a soft, blue fitted T-shirt and a lightweight flannel, showcasing just how perfect his body was. He grabbed a cowboy hat, which complimented his look, further igniting Ginger's thrill of the fact that he was hers—all hers. Ginger slipped into a sunflower-printed sundress and strappy brown sandals. They kissed and walked down three flights of stairs to find most of the family gathered around the kitchen counters.

After eating a light breakfast, Grant and the rest of the Portier men left for the morning ride.

Ginger felt unusually at ease with the Portier women, including the two little ones, Olivia and Gaby. Sybille and Celeste cleared the table while the ladies retreated to the living room. On the buffet serving table, there were mimosas for the ladies and orange juice for the girls, all in the finest crystal champagne flutes.

"Ma chérie, I adore your sundress," Monette said.

"Thank you, Mom—pardon me! Merci, Ette." Ginger blushed. The girls giggled. "And I haven't even had a sip of my mimosa yet!"

"Oh, dearest, I have room in my heart for another daughter. Speaking of which, do you happen to have a sister for my youngest son, Felipe? He's such a playboy. I'm not sure if he'll ever settle down."

"No, I am the only girl. I have a brother. I've been blessed with wonderful parents who have been married for nearly forty years."

"I surmised you came from a loving family. Am I to assume you designed the dress?"

"Oui. It was one of my first designs. To this day, I

still adore it."

Shortly thereafter, Hugo, the chamberlain, let the trio of female coiffures in: Madeline, the hairdresser; Natalie, the nail tech; and Zara, the masseuse.

Olivia and Gaby were excited to get their nails painted. Ginger suddenly felt overwhelmed with the decadent spoiling.

"Don't forget, Olivia, after our nails are dry, we will ride the ponies. Gaby, will you join us?"

"Oui, Madame Ginger. I like you a lot."

"And I like you too."

Meanwhile, Grant and the others rode along the riverbank. Monsieur Portier was slightly ahead of Grant, who rode close to Monsieur Portier's son, Gabriel. They were followed by Maurice, Felipe, and Tomas.

Gabriel said, "Let's make life a bit easier: call me Gabe. And by the way, my father really admires your boots. Do you happen to manufacture those? If not, maybe I can enlist your assistance in finding a pair for his next birthday."

"Unfortunately, I don't make them, Gabe. But I certainly know where to get them, and I'd be honored to send a pair."

"Merci, Grant."

Tomas galloped a bit closer, breaking the two rows of

three riders. "You are from New York, oui? And a Yankees fan, Monsieur Grant?"

"Not really. I prefer the Mets. I can get you a Mets hat, hot off the press, but I'm not touching a Yankees hat."

The small talk continued over the next half hour while they rode at a leisurely pace. Monsieur Portier slowed the ride even further and guided the horses to the cement watering trough.

Each man dismounted his horse, tying it to the trough.

"Grant, we have not yet personally spoken about your clothing line," Gabe said.

"This is true, Gabe. I thought when the time was right, we would."

"And now seems parfait to tell you what my parents thought about it."

"And what are their thoughts?"

"They thought your line was, shall we say, very fashion forward and think it would be an asset to Le Printemps."

"And do you feel you need to see our clothing as well? We can arrange for—"

"No, no, no. Mon père and mère are very successful in choices. I trust their judgment. However, what concerns me is whether or not your company can deliver on a timely basis. We are in separate countries, halfway around the globe. And to be totally honest with you, I had an interesting conversation with a Howard Gold . . . is that his name? He is your partner of sorts, oui?"

"Howard Golden. He's the owner of the company. And I have never missed a deadline with any client. As far as shipping to France, I am prepared to ship internationally. It is already in place in my company."

"Grant, I feel I can be forward, I found him to be ill-mannered and easily irritated with questions regarding performance. After conversing with him, I suggested cancelling your trip. But once mon père spoke to you personally, he felt you were worthy of our time. So in the future, I would prefer to only work with you. Is that a problem?"

"Not a problem at all. In fact, Howard Golden is not involved with all of my work."

"Good. Trust is important in my family. There's one last question."

"Whatever you need to ask, please feel free, Gabe."

"Will you personally guarantee that if we decide to move forward with you, everything will be in a timely fashion?"

"Gabe, Ginger and I are a great duo, and we have an unbelievable team of seamstresses. Although this is through H&M, I am fully prepared to bypass Howard Golden's inequities."

Gabe reached his hand out to shake Grant's. "Then I

will suggest to Papa to place the order with confidence. I look forward to a friendly working relationship, Grant."

They shook hands. "Merci."

"Oh, one last thing, Grant," Gabe said. "I want exclusivity to Paris. Would that create an issue?"

Holding back his emotions, Grant responded, "Not for Ginger or myself. We are on the same page, Gabe."

"Excellent."

After a few more minutes, the men remounted their horses.

Felipe said, "Let's race back to the stables. Come on, Tomas. You have nothing to worry about. I gave you the fastest horse this time." He took off.

Gabe slapped the backside of his horse and screamed, "Yippee-kai-yay!"

Maurice tried to mimic his brother's enthusiasm, but it came out, "Eee-yay-kai-yipee!"

Grant leaned into his horse and whispered, "Let's get them, baby." He sped off.

Monsieur Portier lagged behind and happily soaked in the vision in front of him. Though it seemed too good to be true, sometimes, things just are—good and true.

Grant passed Felipe, who was the leader of the pack, leaning into his horse like he was a jockey. Grant looked back and saw Monsieur Portier way behind everyone. He gently eased up on his horse until he was next to Gabriel.

Gabriel smiled at Grant. "I see you have many talents, Grant. I won't tell my boys you let them win."

By the time the two arrived back at the stables, the brothers were arguing over who actually won.

Madame Monette announced that dinner would be served around seven and everyone was free to spend their time as they wished.

Grant retreated to the guest room to find Ginger lying in bed covered by a thin sheet. It seemed she was sleeping, so he decided to shower before crawling into bed with her. Grant entered the shower, and all he could think of was Ginger's naked body just a few feet away from him. He showered the smell of horse off his body and wrapped a towel around his waist.

Walking into the bedroom, he found Ginger with her knees bent and spread, fingering herself; her eyes were closed and she was licking her lips. She opened her eyes when she felt his presence and looked at him. Unabashedly, she did not stop pleasing herself because it clearly aroused him.

Grant's cock was instantly hard as he climbed into bed with her. He sucked her perfectly pedicured toes while she brought herself to orgasm. They fucked around with each other's bodies for almost two hours.

Chapter 55

Grant gave Ginger a recap of his conversation with Gabe while they dressed for dinner.

"Gabe has made it clear to me that he doesn't want to deal with Howard again."

"Neither would I if I had any say."

"And he asked me to personally guarantee a timely delivery."

"So it sounds like they want to work with us. But what if Howard screws everything up?"

"Then we leave his ass high and dry and go to Terri."

"Yeah, Terri will take care of us."

"But it would be a big change for us. We'd have to save money for a while to get everything in place and in motion."

"Listen, bébé," Ginger said, "if you don't have enough money, you know I have my own, and even my dad can help us. This is our *dream*. Let's make it our *reality*."

He kissed her passionately. "My beautiful, smart girl."

They finished getting ready and joined everyone for dinner. Dinner was another amazing French gourmet delight starting with the most delectable escargot appetizer and freshly baked baguettes. The children and adult tables were rowdy and filled with laughter. The vino flowed like water, and time flew by. And the brothers still bickered over who won the race.

After the children settled down for the night, the adults sat out on the porch and enjoyed the cool evening air.

Monsieur Portier walked behind the outside bar, retrieved a bottle, and popped the cork. He cleared his throat, and everyone quieted to listen.

"My dear family and friends, I would like you all to join me in a toast." Everyone gathered while Gabriel poured the champagne.

"Gabe and I have spoken in regards to working with Monsieur Grant and Madame Ginger. We have decided to move forward with their line of clothing," he said while lifting his glass. "Yet no further business discussion tonight, other than a toast to you both: may we have a long, prosperous, and happy friendship."

The last two couples were winding down the evening on the porch.

"I don't suppose you will turn down a glass of brandy, would you, Grant?"

"Most certainly not, Gabriel. Is that a bottle of Armagnac?"

"Ah, so you are familiar with this brandy?"

"Oui."

He poured the brandy and sat back. He addressed Grant and Ginger. "I want to share with you tomorrow something that has affected my heart over four decades. It's a short drive from here, but I believe you might find it interesting." Monette sat on her husband's lap and kissed his cheek lovingly.

"We would be honored," Ginger said.

"I have a feeling it has something to do with Madame Ette."

"Ah, Grant. You are a very intuitive man. Look around. What do you see? My children, my grandchildren, this house, the lands, all filled with *happiness*. Tomorrow, you will see why it is such a gift to me."

Grant looked out the bedroom window, admiring the view of the moon over the tall, waving grass. "It looks like it will be a full moon in a night or two, Gin."

After hearing no response, he turned to see Ginger soundly asleep.

He looked back out the window and saw a shooting star. *I guess I'm supposed to make a wish now.* "My wish is that I never lose the love of my life again," he whispered.

He climbed into bed and wrapped around Ginger's warm body, the moonbeams dancing through the window. He fell fast asleep; finally, a dreamless night.

Wrapped up in a bathrobe and a towel on her head, Ginger kissed Grant's cheek. "Wake up, mon amour."

Grant rolled over and stretched his arms over his body. The covers slipped down just below his waist, showcasing her favorite muscles. "Grant Robinson, I fucking love and lust you."

She jumped on top of him and covered him with kisses, tickling his waist, feeling an erection starting.

"Oh no, Prince Erector Set. We have no time for that—as much as I want it. Monsieur Portier is surely waiting for us by now."

After breakfast, Fabio drove the two couples farther into the farmland. Nearly twenty minutes later, they were at the edge of the town of Incarville.

"I have visited this particular spot every year on the thirteenth of August since 1944. This year's visit was extremely emotional because it was also the day we were able to purchase this piece of land."

They stepped out of the limo into the lush farmland. Immediately, Grant felt uneasy. Ginger felt his body stiffen. She looked at him, trying to gauge his demeanor.

There were small groupings of old trees that provided shade to livestock and the wild birds that were singing in them. The freshly cut hay and summer flowers all added their aroma to the air.

"This, my friends, is where a very important part of my life begins, a story to tell, if you will."

Fabio placed a wreath of purple, blue, and pink flowers against a collection of rocks. Watching Fabio, Ginger felt something yet had no idea what it could be. Grant was still distant and quiet.

Gabriel looked toward the sky, smiled, and then wrapped his arms around Monette. He kissed her forehead. "When I was a youngster, just a boy at the time, I saw something that changed my life. It was during World

War II. I watched American planes heading toward the rail bridge to bomb it. They were attempting to stop the Germans from reinforcing their troops." He pointed in an easterly direction. "I witnessed the lead plane get hit by German antiaircraft fire just over the town. The *Fifinella*, as I later learned it was named."

Grant's eyes widened as Gabriel said the name.

"The pilot continued his bombing raid despite the fact that his plane was fatally impacted. Somehow, he managed to keep his plane in the air long enough to allow his crew to jump from the dying aircraft.

"The pilot managed to maneuver the fiery plane safely away from the town. I watched as a final crew member jumped, thinking it was the pilot. The plane went down in this field, and in so doing, it saved the lives of the villagers." Gabriel pointed all around him.

"I later learned that the pilot went down with his aircraft. Now that we own the land, I am going to erect a memorial for him, Thomas P. Smith Jr., to keep his heroic sacrifice alive."

Ginger was teary eyed at this point, and Grant looked ashen. She was shocked at his demeanor.

"This man sacrificed his life to save a whole village. Imagine who he left behind." He gently grasped Monette's chin and kissed her.

"Consequently, as I briefly mentioned, that moment

in time changed my life. Understand, my Ette lived in this village the pilot saved."

Grant said nothing, so Ginger chimed in. "Monsieur, merci for sharing that with us."

"Madame Ginger, one of the reasons I decided to search for a business connection in America is due to this man and what he represents. Perhaps it may mend some broken hearts he left behind."

Grant's brain was desperately scrambling to analyze everything. The puzzle pieces instantly fit together: *Dan was buying property from a Mr. Smith, who lost his brother, a B-17 pilot, during World War II. The name of the plane in the picture was* Fifinella. *And Mr. Smith said his brother's name is Thomas. Thomas Smith. The same Thomas Smith from my dreams?* He felt shockwaves throughout his entire being.

He cleared his throat and said, "Monsieur, I told you I spent summers in Baraboo, Wisconsin. Nearly a month ago, I was visiting my cousin, who purchased a farm that belonged to a family named Smith. They lost a family member during World War II in a B-17 crash. His picture still sits on their mantel."

"Are you inferring that this Smith family may be related to Thomas Smith? Are you able to find out?"

"It would seem a long shot, but I will inquire. I can call my cousin, Dan, from your home, if you wish."

"The more I know, the better; the sooner I know, the sweeter."

Back at the Portier retreat, Gabriel said, "There is a telephone in the kitchen. You remember the country code for the states, mon fils?" Gabriel had just referred to Grant as a "son" in French.

"Oui. I will be right back. Merci." Grant's voice was slightly trembling.

Ginger, Gabriel, and Monette sat at the table on the porch right outside the kitchen, where they could hear Grant's side of the conversation: "Hey, Dan. It's Grant. Yeah, buddy, I'm good. You? Great. Listen, I'm in France and I need some info . . ."

Monette asks Ginger, "Ma fille, what are your plans for the rest of your stay in France?"

"We have many things we'd like to see. Especially the Eiffel Tower. May I ask, what does 'fille' mean?"

"It means 'daughter.' You have called me 'mother,' after all."

"Ah, oui. So how do I say 'mother'?"

"'Mère.' And just in case you're wondering, father is 'père.'"

"Merci, mère. You both have been such gracious

hosts. And your family is lovely."

Grant returned to the porch. "My cousin will be calling back as soon as he has information. He will contact Mr. Smith about his brother."

An hour later, Sybille answered the phone. "Monsieur Grant, the telephone is for you. Dan Johnson."

"Merci, Sybille."

The three sat silently, overhearing Grant's side of the conversation. "Oh? Oui. I mean, yes. Okay. Do you mind speaking with Monsieur Portier? Great. Hold on."

Grant walked the few steps back to the porch. "My cousin would like to speak with you, Monsieur. He has some information you may find interesting."

"I'll be happy to speak with him. You, mon fils, however, look like you need a sip of brandy—or maybe something a bit stronger?"

Chapter 56

It was early that afternoon when they departed from the Portier retreat. As much fun as they'd had, Ginger and Grant were looking forward to some alone time in Paris.

"Monsieur, Mademoiselle, the Portiers have insisted on treating you to a special night of dining at the Eiffel. They have instructed me to make the arrangements. Would you prefer tonight or tomorrow? Keep in mind, tonight is a full moon."

Ginger and Grant looked at each other and answered in unison, "Tonight."

"C'est parfait. I suggest that we meet in the lobby

around seven thirty. That way, you can watch the sunset and the moonrise; the mind cannot conjure mother nature's beauty until you've witnessed it."

"Merci, Fabio."

"May Grant and I have some privacy, please?"

"Of course, Madame."

The glass partition allowed Ginger and Grant to be alone. She crawled on top of Grant, straddling his upper thighs and hips. He began to slide his hands between her legs, but she stopped him. "Grant, what's going on? Is something wrong?"

"Nothing's wrong, babe." He turned away from her.

"Something *is* going on and you aren't telling me. What happened to you this morning when we visited Incarville?"

"Gin, if I told you, you would probably want to jump from this moving limo and run as far away from me as possible."

"Try me."

"Before I tell you anything, please promise me that you will not leave me. I will go for help, counseling, whatever it takes. But I cannot lose you."

"You're scaring me, Grant. What is this about? Your past? I thought we were supposed to leave the past as the past."

"You haven't promised me you won't leave me, Gin."

"I want to be with you forever. I am *not* leaving you. But you better spill it, because you're making me crazy over here."

He took a deep breath to calm his nerves and collect his thoughts, and then he began. "Remember when you said you were having a déjà vu at the park a few weeks back?"

She looked at him blankly for a minute before recalling the moment. "Yes, yes, I remember. When you were packing up the basket, right? It felt like I'd seen you do that before."

"Well, I'm having one of those on an epic scale today." He looked around and said, "Is there any alcohol?"

"Let me look, my love. Sounds like we may both need a drink. Here's a bottle of chilled vodka."

Ginger handed him the bottle. "Let me find some tongs for the ice."

Grant gulped down at least three shots worth of the clear liquid before she even touched the chilled tumblers. Ginger looked at him cautiously and prepared two glasses.

"Gin, remember how I told you that I've had dreams? They are vivid dreams. They started about a month ago, when I flew to Dallas to meet with Steve and Rebekah Scott. That night I had my first—oh shit!" Grant laughed. "It was August thirteenth. Just another coincidence."

"To what?"

He sipped his vodka. "Everything. Anyway, I started

dreaming of a young man in the army stationed in England during World War II. At first, I thought these were just dreams because my father made me watch every damned war movie possibly made about World War II. But get this, Gin, the soldier's name in my dreams was *Tommy*. Oddly enough, that was my secret name for myself during my childhood. My parents got angry whenever I told them my name was supposed to be Tommy instead of Grant."

"Tommy, huh? I could see you as a Tommy."

"Really? Anyway, I ignored the dreams at first, thinking I was just under a lot of stress from the Neiman Marcus account and my upcoming divorce. On top of that, Ronald Reagan was an actor in some of those war movies, and he's running for president.

"The dreams kept weaving into a full-blown story. They were so real that they began spilling over into my conscious thoughts."

He paused. "You sure you want to hear all this?"

She nodded.

"So this Tommy met an English girl who worked at a pub, and they instantly fell in love. Neither of them had ever been so in love before.

"So here's where it gets really weird: Tommy's plane was named the *Fifinella*. The same plane Gabriel was talking about this morning. When he was talking about that pilot, I felt like I already knew what he was going to say."

Grant shook his head. "I don't understand *what's happening. Can all* this be coincidental? The Smith family in Baraboo? The plane crash in Incarville? And there's so much more! I mean, am I going insane? What the fuck is this all about?" His voice suddenly filled with frustration and anger. "And there's so much more!" His eyes began to tear up.

Ginger wrapped her arms around him. "Grant, baby, take it easy, my sweet soul. You're not crazy. We'll figure it out. Together. I *want* to hear the whole story, when you're ready. Deal?"

"Deal, my sweet Ginger. I love you so much."

"I love you. Now rest, my love." She moved her body next to his, and Grant relaxed in her embrace.

As she pet his head, Ginger wondered if her recent dreams fit with his in any way. *I wish I could remember them. It was in England, right? Beyond that, I can't remember much.*

Ginger showered and braided her wet hair. Dressed in a black-and-gray printed jumpsuit with thin shoulder straps, she paired the outfit with her black patent stilettos.

Grant was dressed in a light-gray button-up dress shirt paired with his black dress pants. His shoes were also a patent leather with a matching belt.

"You look amazing," Grant said. Ginger could tell that Grant was in better spirits after his nap. He began to put on his tailored black blazer when Ginger wrapped her arms around him. "Monsieur, are you trying to seduce some hot, French women tonight? After all, you are very delicious looking. You make my mouth water."

"French women usually don't shave under their arms, remember? Not my type. But you, my love, are truly my type."

They kissed, and Grant stepped back to twirl Ginger around, visually devouring every inch of her body. When he was finished, she curtsied, and Grant bowed, stretching his hand out to take hers. "Madame, our motor carriage awaits."

"Monsieur Grant, Madame Ginger, you look splendid," Fabio said, holding Ginger's hand and assisting her into the backseat. "Everything is arranged. My cousin Kari is awaiting your arrival."

"Merci, Fabio," Grant responded, holding Ginger's hand tightly.

Fabio pulled into what Grant referred to as the 007 entrance—only for those in the know. Kari met Fabio at the driver's door of the limo.

"Please wait a moment, mes amis," Fabio requested.

Grant took advantage of the moment and kissed Ginger again, leaving her to reapply her lipstick.

"Oops. Sorry, love."

"No, no, mon amour. I love to kiss you. And I don't mind freshening my lips after your kisses. I've always been a girlie girl."

"God, you're pretty, Gin. The prettiest woman I've ever seen."

She giggled. "Merci, mon amour."

"Tu es ma Venus," Grant responded.

"French is the most romantic language. So what does that mean?"

"'You are my Venus.' I was practicing that line while you were singing in the shower."

"Okay, Prince Smart-Ass."

"There's the Ginger I love. Such spark, such passion." He kissed her cheek.

"Such . . . such . . . oh, screw it, whatever." They both laughed. "But I do love how much French we have learned in less than a week. Paris, mon amour!"

They leaned into each other for another kiss.

Chapter 57

The setting sun had the sky ablaze in yellows and oranges. The spray of clouds reflected the pink and faded into magenta and purple, barely separated by the faintest ray of red. Above the clouds, the sky was turning from blue to a dark and romantic black, which began to shimmer with stars as the moon began its ascent.

Grant and Ginger sipped champagne and enjoyed the view from a private table at the Champagne Bar at the top of the Eiffel.

Grant raised his glass to Ginger.

"Un autre toast, mon amour?"

"Oui. À l'amour de ma vie," Grant said.

Ginger responded, "À mon âme soeur."

They clinked their champagne flutes.

"You, Ginger Madison, *are* my soul mate."

Kari approached and said, "Mes amis, your table for dinner is ready when you are."

"Merci, Kari," Grant responded.

Kari took them down to the second platform of the tower where Le Jules Verne restaurant was located. They were seated at a table with another magnificent view of the city. Kari advised them that they need not worry about ordering, for he had the chef prepare a special menu for them.

"What, are we movie stars?" Ginger giggled.

Kari laughed. "You are VIPs tonight. Tristan will be taking care of your needs for the rest of the evening. However, when you are ready to depart, please have him inform the maître d', Jean Paul, and I will arrange with Fabio for your return to the Hilton. Bon appétit."

After some savory hors d'oeuvres and their fourth bottle of champagne, Ginger found the courage to ask Grant to expand further on his dreams.

"Here? Ginger, I—"

"What's the difference? Here, there, anywhere? With green eggs and ham? Just tell me."

Grant decided to share more details than he originally

planned to. Nearly inebriated himself, he figured she wouldn't remember in the morning anyway, so he acquiesced.

"Okay, I think I left off where the two couples were madly love in love."

"Oui, oui, I recall."

"But some of the dreams have blended together, yet a few stand out."

"What stands out the most?" she asked, draining her flute.

"Well . . ." He cleared his throat. "You know how in most sex dreams you don't actually have intercourse? It's just grinding?"

"Oh, do tell!" She leaned her head on her folding hands with excited eyes.

"Well, in these dreams I had vivid sex on multiple occasions. One time, I even woke up to a fist full of cum."

Ginger's demeanor transformed from excited to appalled in the blink of an eye. Grant didn't notice her reaction, even when she sat back and crossed her arms. The alcohol was clouding his judgment.

"And I specifically remember one time after a night of wild, passionate sex with her, I awoke half expecting her to be lying next to me. I could smell her essence—her hair, her skin. I could almost feel her body spooning mine."

Grant paused for a second to sip his drink when he

finally recognized Ginger's countenance. She stared at him intensely.

"It sounds like you love her."

He didn't respond.

"Do you love her, Grant? I thought *she* was just someone from your dreams? *Dreams* that affected your emotions earlier today."

"I guess on some level I am."

"What exactly does *that* mean? Every time you're intimate with me, are you fantasizing about her? A girl from your fucking dreams?"

She stood up, threw her napkin on the plate, and said loudly, "Grant, I can deal with a Tina, an Abigail, a Sarah, even a ridiculously insecure ex-wife. But how am I to compete with a spirit?"

"Gin, wait. I was just—"

"Just what, Grant? Just breaking my heart? I suppose you almost married the wrong one—again!" She removed her engagement ring and dropped it in his champagne flute. Then she stormed off.

Grant watched Ginger leave. The fear of losing her filled his entire being. He envisioned Rodin's *Gates of Hell*, the demons screaming, "Abandon all hope, ye who enter here," over and over. His heart beat heavily against his chest, and he found it difficult to breathe.

Tristan approached after the commotion. "Are you ill,

Monsieur?"

"No, no, Tristan. Could you hold the main course for a bit? Madame had to step outside for fresh air—perhaps too much champagne."

Tristan nodded. "I will bring un verre d'eau froide. It may help her."

"Merci."

Grant retrieved the ring from the champagne flute and mustered up the courage to look for her. With the glass of water in hand, he stepped outside and found her on the balcony. Her back was to him. She was talking to a tall, attractive Frenchman. She leaned toward him and kissed his cheek.

Grant felt sick. Everything spun around him, and he grabbed for the door handle to steady himself.

He wanted to speak to her, but she was laughing with the stranger and puffed a cigarette.

My God, he thought. *Who is she? Didn't we agree that these dreams would never affect our relationship? I knew I should have never said anything.*

He made his way back to the table and dropped the ring back into *her* flute.

Tristan approached and asked, "Monsieur, is now a good time for your main course?"

"I apologize, Tristan. But it seems Madame has made arrangements that do not include me." Grant took out two hundred francs and handed it to Tristan without uttering another word.

Grant slowly walked down the long set of stairs. At the bottom of the tower, he exited and wandered down the path into the Champ de Mars—Paris's version of Central Park.

Finally, he reached a cluster of trees whose leaves shimmered in the moonlight. Sitting on a bench, he could no longer contain his pain and began sobbing into his hands.

He relived a moment as a boy when he climbed to the top of a tree in Wisconsin after his mother passed, curling up in one of the branches and letting the gentle breeze rock him back and forth. That young soul inside him was seeking solace from terrible heartbreak—again. The overwhelming emotional pain had him desperate for any comfort. He just lost his true love, this time as a grown man. After some time of crying on the bench, Grant decided to make his way back to the hotel.

"Monsieur, you look lost."

A young woman approached him from the shadows. She looked to be in her early twenties. In the moonlight, he could see her blonde hair and beautiful body; however, her provocative clothing made it clear that she was a prostitute. He would have normally walked away, but he needed to feel something, *anything*, other than rejection.

"I am beyond lost."

She inched into his space.

"Monsieur . . ." She touched his arm.

"So lost that I've abandoned all hope of ever finding my way back to happiness."

The young woman looked at him. "Is it your heart that you lost?"

"And my soul. You should be afraid of me. Maybe I'll steal yours since I have none."

She rubbed his soft, tear-streaked cheeks and studied his face. "Monsieur, I am a lost soul as well. Maybe together we can become, shall we say, *unlost*?"

Grant sadly laughed. "If it were only that easy. Unfortunately, mine cannot be recovered, for I gave them to someone I love."

"Let our passion soothe us. You remind me of a man whose heart and soul I broke in my past. Let me do penance by giving you my body for free tonight."

He heard a voice in his head—or maybe just the breeze rustling the leaves—say, *Grant go back to Ginger. Now.* "No. I haven't lost all hope—I'm not letting go!" He handed the young woman some francs and ran toward the Eiffel.

Chapter 58

Ginger stood by the railing, making sure to be out of Grant's sight. She didn't want to hear another word from his mouth about the damned dreams—she didn't even want to look at him. Staring out over the city alone, she tried to gather her thoughts.

I finally found a man who I thought understood me, shared my dreams, and wanted to create a life with me. How did a toast to our future end up with him being in love with a woman from his dreams? Am I destined for unhappiness?

She felt betrayed and confused all at the same time. She looked down at the ground below when she heard a man's voice.

"Pardon me, Mademoiselle?"

"Yes?"

"Have you lost something?"

"Oui."

"Je m'appelle Armande. I work at the Jules and am on break for a moment. Would cigarette smoke bother your quiet reflection?"

"No, no. Please." She hesitated. "May I smoke with you?"

"My pleasure. It is a clove."

"Even better." Ginger took a puff and started coughing.

"So Madame, what is it that you have lost?"

She took another puff. "Lost? Oh, yes. I feel like I've lost . . . everything."

"I see. You have no intention to jump, correct?" Armande grinned.

Ginger returned his smile and shook her head no.

"That is a good choice. You have lost Love. Is that your affliction?"

"Oui," she softly said.

"I often find someone standing where you are. Each seeming to ponder Love just as you, as if waiting for some answer to appear from the sky. I always ask myself, is Love beautiful, or is She painful?

"I have always found Love to be intoxicating, like drowning in the finest wine. Trouble begins when you sober up from Her affect. You think it to be a mistake. At times, oui. She doesn't care about *why* you are one with Her, all She wants is to *be*. You can want Her, but She must choose you. Perhaps She, Love, is meant to fulfill a cosmic design unknown to us. Madame, trust me, in Her truest form, She does not make mistakes."

Ginger stared at him for a moment. "Armande, you speak of love like it is a living being."

"Oui, I do. Only a woman knows where love begins . . . in the soul. Do you see why I call Love a female? *She* is painfully beautiful."

"Yes. I love him so much, but there seem to be endless issues. Tonight, he told me about a woman from his dreams that he loves on some level." She began to sob, and he pulled her into his arms.

The two looked at each other, and then Armande released her. "And to think I was afraid you were going to jump. I always wondered what I would do if it actually happened."

They both laughed.

"Well, Monsieur, thank you for saving me." Ginger kissed him on the cheek.

"So, Love has found you. Now be very careful how you treat Her. She is imperfect and fragile. Love will not endure if you lose faith. Love is not just about a moment but also about the past and the future of who we are."

A soothing silence followed as Armande finished his clove cigarette.

"Mademoiselle, trust Her. Now, I must excuse myself, for my break is over." Armande kissed Ginger's hand and walked away.

Left alone, Ginger reflected on what Armande said and realized how much she overreacted.

I love him so much. Past. Dreams. Craziness. Everything!

She walked back into the dining room: the table had been cleared away. "Tristan, where is Monsieur Robinson?"

"He has left, Mademoiselle. He said you made other plans that did not include him."

"I don't understand. Did he go to the bar?"

"No, Madame. He left the Eiffel. However, I believe you dropped this in your flute." Tristan placed the ring in her hand. "If there is anything else I can assist you with, please let me know."

Ginger sat at the bar and ordered a dirty martini. She put her ring on her finger, picturing Grant's eyes. *Where is he? The hotel? Why did he think I made other plans? Oh my God . . . he must have seen me with Armande!*

Ginger panicked, slammed back her martini, and ordered another. Then, a hand lightly touched her back, and she fiercely whipped around. Grant looked slightly disheveled, his eyes red. "Ginger, I will always be in love with you, whether you choose to be with me or not."

She jumped up and hugged him tightly.

"Please forgive my harsh reaction earlier, Grant. There is no one else I want other than you. I love you."

Grant took a deep breath. "As long as you forgive me."

They kissed, and Grant sat down on the bar stool while Ginger leaned into him. "Bébé, the man I was speaking to on the balcony was just—"

"It doesn't matter. Because I love you."

"As I love you. Always and all ways."

"I see you're wearing your ring."

"Of course I am. I should never have taken it off."

They kissed again. "Mon amour, why had you never told me about these dreams before?"

"Your reaction is exactly why. The possibility that I could lose you . . ."

"I am sorry for that. Would you please finish telling me about them?"

"After what just happened?"

"Yes, I need to hear them. They are a part of you."

"I will, but only if you remember that these are just dreams."

"I know. But they emotionally affected you this

morning, and I need to understand why. Though if you would please leave out the intimate details . . ."

He nodded. "Tommy was deeply in love with her, and she didn't want him to leave for that mission. She had a feeling it would be his last. And it *was* his last mission. But hearing the story earlier today, and then speaking with my cousin Dan afterwards . . ." He took a deep breath. Ginger caressed his face.

She leaned into him. "Oh, so you actually had a dream about his last mission?"

"Yes, every detail. Even beyond what Monsieur Portier spoke of—Tommy's last words, telling his best friend, the navigator, to give a message to the love of his life."

"What was the message?"

"That he'd be back for her the next time around."

Tears filled his eyes, and he laughed just to keep from crying.

"Oh, Grant, I'm so, so sorry. What do you think all those dreams mean? We all have dreams. I've had some crazy ones lately, but the details have vanished."

"I really don't know. Believe me, I wish I did understand them. It feels like I found a diary that someone left behind, and it's like someone *really* wanted me to read it."

Ginger and Grant sat in silence. Grant hoped he told

her enough, although there was more, like names and places. Ginger wished she could ask more questions, but she had a feeling that she should leave it be for now.

Finally, Ginger broke the silence. "Are we going to have a big wedding or just family? I'm open for anything—even Vegas!"

"Will Aunt Sadie go to Vegas?"

"Well, mes yeux bleus, I think she'd go anywhere you are."

"Yeux bleus?" Grant inquired.

"Blue eyes."

"I love you, Ginger Madison, my fiancé." He held up his drink.

"And I love you, Grant Robinson. You're already my husband in my heart."

Not much later, Kari appeared, saying, "Fabio is waiting for you downstairs. I will escort you on the executive elevator when you are ready. Am I to gather that your evening was everything you imagined?"

"And more," they said in unison. They looked at each other and laughed. It wasn't the first time they'd mirrored each other's words, but it meant even more after that night's emotional rollercoaster.

Riding down the elevator, Kari said, "Monsieur, the moon is fully above the horizon, and it would go against luck if you don't kiss your love under the full moon on la

Dame de fer."

Grant gently leaned into Ginger, grasping her face with both hands. "Mon amour." The kiss they shared was tender yet passionate. Their tongues sweetly danced. She sucked his tongue, he gently tugged at her bottom lip. Ginger moaned with happiness as they floated down the Eiffel, locked in a passionate embrace, even after the elevator came to a stop.

Kari waited a bit and finally cleared his throat. Both finally realized they were on the ground level.

Grant handed him a folded bill and said, "Merci, Kari."

Chapter 59

Ginger and Grant entered their suite midkiss. The emotionally charged evening had drawn their souls together, melding them into one. Lost in each other, they found their way to the bedroom. Clothing lay where each piece was tossed, leaving a trail from the door to the bedroom. Her jumpsuit was torn and discarded; his pants a crumpled mess near the bed.

Their lovemaking was sweet yet passionate, like the first time they were intimate in New York.

Lying on the bed, Ginger spread her legs. She trembled with desire when his tongue parted her lips.

Ginger moaned with physical need while she grinded and climaxed on his face. She pulled at his hips, guiding him upward until he straddled her face with his cock. She welcomed his velvet, steely length into her mouth, letting her tongue play with the tip. Sucking him while twisting her hand around his girth, she brought him to his first orgasm of the night.

Lying back to breathe, it was then that the rays of the full moon began to fill the room.

"Bébé, look! We are lying in the moon's ray." Ginger reached over and turned off the lights, allowing only the moon to illuminate the room and their bodies.

"I love you so much, sweetheart—even the cosmos is lighting our way."

After popping the cork on a bottle of champagne, their kisses turned carnal.

Ginger and Grant continued to explore more of each other's body, and finally she begged for the naughtiness of anal pleasure. Ginger lay missionary style, and Grant tenderly penetrated the tip of his cock inside her ass, slowly gauging acceptance through her eyes. Once the initial pain of his size entered her completely, she grasped at his ass cheeks, pulling him deeper into the forbidden entrance. Finding an unknown yet instinctive rhythm, she came intensely, nearly losing her sight from such physical delight.

After sharing a sensual shower bathing each other,

they snacked on room service and laughed at the size of the jumbo shrimp cocktail.

On the chaise lounge, elated with their mental reconnection, Grant and Ginger couldn't keep their hands off each other's naked bodies. While she rode him feverishly, they began climbing toward a mutually explosive orgasm, which suddenly unraveled them into an entirely different experience.

At the peak of their combined climax, their souls were joined together on a level neither had ever felt before. It was as if there was no measure of time—two souls as one sharing an out-of-body experience.

Ginger breathlessly asked, "Did you see that . . . feel that? What just happened?"

Grant whispered, "Yes. Yes, I did . . . Rachel?"

"You are my sweet Tommy!"

"The moonlit bedroom in your cottage, my sassy Brit!" A nervous laugh escaped him, "So, Gin, these aren't just dreams; they're memories of . . ."

"Our past lives? Wait! Tommy, you helped me plant the flowers in the garden of my cottage."

"It was raining earlier that night when we made love for the first time."

"And I was instantly in love with you, my fly-boy, the moment I laid eyes on you. Oh my God, Tommy! I can remember everything now, it actually happened! Our first kiss—the one when you were leaving the pub."

"Did I tell you about that?"

"No. But I know I warmed a piece of apple pie for you and gave you a cup of coffee, because you Americans didn't drink tea."

"Are we fucking crazy?"

"Hell, yes! But it's okay, right?"

"I promised you that I would find you again!"

"For the short time I lived after your death, I was heartbroken. Alex was dear to me, but it wasn't enough. I spent every moment wishing you had come back to me. I lost you . . . you were shot down! Oh my God, Tommy—Grant—Tommy . . ."

He held her in his arms as she sobbed, "I thought I was going crazy! I've had some dreams too. But now I remember too much! I'm sorry I killed myself—I just couldn't bear the pain any longer. You and Izzy were gone."

"It broke my heart to lose you, Rach. I'm so sorry. I was drawn to you since the first time we met in Chicago. I thought about you so many times but never reached out. And now . . ."

"My sweet Tommy. I loved you then with my entire being, my soul. But here we are. Again. In the now. Please don't leave me ever again, Grant."

He held her tighter. "Rachel, Ginger, my sweet love, I am never leaving you. I promise. I'm yours. Always and all ways."

"You kept your promise to me. You came back for me."

He nodded. "And now I feel like I'm *awake* for the first time in this life."

They lay in silence of the moonlight, wrapped in a deep embrace.

Grant/Tommy and Ginger/Rachel sipped coffee Monday morning on the balcony of the Hilton, enjoying the rising sun glisten off the Eiffel.

"So, crazy question. What should I call you? Ginger or Rachel?"

Ginger nearly spat her coffee out with laughter.

"I thought it was a crazy question, not a funny one, mon amour."

"Well, the thought *is* hilarious."

"Yeah, you're right. But I do have a serious question for you."

"What's that, my fly-boy?"

"Sure you still want to be my wife? After all, I'm as crazy as they come."

"Oui! And, bébé, call me whatever name you wish, because now I know who I really am—who you really are—from our past life and current life and all the lives ahead of us, the one you've kept your promise to, the one you've dreamt of for almost a month, Grant, Tommy, whoever the hell you are. I love you."

"Rachel, Ginger, I love you. I thought the dreams were a curse, but now I am grateful."

"I'm grateful you shared them with me. Do you think that's why I was finally able to see what I saw last night?"

"Maybe. But either way, we know now."

"It was the first full moon since your dreams began."

"The cosmos. Who knows."

They spent a few moments in silence, holding hands, just lost in each other's souls.

"Sorry to break up our reunion, Mrs. Robinson—Mrs. Smith, but it's time to get dressed. The Portiers will be here in less than an hour. However, I think we should stick to our current names—at least in front of them."

"Tommy, how about getting married in England? I know of an old pub, or perhaps a cottage with a garden—if they're still there."

"Whatever, whenever, however you wish, m'lady." He kissed her and began to rub her ass.

"Tommy! As you said, we don't have time right now. Besides, I'm a little sore from last night." She removed his hand from her robed ass.

The knock on the door came promptly at ten a.m. They took a deep breath, looking at each other for a moment and holding hands. Grant opened the door to see Monette and Gabriel holding hands as well.

"Bonjour, bonjour, Monsieur, Madame."

Immediately, Monette reached for Ginger with arms wide open. Gabriel and Grant hugged like a father and son.

"Mère, it's fantastique to see you again. You look belle, per usual."

"Merci, my little one."

"We loved our time at your retreat and meeting your beautiful family."

"Ma fille, it was our pleasure as well. Vous êtes les bienvenus."

Both couples headed toward the dining table for brunch, which room service had perfectly displayed buffet style.

After the pleasantries, Monette interrupted Gabriel. "Mon amour, Gabriel, veuillez tell them about our family meeting. I can no longer wait."

"As mon amour just spoke of, we had another family meeting. It lasted a few hours. But first, Monsieur and Madame, I wanted to inform you that your cousin, his family, and Monsieur Robert are flying into Paris to be our guests next month for a week. We are looking forward to meeting Thomas P. Smith's younger brother. We will be celebrating Monsieur Thomas's life with him."

Grant smiled, his eyes tearing up, and could only nod before speaking. "That pleases me, Monsieur, more than you know."

"He is bringing the picture of which you spoke with him, along with some others so we can see who Thomas was."

"Merveilleux!"

"Mon amour, veuillez, tell them, or I will!"

Gabriel said, "Before we place the order with you, we have a business proposition for you to consider."

"Oui?" Grant responded.

"Nos enfants—our children—our family has decided to make you an offer. We believe in your passion and work ethics. We wish to form a partnership with you and back you in your own private-label company."

Chapter 60

The ground was covered with fresh snow. As the children opened a mountain of gifts, Grant and Ginger stepped back to soak in the moment.

Ginger whispered, "Isn't this beautiful, Tommy?"

Grant said, "Rachel, if someone would have asked me a year ago how I would be celebrating Christmas this year, I would never, ever have dreamt it would be this. This is more beautiful than I ever imagined." He kissed her on the cheek.

"My sweet Tommy, if someone were to ask us about the beginning of our relationship, where does our story begin?" She paused for a moment, then added, "I wonder where it will end."

"It will never end; we'll always be together. We are soul mates."

"Oui, mon amour."

They looked at the shredded wrapping paper and bows covering the floor of the Portier family farmhouse. Ginger listened to her father in the background speaking with Gabriel. "I never made it to France when I was in the service . . ." Her mother was again thanking Monette for inviting them to celebrate Christmas with their new extended family.

Lyla jumped into Ginger's arms and said, "You are so sweet, Mommy Ginger. I don't mind sharing Daddy's heart with you."

"Oh, baby girl, that means the world to me. If you only knew how much he loves you and Jason. One day, if you become a mommy, you will understand. But for now, merci beaucoup, ma fille. Je t'aime énormément."

"And what does that mean?"

"'Thank you very much, my daughter. I love you. A lot.'"

Grant was just inches away from his two favorite girls in the universe. Although they were whispering, he could hear every word and couldn't imagine how his heart fit in his chest.

Just then, Jason ran up with his newest Lego set. "Daddy, can we build it now?"

"Of course, son!"

Sybille found Lyla to tell her that her mother was on the phone and needed to speak with her right away.

Grant watched Lyla while she spoke with her mother. He noticed how her happy demeanor morphed into something he couldn't describe. Lyla wasn't speaking, only listening. She wiped away tears when she hung up the phone. She noticed her father looking at her and turned away.

Debut . . .

Like We Always Do

A Note from Deb & Ray

To our wonderful readers,

Talking is where ideas are hatched; following through with the ideas is where stories are told . . .

Ray and Deb share an interest in past lives. They would swap stories about what they thought may have been past-life experiences they each had, at times wondering, as we all do, why certain places one has never visited feel familiar or why one immediately has a connection, good or bad, with a person one has never met before—sometimes without a word being spoken.

In 2012 Ray visited France to see his son's art exhibit. He scoured the Internet, searching for different places to see during his stay. In the course of his research, he stumbled upon a picture of a woman in Incarville, France, standing next to a memorial for First Lieutenant Thomas P. Smith, a B-17 pilot killed in action on August 13, 1944, in World War II. The memorial had an inscription describing how he sacrificed his life to save his crew and a small village.

Ray and Deb felt an otherworldly pull to Thomas P. Smith. Something nearly screamed at them that a story needed to be written about this brave hero, who died on his plane, the *Fifinella.* Does it matter whether it is fact or fiction?

We hope you enjoyed *Twisted in Time.*

Thank you.
Life Only Has Beginnings,
Deb & Ray

Visit MysticScribblers.com for updates and interesting past life information. Be sure to subscribe to The Mystic Scribblers Podcast on your favorite provider.

Have you had past lives? Find out. Take the past life questionnaire.

If you enjoyed this book, help others find it so they can enjoy it too.

- **Recommend it:** Please help other readers find this book by recommending it to friends, readers' groups, and discussion boards.
- **Review it:** Let other potential readers know what you liked about this book.

Made in the USA
Middletown, DE
16 January 2022

58822466R10279